No Lesser Measure

* * *

FREDRICK W. BOLING

ISBN 978-0-9722808-7-7

Published by:

BIGHORN PUBLISHING
35 La Canada Way
Hot Springs Village, AR 71909

Printed in the United States of America

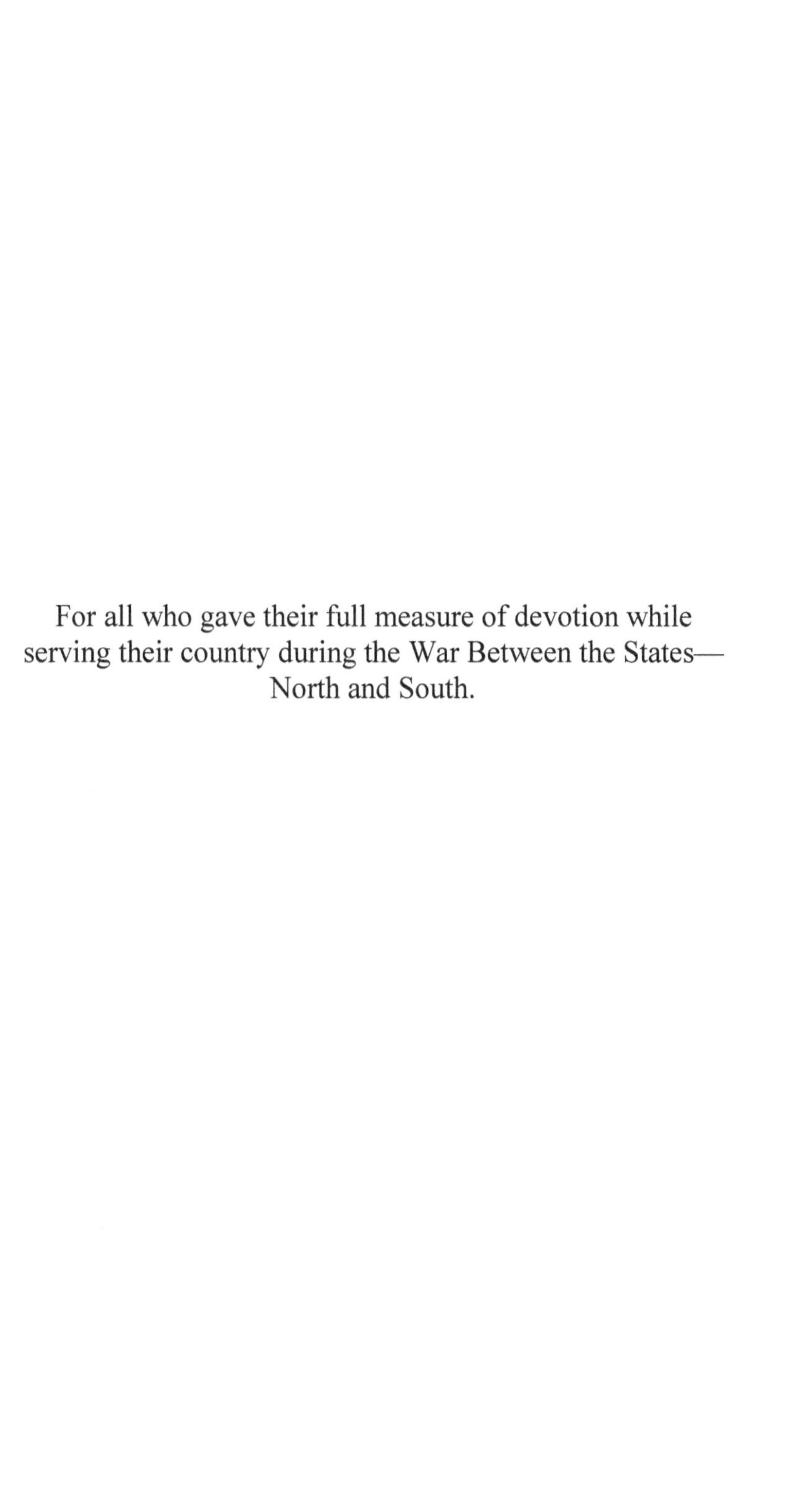

PROLOGUE

To: Historical Archives of South Carolina,
          Charleston, South Carolina.
From: John H. Pendleton

More years than I care to count have gone by since we answered the call to fight the Northern invaders. Most of the skirmishes, battles, days and nights of marching barefoot along muddy or dusty roads and suffering from fevers and dysentery have faded into the recesses of my memory. However, one day remains as if it had only been yesterday — the afternoon of the third day of July in 18 and 63 near Gettysburg, Pennsylvania.

Silence hovered over the killing field as our tattered gray ranks stepped in measured cadence toward the Yankee's line along Cemetery Ridge. The heat and a pall of impending death oppressed us on that horrible day. The sun was obscured by a veil of acrid smoke from belching cannons and dust rising from our ill-shod feet. "I reckon this is it," Hank Johnson said as we marched behind our frayed battle flags.

All semblance of order dissolved before I could answer. Cannon shot and canister, ripping through flesh and bones, hissed like geysers of steam in the midst of our long gray line. Each exploding fireball created vacancies where sweating men had been only seconds before. Every sweep of these sickles of death gleaned untold numbers of our young men grown old by war into eternity.

We lunged onward, blinded by smoke, dust, and fear, into a holocaust of Miniéballs screaming from thousands of rifles. Men groaned and crumpled all around us.

Time disintegrated into a void for Hank and me as a shell exploded above us. Cascading tongues of fire sprayed our company with searing shards of shrapnel. The violent concussion rendered me senseless, unaware of anything.

Then pain, ascending from my mangled right leg, wrenched me from a dark abyss of nothingness. Each jolt of the litter sent new waves of agony that lodged in my gut until the sickness, bitter and sour, spewed between my clenched teeth. "Set 'im down till he's done pukin'," one of the bearers said.

"Can't wait," another said, "Doc's ready t'cut off that leg."

I continued to retch until someone shoved a gauze mask reeking with chloroform over my mouth and nose. The pungent, sweet vapors slithered into my lungs, severed the cords of nausea, and swept away the pain. Like a velvet blanket, sleep wrapped itself around me and deafened my ears to the surgeon's saw cutting through bone.

I felt no pain, but streaming visions of days gone by haunted me like ghosts from the past. I experienced brittle cold, searing heat, an empty belly, and marching barefoot into battles across North Carolina, Virginia, Maryland, and Pennsylvania. I saw Mother weeping as Father read aloud a letter from Stephen R. Mallory, Secretary of the Navy, informing us that my older brother, Andrew, was missing. His ship, the C.S.S. Sea Bird, was either sunk or captured in Albemarle Sound. I relived anguish felt the morning I left home, my mother being certain I would never return. Again, I met Hank Johnson in Charleston the day we both volunteered. Even though we fought side by side for two years, his features were murky as a photograph faded by time. I kept stepping closer, trying to see more clearly, but his appearance dissolved like fog on a summer morning.

The voice of a young woman awakened me. "Are you feeling better?" she said, setting a wicker basket filled with cotton lint and rolls of muslin dressings on the table.

I blinked sleep from my eyes, trying to clear my mind. "Yes, ma'am — better."

"That's good, it's time to change your dressings."

"Dressin's?"

"Yes — your leg."

I lifted the sheet. "My leg? Oh."

"I'm so sorry," she said, looking away.

I gazed beyond her at the row of injured men lying on canvas cots. Some of them were moaning and thrashing about while others lay quietly with faces blanched from bleeding wounds. "What is this place?"

"It's the old dorm," she said, pulled the sheet aside, and began to remove blood-soaked bandages from the stump that once was my right leg. "I'll try not to hurt you."

I stared at my bandaged thigh, determined to keep my composure. Anger flushed my face and clenched my fists. I was alive but wished I wasn't. "What's the old dorm?" I asked, not really caring.

Without looking up from her task, she continued to cut through bandages that were stiff and brittle from congealed blood. "It's a residence for our students here at Pennsylvania College."

My mood turned sullen as she changed the dressing. My thoughts returned to the killing ground where I was maimed. I had no idea what happened to Hank or our charge against the Yankee horde. He was probably dead, torn apart by canister or exploding shells fired at point-blank range. He might be wounded and here in this same hospital, or carried back to our line on Seminary Ridge. He could have completed the charge, helped overwhelm the Yankee line, and sent them scurrying back to Washington City. I pondered these possibilities only to realize that our charge probably fell short. "Are all these men, Yanks?" I asked, gesturing toward the long row of cots.

"Yes — they are."

"Any of my people here?"

"No, you are the only one."

She completed her task, placed all of the bloody bandages in a sack and picked up her dressings basket. She smiled and placed her hand on my shoulder. For the first time, I became aware of the young woman who was attending my needs. She could have been no older than I, which was nineteen years. Long, golden ringlets falling loosely across her shoulders framed her features. Kindness reflected from her eyes that were bluer than South Carolina's bonny flag. Her gentle fingers squeezed my shoulder as she asked whether I needed anything before she left. I was taken aback a bit by her pleasantness. After all, I, a rifleman in General Lee's army, intended to wreak much destruction upon her people. Maybe she didn't understand why we were intent upon our pillaging foray. Was she aware of the Yankee's atrocities that were being committed daily in the South? Did she know that our army was marching barefoot or on footwear held together by twine, thong, or wire? We heard that her town had a shoe factory — that is why we came. We needed shoes, even Yankee shoes.

"I need a shoe," I said, pointing at my callused left foot.

At first, she seemed surprised at my request, but a quick pat on my shoulder told me she understood. "Of course, what size do you wear?"

"Whatever I can squeeze my foot into, a nine or ten works best."

A wounded man lying on a cot across the room spoke up. "You can have my left shoe — won't be needin' it no more."

I rose up on my elbows to look at the fellow who was propped up on a pillow. His hair was disheveled and red as Georgia clay, and at least one thousand brown freckles covered his face. He threw back the sheet and pointed at a short stump, the only remnant remaining of his left leg and thigh. "You Rebs blowed mine clean off."

I thanked him for the offer, but knew his shoe was long gone. It probably wound up in a discard bin, thrown there by a litter bearer or surgical attendant.

As she walked away, seeming to be intent upon the needs of her next patient, I realized I failed to get her name. I called after her, "I'm John Pendleton — what's your name?"

"Penelope Gresham — I'll be back tomorrow, John Pendleton." Then she smiled. "With a nine or ten shoe."

The next day, as promised, she returned carrying a size nine shoe with plenty of wear left in it. That shoe became not only sturdy footwear but it also would gain a new friend for me, the redheaded Yankee whose leg had been blown away by my people. He asked to examine the shoe to determine whether it might be the one he had promised. Of course, it wasn't. He tossed the shoe back to me. "No — that's not mine, John. I inked my name, Timothy O'Brien, on the underside of the tongue."

He seemed disappointed, but chuckled when I said, "I'd give you my right shoe, Timothy, if I had one, but I haven't had shoes for over a week. Mine became more twine, thong and wire until there wasn't any more leather that could be mended."

"It's Tim — only me mother calls me Timothy."

His response caused me to pause, to remember the time Hank and I boarded the train in Charleston. I introduced myself after noticing Henry Johnson stenciled on his haversack. "Only my mother calls me Henry," he said, "just call me Hank."

Some day, within the providence of the Almighty, I pray to once again grip his callused hand and say, "Hank! It's good to see you again." But, in case that isn't to be, I have set down a recounting the best I can of my life after

Gettysburg. Maybe, the time will come when Hank will have the opportunity to read it. But if that never can happen, I pray he rests in peace.

My recovery was enhanced by the care I received from Penelope over the ensuing weeks. Each day her gentle hands and effervescent smile brought healing to my wounded body and soul. Our relationship grew until I realized life spent apart from her was unthinkable. I prayed daily for God to allow us to continue to be together, but doubted it could come about. Would our love survive the terrible war that was engulfing our lives? Only God held the answer.

John Pendleton
Hank Johnson's brother-in-arms

CHAPTER ONE

Gettysburg, the killing ground, the old dorm and rows of Letterman hospital tents lay far behind us. Our prison train traversed southern Pennsylvania, crossed a steel trestle bridge spanning Susquehanna River and headed for Philadelphia. As we approached the city, our guards closed the boxcar's doors. The temperature climbed, becoming more and more unbearable as our train slowed. I clutched my haversack, which contained my journal, a pair of socks, a bar of pine tar soap, pencil and pad of paper, comb and a new leather-bound New Testament — all gifts from Penelope Gresham.

The train switched to other tracks several times before backing down a spur beside Delaware River. Our motley ranks attired in all shades of butternut and gray were then mustered onto the wharf. My god but we are a forsaken lot, I thought, gazing up and down our bedraggled line. There were men who had empty sleeves. Others were unable to walk or even stand without the aid of a crutch, a poor substitute for an amputated leg. And their eyes, such anguish I had not seen before, were downcast and filled with agony. A few heads were swathed within bandages covering eyes that would never see another sunrise or behold faces of loved ones. A pall of dark despair fell over me as if the light of day had been blotted out by a total eclipse.

"I'm Captain Bailey, General Schoeph's adjutant," a tall, gray-bearded Yankee officer said, rousing me from my depressing mood. "Any attempt to escape will be a fatal mistake. Sergeant O'Hara, board the prisoners."

"Yes, sir — Rebs, right face," bawled a burly, ruddy-faced fellow with blue master sergeant's chevrons covering his sleeves. "By the line, board the Delaware Queen."

While hanging onto my haversack, crutch, and the gangplank's rickety railing, I climbed to the main deck. When all of us were boarded, two long blasts from the boat's whistle echoed up and down the riverfront and our guards swung away the ramp.   The massive stern paddlewheel churned, causing our riverboat to begin its course out into a deeper channel of the river. We were headed for Pea Patch Island sixteen miles south of Philadelphia.

Since we were given freedom of the boat, I climbed a stairway to the upper deck, which vibrated as each blade of the paddlewheel slammed into the river. Upon reaching the railing, I watched frothy wakes rolling away from the bow toward shore.   Soon, my forward visibility became obscured.   An opalescent mist rose from her bow as Delaware Queen plowed through rolling white-crested waves.

Disturbing recollections came to mind concerning my brother, Andrew, who had been missing for such a long time. How Mother and Father must have felt with the wounding and capture of yet another son. If they had not received letters I posted in Gettysburg, the Army would only be able to inform them that I was missing in action. I became lonelier as I pondered the fate of Hank Johnson, my comrade in arms. The loss of a leg did not compare with losing my closest friend. I whispered a prayer for him — uninjured, I hoped — alive if not.

I was roused from my musings by the voice of a Yankee guard standing beside me. "Thinkin' 'bout home?"

His accent was unmistakable — South Carolinian. I snapped my head around to see who was speaking. He was a Negro wearing a private's Yankee uniform and a squared regulation kepi. When our eyes met, he grinned. "Is that you, Marse John?"

"Jacob?"

"Yes, sir. This be Jacob."

I grasped his shoulders. "How did you get here?"

"After you left, I ran away and joined the Yankee Army. They made a guard out of me. Where did you get captured, Marse John?"

"Gettysburg — that's where I lost my leg."

He glanced at my crutch. "That's bad."

"What is Fort Delaware like? Do they treat our people decent?"

"It's terrible. They don't have 'nough to keep body and soul together. The food is worse than what your daddy fed the pigs and most ever'body is sick. Not enough clothes for winter and them that don't die from sickness dies from cold. It's a bad place, Marse John."

I'm sure my dejection caused him to pat my shoulder. "Now, Marse John, you can live through this if you make up your mind. Many South boys do by bein' smart. Jacob's goin' to help. Remember that, Marse John."

He walked away saying that he needed to keep moving because of a standing order not to associate with prisoners. Once again, I was alone with my thoughts as the boat continued downriver toward Pea Patch Island and its miserable tenant, Fort Delaware Prison.

Scattered lights appeared along the shore as darkness enveloped us. Millions of stars soon filled a cloudless sky. Despite the warm night, rising sprays permeated my shirt and winds rushing by me brought a chill. Yet, I clung to the railing, striving to collect my thoughts and overcome a feeling of dread. Going into battle did not compare with my apprehension. In the mist, I saw visions of Hank Johnson — the Old Dorm where my right leg was amputated — Penelope Gresham who ministered to my needs — and Tim O'Brien, my wounded Yankee friend. I felt helpless, a captive of utter despair. These had become the most important persons in my life. The destination of the boat was clear enough — one of the most detested Yankee prisons where men were broken and starved.

I remained deep in thought until our boat rounded a bend in the river. For the first time, I saw a place which I feared would end my life. It was a stark and foreboding island prison with timbered walls surrounded by swirling currents of Delaware River. Could anyone escape from such a place? If sentries' rifles failed to kill me, would I drown before reaching solid ground? Nevertheless, hope for freedom, enough food to relieve my grinding stomach, and warm clothing and blankets to shield me from coming winter filled my thoughts.

Gradually, the boat slowed, easing us toward a sparsely lit island pier. We moored and a slippery walkway swung about as the guards ordered us to muster on the wharf. I leaned over to pick up my haversack, which I had set down in order to grasp the railing during our voyage. It was gone along with all of my earthly possessions. One of my fellow prisoners had already set about his plan for survival by stealing it. Now, I possessed nothing but the clothing on my back and a good shoe on my left foot.

"Tenshut!" Sergeant O'Hara yelled, strutting in front of our bedraggled group.

"Go t'hell," a lone voiced growled in response. I admired its bravery, but feared retribution would come to all of us swift as a slashing saber.

"Which one of you Rebel trash said that?" O'Hara bellowed.

There was no response, not even a whispered taunt.

"There's one thing for certain," he barked. "Your butts belong to Sergeant O'Hara from this moment until you either die or escape from this place – which ain't goin' t'happen. Now form up and march by columns of two toward the prison gate."

Several Yankee guards prodded us with rifles as we struggled from the pier toward Fort Delaware's rough-hewn prison walls. "Move it, Reb," and "Your arse belongs t'me," were a couple of their favorite taunts. The coolness of my spray-soaked shirt soon felt comfortable. The night was hot and humid, which made my efforts to hobble along quite taxing. Several amputees fell from exhaustion, and then the Yankees loaded us onto wagons for the remainder of our march.

The stark reality of my incarceration hit me like the shoulder-jarring recoil of a musket as the massive wrought iron gate to the fort clanged shut behind us. We assembled and Sergeant O'Hara pitched us a sarcastic greeting with gusto, "Gladiators of the South, welcome to your new home graciously provided by the United States of America. You have already been warned about any attempt to escape. The guards have orders to shoot to kill anyone trying to leave the confines of this prison. The night is warm and you can spend the remainder of it here in the quadrangle. Following muster in the morning, you will be searched. All belongings will be confiscated, and then returned if no contraband is found. Good night gentlemen, sweet dreams."

I searched for some soft ground to spend the night on, but found none. It was during this first night of prison life that I began my descent into an internalized existence. The stench of accumulated filth was overpowering, but my sense of smell soon ignored such useless information. The night was filled with distressful utterances. We were like a bunch of caged animals, lashing out at anyone who we perceived to be encroaching on our chosen places. Fortunately, most everyone accepted the fact that one spot was as good as another. The haranguing subsided as we endured until first light.

Following muster, the searching of our belongings and assigning us to our barracks, Sergeant O'Hara roared all of the prison's rules while pacing back and forth in front of us. The most threatening was, "If you slave masters get closer than six feet to the stockade, one o'my dear lads will penetrate your backside with Yankee lead."

All of our officers were then separated from us and housed within barracks assigned for their use. A fence encircling their area incarcerated them in a prison within a prison.

The prisoners of my barrack were assigned to a Mess of our own, which was an area designated for cooking outside and away from all wooden structures. We were issued a log about eight inches in diameter by ten feet in length for building cooking fires. The log had to last one week. Guards hewed strips of kindling from it and stacked them in seven piles, not trusting any of us with an axe. We discovered prison slop goes down a lot easier if it is hot — so we guarded our kindling like a mother hen shielding her chicks.

My journal in which all of my experiences in Gettysburg were set down was gone, lost when my haversack was stolen. I complained to Sergeant O'Hara, but to no avail. "Y'er all a bunch o' thieves. Go steal another'n."

Of course, there was no way I could tell that low-life Yankee where to go, but I mentally sent him to the dark waters of River Styx.

My barrack of recent construction was poorly assembled. There were spaces between siding boards that would allow wind, rain and snow to penetrate the wall. My bunk was a wooden platform with legs that elevated it about six inches above the floor. Three additional bunks were built atop each floor bunk. Above every tier of bunks was a ventilator shaft designed to provide free flowing fresh air. My bedding was a coarse, gray woolen blanket. It was no different from what I had been used to while serving in the field, so that seemed of little consequence. I, however, wasn't prepared for how cold and miserable the coming winter would be on Pea Patch Island in the middle of a frozen river. Also, a persistent rumor about epidemics of typhoid fever and smallpox spreading through other barracks was disconcerting. Escape became the only option worth considering.

* * *

I was reluctant to make friends during those early days at Fort Delaware. Having lost Hank was taking its toll, making me unable to get close to another soldier. However, out of necessity, I became interested in one of my bunkmates. If escape from that hellhole was possible, I needed a partner. Cade Arthurs slept in the bunk just above mine. I wasn't certain he was the right one, but getting to know him was a start. We began to talk to one another, mostly about home and what we would do when freed by Gen'ral Lee. Up until then, I prayed Gen'ral Robert would get me paroled through prisoner exchanges. But the rumor was that the Yankees had halted all paroles.

Cade was an affable sort, prone to bragging about his service with J.E.B. Stuart's 1st Virginia Cavalry. I'm sure he, at one time, was a disciplined cavalryman, but getting captured had most likely changed him. He was of average height and slight of build, somewhat like me. His eyes were the most striking thing about him. His gaze would cut through me like cold steel of a lance. I was acquainted with that kind of wildness in men's eyes who had escaped death during battle.

Our first conversation didn't take place for a couple of days. Well, it was a conversation of sorts. We were both hibernating from reality within the security of our blankets on our bunks when he began to tell how he was captured.

"Taint no way you can stay on a bucking horse and swing a saber or fire a pistol."

I just lay there waiting for him to say something else, but not a word came from him. "That right?" I finally said, leaning over the edge of my bunk.

"I tried to rein him down, but he was determined to get the hell out of there."

"What happened?"

"Lost my saber and pistol. Then he wheeled and charged toward Custer's Wolverines."

He fell silent. I decided he might be talking in his sleep, so I let him sleep or ponder, whichever he was doing.

Cade's comments got me to thinking about my own capture west of the Yankee's line on Cemetery Ridge. There wasn't any recollection of how it came about since I was unconscious at the time. My first awareness was being toted on a litter toward an unfamiliar odor, which I discovered to be chloroform wafting from a room in the "Old Dorm" at Pennsylvania College. I was pondering how much better breathing its vapors were compared to biting a lead Miniéball when Cade slammed a fist against the frame of his bunk.

"The next thing I knew," he bellowed, "me and that knothead was chargin' through the Yankee's mounted reserve. Pennsylvania sky separated my butt from the saddle as I rode air for a lot o' yards. I had no choice about surrenderin' when all I could see above me were blue uniforms and sky."

I didn't say so, but there was little concern on my part for Cade's confessions. The only battle remaining for me was survival. I needed to make a decision before frost changed summer greens into autumn hues. I continued to ply Cade with questions hoping to ascertain whether he had a driving desire to avoid spending winter in prison.

Toward the middle of September, nights became chillier. Cracks between boards on the barrack's wall whistled and hummed as winds fingered their way between them. I now had grown a scraggly beard, which was infested by critters that took up residence in every hairy area of my body. Decision time arrived on the seventeenth when a Yankee guard distributed my mail. He sailed an envelope as if it were a boomerang toward my bunk. "Thanks," I said, catching and ripping open the letter. I detected the distinct aroma of lilac, Penelope's favorite. I savored the paper's texture as my fingers slipped beneath the open flap, pulled out and unfolded her letter.

> Dear John — today has been just like every other day since you left — desperately lonely. Each morning as I awaken, I wonder if you are well, getting enough to eat, keeping your spirits up, whether you are missing me. Papa deposited money in your sutler account, so be sure to buy whatever you need. He also has written to the Commissary General of Prisoners, William Hoffman, requesting that you be paroled through the next prisoner exchange. If so, he has asked that you be allowed to enroll as a student here at Pennsylvania College. We hope to have a response before the onset of winter. I pray for you every night. Please write.
>
> Affectionately,
> Penelope.

Her letter lifted my spirits. I'd feared she wouldn't write, let alone convince her father, the president of Pennsylvania College, to intervene in my behalf. Quite suddenly, escape became less of a priority, but it remained a necessary option.

Smallpox struck our barrack on September twentieth when a prisoner transferred from Hilton Head Island came down with the disease. The poor fellow was taken to the smallpox hospital, but this did little to allay the dread gripping me. Cade's moaning and complaining of a severe headache awakened me several days later. I got up and discovered he was suffering from a raging fever. Throughout the night, I secured water from the barrack's barrel in an effort to quench his burning thirst. He couldn't arise and respond to reveille and muster the following morning.

I reported Cade's condition to one of the guards. They came with a litter and carried him to the smallpox hospital. That was the last time I saw him. I learned later he had died within a week of taking ill. I was devastated. My hopes for escape were dashed. How could an amputee escape on crutches from the hellish confines of Pea Patch Island?

My turn with smallpox came on the eighth of October. I awoke with the most ferocious headache I'd ever experienced. My entire body was on fire, and every fiber of my being ached beyond description. A high fever remained unquenched from drafts of cold water. My mind lapsed in and out of terrifying dreams. I have no recollection of being carried to the smallpox hospital. The first couple of days I was unable to eat. Water remained my greatest need. No medicines were available for treatment. At least, none were given. The Yankee doctor was an unsympathetic scoundrel. He hated Rebs and often said so. He was totally negligent in my care, which probably was to my advantage, considering his hatred.

On Sunday, red bumps appeared on my arms, shoulders and face. My fever subsided and I began to feel better. I was able to eat some of the slop attendants brought to me. Since Penelope's father deposited money in my prisoner account, I could have purchased edible food from the prison sutler, but the doctor refused to prescribe any. I overheard him talking with my attendant. "Don't worry about him," the doctor snarled. "It would be a waste of good food. He's showing signs of *black smallpox* and isn't likely to survive. Give him whatever comes from the cookhouse."

"Black smallpox? What is black smallpox?" I muttered to one of the guards.

"Well, Marse John," he whispered, leaning down close to my ear. "It's jus' a worse kind o' pox."

"Jacob?"

"This be Jacob. You res' now, Marse John."

"Y'don't know how happy I am you're here."

He patted my shoulder and walked away, probably not wanting to reveal he knew me. But I was comforted he was looking out for me the best he could.

There was now a raging epidemic going. The hospital was filled with ill men. Several died every day, but new patients took their beds. My disease worsened as a rash progressed to blisters over most of my body. Itching became almost unbearable. It was at this time that the fever returned with a vengeance. I became more and more confused about where I was until progressing into a stuporous state. I was so sick that the thought of death lost its intimidation. The doctor's prognosis became a definite possibility as I sank deeper toward a comatose condition.

Dreams changed as my illness worsened, becoming a vicarious source of comfort. Once again, I lay with Penelope on cool green fern growing along Steven's Run and felt her softness within my embrace. I marched with Hank through the lush Shenandoah Valley and experienced the sweet fragrance of hyacinth. Jacob and I fished in

Cooper River and smelled earthy odors along its banks. In the tranquil cool evening, my sister, Priscilla, and I walked beneath giant limbs of massive live oaks, and listened to our servants sing as they prepared an evening meal in our cookhouse.

Following the amputation of my mutilated right leg, Penelope Gresham loaned me a book, **A Tale of Two Cities**. I became so impressed by the opening paragraph penned by Charles Dickens that I committed it to memory. Now, as I lay in the darkness of near-coma, those lines kept running through my mind. *It was the best of times, it was the worst of times, it was the age of wisdom, it was the age of foolishness, it was the epoch of belief, it was the epoch of incredulity, it was the season of Light, it was the season of Darkness, it was the spring of hope, it was the winter of despair, we had everything before us, we had nothing before us, we were all going direct to Heaven, we were all going direct the other way.* I found the words apropos for our time, for my struggles. They streamed before my eyes as if they were emblazoned on the tail of a comet. They faded and once again I was lying on an "Old Dorm" cot. While awakening from the effects of chloroform, I felt someone unbuttoning my breast pocket. "The Lord has been with you."

"What did you say, sir?"

"This Testament saved your life."

"It did?"

"A sliver of shrapnel almost pierced it."

I managed to rise up on my elbows and peer at a man sitting beside my cot.

"I'm Chaplain Janeway with the Eleventh Army Corps," he said, holding up the small leather-bound book. "You are a Christian?"

"Yes, sir, Bishop Dossy gave it to me when I was confirmed."

"Well, it has served you well."

He then opened its back cover and read names of our Yankee relatives penned by my mother before I left Charleston. At the time, neither she nor I had any idea a need would arise for me to contact any of them. "Who is Doctor Todd Martin of Gettysburg?"

"He's my mother's cousin."

"Would you like for me to let him know about your injuries?"

I hesitated, not knowing Todd, but decided it would be a way to let my parents know I was alive. "Yes, sir, I'd appreciate it."

"Is there anything else I can do for you?"

"Hank Johnson was beside me when I was injured. We are members of Gen'ral Pettigrew's Division. If there is any way you could locate him, I would be most grateful."

"That would take a miracle, but I will do my best."

The imagery faded and I slipped back into febrile delirium. I remained unaware for at least two days except when an attendant plied my lips with water. I would gulp all of it and beg for more. This ravenous thirst continued until the fever broke. When that moment happened, I became determined to make a liar out of my Rebel-hating physician.

The course of my illness lasted about three weeks before I was allowed to return to my barrack. The only signs remaining were purplish scars scattered over my face, torso and limbs. My stamina was severely depleted, which would require several weeks for me to recover. All the time as I regained new strength, escape became a burning obsession. Fear of death from a Miniéball or drowning in Delaware River would not deter me from being free again.

CHAPTER TWO

While walking near the officers fenced prison enclosure, I saw two men seated on the ground, leaning against a barrack wall. One of them had a scraggly red beard and wore the tattered blouse of a Confederate Naval officer. I stepped closer to the fenced enclosure in an effort to see him more clearly. He raised his gaze to meet mine when I spoke. "Excuse me, sir, are you a naval officer?"

"Yes, I am."

I wondered whether this fellow might have served with my brother, Andrew? I took a couple of steps toward the fence. He held up his hand in a warning gesture. "Don't come any closer — the guards have orders to kill if you step inside the six foot line."

I was grateful for his warning. A week hadn't gone by since a prisoner was killed who had ventured into the *dead zone* near the prison gate. "No — I won't, sir."

"You sound like a South Carolinian," he said, striving to stand up.

That is when I had a strange feeling I knew this man. We stared at one another for several moments. His baldhead, rimmed by matted red hair, was flecked with brown freckles. He was pallid, emaciated and unsteady. "Yes, sir, I am from Charleston — and you?"

His expression changed from a mask of depression into one that was alert and inquisitive. "Charleston — do I know you?" He asked, shielding his eyes from the noonday sun.

I eased nearer to the *dead zone* and peered at him. As we stood staring at one another, the realization struck me that the ravages of war had affected both of us. I certainly had changed.   "Don't know — your voice sounds familiar."

"So does yours," he said, stroking his beard. "Could you be my little brother, John Pendleton?"

Could this be my brother who had been reported missing after his ship, The CSS Sea Bird, disappeared with all hands while on patrol? "Andrew?"

"Yes — John?"

"Yes, I'm your brother, John "

While leaning on my crutch, I was ecstatic but also sad — sad because my brother was obviously quite ill or starved — maybe both. My right leg was probably buried in a pit with many other mangled limbs near the "Old Dorm" in Gettysburg. We were prisoners in a despicable hellhole. I was ecstatic because I found my brother who had been feared dead. And I survived a smallpox epidemic that killed many fellow prisoners.

There we stood, separated by a fence, twelve feet of the prison's *dead-zone*, unable to embrace one another. Time stood still while emotions had to be restrained. I was tempted to lunge toward the fence, shove my hand through its wire mesh and touch my brother. Andrew stood ever so still and lifted his hands with their palms facing me. "Better leave, John. A guard is walking toward you."

He was right. We could not tarry at the fence any longer. If the guards became suspicious, we would not be able to meet again. "How about tomorrow? Can we talk then?"

"Sure. I'll be here," he said, turned away and rejoined his friend.

We changed the meeting places every day so as not to arouse any of the guards' suspicions. Our conversations covered what had happened to us since Andrew left home and joined the Confederate Navy. I learned that his ship had run aground on a sand bar in Albemarle Sound. He and his First Mate tried to reach Confederate shore batteries, but their dingy capsized when a wave pitched them against a boulder. Andrew's leg was broken, but they managed to reach dry land. His First Mate then discovered that all of the shore batteries' cannons had been spiked and abandoned. Both of them were captured later in the day when a Yankee gunboat seized The Sea Bird and its crew, and sent a dingy with armed sailors ashore.

Andrew spent several weeks in a Yankee hospital, and then was transferred to Fort Warren Prison in Boston Harbor. He was caught trying to escape and placed in solitary confinement on a starvation diet. Scurvy and malnutrition soon loosened his teeth, and also caused both knees to become swollen and painful. His once robust physique became gaunt, stooped and tremulous. I was concerned for his surviving much longer in a Yankee prison environment. How could I carry out an escape now? Leaving Andrew was impossible. Escaping together seemed beyond hope — only a miracle could gain our freedom.

* * *

Saturday, the fourteenth of November, was a cloudless day. The warm sunshine felt good on my shoulders as I walked to meet Andrew at the fence. While I plodded across the quadrangle with aid of my crutch, Sergeant O'Hara came hurrying toward me. "Pendleton," he yelled. "Come with me."

What could be so important? I turned about and followed O'Hara toward the administration building. "What's wrong?" I asked, fearing some reprisal for my frequent meetings with Andrew.

"Don't know."

O'Hara's curt reply was no surprise. He reveled in keeping prisoners on edge, causing us to wonder when retributions would occur for infractions that were impossible to avoid.

When we reached the stairway to General Schoeph's office, O'Hara stepped aside. "After you, Pendleton," he said, pointing up the steps.

I gave him a tacit nod and obeyed. My climbing steps on one leg and a crutch wasn't to his liking, so he kept poking me in the back with his finger. "Hurry up — the General ain't a patient man."

The door at the head of the stairs opened into General Schoeph's offices. His adjutant, Captain Bailey, was seated at his desk poring over a record book. O'Hara and I stood at attention awaiting Bailey's recognition. He closed the book, leaned back in his chair and gazed over rims of pinch-nosed spectacles. "Thank you, Sergeant, that will be all."

O'Hara left me alone, facing the steely glare of Schoeph's adjutant. He stood up and motioned for me to follow him into another office where the General's clerk acknowledged us. "Go right in, Captain Bailey."

I had never seen Schoeph before and wondered what kind of man I would meet on the other side of his office door. Bailey told him who I was and left after the General returned his salute. Schoeph's hair, mustache and beard were slate gray and neat. He appeared to be middle aged, slightly built and quite handsome. He leaned back in his chair and looked at my crutch and empty right pant leg pinned to my waistband. "Have you been sick, Pendleton?"

"Smallpox, sir."

"Well, you seem to have recovered."

"Yes, sir."

He nodded and picked up a sheet of paper from his desk. "You have a visitor waiting in the staff room."

"Visitor?"

He slid the sheet across his desk. "He has brought you a blanket, some clothing and canned food. The items are listed here," he said, handing me a pen. "Please sign it, and then my clerk will take you to see your visitor."

I dipped the pen in his inkwell. "Who is my visitor?" I asked, scratching John Pendleton on the line indicated by an X.

"Doctor Alonzo Gresham, the president of Pennsylvania College."

Then I understood why the General, instead of some lower ranked officer, was in charge of my visitation. Penelope's father had been interceding in my behalf with Schoeph's boss, General Hoffman. Realizing the edge this provided me was quite encouraging.

"Thank you, General," I said, handing back his pen.

He dismissed me into the care of his clerk, and then I was escorted down a long hallway. My anticipation mounted when we reached a door with STAFF ROOM stenciled on its window.

The clerk opened the door and waited as I hobbled past him. "You are to remain in this room until I return," he said, closing the door behind me.

To my surprise, the room was empty except for a dozen chairs arranged around a long oaken table. A large potbellied cast-iron stove squatted next to the far wall, but a chill in the room testified to its lack of use on this crisp fall day. I wandered about the room, scrutinizing several framed photographs on the walls. They were all of Fort Delaware Prison and its Yankee officials. Viewing them was just a means of passing time while waiting for a visit with Penelope's father. None of them held any interest for me until I reached a framed representation of the prison. It also included the Delaware River, which surrounded Pea Patch Island. An inset in its lower right corner caught my attention. A scale of one inch to fifty feet testified that this drawing had been accomplished by a qualified cartographer. He included every stockade guard tower that encompassed the prison. All buildings, fenced enclosures, latrines, cisterns and burial grounds were labeled and drawn to scale.

Architecture and cartography were two of my favorite subjects while spending four years at Eton College in Berkshire, England. Most planters' sons were sent to England upon reaching the age of twelve for their formal education. This was true for all plantations along the Ashley and Cooper rivers in South Carolina. That schematic outlay was all that I needed to put together a plan of escape in my mind. I had to memorize every detail, since there was no way to copy it, but was such a feat possible?

The answer came in an instant. Familiar sounds of rifle fire erupted from somewhere in the prison. Unintelligible shouts joined into the melee. My first thought was that a prisoner had violated the six foot no-man's zone. When I peered through a window, the commotion became clear. A prison riot was in the making. I became witness to a mob of desperate men, so enraged by their oppressors that reason could no longer restrain them. Their fear of death must have evaporated like an early morning fog hanging over the Cooper River, which coursed across our plantation. The Yankees were discovering that our men, though starved and sick, had been pushed beyond benign submission. A foul bowl of soup and hardtack filled with weevil, though wolfed down by starving prisoners, emaciates, and enfeebles both mind and body. Even so, all of the maltreatment had emboldened them to seek relief — death by a Miniéball being preferable to a strung-out demise on Pea Patch Island.

My observations ended when General Schoeph's clerk slammed open the door. "Come with me, Pendleton."

"Wait a minute," I said, hesitating to obey his curt command. "Where's Doctor Gresham?"

"Come along — your visit's been cancelled."

By the time Sergeant O'Hara shoved me through my barrack's doorway, the riot was quelled. Bare hands can be of little effect against pistol, rifle and sword. Eighteen of my compatriots paid the ultimate price, while an unknown number suffered various wounds, some that ultimately killed them. My missed visit with Penelope's father and being unable to commit the prison schematic to memory weighed upon me for several weeks.

We were allowed freedom of the prison quadrangle when the turmoil subsided and normalcy return to Delaware Prison. It was then that I returned to the officer-prisoners' compound. All was for naught. Not a single imprisoned officer was to be seen outside of their barracks. The riot had not spread to their enclosure, so I was quite certain Andrew had not been involved. The Yankees were making certain that we common prisoners would have no contacts with any of the officers. I could only cling to the hope that my brother had not succumbed to the afflictions that were consuming him.

December came and went. Christmas was a memory, one that held little joy. Sergeant O'Hara, bless his black Irish heart, tried to make amends with us by passing out sticks of horehound candy. "Happy Christmas, Rebs," he intoned, over and over, while distributing his treats. I must say that his efforts met with some success. From that day on, whispered insults laced with profanity diminished as we stood muster each morning, many of us barefoot in the snow.

Every day, no matter the weather, I returned to the fence where Andrew and I had met. Failing to catch even a glimpse of him for over two weeks, I decided to make an inquiry. No one knew I had a brother imprisoned on Pea

Patch Island. My fear of the Yankees finding this out was reasonable, since they forbad any contact between imprisoned officers and lesser ranked men. The question as to what would be their response if they gained that information was disturbing. Yet, I was being driven to do whatever was necessary. My opportunity came following muster on January 25th. Sergeant O'Hara appeared to be in a more jovial mood after he dismissed us to return to our barrack. I stood in place, standing at attention the best I could on a crutch and one good leg, while my fellow barrack mates walked away. O'Hara glared at me for a moment. "Didn't you hear me, Pendleton? You're dismissed."

"Yes, sir, I know."

"Well, get your butt back into the barrack."

"I will, sir — if I can first have a word with you."

My request must have caught him off guard. He stepped closer to me, close enough for his red beard to tickle my chin. "Well, bless me mither's grave, if this sorry Reb ain't fixin' to ask a favor. What's on your mind, Pendleton?"

"Begging your pardon, Sergeant O'Hara, I do have a favor to ask."

There we stood, eye to eye, a one-legged Confederate prisoner, dressed in tatters and a Yankee sergeant whose breath reeked of Irish whiskey. I stared at his face and watched a widening grin lift the corners of his drooping mustache. "Well now, Laddie, just what might y'be wantin' to ask, and why should I be listening at all?"

That was the first time he called me anything but Reb or Pendleton. And his smile was also something new. I wondered whether he was amused or maybe tweaked by my assumed humility. It didn't matter. I needed to ask about Andrew. "Sir — my brother, Ensign Andrew Pendleton, is confined in the officers' prison compound. I haven't been able to contact him for weeks. I need your help."

O'Hara, bemused by my request, stepped back and placed his hands on my shoulders. "So — you've a brother here. How old are you, Laddie?

"Nineteen, sir."

"Nineteen is it? When did you enlist?"

"Two years ago, sir."

He removed his hands from my shoulders. "Where did y'lose your leg?"

"Gettysburg — July third — near the cemetery."

"You're one of Pickett's boys?"

"Yes, sir, General Pettigrew's Division."

The countenance in his eyes hardened. "Well, Laddie, you lost a leg there," he said, his voice now weighed down with emotion. "I lost a son — killed defending Little Round Top."

As I watched him staring down at the snow-covered ground, his shoulders began to shake. He squeezed his eyelids trying to hold back tears that could no longer be restrained. I was overwhelmed by sorrow for this gruff, oft times abusive man, who treated all prisoners with vitriolic disdain. Embolden by sympathy for his grief, I did the unthinkable. I grasped his hand in mine and firmly conveyed my condolences the best I could. "I will pray for you and your son."

He looked up at me, nodded, and gripped my hand. "I'll get back to you regarding your brother."

I returned to my bunk to ponder what had just occurred. The reality of war and its terrible affect upon everyone, no matter the colors under which we served, had become clearer to me and would remain so the rest of my life. Sergeant O'Hara and I experienced an inexplicable encounter between a captor and prisoner, one that would change both of us. From that day on he called me, Laddie. Never again was it Reb or Pendleton.

*　*　*

The winter of my despair crept by like an inching snail. January and February came and went, leaving behind memories of trying to cope with overwhelming boredom, disappointment and misery. Every time I managed to visit the officers' compound, no loitering prisoners were seen outside their barracks. The Yankees must have blamed them for instigating the riot; otherwise, such a severe lockdown would not have taken place.

We endured sporadic outbreaks of camp fever, which I later learned were conveyed to us by every soldier's nemesis, body lice. Hours were spent searching for and squashing vermin found in bedding and clothing. As I tried to sleep, they crawled from hiding places to feed on my skin. Their blood-sucking forays produced red welts that itched almost more than I could endure. My body was covered with weeping excoriations that resulted from fingernails seeking relief while I was trying to sleep.

I was sitting on the side of my bunk, busy with a delousing project, when Sergeant O'Hara paid me an overdue visit. Several weeks had transpired since our encounter following muster. Little hope remained for any word about Andrew. O'Hara stopped beside my cot, but apparently thought better of sitting down. Lice have an ornery habit of changing hosts when given the slightest opportunity. "Well, Laddie, he said, tapping my shoulder. "If you'll stop your bug killin', I've something to tell you."

His terse comment came as I was pulling a pesky intruder from beneath the waistband of my drawers. "Let me guess," I said, trying to sound sarcastic, and then squashed the louse, wiping its remains on my britches. "General Schoeph has signed an order for my parole?"

"Now, Laddie, watch your tongue. It's about your brother I'm speaking."

Overwhelming apprehension squeezed my insides, not unlike that which I had experienced before marching into battle. I tried to read O'Hara's eyes, hoping to be reassured he bore good tidings. The answer wasn't there. His demeanor had been hardened by physical and spiritual poverty that was rampant in Delaware Prison. One thing was certain — I was his prisoner — he owed me nothing.

"I apologize, sir."

"Aye, and you should, Laddie. General Hoffman, has ordered all prisoners in the officers' compound to be removed from Delaware Prison."

"When, where are they being sent?" I said, reaching for my crutch.

"Tomorrow, to Johnson Island Prison."

"Where's that?" I asked, stood up and faced O'Hara.

"It's a small island in Lake Erie about a mile offshore from Sandusky, Ohio."

It was impossible to express the extent of my disappointment. Escaping from Delaware Prison would be a formidable task, but easier when compared to Johnson Island Prison. Nearly all of the prisoner exchanges had ceased by the spring of 18 and 64. I held little hope for Andrew's survival, no matter whether he was in Delaware, Johnson or any other Yankee prison. "He will die there," I said, sighed and leaned heavily on my crutch.

"Aye, Laddie, that he might."

"Is there any chance for me to see him ... before he's moved?"

"Not likely," he said, hesitated and then started to walk away.

A litany of emotions — fear, anger and panic, coursed through me as O'Hara strode between bunks toward the barrack's exit. Without thinking, I pursued him as fast as one leg could carry me. "Sir," I yelled, now emboldened by a burning desire to see Andrew before his leaving. "Wait! Please?"

O'Hara turned to face me. "Laddie," he said, gesturing for me to stop. "I'll do what I can, but that may not be enough. It's all I can do."

He left after I thanked him for being willing to intercede in my behalf. The hours passed even slower than usual as I waited for O'Hara to return. Pacing the full length of the barrack over and over seemed to help relieve my apprehension. Hope finally dwindled away until despair returned me to my bunk where I prayed, venting anger and frustration by the only available means left to me. It was the darkest hour of my imprisonment. I don't know whether God listened to my chastising prayer or not. Since then, I have often asked Him to forgive my haughty attitude.

Daylight gave way to darkness without any word from Sergeant O'Hara. My wretched bunk threatened to become a refuge of sorts, a cocoon where misery could be hardened into a venomous predator. I had observed this metamorphosis in several fellow prisoners since arriving at Delaware Prison. Such phenomenon often led to self-deprecating, even suicidal or homicidal behavior. I spent the night engaged in a moral battle with the demons lurking within my mind. When dawn broke, I crawled from my cocoon and awaited muster — a final moment to plead my case with O'Hara.

Following muster, my fellow prisoners returned to our barrack while I remained at attention, refusing to be dismissed without speaking with Sergeant O'Hara. Several mumbled disparaging remarks, most of them questioning my sanity, but my determination disallowed any reply. When O'Hara finished comparing the prisoner count with his list, he spoke to me. "Well, Laddie, blessings of the Blarney Stone has come your way."

Of course I knew his meaning. Irishmen believe anyone who kissed the Blarney Stone was empowered with eloquence and persuasion. "I can see, Andrew?" I shouted.

For the first time, I saw a self-satisfied twinkle in O'Hara's eyes. "General Schoeph's adjutant has agreed to a meeting in his office between you and Andrew this morning."

My spirits soared. The remnants of a depressing night disappeared like smoke from a bivouac campfire during a winter storm. "When?" I asked, trying to contain my enthusiasm.

"Before noon, I'll come fetch you."

Sergeant O'Hara came for me as promised just before noon. I was again reminded of the situation Andrew and I were forced to endure. The Yankee flag and below it a brigadier general's ensign were snapping in the wind atop Delaware Prison's flagpole. How I wished to again see the stars and bars or South Carolina's bonny blue flag streaming over our campground. Apprehension replaced my nostalgia when we were confronted by two Yankees standing guard at the doorway leading to General Schoeph's office.

Once in Schoeph's outer office, his adjutant, Captain Bailey, leaned back in his chair and scrutinized my unkempt presence. "Thank you, Sergeant, you're dismissed. Please take a seat, Pendleton," he said, pointing at a chair in front of his desk.

Bailey began to shuffle through a stack of papers. He finally stopped, pulled one from the disheveled pile and handed it to me. "What's this?" I asked, peering at an official appearing document.

"Go ahead and read it," he said, gazing at me over his spectacles. "You can read?"

"Yes, sir, I can," I replied, trying to ignore his condescending attitude.

Bailey occupied himself with his stack of papers while I concentrated on the document. I don't recall its exact wording, but will try to convey it the best I can. It was *General Order Number twenty-five by William Hoffman, Maj. Gen. U.S.A. All Confederate prisoners who retain officer grades are hereby to be confined within Federal prisons that house only prisoners of such status. From this date, there will be no contacts allowed between these and prisoners of lesser grades. March fifteen, 18 and 64. William Hoffman, Maj. Gen. U.S.A.*

The meaning of this document was devastating. There would be no meeting between Andrew and myself. Sergeant O'Hara had been duped. I handed it back to Bailey without commenting. He dropped it on his desk and gazed at me. "Do you have any questions, prisoner Pendleton?"

"No, sir, you have made your position quite clear. May I return to my barrack?"

He nodded and called for one of the guards standing at his door to conduct me back to my humble abode. It was a bad day, one that I shall never forget.

* * *

I didn't get to see Andrew before he was sent to Johnson Island Prison. When the sun set on that date, I was certain he and I would never meet again on this side of the abyss of death. Since I was now alone, so to speak, within the confines of Delaware Prison, escape was ever-present with me. Within the realm of providence, Jacob re-entered my story. It was only a few days following my encounter with Captain Bailey that fate did a turnabout for me. I was languishing within the cocoon of my hatred on an otherwise bright spring day when Jacob shook my shoulder, rousing me from my respite. "Marse John," he urged. "Wake up."

As I roused from my retreat, the familiar features of my childhood companion stared down at me. "Jacob, is that you?"

"This be Jacob. I have a plan. Be back, maybe tomorrow."

As I rose up on my elbows, Jacob hurried away, striding between the bunks of prisoners. I called to him. "I'll be here. God bless."

CHAPTER THREE

At about five a.m. on Friday, March eighteenth, my life changed forever. I was experiencing one of my nightmarish dreams, which haunted me since our final charge at Gettysburg. It was during these dreams that I crawled about the killing ground, searching for my companion-in-arms, Hank Johnson. Our dead, some mutilated, lay in distorted heaps where they were ripped apart by Yankee cannons firing pointblank canister. The wounded groaned and pleaded for water — and their mothers. The carnage was beyond description, no words being adequate to convey such grotesque depictions. I inched among the dead and wounded, searching endlessly for Hank's familiar features but to no avail. I was awakened by my voice calling, "Hank — Hank — Hank!"

I wiped stinging sweat from my eyes and thanked God for awakening me from another ghoulish nightmare. It was then I found a long object wrapped in a blanket lying next to me. It required a bit of courage to unwrap and expose this uninvited intruder, but as curiosity guided my fingers I discovered a wooden prosthetic leg. A folded piece of paper was stuffed into its sleeve designed to fit over a remaining stump. I knew it was from Jacob before unfolding and reading his note. I was thankful my father allowed me to teach Jacob how to read and write, a privilege usually denied to all slaves. *This wood leg belonged to a guard, Private McLean. He killed his self yesterday. You can throw away your crutch. Jacob.*

He later told me that McLean's right leg was amputated during the battle at Shiloh Church, Tennessee in 18 and 62. I never learned the fellow's motive for suicide, but it may have been fueled by the wretched life of a guard in Delaware Prison.

Jacob's gift was a godsend. The artificial leg was unique, designed with a metal hinged joint at the knee. A leather sleeve extending about twelve inches in length above the knee was constructed similar to a boot top secured with thong laces. I slipped it over my stump, pulled the laces taught and tied them together. It fit well, but the hinged knee buckled when I tried to stand up. I fell several times before discovering how to lock and unlock the joint. When unlocked, a coil spring in the joint allowed my lower leg to function almost as well as one of flesh and bone.

Getting used to a prosthetic leg was not easy; however, its previous owner's amputation above the knee had been identical to mine. Even so, my stump became blistered and quite tender. I tore a piece from my rotting blanket, folded and inserted it into the prosthetic's receptacle which corrected this problem.

On Sunday, the twentieth of March, Jacob told me that his plans for my escape were nearing completion. Over ensuing weeks he brought me written directions, the dead guard McLean's uniform and identity papers, some Yankee money, and a railroad map of Maryland and northern Virginia. I was able to stow all of it under my bunk until needed early in May. The plan was simple, yet risky to carry out. Four guards were to be transferred from Delaware Prison to Old Capital Prison in Washington City. I was to be one of them, assuming the dead guard McLean's identity.

All during April I walked most waking hours to toughen up my stump and gain a more normal gait. During these walks I tried to unravel the mystery surrounding Jacob's escape plans. He refused to reveal who was helping him, claiming it was too risky before my day of escape was for certain. In case the items beneath my bunk were discovered, I couldn't be made to reveal any accomplices other than Jacob.

The answer came on Sunday, the tenth of April, while I was waiting at the mess woodpile for another noon meeting with Jacob. I was sitting on a log awaiting his arrival when Sergeant O'Hara came across the quadrangle toward me. As I stood up, he stopped, glanced at several prisoners who were gathering wood nearby, and motioned for me to walk to him. "Laddie, it's time for us to have a wee talk."

"What about, sir?"

"Jacob's plan."

"Plan — sir?"

"Aye, let's take a stroll together while I explain things."

"Sure," I said, anxious to get answers to all of my questions.

"You seem to be doing well with McLean's leg. How long can you walk on it now?"

"As long as necessary."

"Good, but keep at it."

"I will, sir."

O'Hara explained the entire plan as we walked the perimeter of Fort Delaware Prison. We stayed close to the six-foot "kill zone" to avoid any prisoners or guards who might overhear our conversation. Everything appeared to be in order. Before first light on Monday, the second of May, I was to become a Yankee guard, Private Ian McLean, by donning the dead soldier's uniform. Sergeant O'Hara intended to document my presence at muster while Jacob and I headed for the prison gate. He and another guard of his choosing planned to join us on the pier. All of us were scheduled to board the riverboat at seven a.m. for our journey to Washington City. He hadn't decided who the third guard might be, which was quite worrisome. We agreed it could be too risky for any further meetings. Before we parted, I asked why he was risking so much to help me escape. His reply was, "You're not needin' to know — just yet. In due time, Laddie, I'll be tellin' ye."

Apprehension began to increase during the final week of April. I was unable to sleep the entire night before making my exit from Delaware Prison. I didn't remove my prosthesis; wanting no delay in getting dressed and assuming a new identity come dawn. I pocketed all of the accoutrements for escape, rolled into my tattered prison blanket for the last time and stared into the darkness. It was the longest night I ever spent.

Before muster on Monday, I donned McLean's uniform and waited on my bunk for Jacob to arrive. Finally, the barrack's east door opened. Jacob, silhouetted by early daylight, slipped through the doorway. He closed the door and walked between bunks toward me. Before he could shake my shoulder, I sat up, eager to head for the Delaware Queen.

"Good morning, Jacob. I'm ready," I whispered, not wanting to awaken other prisoners.

"It is a good mornin', Marse John. Time t'go."

"Is the riverboat at the pier?"

"No, but it's supposed to dock about seven with a load of prisoners."

"Do you know who the third guard is?" I asked, apprehensive about whether he would be someone we could trust.

"Yeah, he's Corporal Dickerson. Sergeant O'Hara says he's the dumbest guard in this here prison."

"Has Dickerson ever seen me — know who I am — know Private McLean?"

"I don't know, Marse John, but we gotta trust Sergeant O'Hara. He'll be jus' fine."

Three familiar blasts of a riverboat horn echoing up and down the river interrupted our conversation. "We gotta go," Jacob said, yanking my sleeve.

We slipped out of the barrack and headed for the prison gate. All of my walking had toughened and strengthened me enough to keep pace with Jacob. We reached the gate, where a guard looked at our papers. He eyed me a couple of times. "You boys are damn lucky," he said, handing me my identification. "Wish O'Hara had picked me to get away from this scum pit. We'd best shoot all these stinkin' Rebs and shut down this place."

I nodded, afraid to speak and reveal my South Carolina drawl.

"Might think about that," Jacob said. "Guardin' Rebs be better than fightin' em."

"Yeah — could be," the guard said, opened the gate and waited for us to walk on toward the pier, and my freedom.

While Jacob and I waited on the pier, several Yankees began to unload Confederate prisoners from the Delaware Queen. One of the prisoners glared at Jacob and me with hatred emanating like fire from an erupting volcano. I almost yielded to an overpowering urge to yell, *I'm not a damn Yankee — I'm a Reb just like you.*

My urge vanished when I saw Sergeant O'Hara striding toward us. He was accompanied by another Yankee wearing corporal chevrons on his sleeves. "McLean and Pendleton," O'Hara said, "Meet Corporal Dickerson."

It was startling to hear Pendleton being spoken, having forgotten for a moment that all of our slaves were given the family name. Of course, he was addressing Jacob, not me.

O'Hara proceeded to give us our traveling itinerary. "As soon as all Reb prisoners have cleared the pier, we'll board Delaware Queen for Philadelphia. Once there we'll catch a Philadelphia-Wilmington-Baltimore train headed for Washington, D.C. We should get there tomorrow morning where we are to report for duty at Old Capital Prison."

Corporal Dickerson kept glancing at me all the time O'Hara was speaking. *Dickerson may be a dumb oaf, but his interest is disturbing,* I thought and wondered how to divert his attention away from my accent. The answer was soon coming — my manner of speech could not be explained away to even a stupid Yankee. I decided to become dumber than Dickerson, to rely on shrugging, nodding or uttering unintelligible grunts when spoken to.

As the riverboat pulled away from Pea Patch Island, I stood at the forward rail, faced a rising mist, and listened to the boat's paddle wheel slapping the Delaware River. I pondered what lay ahead. A litany of questions coursed through my mind. Why was Sergeant O'Hara risking his life to help me escape? Was he doing it for me, Jacob, or some other reason? Just who is Dickerson? Has O'Hara covered my identity with him? What would happen to Jacob if my true identity were discovered? On and on, disquieting questions mirrored the anxiety building within me. I gripped the railing and exhaled a vow. "God willing, one day I will return to Gettysburg — and Penelope."

* * *

Our train pulled into Washington Station at four o'clock the next afternoon. We experienced an uneventful journey except for an unsettling five hour layover in Baltimore. During the previous night, Confederate sympathizers tried to blow up the B&O Patapsco River Bridge south of Baltimore. The city had remained under control of the Yankee army since secessionists rioted during April of 18 and 61. An angry mob attacked Massachusetts militia marching from PW&B station across town to the B&O station. The same Yankee troops returned three weeks later to take possession of the city. Despite heavy-handed military control, southern sympathizers tweaked Yankee noses by sabotaging bridges and telegraph lines. Their attempt to blow up the bridge accomplished little other than to delay our rail travel to Washington City for several hours.

I needn't have worried about Dickerson whose problems must have been greater than mine. He chose to resign from guard duties and the Yankee army during our layover in Baltimore. Fatigue caught up with us a short time following our arrival at the PW&B station. It was while all of us, except Dickerson, were sleeping on stationhouse benches that the dumbest soldier in the Yankee army decided to take leave of our company. Sergeant O'Hara was one irate Irishman when Jacob awakened us with the news of Dickerson's disappearance. O'Hara bellowed all of the profanity I'd ever heard — and then some — as we searched the station and surrounding area.

It was of no avail. Dickerson was gone. All during our searching, I kept berating myself for failing to do the same. He wasn't the stupidest oaf in the Yankee army after all. It was an imposter by the name of Private McLean.

Before boarding the train bound for Washington City, O'Hara reported Dickerson's desertion to Captain Weigel, the provost marshal of Baltimore.

* * *

We checked into the Old Capital Prison guardhouse around five p.m. It was located on the corner of Pennsylvania Avenue and East First Street, facing the Capital building and East Capital Park. My stump was quite painful by this time, which caused me to limp more than usual. Sergeant O'Hara explained the absence of Corporal Dickerson and my infirmity to Prison Superintendent Colonel N. T. Colby. Out of consideration for my disability, the superintendent assigned me to mess duties. These included procurement of meals that were ordered by moneyed civilian prisoners from nearby restaurants. Most of these individuals were political detainees whose loyalties were questionable. Thanks to Lincoln's habeas corpus suspension, they were incarcerated while undergoing investigations into alleged nefarious activities.   Upon their confinements, all money and valuables were taken and receipted by the superintendent. They could withdraw cash from these funds to pay for legitimate expenditures like food, cigars and wine. Most of the military prisoners lacked funds for purchases, so they received prisoners' rations. These were far superior to Delaware Prison's fare of an occasional fried rat, pickled beef, hardtack crackers and moldy rye bread.

O'Hara assumed sergeant-of-the-guard duties and Jacob, who advanced in rank to corporal, was responsible for third and fourth floor sentries. We were consigned to ground quarters reserved for all sentries who were supplied from infantry regiments stationed at Forts Stanton, DuPont and Carroll. A steady turnover of guards precluded any chance of getting acquainted with them.

During the first week of my assumed identity, I practiced mimicking O'Hara's Irish brogue, hoping to mask my South Carolinian drawl. The result failed to meet any objective intended, but did achieve an element of success. Only a few raised eyebrows occurred each time I met a new guard or prisoner with the usual introduction. "Top o' the day to ye. Me name's Ian McLean. To whom might I be speakin'?"

All went well the first week as I became oriented to carrying out my duties. I was assigned a team and ambulance with which to pick up orders at several restaurants. While driving Washington streets, I was impressed by the numbers of Yankee troopers. Nobody seemed to notice me. I was just another Yankee soldier who was performing his assigned tasks — hardly worthy of suspicion. Yet, there could be little comfort, realizing my absence from Fort Delaware Prison was discovered by now. What if some prying eyes should find there were two Ian McLeans, one buried in Fort Delaware Cemetery and another transferred to Old Capital Prison? If exposed, I would be charged with spying, subjected to a speedy trial and shot. O'Hara and Jacob would suffer the same fate. The only solution was for me to disappear — and soon.

* * *

On Sunday, the fifteenth of May, Sergeant O'Hara entered his office while I was seated beside his desk reading restaurant orders for the next day. "Top o' the mornin' to ye, Laddie."

"Aye, Sergeant, 'tis a fine day," I said, trying to mimic his manner of speech.

He slipped an envelope from inside his blouse and handed it to me. "After readin' what's inside — burn it."

"Burn it?" I asked, puzzled by his request.

"Burn it! You'll know why," he said and opened the door to leave. "I've a need to speak with ye, later."

I nodded, tore open the envelope and pulled out two sheets of paper. One was a letter addressed to me from my mother's cousin, Doctor Todd Martin. It was dated January third, 18 and 64 at Gettysburg, Pennsylvania. From the best of my recollection, this is what he wrote:

> Dear John,
>
> I apologize for not visiting you prior to your departure for Delaware Prison. I did not learn of your injury, nor about your being cared for at the Old Dorm until after you were transferred. However, I posted a letter by private courier to your parents as soon as Chaplain Janeway informed me of your circumstances. I do not know whether they will receive it, the war going as it is. About the only means of letters getting into the Confederacy are by private couriers who are scarce and quite unreliable.

I am posting this letter to my brother-in-law, a Sergeant stationed at Fort Delaware. He is a most trustworthy gentleman, the only brother of my dear wife, Kathleen. I regret to add that she passed away on August 5th, one month after your General Lee saw fit to attack Gettysburg. I trust you will ultimately get to read what I have to say.

In another letter, which accompanied this one, addressed to Kathleen's brother, I enclosed a draft for sufficient funds to cover the arranging of relief for your situation. The loss of his son, our nephew, Private Michael O'Hara, during the battle that inflicted your injury was a difficult burden for Kathleen, her brother, and me to bear. I abide no animosity toward you for his death — quite the contrary, we are all victims of this terrible conflict.

You will be contacted at the proper time to communicate information regarding arrangements for your future care. I trust all efforts to provide you with relief from a most trying situation will be successful.

Your Obedient Servant and Cousin,
Dr.Todd Martin

The second sheet bore an itemized listing that clarified Doctor Martin's vague references to relief and future care. I memorized the list, opened the potbellied office stove and committed envelope, letter and list to its flames.

I sat at O'Hara's desk, worrying what was going to happen on the following morning, the sixteenth of May. Somehow, Doctor Martin had managed to make arrangements for my escape, for which he could become a resident in Old Capital Prison — maybe even charged as a spy. These thoughts were most disconcerting.

My meditation was interrupted when Sergeant O'Hara returned. "Well, Laddie, have ye burned everything?"

"I did."

"Ye memorized the list?"

"Aye."

He locked the office door. "It's time for us to talk."

I followed him into an adjoining room where all prisoner records were filed. He locked that door, and turned to face me. His blue eyes were now clear — no longer bloodshot from too much whiskey. I suppose getting away from Delaware Prison removed his need for alcohol. I glanced about the room, apprehensive about our being overheard. Of course, we were alone, separated from everyone by two locked doors; however, uncertainty caused me to hesitate.

"It's all right, Laddie. We're safe here."

I stepped to the window that framed a view of Old Capital Prison's courtyard, which was barren, stark and foreboding. It reminded me of my desolate situation, the utter depravity of being confined without hope. What price was I willing to pay for freedom? Whatever it required was my response — yet, I wasn't willing to apply that prerequisite to those who were trying to help me. I sort of understood the motives of each one, O'Hara, Jacob, and Doctor Martin. I was immersed in reflections when the heavy hand of Sergeant O'Hara squeezed my shoulder. "Listen to me, Laddie. If you're thinkin' about backing out, it's too late. John Pendleton is dead and buried in Fort Delaware Cemetery."

I spun around to face him. "Dead? Buried? Here I stand, alive and breathing."

"Aye, but you are Private Ian McLean, Company I, 58th Indiana Volunteer Infantry, assigned as a guard at Old

Capitol Prison. The burial records of Fort Delaware Prison have no entry for Ian McLean — but it does have one for a Rebel prisoner named John Pendleton. Do y'understand, Laddie?"

So — I am for certain a damned Yankee, I thought. *Now, if Ian McLean gets caught, I'll be a deserter — not an escaped prisoner — maybe a spy if the ruse is discovered. The penalty could require facing a firing squad.* "All too well," I replied. "I pray John Pendleton will rest in peace."

* * *

I reined my team down the alleyway behind Willard Hotel around eight o'clock the next morning. Everything appeared usual as I parked my ambulance next to the hotel service entrance. I yanked the doorbell cable. An unfamiliar security officer opened the door. "Top o' the mornin' to ye, sir," I said, handing him O'Hara's requisition for two bottles of wine and a box of Havana cigars.

He nodded and peered at O'Hara's signature. "Wait here, Private, until I get this approved."

This is unusual, I thought as he closed the door. I've not seen this fellow before. Sergeant O'Hara's signature has never been questioned. Well, if he doesn't come right back, I'm leaving.

I didn't have long to wait before the door opened. There stood a middle-aged gentleman — not the security officer who had questioned O'Hara's requisition. My immediate thought was that a Pinkerton agent was about to arrest me. Too scared to speak, I stood at attention awaiting my fate. My perceived adversary's eyes scanned me up and down before he finally spoke. "Were you at Shiloh, Private …?"

His greeting came as a shock. The question was number two on O'Hara's list. *This man may be someone sent to initiate my escape,* I thought, *or he could be a provost marshal's agent.* Well, it didn't really matter. I had no choice but to trust him with the prescribed reply. "No, Gettysburg."

"Private Pendleton?"

"John Pendleton, sir."

"Hello, John," he said, smiled and extended his hand. "I'm Doctor Todd Martin."

When I grasped his hand, he pulled me into an awesome embrace. "Thank, God, John," he said and released me. "Now, we must not tarry. I have a change of clothes for you in my room."

"What about the team and ambulance?"

"Don't worry. It's all been taken care of."

Not needing to know the details, I nodded and followed him into the hotel, up a flight of stairs and down a hallway to room number 210. Todd gave me a towel and a bar of soap, and then led me down the hallway to a bathroom where I enjoyed scrubbing away a year's accumulation of grime. It was an indescribable relief to remove and discard my dead benefactor's uniform in exchange for civilian clothing. After taking care of my physical transformation, Todd invited me to join him in the dinning room. I ordered and devoured fresh oyster stew, schnitzel, Hungarian noodles, steaming oolong tea, and a cherry tart for dessert. I had forgotten such luxuries existed.

We returned to Todd's room where he explained how my escape plan would unfold. "We board a train at one-fifteen p.m. bound for Harper's Ferry. We will spend the night in McGreggor's Inn. You have a horse, tack gear, and bedroll waiting for you across the street at McGreggor's Livery and Feed. That is when you head south and I board a train bound for Gettysburg. The rest will be up to you and the mercies of God."

He then pulled an envelope from his travel valise and handed it to me. "This is from Penelope. We have enough time before leaving to catch our train for you to read, and then write a reply, which I will deliver for you."

I pondered the envelope, a bit anxious about what Penelope had written. Had she been offended by not hearing from me? I hoped she understood why? Well, the only way to get an answer was to open and read her letter.

> My Dear John,
>
> By the time you read this, your escape from prison will be beginning. Doctor Martin has assured me that he has managed to get it all accomplished, and there is nothing for us to worry about. I pray he is correct.
>
> I miss you every moment of the day. The memories of our spending time together on elm shaded campus grounds and the north portico of Old Dorm are precious. I loved listening to your southern drawl while you told me about your growing up years spent near Charleston, South Carolina. I would so much enjoy seeing and experiencing the grandeur of live oaks whose limbs drip with Spanish moss. Your poetic descriptions of life along the Cooper and Ashley rivers should be written down for everyone to enjoy. Maybe, some day — you will get that opportunity.
>
> Until we meet again, you are in my every prayer. Love, Penelope

I folded and pushed the letter into my breast pocket. Todd handed me a pad and pencil with which I wrote my reply. It was not a long note as I recall — just that I loved her with all my heart and counted each day as loss until we could be together again. I placed it into an envelope, sealed and gave it to Todd for his safe keeping and ultimate delivery to Penelope.

"Well, John," Todd said, handing me a valise. "I've packed most everything you will need to start on your journey. It's time to check out and catch our train."

I was so overwhelmed by emotion that my voice cracked with each effort I made to thank him for all he was doing for me. I was relieved when he patted my shoulder and spoke with compassion in his voice. "That's all right. I understand, John. Let's begin your trip toward freedom."

CHAPTER FOUR

I opened the cover of my gold watch Todd gave me when we parted at McGreggor's Livery and Feed. Its miniature music device began to play familiar strains of Lorena, a song whose lyrics expressed every soldier's yearning for happier days. The hour was half past six. I snapped shut the cover and glanced westward toward forested Blue Ridge slopes. The sun, now lingering just above the mountains, cast long shadows across the Appalachian foot hills. The mountain air, laden with whippoorwill calls and sweet aromas of azalea, evening primrose and mint, filled me with gratitude. At last, my spirit was being renewed, having been ransomed by Todd, Jacob and Sergeant O'Hara from a hellish existence within Yankee prison walls.

By this time, Todd should be back in Gettysburg — probably handing my letter to Penelope and telling her about my escape. The thought yanked me back to reality. My journey was destined to carry me more miles away from Penelope than I wanted to count. I wondered whether we would ever see each other again. Could I dare rein my horse around and risk recapture trying to cross the Potomac, Maryland, the mountains and valleys of southern Pennsylvania? The answer, bitter to swallow, came quickly. Too many had risked their lives and liberty for my chance at survival and freedom. If I were captured north of the Potomac River, it could spell disaster for my benefactors.

I needed to find an out-of-the-way place to camp, one where smoke from a campfire would not attract attention. The area was loaded with Yankee and Southern units eager to control the Shenandoah Valley. Northern invaders wanted to render it desolate — my people hankered to send them scrambling back across the Potomac.

I reined my horse, a solid sorrel gelding, quite a distance away from the roadway into a grove of oak and dogwood. There, I discovered a spring fed pool secluded among rocky outcroppings and mountain laurel whose lavender buds were about to break into full bloom.

I prayed it would be far enough from the road for me to remain undiscovered by friend or foe. Determining the difference between them was often difficult. Both Yankee cavalry and Confederate guerrillas roamed across northern Virginia. The Yankees, some of them deserters, pillaged and burned public buildings and private homes. Bushwhackers and highwaymen who held no allegiance to North or South, raped, murdered and plundered at will. Horses were prized possessions; consequently, a good mount was subject to seizure by guerrillas and Yankees or being stolen by bandits.

I watered and hobbled my horse before unrolling the saddle pack Todd purchased from McGreggor's Livery and Feed. It contained basic needs: a nosebag for feeding grain to the horse, a sack of oats, cooking utensils, bags of bacon, coffee, sugar, dried apples, hard crackers and corn meal, canned oysters and sardines and a jar of molasses. I then fed the gelding before gathering dry wood to build a campfire. My supper was coosh, a combination of fried bacon with a tasty sauce made by adding corn meal to the grease. It was a simple meal that stuck-to-your-insides, a common fare for us during bivouacs and extended marches.

I crawled into my bedroll and fell asleep pondering many nights spent in the field before being captured at Gettysburg. Many of them were of one or another extreme. Some were during blizzards, so cold sleep would not come. Others were oppressive from heat, humidity and swarming mosquitoes. Not a few were interrupted with trips to a latrine trench in response to belly cramps and dysentery. I have no idea how long I had been sleeping when awakened by cold steel being pushed against my neck. "Empty yer pockets, Reb," a harsh sounding voice threatened. "Or we'll empty 'em for ya."

Sensing the cold steel was a revolver barrel; I nodded agreement to my assailant's request and sat up. He pulled away his gun. Three men wearing combinations of Confederate and Yankee blouses and kepis surrounded me. My campfire, having been rekindled by the bushwhackers, lit up their faces. They appeared to be enjoying my predicament with laughter and jovial banter about the loot I was providing them. The only item I kept was a knife hidden in a pouch on my prosthesis. They got everything including the gold watch Todd gave me.

My story could have ended then if it hadn't been for my prosthesis. The leader leaned down to scoop up my possessions. "How'd you lose yer leg?"

"Gettysburg — Pickett's charge."

"You're a Reb?"

"Pettigrew's Division."

"You're desertin'?" he asked, stuffing all of my belongings into a haversack while his cohorts set about saddling the gelding.

"Reckon so," I lied, hoping my robbers were deserters who would sympathize with my predicament.

He scowled at my reply. "Hah — y'ain't got much smarts. Next time make a cold camp."

They rode away leaving me to ponder my stupidity. I chucked more wood on the campfire and waited for dawn.

* * *

I headed south at first light. My plan was to avoid public roads and open fields by following game trails that traversed forested mountain slopes. Having lost my horse and supplies to the bushwhackers forced me to rely on survival tactics learned while serving in the Army of Northern Virginia. The greatest problem facing me was walking across steep terrain for many hours on a prosthetic leg. Before leaving camp, I fashioned a sturdy walking stick with my knife the marauders had overlooked.

It was about sundown when an imminent change in the weather was ushered in by a cold wind sweeping through the woods. Lightning streaked and thunder rumbled amid dark, ominous clouds rolling across crests of the Blue Ridge Mountains. A pelting rain propelled by swirling winds began to sting my face. I didn't fear the rain, just lightning. I experienced its terrifying presence during a mountain storm in this same area while we were marching toward our invasion of Maryland and Pennsylvania. Several men and horses were killed when a fiery bolt slammed into the tree under which they were seeking shelter. I had to find a refuge before the storm's full force arrived.

While hurrying down a trail toward lower country, darkness began to engulf me as storm clouds blotted out the setting sun. The storm's fury was getting closer. Like the roaring of a hundred artillery batteries, a thunderous staccato of sound pained my ears and shook the mountainside. The pungent odor of ozone generated by each lightning strike permeated the air. When I had almost given up finding shelter, a beckoning light flickered beyond the trees like a lighthouse summoning a floundering ship.

My pace quickened, being driven by the need for a safe place to weather such a storm. Upon reaching a mountain meadow, the light's source became apparent. There was a farm house, barn, corral and shed near a copse of oaks in the center of the clearing. A bolt of lightning slammed into a tree behind me just as I reached the nearest building, a tack shed with two horse stalls attached. I entered through a side door, found a pile of loose hay and several saddle blankets hanging on wall pegs.

I stripped away wet clothing, hung them on wall pegs, wrapped myself in horse blankets and bedded down in the hay. The blankets reeked of stale horse sweat, but I soon forgot about its pungency as my shivering subsided. I became oblivious to the storm raging outside as my exhausted body yielded to an overpowering need for sleep.

I was awakened the following morning by someone slamming shut the back door of the house. I jumped up and peered through a crack in the wall. An elderly woman with a gray shawl tied over her head was walking toward the shed. There was no way I could avoid a confrontation with her, so rather than having her find me, I decided to go meet her. I hesitated. There wasn't time to put on my clothes. What would she do if a nearly naked man with a prosthetic leg and attired only in horse blankets came to meet her? Realizing the shock would be greater for her if I stayed in the shed, I eased open the door just enough to poke my head through the opening. "Please don't be scared, ma'am," I said, trying to emphasize my South Carolinian drawl.

She stopped and pulled the shawl away from her face. "Who are you? What are you doin' in my shed?"

"I'm John Pendleton, ma'am. I took refuge from the storm in your shed last night — hope you don't mind."

"I don't mind. Where are you from, John Pendleton?"

"South Carolina, ma'am."

She took a couple of steps toward me. "Might you be a deserter? I can tell you ain't a Yankee."

"I was in Gen'ral Pettigrew's Division. I lost my right leg and got captured at Gettysburg, but escaped several days ago."

Her face broke into a smile. "Well, I do declare. You mean to tell me you came this far without gettin' caught?

This part of Virginia's been swarmin' with bushwhackers and Yankees for the past week."

"Well, I haven't seen any Yankees, but bushwhackers stole my horse and supplies night before last."

"Then you're afoot?"

"Yes, ma'am."

"Without a right leg?"

I eased the door open enough to show my prosthesis. "Yes, but I get by using this one."

I guess a portion of my nakedness showed as well. She looked away for a moment. "Get yourself decent, John Pendleton, and come on in the house. I'll get breakfast cookin'."

"Thank you, ma'am. I appreciate that."

"Don't keep callin' me ma'am. My name is Sarah. Sarah will do just fine," she said and returned to the house.

I dressed in still damp clothing, walked to the house and knocked on the back door.

"No need knockin', John. The door's unlocked."

When I opened and stepped through the doorway, a muffled growl greeted me. Lying beside the fireplace hearth was a large black dog gnawing on a shank bone. "Now, Captain," Sarah said. "John is our guest. Keep your growls to yourself."

I slid a ladder-back chair away from the table and sat down. "A good lookin' dog," I said, trying to hide any apprehension in my voice.

Sarah busied herself preparing our breakfast. "He's a good dog — belongs to my grandson."

"Is your grandson in the Army?"

"You say you were at Gettysburg? He was there, too. We got a letter from his captain a few weeks ago sayin' that he had been missin', and probably captured. Nobody for certain knows what happened to him."

"What general did your grandson serve under?"

She looked up from tending a cast-iron skillet and pushed silver tresses away from her face. "Jeb Stuart — why do you ask?"

"The First Virginia Cavalry?"

"That sounds right."

"What is your grandson's name?"

"Same as mine — Arthurs."

My heart sank as she spoke. Cade, my Fort Delaware prison mate's last name was Arthurs. I probably was sitting in his grandmother's kitchen, having been invited to breakfast after spending the night in her tack shed. As I pondered how to reply without causing her another shock, I decided to postpone the issue until we became better acquainted. I was certain the prisoner I knew was her grandson, and he was dead from smallpox — the news was going to break her heart. Sadness penetrated my soul as Mrs. Arthurs set a steaming plate of scrambled eggs, sow belly and corn dodgers before me. "Thanks," I said as she poured coffee into my cup. "I never saw any of our cavalry during the battle."

With breakfast finished, I gathered my plate, cup and utensils together and set them in a dishpan on the cabinet counter. "No need t'bother, John," Sarah said, dipping water into a kettle. "I'll wash 'em later. Just set and we'll talk while I cook a ham bone in a pot of beans and mix up some cornbread."

"Yes, ma'am," I said and reached down to pet Captain, hoping he wouldn't growl or snarl at me.

"It's Sarah. I told you to forget the ma'am."

Captain continued to gnaw on his bone as if I hadn't touched him. A couple wags of his tail said it all — *thanks for the pats, but I'm busy.* At least, that was my impression.

Sarah was in a jovial mood as she tended her chores. She did most of the talking while Captain slept and I listened. I marveled at her innate ability to paint word pictures, which reminded me of descriptive narration I'd studied at Eton College in Birkshire, England. "You're fortunate," she said, wagging a mixing spoon at me. "We had an early springtime blizzard in March. It's good you didn't come along then. It sort of snuck up on us. There was a low overcast when I awoke the mornin' it hit. Right soon the sky was filled with white flakes flutterin' through the windless air to alight on naked tree limbs and backs of my four milk cows. My stove had heated the window panes enough to melt the snow as it pelted against 'em, but it soon froze. Ice built upon itself, distortin' the outside world into grotesque shadows, which became murky and uninterestin'. Well, John, you ain't interested in my talkin' about the weather. Tell me about your family."

Sarah stayed busy while I told her about growing up on our plantation north of Charleston and most everything that had happened to Andrew and me during the war. I avoided bringing up her grandson, not wanting to convey sadness into her life, not just then. I knew she had to be told, but I was praying for a more fitting time.

While I was talking, she began to hum a song whose melody was unknown to me. "That is a pleasant tune," I said, interrupting my story. "What is it called?"

She slowed the speed of her mixing spoon in a bowl of cornbread fixings. "Abide With Me," she said and hesitated. "My husband, George, God rest his soul, loved that song. He'd ask me to sing it for him every day after he took to his bed with consumption two years ago. The night he lay dyin', he called out to me, 'Come sing my song, Sarah.' He went on to be with the Lord while I was singin'. I guess it's been takin' George's place here in this lonely house since then. Do you sing, John?"

"Yes, our family would gather around and sing while my mother played the piano."

"That's nice. Can you play any instruments?"

"I can strum a little on a banjo."

She clapped her hands, hurried from the kitchen and returned clutching a banjo. "This is George's. It ain't made a sound since he passed. Would you play me a tune — I surely do long to hear its singin' strings one more time."

"This is a mighty fine instrument," I said, reaching for the banjo.

"You'll have to tune her up — can't wait to hear her warblin' soul again."

The banjo, indeed, was beautiful. Diamond shaped ivory inserts were inlaid between the frets. Its tuning knobs were carved ivory. The body was polished rosewood; however, the skin was stained and worn from being struck by strummer's fingers. I plucked each string and found they were near to a true pitch. I tuned each string and began to play, *The Berry Patch Dance*, a folk tune learned as a youngster. Sarah began to clap and skip about the kitchen. Captain awakened, jumped about and barked as he pawed at the kitchen door. I suppose he thought we had lost our senses and wanted to escape from such antics. Sarah didn't miss a step as she opened the door and Captain made a quick exit.

I finished the lively tune and began to pluck, *Come, Ye Disconsolate*, a hymn my mother loved. To my surprise, Sarah began to sing with a clear soprano voice the words of that old hymn. As the last note faded, I knew the time had come for me to tell her about Cade. I sat staring at the banjo as she returned to her work, picked up a spoon and poured cornbread fixings into a baking pan.

"You have a beautiful voice," I said and laid the banjo on the table.

"Thank you, John. I ain't done any singin' since George died. Our church is about the only place where I've done any — now, we don't have regular services, except when a visiting parson rides through."

She opened the cookstove firebox, stoked the fire with a poker and dropped in several sticks of wood. "The cornbread will be ready afore long," she said, sliding the pan into the oven.

I tried to speak, but words froze on my tongue. She lifted the bean pot lid and began to stir its contents. "The ham and beans are nigh done."

I took a deep breath and tried to muster faltering courage. "Sarah," I began. "I ah, ah, need to ah, ask you something."

She seemed to sense my distress while wiping her hands on a towel. "You can ask anything you need," she said with a note of compassion in her voice. "What is it?"

"You said your grandson was missing at Gettysburg."

"Yes."

"What is his Christian name?"

She frowned and steadied her gaze at me. "Cade. You never saw him — did you, John?"

My distress must have shown itself. She stepped to the table, pulled out a chair and sat down. "You know something about Cade — don't you?

I grasped her hand. "Yes, Sarah, I regret having to give you some bad news."

"He's dead ain't he, John?" she said, gazing at our hands.

"We were bunkmates in Fort Delaware Prison. He took down with smallpox and they put him in the prison hospital. He never returned and I heard later that he died. I wish there was some other way to tell you about this."

Silence fell on that little farmhouse in Loudoun County, Virginia as she wept for the loss of her grandson — I grieved for the anguish I brought to her. A scratching sound on the door brought her time of weeping to an end.

Sarah dabbed each cheek with her apron and opened the door. Captain sauntered across the kitchen and curled up in a corner next to the stove. "The cornbread's ready," Sarah said. "Let's have dinner."

* * *

For the better part of a week, I settled into a routine of sleeping, good food, chopping firewood, hewing shingles and patching Sarah's leaky roof. I told her everything I could recall about Cade, including his humor about getting captured by Custer's Wolverines. Sarah rummaged through George's possessions for items to replace those stolen from me by bushwhackers. She retrieved a canvas knapsack from her tack shed and provisioned it with beef jerky, a bar of lye soap, bone-handled Addis toothbrush, and comb. Other items included were two pair of socks, tin cup, and an oilskin wrapped supply of matches.

The day before I was planning to leave, Sarah insisted that I take one of her horses for my journey toward home. She wrote a bill of sale for one of her two mares, both of which were over fifteen years old. "Kate's the best of my horses. She's yours, so be sure to keep this handy. No tellin' what the Yankees might do if they capture you on somebody else's horse."

I was overwhelmed by her generosity, which made it possible for me to continue my trek to Charleston. "Thanks, Sarah," I said, folding the bill of sale. "I hope that someday I can repay you for your kindness."

"Oh, tut — tut, John. There's one more thing I want you to do."

"Of course. Anything you ask."

"Take Captain with you. Cade would want you to have him, and he'll be a good travelin' companion."

"I hate to take him. He's protection for you — all alone here by yourself."

"I'll do just fine. Don't fret about me."

I was certain she had made up her mind, so there was no need to argue with her. Consequently, I went about cleaning and waxing a saddle for an early start the following morning, Wednesday, the 27th of May.

Saying goodbye to Sarah would be pure agony, which reminded me of the morning I bade my mother and father farewell and boarded a train bound for service in the army. I tried to delay the moment as long as possible by getting all of my gear packed. I then saddled and tied my bedroll on Kate and led her by the reins to the backdoor hitching post. Sarah swung open the kitchen door and walked down the path to meet me. She handed me a bundle wrapped in yellow oilskin. "Here's some ham and biscuits for dinner. Kate's a good mare, sure footed and well behaved. I hate to see her go, but it's hard for me to keep and feed two of 'em."

"Thanks …," I managed to say past a lump lodged in my throat.

"Don't forget, Captain. He'll go ahead of her just the same as when him and Cade went deer huntin'."

"Yes — ma'am."

She wagged a finger under my nose. "It's Sarah, John. No more ma'ams."

The emotions welling within me were striving to erupt, which seemed to shut down all of my mental capacities. In only a week I grew to love this gray headed lady who had become my surrogate grandmother. I doubted we would ever meet again this side of death. While I was struggling to maintain control, Sarah held out a folded piece of paper. "This is a map. I drew it for you this mornin'. Just follow the marked roads and they'll get you across Goose Creek toward Snicker's Gap in the Blue Ridge. That's as far as I know anythin' about. You're on your own from there on."

All I could do was nod, being unable to speak. We reached for and embraced each other. "I'm prayin' for your gettin' home safe," she said, pulling my face against her cheek.

"Goodbye and thanks for everything."

"Goodbye, John," she whispered and patted her callused hand against my cheek.

We parted our embrace. I stepped into my stirrup and mounted Kate. Sarah held her folded hands beneath her chin. "You're more than welcome, John. Thanks for tellin' me about Cade, and for playin' George's banjo for me. Keep out of sight of them Yankees. Once in the Shenandoah, you'll be safe. Oh, there's a ham bone in with your dinner for Captain."

"God bless you, Sarah. I'll always remember you," I said and reined Kate about. "Come on Captain, let's be going."

* * *

Once I reached Goose Creek, Snicker's Gap and access to the Shenandoah could be found without difficulty. My division had taken that route on our march to Gettysburg. I kept on the roadways most of the time, only leaving for cover on two occasions to avoid approaching Yankee cavalry patrols.

My good fortune in avoiding patrols then took another turn. I cold camped within a copse of oaks near Goose Creek late in the afternoon and was enjoying Sarah's ham and biscuits. Captain stopped gnawing his ham bone and growled. Three riders were approaching through a walnut grove on the other side of the creek. I'd made another mistake by hobbling Kate in a grassy meadow about 100 yards from camp. They sighted her, reined to a stop, and remained motionless for a few moments. There was no choice for me except to feign friendliness toward them. "Keep your growling to yourself," I said, stroking Captain's shoulder.

I continued to observe them as they parleyed together. Finally, one rode toward the creek until reaching water's edge. "Hello the camp," he yelled.

Captain and I walked out of the woods toward our visitor. "Hello," I yelled, and then admonished Captain, "Steady — stay — steady."

The rider swam his horse across the creek, spurred him up the bank, and trotted to meet me. He was attired in a scruffy Yankee private's uniform and cradled a carbine in the crook of his elbow.

I waved, hoping to appear friendly and unafraid. "I'm John Pendleton."

"Do you have any identification, Mr. Pendleton?" he said, stepping out of his stirrup.

"Just this bill of sale for my mare," I said, pulling it from my pocket.

He jerked off a glove, accepted and unfolded the paper. He glanced at me once while reading it. "This states you are Mrs. Arthur's grandson. Is that correct?"

"Yes, sir, I am."

He frowned and handed the paper back to me. "Where are you headed?"

"Berryville to fetch medicine for my ailing grandmother."

"Well, John, it looks like you've got a good place to camp — mind if we join you?"

Before I could reply, he whistled and waved for his companions to cross the creek.

"No, sir, I don't mind," I said, not having any other choice.

Captain didn't cause any trouble, but he never ventured far away from me as we returned to camp. The Yankees were armed only with Colt Army revolvers and Spencer carbines. I wondered why they weren't wearing traditional sabers since their kepis were trimmed with crossed cavalry swords.

My uninvited guests began to act more friendly after we built a good campfire. The first one to cross the creek squatted by the fire and filled his pipe with tobacco. He pulled a brand from the fire and lit it. Between puffs, he began to speak. "Well, John — since we're goin' to be together tonight — I reckon we need to know each others names. I'm Fenton Beavers."

"Pleased to meet you," I said, shaking his hand.

I circled the campfire, exchanging names and shaking hands with his compatriots. They made the usual responses and we settled down to an evening of idle conversation. Their supper was made up of bacon and hardtack biscuits crumbled into a pan of bacon grease. I didn't dare mention my Confederate preference for coosh, the same concoction except using cornmeal instead of hardtack. Their demeanor and conduct raised my suspicions as to whether they were who they claimed to be. They had little interest in me — not even a comment about my limp and squeaking prosthetic leg. A genuine soldier would quiz to determine what a lone man with a dog, a horse, and without any weapons was up to. I decided they were foragers, scouts for a raiding party, or out and out deserters. I was determined to not turn my back on them, so spent a sleepless night rolled up in my bedroll. Captain curled up next to me, showing no belligerence toward them, for which I was grateful.

The night grew chilly as our campfire waned. I lay staring at red embers as they gathered gray ash and finally died. My thoughts turned to Penelope, Jacob, Sergeant O'Hara and Todd. I regretted any additional problems I might cause them to endure. Over and over, scenarios of being captured and returned to prison arose out of my subconscious like steam from a boiling cauldron.

The coming of dawn was welcome, bringing a measure of relief from an ill spent night. The Yankees got up, ate breakfast, saddled and then mounted their horses. Without a thank you and only a terse goodbye, my uninvited guests rode out of camp toward the east. Their true identity and mission remained unanswered, but I was grateful for being able to continue my journey.

As we ascended the eastern Blue Ridge slopes, I urged Kate toward Snicker's Gap, hoping to reach Shenandoah Valley by noon. Captain, his tail flopping to and fro, scurried ahead of us. The countryside was now populated with hardwoods and pines. When Hank Johnson and I marched through here the previous June, everything was just like today. It was verdant and laden with aromas of daffodil, mountain primrose and forget-me-not. Kate seemed to sense my urgency by maintaining a steady pace in spite of the steep ascent. When we reached the summit of Snicker's Gap, the expanse of Shenandoah Valley unfolded before us. Captain began to growl, a certain warning something was amiss. Kate began to snort and perk her ears. I stepped out of my stirrup, not wanting to be astride a frantic mare if a predator was at hand. I held the reins taut and led her off the trail into a secluded area among loblolly pine and mountain laurel. I caught site of red, white and blue through a break in the trees along the road. If columns of Yankee cavalry were riding through the gap, my bid for freedom might be at an end. I prayed, tried not to move, make any sounds, or even breathe. A simple whinny by Kate or one yap by Captain would seal my fate.

CHAPTER FIVE

I was relieved when cavalrymen rode into view bearing our red, white and blue CSA battle flag atop a color bearer's staff. As I led Kate and Captain into the open, two troopers left their column and trotted toward me. I cautioned Captain to stay, and waited. One of them, wearing sergeant's chevrons, dismounted and handed his reins to the other trooper. "Hello, you live around here, son?" he said, walking to meet me.

"No, sir, South Carolina."

He frowned and held up his hands, gesturing for me to stand still. "You sound like a Carolinian. What's your name?"

"John Pendleton, General Pettigrew's Division. I lost my right leg at Gettysburg and spent eight months in Fort Delaware Prison. I managed to escape and am tryin' to get home."

"Your right leg?"

I pulled up my trousers so he could see the prosthesis. "Yes, sir."

"I'm sorry, John. You're welcome to ride with us. Yankee scouts are in this area."

I glanced at the column of riders. None wore the same uniform, being attired in gray or butternut trousers along with blouses of various blue or gray hues. Some wore blue or gray kepis, but most wore hats, some of which were adorned with a large feather or plume. Their varied uniforms were not unusual; however, hat adornments of such were usually worn by general officers like JEB Stuart. "Which cavalry are you, sir?" I asked, reluctant to get involved with a group so diverse in appearance.

He chuckled at my apparent reluctance. "I'm Sergeant Benjamin Moore," he said and pointed at his compatriots. "We are Company D — Forty-Third Battalion — Virginia Cavalry."

Of course I accepted his offer, but had some concern about Captain. He was obedient to my commands, always refraining from barking at or showing any belligerence toward strangers. However, I was certain one mistake by him would be his last.

My benefactors turned out to be a unit of Lt. Colonel John S. Mosby's Rangers. I was to remain with them for six weeks as they went about harassing Yankees. Captain behaved himself and was soon adopted by the men of Company D as their mascot. He supported himself by foraging rabbits and an occasional squirrel. The unit only camped together for three or four nights before "holing up" in homes of friends or relatives. A majority of Company D were Maryland secessionists with relatives scattered throughout northern Virginia. They would assemble again when summoned to participate in another round of raids. These tactics made their capture difficult, but branded them as outlaw guerrillas, subject to summary execution if apprehended — a disconcerting reality if I should be taken prisoner while in their company.

During these times of dispersion, Captain and I shared hiding places with members. It was during one of these times that I learned about the three Yankee imposters who had spent the night in my camp. They were troopers of Company D, who on occasion would don Yankee uniforms in order to ferret out promising targets for Ranger raids.

While Captain and I were "holed up" with Rangers Pete and Roy Conklin at the home of their aunt, Mrs. Faith Conklin, in Fauquier County, they introduced me to horse artillery. Several light howitzers had been captured and hidden in her barn. We studied tactics and the mechanics of deploying, unlimbering and firing cannons laid out in several Virginia Military Institute texts. We also practiced "dry runs" in the barn until I could do it blindfolded.

During this interlude, Mosby, who the Yankees called The Gray Ghost, came to parley with Pete and Roy. He was slight of build, spoke with a pleasant Virginia drawl, and emitted an aura of self-confidence. A well-trimmed black beard and mustache graced his somewhat gaunt features. The most striking thing about him was a steely gaze he fixed on me during our conversation. My experiences during and following Pickett's charge on July 3rd was of considerable interest to him. He was so compelling that I volunteered to become a cannoneer in Company D, but he refused my services. "You've sacrificed enough, John," he said, probably trying to spare my feelings. I realized the Rangers were raiders whose success depended on speed and surprise. Anyone with my disability would be more of a liability than an asset for them.

On Monday, July the fourth, Pete and Roy left to reconvene with the men of Company D while Kate, Captain and I headed south. My only security was a passport signed by Lt. Colonel Mosby, requesting my unfettered passage through all areas controlled by C.S.A. forces. The document could also guarantee my demise if discovered by the invading Yankees.

* * *

I crossed Rapidan River at Madison Mills on the seventh of July and headed toward Pamunkey River and Mine Run. I rode into a farmyard just outside the village. A white-haired gentleman whittling a stick was sitting on the porch. "Good afternoon, sir," I said, reining Kate toward the house.

He continued to whittle without looking up. "Afternoon, sonny."

"Can you tell me whether General Lee's forces are here about?"

"Nope. They were here durin' the winter, but pursued the Yankees after thaw."

"How long have they been gone?"

He leaned back a bit. "Where've you been, sonny?" he said, peering intently at me. "Gen'ral Lee's been whuppin' Yankees from the Wilderness to Petersburg since first o' May."

If the Yankees had reached Petersburg, Richmond was in danger. I thanked the old man, reined Kate about and headed south.

It appeared the invaders now controlled Virginia from the Potomac almost to our capital and beyond. No longer could I travel public roads, but needed to traverse out of the way places. It slowed and frustrated my progress, but I was fortunate to have Captain with me. He always assumed lead several yards in front of Kate, similar to scouts riding ahead of a cavalry column. When sensing danger, he would stop, remain unmoving and growl until I reached him. I might have been captured and executed or returned to prison except for his keen senses.

My journey to Richmond was accomplished on the nineteenth of July as I neared Fort Stevens east of the Richmond and Petersburg Railroad. A field, through which I rode, was overcast by smoke from mess fires. Cannons were limbered and aligned in a clearing within a hillside grove of trees. The setting sun's rays reflected red and orange from polished bronze and steel gun barrels. A crimson battle flag fluttering atop an earthwork's staff denoted an officer's bunker. When I reached it, a Negro man appeared in the doorway, holding a tin plate, cup and utensils.

"Is this the commanding officer's quarters?"

"Yes, sir," he said, bowing in the manner of an obedient servant.

"I'd like to speak with him."

A bearded man of about twenty-five years with piercing brown eyes set beneath bristled brows appeared behind his manservant. "I'm Major Graham. You say you'd like to speak with me?" he said and eased aside his orderly. "Go fetch my supper, Josh."

I pulled Colonel Mosby's note from my pocket and handed it to the major. He unfolded, read it, and then eyed me. "Are you Private John Pendleton?"

"Yes, sir, I am." I continued to explain my service, injury, imprisonment and escape.

"Colonel Mosby writes you're a qualified cannoneer."

"Just mountain howitzers, sir."

"I could use another man in my battery."

I pondered his meaning. Survival and getting home would be enhanced by joining friendly forces. There were no areas free of Yankees between Richmond and Charleston, South Carolina. To continue my solo journey at this time and place seemed to be pure folly. "I'm willing if needed," I said, resigning myself to defending what was left of the Confederacy — and my best chance for staying alive.

"I'm placing you in Sergeant Bob James's mess. You'll find his quarters over where our cannons are deployed."

"Thank you, sir."

"Best keep an eye on your dog," Major Graham cautioned as I started to mount Kate. "Some of my men are hard up for meat. They've been known to eat such critters."

His admonition caused me to step out of my stirrup and assume a defiant stance. "Beggin' the Major's pardon, that'll not happen while I'm alive, sir."

* * *

Major Graham advanced my rank to corporal and assigned me to the crew of a captured 12 pound Napoleon howitzer. Kate was teamed with four horses and a cantankerous mule to draw and deploy my bronze-barreled gun and limber.

All forts defending Petersburg and Richmond were in the thick of it. Two divisions of Yankee cavalry crossed the James River and began harassing our people. The main conflict occurred at Darbytown on New Market Road. Several batteries from neighboring forts had to fight skirmishes close by with Sheridan's troopers.

I discovered little difference between working a mountain howitzer and larger cannons. Napoleon 12.3 pound solid or explosive shot could be propelled over 1,500 yards. Frontal assaults required the use of canister, a cylinder filled with everything from nails to ball shot. As an infantryman, I had lost my leg to this horrible bludgeon at Gettysburg. It was of some relief to be serving on the other end of this weapon.

My first action as a cannoneer occurred on the thirtieth of July. During early morning hours, I was awakened by an explosion, the magnitude of which was and remains beyond description. Captain erupted into frenzied high-pitched barking. Bugles and drums blasted their call for us to assemble and man batteries. Within an hour we reached the crater where Yankees exploded tons of powder burrowed beneath our lines. The blast annihilated a battery and over one regiment of Confederate infantry. The crater swarmed with confused Yankees. Their officers failed to anticipate our rapid counter attack. We unlimbered and deployed several cannons within point blank range. Our bombardment turned the crater and surrounding grounds into a hellish cauldron, killing and maiming wave after wave of invaders. Many of them were Negroes, whose presence sent gray-clad infantrymen into a frenzied killing spree.

My job was to help unhitch horses, and lead each team away from action to the rear. I occupied a position drenched with danger. A Negro Yankee escaped from the crater and avoided getting shot or captured while running toward me. I didn't even possess a weapon with which to parry a thrusting eighteen-inch bayonet. My demise seemed inevitable.

The next few moments were not unlike Ahab's encounter with Moby Dick, the great White Whale: *The White Whale churning himself into furious speed, almost in an instant as it were, rushing among the boats with open jaws, and a lashing tail, offered appalling battle on every side.* In that instant, I knew the emotions coursing through Melville's Ahab. The Negro Yankee, his eyes filled with terror, careened toward the caisson horses and mules, and me. Like a charging squad of raging infantrymen, he bellowed oath after vile oath while lunging forward. His intention was clear as that of the surgeon who amputated my mangled right leg. Without any conscious thought, two years of infantry training and battle know-how took command of my body. While trying to crouch low to avoid eighteen inches of piercing steel, my spring-loaded prosthetic knee joint buckled. As the bayonet grazed my left side, the Yankee recoiled and hesitated. The last moment I remember of that event was a rifle butt hurtling toward my head.

* * *

I was not aware of anything for several hours, during which time I was transported to Wayside Hospital in Petersburg located near Southside Railroad Depot. There I remained in a stuporous condition for two more days. It was during this twilight of consciousness that I experienced a visual phenomenon, which can best be described as an apparition — or maybe — a vision.

I was confirmed into full membership at St. Michael's Church in Charleston, South Carolina, by Bishop Treetor Dossy when I was a lad of thirteen. Bishop Dossy was very close to our family for many years. He presided over the marriage of my parents and christened my brother Andrew, my sister Priscilla, and me. Our family was devastated when he died an untimely death during a cholera epidemic a short time following my sister's confirmation. He was a saintly man who took the burdens of others upon himself. When he came to me during my ordeal, I was not surprised, nor did I question the reality of his appearing. It was unthinkable for me to believe he no longer existed, a man of God who devoted himself to all unfortunates. So, let me tell about his coming to me during my journey between life and death: Out of the darkness of my afflicted world came a brilliant light, which enfolded me with an overwhelming presence of peace and love. There was no pain, no fear, only complete tranquillity. I have not known such awesome love either before or hence that time of supernatural visitation to my bed of misery. In the distance, an apparition of Bishop Dossy carrying a shepherd's staff walked toward me. The nearer he came, the more I experienced complete serenity. When only a short distance separated us, he stopped, smiled and raised his staff. "John, the Lord has sent me to anoint you with his everlasting love for all lost souls. He has ordained you to be His messenger, a purveyor of His gospel to the lost and afflicted. Your life has been extended for the fulfillment of His purposes."

He then touched me with his staff and said, "Rise, stand upon your feet for I have appeared unto you for this purpose, to make you a minister and a witness." He then disappeared, but the aura of peace remained with me until I was aroused by Captain's tongue lathering my bruised left cheek.

I returned to my battery a changed man. The oath to serve my country took on a new meaning, an obligation of which I could not shirk in any manner or means. Once again, I committed myself to serve in the trenches during our defense of Petersburg and Richmond. It was destined to be an ordeal of indescribable proportions. Only the companionship of my faithful dog, and assurances bestowed upon me by Bishop Dossy sustained me.

I recovered from my head injury with no subsequent infirmity. My obligation at that time was to fellow countrymen and the Confederacy. Once the war ended, my life would be committed to serving God and His church.

CHAPTER SIX

The winter of 18 and 64 found our impoverished legions gathered within meandering trenches east of Richmond and Petersburg. We were once proud and youthful soldiers that almost four years of unrelenting war had reduced to emaciated old men clothed in tattered gray. Stained and shredded battle flags flapped in frigid winter winds — the agonizing chill of which pierced our shabby rags. The Yankees waited. We waited. They grew fat. We grew gaunter as each day came with little more than a mouthful of food to sustain us. Captain whined through long freezing nights from creeping starvation and bone-breaking cold. Until this day, I do not understand why he did not desert me and our crevasse of misery. But, he remained steadfast as a sentry by my side, sustained only with meager portions of food provided by Sergeant James and myself.

Progressive attenuation sapped not only our energy, but impoverished our determination to gain ultimate victory. Each day the Yankees mounted skirmishes at various points along our lines. They must have thought these were demoralizing for us, but we looked forward to such breaks in our monotonous existence. The only hope for victory lay with the invaders. I prayed they would give up on conquering us and negotiate for peace. Otherwise, death from starvation and diseases might well be our lot if we remained in those squalid trenches much longer.

Silence reigned throughout our positions during the Yankee's Thanksgiving Day. They feasted while we starved, yet both observed a spontaneous truce with no hostilities.

New Years was supposed to be our day to feast while the blue hoard left muskets stacked and cannons silent. Ladies of Richmond were to prepare us a spread that would be the envy of our enemies. The day passed as slow as a deathbed wake. Nightfall came. Still we waited. Hope had almost died when wagons arrived filled with boxes of food. We lined up to receive our long awaited banquet. Instead of anticipated goodies, we were handed a sandwich made of a thin sliver of ham between two slices of stale bread. "May I have one for my captain?" I asked as I took mine from a gray headed lady whose sad countenance mirrored our plight.

"Where is your captain?"

"He's asleep, ma'am," I lied, hoping to get much needed food for my faithful dog.

"Bless him. Is he sick?"

Her emotion caused me to pause, to ponder guilty pangs, but they soon passed. "Yes, ma'am — dysentery."

"Tsk! Tsk!" she clucked. "Is he being attended by your surgeon?"

I would have to run up against a Good Samaritan. My subterfuge had gone too far for me to back down. A familiar conscience-pricking adage came to mind: Oh, what a tangled web we weave, when first we practice to deceive! "Yes, ma'am, but he doesn't have any more opium."

"My husband is your regimental surgeon. You wait right here while I get medicine for your captain."

I was tempted to make a hasty retreat before she returned, but thought better of it. Captain was in dire straights and needed food. The problem was how to handle a situation that was billowing out of control. A corporal would never be entrusted to deliver scarce medication to a sick officer, but maybe my benefactor would let me take it to our company surgeon. If not, she would ask me to take her to the surgeon's tent. What could I say to him? None of my officers were ill with dysentery. I had no idea whether our surgeon was out of opium pills. What would he do if she handed him medication for an officer suffering from a fictitious illness? I needed to make a quick decision — confess or stand firm.

I decided sharing my sandwich with Captain would be a wise decision. Just as I started to return to my trench, the dear lady returned empty-handed. "I'm so sorry," she said. "My husband sends his regrets to your captain. There is no more opium in Petersburg or Richmond."

I struggled to show a glimmer of disappointment instead of relief for her bad news. "My captain will understand, ma'am. He will appreciate your trying to help him."

She nodded, reached into a basket, pulled out two sandwiches and handed them to me. "Please give him these. He needs nourishment. I will be lifting him to the Lord in prayer."

"God bless you, ma'am."

While walking back to the trench where Captain was sleeping, I pondered my good fortune — one legitimate and two ill-gotten ham sandwiches. Just when I reached our earthworks, I paused and glanced skyward. The cloudless heavens were filled with millions of stars. As I breathed a prayer of thanksgiving, the sounds of Yankees singing wafted from the east across the field where no man could survive. I stood listening to their rendition of Auld Lang Syne and longed for the touch of my mother, and Penelope, one more time.

* * *

The attrition of winter, frequent skirmishes and diminishing provisions took their toll during January and February. Our bodies were melting away as the ravages of starvation reaped its harvest. Many of us became sick with various maladies. A simple scratch often became a festering sore. Vermin crawled at will within our frayed and rotting clothing. Like every Southern soldier, all of my strength and determination was centered upon survival. Every ensuing day was a copy of the previous one — existing long enough to greet a new sunrise.

Winter was beginning to release its grip during the month of March. The days grew milder and nights less tormenting. We were anticipating renewed general assaults by the invaders as spring began to thaw the countryside. A short time after noon on April first, the Yankees attacked and defeated our right flank entrenchments at Five Forks, which were manned by my old division.

The following morning, an artillery bombardment followed by a massive infantry attack was launched by the enemy on Fort Mahone east of Petersburg. Fort Gregg, about three miles to the west, fell following an overwhelming assault. Also, the Boydton Plank Road and Southside Railroad were cut, which made Petersburg's defense untenable.

Word by couriers spread up and down our entrenchments about the calamities befalling Five Forks and Petersburg. We only had enough able horses to hook up two caissons with ten pound Parrot cannon. To my good fortune, Kate was one of them. She was thin, but no more than any of the others.

At about ten o'clock in the evening, we began our retreat through Richmond. I looked up and breathed a prayer, "Thank you Lord for delivering me out of that godforsaken cesspool."

While crossing James River's Mayo Bridge, several tremendous explosions along the waterfront caused the bridge to groan and shudder. Richmond continued to burn during the remainder of the night. All the while we were traveling westward, billowing flames lit up the eastern horizon. This conflagration continued until dawn when

Richmond's disintegrating silhouette became obscured by undulating clouds of black smoke.

Our trek toward Amelia Court House progressed at a good pace, considering the depleted condition of men and horses.   Our hope for promised rations at that town sustained a more rapid march than we would have been able to maintain.   Despite his weakened state, Captain trotted to the front of my caisson.   The roadway was clogged with our retreating army, hundreds of civilians, government officials and members of congress. Most were on foot. Some carried luggage. Others pushed carts or wheel barrows. It did not take long for the roadside to be strewn with most of these abandoned items.

We marched the entire day and night of Monday, the third of April, arriving at Amelia Court House on Tuesday morning. We parked our caissons and awaited distribution of rations we had been promised. None came. They were sent to Richmond where the blue hoard confiscated them. About three or four hours before noon, several forage wagons pulled into our area and began to dole out two ears of hard corn to each of us. My gums bled and teeth ached after trying to gnaw on my ration. I gave up following several futile attempts and fed the remainder to Kate.

Close to ten o'clock in the forenoon, we were startled by a sudden earth-shaking explosion that brought us to our feet in preparation to do battle.   Sergeant Bob James remained seated while continuing to whittle on a stick of wood. "That ain't anything, John. They're blowin' up ammunition our played-out horses can't haul no farther."

We were so drained of strength that our retreat needed to be halted until foragers could secure food. We unhitched our horses, watered them in a creek, the name of which was unknown to me, and then tethered them nearby. Captain and I lay down beneath a spreading live oak tree. He soon began to snore while I gazed beyond limbs draped with

Spanish moss at springtime clouds puffed like cotton bursting from open bolls. The countryside seemed to be peaceful and full of promise, except for our presence. A southerly breeze laden with aromas of burning wood and sweating horses overpowered gentle fragrances of a nearby garden.

My thoughts turned to Penelope and the day when I could return to Gettysburg. I struggled to frame her face in my mind's eye. Her presence scintillated like a rippling reflection upon the surface of a windswept lake. As I concentrated on her features, azure blue eyes and golden ringlets beckoned me to draw nearer, so near that her image became clear and distinct. Many days, weeks and months had gone by since we said our farewells at the Gettysburg train depot. During many a frigid night I yearned to be warmed by her embrace, to experience anew the scent of lilac wafting from her hair. Like those times, my nostalgic musings faded away as sleep brought a renewing interlude to the mayhem of war.

When I awoke, Captain was gone. I suppose he decided to seek a more tolerable existence elsewhere. "Goodbye, old friend," I muttered to myself. "I pray God will keep you safe."

None of our foraging wagons had returned by first light the next morning. We marched westward after being ordered to resume the retreat. About three miles out of Amelia Court House, the right wheel of my cannon broke apart. Since there were no replacements, the ten pound Parrot cannon was abandoned. Sergeant Bob James and I along with four other fellows in our battery were happy to ride instead of marching on foot. It was good to be astride Kate again.

We headed north of Jetersville to avoid Yankees that were reported to be just south of the town. The countryside was littered with discarded items, including muskets. All day long I rode by men sitting either on logs or bare ground. Our army was dissolving. The end was near, but I didn't want to quit. I patted Kate on the shoulder just to let her know of my concern. I kept urging her on until it was too dark to keep going. "Let's camp here," I called to Bob, but he didn't answer. "Sergeant," I yelled. Still there was no reply.

I was alone. Had I taken a wrong turn, being too tired to realize where Kate was heading? A springtime downpour of rain began. Lightning bolts slashed fiery paths across the sky, which were followed by tumultuous thunder claps. I dismounted and led Kate by the reins, fearing she might lose her footing. Slick mud was turning into slippery slime. She, as well as I, were growing wearier. We were lost, separated from friend and foe alike.

A brilliant lightning flash revealed an unpainted pole shed about ten yards from the road. "Thank, God," I said to Kate. "Let's get out of this storm."

* * *

Morning came, overcast and gloomy. The heavy downpour abated until only a drizzle remained. My bed of moldy straw stunk like a stagnant pond. I was wet, shivering and irate. Why was I participating in the retreat of a defeated army? Why didn't I head for home? Who would call me a deserter? What would it matter if they did? The more questions I pondered, the angrier I became. I lunged from that sordid bed, determined to mount Kate and rein her toward Charleston. My prosthetic leg collapsed. The muck and mire of Petersburg's trenches had rotted all of the leather causing it to rip apart. Despondency replaced anger as I pondered how to repair the broken prosthesis.

The frayed leather was too disintegrated to mend, even if any thong, string or wire was available. Repair was impossible, but its future restoration could make it a serviceable limb once again.

Kate was no longer in the shed. I managed to stand up and hobble to a pole supporting the shed's roof. I could see her through the trees down by a nearby creek. While I was mulling over what to do next, she neighed. Then I sighted a horse and rider about fifty yards to the south. He reined to a halt, no doubt concerned whether the horse which had whinnied belonged to friend or foe. Much to my relief, the rider wasn't wearing blue; however, I was unable to make out his features. I wanted to call to him, but decided to wait until he saw Kate — no need to take a chance on getting shot.

It seemed as if time stood still while I clung to the pole, stripped of its bark and polished from cattle rubbing off pesky cockleburs. The drizzle ceased as a chill wind pushed misty fog through the copse of surrounding live oaks, draping a murky shroud over the rider and his horse. I didn't know whether he had seen me. Without any doubt the fog blocked the shed and me from his view. Then I caught a glimpse of something coming toward the shed. Being much smaller, it could not be the rider's horse. I braced for an attack by the critter, maybe a black bear. I was surprised and relieved when Captain emerged from the haze. "Captain, where have you been?" I yelled, released my grip on the pole and sat down as he leaped toward me.

He yelped and licked my face over and over while I examined him. There were no wounds and he was less gaunt, good evidence that he found food.

Sergeant James led his horse to the shed, kneeled down and patted Captain's shoulder. "Hey, John, I knew old Captain would find you."

"Yeah, he's got a keen nose."

"I reckon so," he said, opened his haversack and pulled out a plump mallard duck. It was plucked, cleaned and ready for a skewer.

"Where did you get that bird?"

"Captain."

"He caught a duck and didn't eat it?"

"Sure did. I holed up in a barn during the storm. I was gettin' ready to mount up this morning when Captain came trotting down the road with this duck in his mouth. He's a determined hunter and no deserter."

That comment lodged in my gut. Only moments before, I was willing to shuck my responsibilities and head for home. "He sure isn't," I said, hugging Captain and planting a kiss on his forehead.

Bob then noticed my empty trouser leg. "What happened to your prosthesis?"

"It's broken and can't be fixed without good leather."

"That's bad," he said, glancing at Kate grazing near the creek. "You're going to need a saddle."

"Yeah, but finding one out here isn't likely. Let's cook that duck."

CHAPTER SEVEN

Friday morning, the seventh of April, dawned clear and pleasant. Bob rode toward Appomattox Courthouse at first light in search of a saddle for Kate. Since his being able to find one was doubtful, I rummaged about for something with which my prosthesis might be repaired. Riding Kate bareback would be possible if there could be a means to hold the limb in place.

While pondering what was available, Kate's leather reins came to mind. Did I cut too much from them when we abandoned the cannon? I stared at her bridle hanging from a wall peg where I hung it during the storm on Wednesday night. There appeared to be about six feet of each rein remaining. Would there be enough?

I retrieved the bridle, sat down next to my broken prosthetic limb and pondered how to accomplish the task. The only anchoring devise available was my belt. If I could loop a length of rein over my belt and through the hinged knee joint, it would secure the limb to my stump. The task would require about thirty inches of leather strap, leaving enough rein to guide Kate.

I accomplished the job a short time before noon and was waiting for Bob to return. Sporadic cannon fire to the east toward Amelia Court House seemed to be getting closer. Capture would be my lot if I remained in this place much longer. When another hour passed, it became obvious that I needed to straddle Kate and head west.

My improvised prosthetic support served me well. I was able to ride with reasonable balance and comfort. There was no way of knowing how long it would take to catch up with our army, so I was determined to keep going.

By dawn the next day, I reached an encampment of General Gordon's forces north of Appomattox River. At about that time, our invaders began to assemble south of the river. Gordon's men set ablaze the bridge over which I just crossed. We then abandoned camp and headed west, not knowing where General Gordon would order his men to make a stand or join the main body of our army. Yankee pressure upon us was less severe during most of the day.

I kept looking around, hoping to see Bob, but there was no sign of him. Fearing he might become wounded, captured or killed, I muttered a prayer asking God to spare his life and keep him from harm.

We set up camp that evening northeast of Appomattox Court House. I watered Kate and fed her corn one of the foragers gave me. Around eight o'clock in the evening, cannon fire rumbled and musketry crackled southeast in the direction of Appomattox Station. The sounds were short lived with relative quiet remaining throughout the night.

To the south and southwest, thousands of Yankee campfires flickered across the countryside. The numbers were foreboding. Supplies of food were rumored to be awaiting us in railcars at Appomattox Station. Now, the overwhelming number of invading Yankees could block us from getting them.

I tethered Kate and then bedded down with Captain for the night, intending to keep to myself. The end was at hand. All I wanted to do was sleep, to escape my sordid existence if for only a few hours.

Battle sounds from the west awakened us at dawn. A number of infantrymen jumped up, assembled, and marched double time out of camp. The sounds of fighting ceased about eight o'clock. The hour was heavy with anticipation. What was happening? No one knew. We waited.

A dense morning fog enshrouding our encampment began to fade away until only a few cumulus clouds remained. Scattered musket fire resumed to the south and west. Time dragged by with no orders received to form up and move out. Around noon, rumors about imminent surrender by General Lee became rampant.

All sounds of battle ceased in early afternoon. Later on, wagons filled with rations and feed for horses began to arrive. All of their canvas tops were stenciled with U S A, which was certain proof that we had surrendered and were prisoners of our dreaded enemy.

The next morning, we received orders to remain in camp. A colonel on General Lee's staff called us to muster at ten o'clock to read General Order No. 9, a farewell message from General Lee. Many of us wept as we listened: *After four years of arduous service, marked by unsurpassed courage and fortitude, the Army of Northern Virginia has been compelled to yield to overwhelming numbers and resources.*

I need not tell the brave survivors of so many hard fought battles, who have remained steadfast to the last, that I have consented to this result from no distrust of them.

But feeling that valor and devotion could accomplish nothing that could compensate for the loss that must have attended the continuance of the contest, I determined to avoid the useless sacrifice of those whose past services have endeared them to their countrymen.

By the terms of the agreement officers and men can return to their homes and remain until exchanged. You will take with you the satisfaction that proceeds from the consciousness of duty faithfully performed, and I earnestly pray that a Merciful God will extend to you His blessing and protection.

With an increasing admiration of your constancy and devotion to your country, and a grateful remembrance of your kind and generous consideration for myself, I bid you all an affectionate farewell.

The only sounds coming from the men were expressions of disbelief, remorse and admonitions to continue the fight. When the clamor subsided, the colonel concluded his statement. "General Grant has agreed to General Lee's request for all officers to retain their side arms. All men, regardless of rank, can retain their privately owned horses. All of you will receive a signed parole sometime during the next couple of days. Day after tomorrow on the twelfth of April, all Confederate forces will stack arms and surrender battle flags to United States forces here assembled. In the meantime an ample supply of rations for both men and horses will be distributed to all of you."

The waiting was over. All of our sacrifices were for naught — a sad day — but I was free to go home. What will I find when I get there? What has happened to my family? Did Andrew die in prison? Will I ever see Penelope again?

* * *

"You're next, corporal?"

"Thank you, sir."

"What's your name?"

"John Pendleton."

"Infantry?"

"No, sir, artillery."

The Yankee parole captain interrogating me, glanced at my crutch, which I managed to obtain from their surrender depot. "Wounded recently?"

"No, sir, Gettysburg."

"Gettysburg?" he said, leaning back from his desk. "And you're still serving?"

I tapped my prosthesis. "This peg leg gets me by."

He wagged his head in disbelief. "Any side arms?"

"No."

"I don't suppose you own a horse, being a cannoneer?"

"I do own a horse."

Again, he stared at me. "Oh. You Rebs run a peculiar army. Where is your horse?"

"She's tethered at General Gordon's encampment."

"You have any papers of ownership?"

I handed him the bill of sale given to me by Mrs. Arthurs. It was my good fortune to have kept it — mainly because of my affection for her. "Will this do?"

He read it, nodded, filled out and signed my parole pass. He handed it and my bill of sale to me. "Where is home, Corporal?"

"Charleston, South Carolina, sir."

"Good luck, John Pendleton."

I glanced at the parole. It was signed, Archibald Fanning, Capt. U.S.A. An impulse, one of total surprise, lifted my right hand in a salute. "Thank you, Captain Fanning."

He returned my salute. "You're welcome, Corporal Pendleton. Via Con Dios."

* * *

On the morning of April twelfth we assembled for a final muster and surrender ceremony. I suppose the Yankees wanted to let us know who had won the war. The stacking of arms and battle flags would be an appropriate finale. It wasn't necessary. General Lee would never surrender unless we were unable to continue fighting.

I prayed the invaders would go back home — but that prayer was not answered to my liking.

I went to the surrender depot following the ceremony where a sympathetic guard allowed me to obtain a worn McClellan saddle and blanket from stacks of discarded equipment. I began to saddle Kate when from behind me came the familiar voice of Sergeant Bob James. "Well, I see you made it, John."

When I turned around, he was grinning. "Bob, where have you been?"

"An artillery burst spooked my horse. He bucked and left me in the middle of a nettle patch."

"When are you heading home?"

"Right away. How about you?"

"Me, too — today."

Bob glanced at Captain. "You goin' to take him with you?"

"Yeah. He's got a home with me for as long as he lives."

We shook hands, a final farewell. I hesitated to turn his hand loose, knowing I would never see him again. "Goodbye, Bob. Thanks for being my friend."

"Goodbye, John. Be sure to go see your Penelope."

"I will, but I've got to go home first."

As our hands slipped apart, Bob reached down and patted Captain. "Goodbye, Captain. Take care of John."

Bob walked down the road toward Appomattox Station without looking back. "May God watch over you, my friend," I said and finished saddling Kate.

I secured my crutch to the saddle, stepped in the stirrup, and swung myself into General McClellan's invention, the hardest, most uncomfortable saddle known to man. I headed for Charleston with my trusted companion, Captain, leading the way. I was amazed. He did seem to have our destination well in mind. We had a long journey ahead of us, over three hundred miles across country, plus fifty more for following roadways and pikes.

* * *

South Carolina was desolate. Sherman's "Total War" destroyed over two hundred years invested in developing the land by our ancestors. Most farm dwellings were reduced to ashes with only stone or brick chimneys standing like lonely sentinels amid blackened ruins. The ever-present stench of ashes and smoke lingered, a silent reminder of our enemy's policy of extermination.

The nearer I came to home, people were living in makeshift shelters of scrap lumber, tree limbs, wagon beds, army tents and dugouts. These sights heightened my concern for family and neighbors.

On Tuesday morning, the twenty-fifth of April, I crossed Cooper River's west fork and rode down the lowlands toward home. Every plantation home along the way had either been burned to the ground or sustained extensive damage. Timberlands were decimated. Only charred spires remained. Likewise, many bridges were gone. Burnt timbers were scattered along banks of streams they once spanned. Fences were also nonexistent, having been torn up and burned by Sherman's men. The mad general extracted his pound of flesh from families who signed the Declaration of Independence from Britain, and later endorsed South Carolina's Secession Ordinance.

The desolation through which I was riding prompted me to visit Jeremiah Middleton, whose plantation bordered ours to the north. The house, built in 17 and 45 by his grandfather, Henry Middleton, was located at the end of a long, live-oak-canopied driveway. Unsettling odors left by Sherman's conflagration of buildings and animals filled the air. When I rode into the front yard, an elderly gentleman was sorting through remains of a once magnificent home. Long white hair falling across his face obscured it from view. "Mister Middleton?" I called.

He peered at me. "Who might be inquiring, sir?" he said, striving to stand erect.

"John Pendleton."

"Did you say, John Pendleton?"

I slid out of the saddle, untied my crutch and walked through debris toward him. "Yes, sir, I'm John. Are you Mister Middleton?"

"Yes," he said, shuffling toward me. "You look awful thin. Wish I could offer you somethin' to eat, but …"

"How is Mrs. Middleton?" I said, reaching to shake his hand.

"She died a year ago — smallpox. Swamp fever killed Sarah and Naomi. You remember my daughters?"

"Yes, sir, Naomi used to play with my sister, Priscilla."

He nodded, and then pointed at piles of rubble, the remains of burned out barns, sheds and slave cottages. "I'm all alone. Everything's gone. They killed the live stock, chickens, and turkeys — chopped down the fruit trees. I'm existin' in a dugout … well … keepin' body and soul together."

"Is my family all right?"

His reply was slow and measured. "John, you've got to understand that nobody livin' here is all right. The Yankees had a special vengeance to mete out. Your grandfather as well as my father signed the Declaration of Independence from Britain. Secession had its beginnin' here and Mad Dog Sherman intended us to experience his "Total War". Your place was no exception."

"My family — what has happened to them?"

"I regret havin' to tell you a Yankee officer shot your father dead. Mrs. Pendleton pleaded with him to stop. He laughed, cursed her, and ordered his men to set your home ablaze."

"Did they harm Mother?"

"No, she's in Charleston with Bishop Dossy's widow. You remember her?"

I nodded, but could not speak. The impact of my father's murder had stifled my voice.

"We're all hurtin'," he said. "All of us livin' along the Ashley and Cooper rivers have lost sorely, but we are goin' to survive — and rebuild — God willin'. Now, you ride on down to Charleston. Your mother needs to see that you're alive."

* * *

I waved goodbye as Kate trotted away from Jeremiah Middleton and his abode of sorrow, and hope. I didn't wish to see the destruction of our home, but needing to visit Father's grave caused me to rein Kate toward Pendleton Plantation.

The destruction through which I was travelling should have prepared me for devastation inflicted by Yankee invaders upon my home. It did not. Our palatial house was now a pile of rubble. All that remained were two large stone fireplaces with their towering chimneys standing amid mounds of crumbled bricks. Oak beams were reduced to fragile slabs of charcoal. Nothing was intact. It was just like the Confederacy. What a waste. The blood spilled, senseless destruction of property, countless families torn asunder and legions of maimed and scarred men were terrible costs we all paid.

I sat under an ancient live oak in our front yard while Kate grazed and Captain hunted along the riverbank. My mind, body and spirit were spent. Father was lying in our family cemetery along with my grandparents. Andrew and I had gone to war. I was returning, crippled but alive. Andrew's survival was questionable; he might even be buried in a prisoner's grave on Johnson Island. My sister, Priscilla, brother, Martin, and Mother were destitute, being cared for through the charity of Bishop Dossy's widow.

Setting aside self pity, I arose and walked down the pathway to our cemetery. There I sat beside Father's grave, placed my hand on its mound of earth and prayed for him.

Captain trotted to my side and lay down next to me. I was grateful he was there, a consoling presence for which I had a great need. While patting my companion, I became aware of the present. A warm breeze blowing across Cooper River replaced the stink of destruction with placid fragrances of springtime. I experienced a gradual return of hope for the future. As hard as humans may strive to inflict their madness upon the earth, they will fail to destroy her. The sites of our lunacy will soon be memorialized with granite monuments erected by man. It was time for me to lay aside the past and strive toward a new beginning. Where that search would lead, I could only question. My present task was to provide for Mother, Priscilla and Martin. "Come on, Captain," I said, rubbing his belly. "Let's make Charleston before dark."

CHAPTER EIGHT

Charleston, lying between the confluence of Cooper and Ashley rivers, came into view as I rode down the peninsula. Our once pristine community with many church steeples towering above neat blocks of residences was in disarray. The Yankee's long siege and their big cannons raining shot and shell into her wrought terrible destruction. Like scattered gravestones, remains of stone and brick walls haunted the landscape. This state of near ruin caused General Sherman to bypass the city during his pillage, torch and destroy foray across South Carolina.

As I urged Kate along the Ashley riverfront toward the Battery, I saw many devastated houses — none unscathed. Streets and yards were cratered like a battleground from exploding artillery shells, stark evidence of the enemy's wanton bombardment of noncombatants.

The evening was calm and warm. Seagulls circling overhead broke the silence with screeching calls. Captain must have been intrigued by new sights and sounds, having never been near the seashore before. He barked and chased gyrating shadows as gulls and pelicans sailed with little effort above the Battery's seawall.

I envisioned Bishop Dossy's home as it was before the war — two stories, gleaming white walls, and a porch extending across the front. Two live oaks with lower limbs bowing to the ground graced the front yard, which was enclosed behind an ornate wrought iron fence. It was quaint, but seemed out of place, being located among grand homes of wealthy merchants.

My reflection ceased when the Dossy house came into view. The exterior was dilapidated and dreary, no longer well kept and cheery like I remembered. I tied Kate to the hitching post, and then followed Captain to the front door where I took stock of my appearance. Similar to the Dossy house, shabby attire hid my gaunt frame and used-up prosthetic leg from view.   While leaning on my crutch, I knocked once, twice, three times before sounds of footsteps approached the door. The latch turned. The door opened just a bit. A subdued voice from beyond it said, "Who's there?"

"John Pendleton."

The door opened some more. "Did you say John Pendleton?"

"Yes, ma'am."

The door flew open and Carrie Dossy stepped toward me with arms outstretched. "Johnnie, dear, dear Johnnie, you are alive."

My crutch fell to the porch as I threw my arms about her. Tears trickled into my matted beard while we stood with our arms locked about each other. From inside the house came my mother's voice, "Carrie, who's there?"

"Come and see, Martha."

I shall never forget Mother's expression when she walked into the doorway and beheld my face above Carrie's shoulder. "Dear, God." she cried. "Is that my John?"

Mrs. Dossy stepped aside. I swept Mother into my arms. Neither of us said a word — the moment was overpowering for both of us. We wept, savoring a reunion that only a mother and her son who is returning after so long an absence can experience. At last, she whispered into my ear, "Oh, Johnnie, how I've missed you. We didn't know whether you were alive or dead."

"I'm sorry. There wasn't the means or way to get letters to you. Where's Priscilla?"

"She's gone with Benton to get fresh milk at Wilson's Dairy. You remember Carrie's son?"

"He was but a lad when I left, but I remember him."

Carrie patted my shoulder. "Johnnie, Martha, let's go into the house. I'll brew some tea and you can talk while I prepare supper."

* * *

The front door swung open and Martin walked in carrying a satchel filled with books. "Look who's here, dear," Mother said, gripping my hand.

We stared at each other. Martin was but twelve when I left to join Colonel Pettigrew's Regiment. He had grown to be quite tall for a sixteen-year-old. I was amazed how much he changed in four years. However, my wasted presence must have startled him.

"Hello, little brother," I said, struggling to stand up.

He dropped his satchel and took a step toward me. "John?"

"Yes, Martin. Whatever is left of me."

We hugged and slapped each other on the back. Martin said, "I didn't think I'd ever see you again."

"That came close to happening a lot of times."

The back door slammed shut. "Get behind me, John," Martin whispered. "We'll surprise Prissie."

Mother clapped her hands. "Oh, yes, and Benton, too."

"What's going on in there?" Priscilla called from the kitchen.

I hid behind Martin's taller and more robust frame as he called, "Come here a minute."

"What are you up to, now?"

"Nothin', I just need you for somethin'."

Being consumed by curiosity, I eased my head aside just enough for a discreet peek. When Priscilla and Benton Dossy stepped through the doorway, Martin pulled himself more erect to better hide me. Priscilla stopped and placed both hands on her hips. "Martin Pendleton, who are you hiding?"

Before he could answer, I said, "Guess who?"

"Johnnie? You're home," she said as I stepped from behind Martin.

"Yes, little sister."

We embraced. There were no dry eyes in Carrie Dossy's parlor. Even Benton, reserved and proper, was swept into laughing and weeping with us. "I knew you were alive," Priscilla said, patting my bearded cheek.

While Carrie Dossy prepared supper, everyone sat in rapt attention as I recalled my experiences. These memories took me from depths of depression to emotional mountaintops. Subjects discussed were: Gettysburg and what happened to Hank Johnson; the loss of my leg; falling in love with Penelope; Todd's helping me escape from prison; meeting Sarah Arthurs and her sustaining gifts of Kate and Captain. My greatest regret was lack of knowledge about Andrew — was he alive — I didn't know.

"He has to be alive. God will spare him," Benton Dossy said, gripping my arm.

* * *

I discovered Bishop Dossy's journals, sermons, and essays while browsing his library. His dedication, intellect and absolute faith in the teachings of Jesus and disciples became a guiding light for me. Many books and treatises were authored by founders of the Reformation — Luther, Knox, Wesley and Calvin. It was during spare hours spent in his library that a deeper and more profound commitment to the ministry undergirded me. If he had failed to keep his memoirs, the loss to me and others would be unthinkable. While reflecting on the need for recording one's experiences, I decided to resume keeping a regular accounting. I penned the following entry, dated June fourth, 18 and 65:

> The mails are reestablished. I will pen a
> letter to Penelope. I'll not write about my

experiences before arriving home, except for the supernatural appearance of Bishop Dossy. How else will I be able to tell her of my commitment to the ministry? There are too many distressing emotions remaining for me to do otherwise at this time. I will begin with expressing my love for her, how I miss her presence daily, and pray we will soon be together.

Despite my father's death and the destruction of our home, I am thankful to be reunited with Mother, Martin and Priscilla.

Charleston is rife with rumors about Lincoln's assassination. A few diehard firebrands express pleasure in the event; which is troubling for me. What recompense might our occupiers inflict upon us? They appear to need no encouragement.

Charleston's future, like every Southern city, is suffering from postwar reconstruction. Many returning soldiers are drifters, because their homes were destroyed. Displaced families have resulted in children being cared for by relatives or neighbors. Like a Good Samaritan, Carrie Dossy opened her heart and home to what remains of my family. Mother seems to be growing younger in appearance and spirit. Being together once again is bringing renewal to all of us. Except, Andrew's circumstances are of prime concern. We are interceding for him in our daily prayers.

My prosthetic leg is no longer serviceable until repairs are made. So, I tossed it into Martin's closet, pinned up the empty pant leg and am relying on my crutch. Benton Dossy has taken it to Charles Billingsly who worked with prosthetic inventor, Dubois D. Parmlee. I hope to get it back soon.

Martin and I have ridden out to the plantation several times to give Captain an outing. Sherman's minions destroyed every structure except the well house. We plan to build a log cabin nearby, so we'll have shelter while erecting a family dwelling. We salvaged three axes, four hammers, and two saws while searching through piles of rubble. We made new handles and sharpened axes and saws. Also, rusty nails were retrieved, a necessity for rebuilding since new ones are unavailable. If there were any, we do not have cash with which to buy them.

Penelope's reply came two weeks later. She and her family were well. Gettysburg had almost recovered from the great battle. Monuments were being erected on the battlefield. Visitors kept hotels, inns and boarding houses busy. The most surprising and welcome news was about Andrew. His release and parole from Johnson Island Prison was obtained by Todd several weeks after my escape. Andrew was convalescing under the care of Todd and his housekeeper. Her nutritious recipes were restoring his strength and good health.

I called the family together and read Penelope's letter to them. Mother raised her hands. "Our Andrew is alive. Thank you, dear Lord."

"God bless Todd," Martin said, embracing Mother.

Priscilla reached for the letter. "Does she say when Andrew is coming home?"

I shook my head and handed it to her. I didn't dare tell them the last time I saw Andrew, he was close to dying. I feared Penelope was trying to ease our apprehension. Even if he were alive, his chances for recovery seemed remote. I excused myself and took refuge in Bishop Dossy's library. No one appeared to sense my distress, for which I was grateful.

* * *

Benton Dossy became a powerful influence upon me during those days. He planned on enrolling in seminary to follow his father in ministry, but the war deferred his plans. He served with our forces at Fort Moultrie on Sullivan's Island. He escaped injuries, but heavy bombardments by Yankee artillery frayed his nervous system.

While sawing logs for our cabin, he expressed a burning desire to resume studies for the ministry. Also, my plans for the future came into question. "John, what do you plan to do now that the war is over?"

I had but one obligation at that time. "Take care of my family."

"What about Penelope?"

The crosscut-saw handle slipped from my grip as I faced Benton. His question jolted my sense of right and wrong, rousing it from a dark corner of self inflicted apathy. For too long I had set aside a question begging to be answered. Fear was controlling me. Fear that Penelope would be repulsed by scars and infirmities left by smallpox, starvation and war. Fear of abandoning Mother, Martin and Priscilla during their dire time of need. Fear that I could not provide for a wife. I had no skills or vocation. I must have been mute for several minutes as these and more concerns swirled like dust devils out of my subconscious. "Are you all right?" Benton said, dropping his end of the saw.

"I don't know. My right leg lies buried with several thousand other limbs somewhere in Gettysburg. Smallpox scars cover my face and body, hidden only by beard and garments. The trenches at Petersburg consumed me, melting away muscle and sinew until you see this gaunt cripple standing before you."

Benton gripped my shoulders but could not speak. I continued with my exhortation of self pity. "How can I ask Penelope to ignore such ugliness? Will she reject me if I do?"

Benton helped me sit on a log, and then sat down beside me. "I can't answer those questions. The only advice I can give you is what you will find in the Bible. Love bears, believes, hopes and endures all things. Love never fails. You and Penelope will find the answers to your questions if you address them in love. I believe you need to go to her now. Martin and I will carry on this work."

Of course, Benton was correct. However, I was unable to accept his advice at that time. I continued to wrestle with my demons for several more weeks. The moment of truth came while I was sitting at Bishop Dossy's desk reading Luther's Smalcald Articles when Benton knocked on the door. "John?" he said, opening the door. "I have something for you."

"Yes. Please come in."

Emotion stilled my tongue as he entered, carrying my wood, steel and leather leg. He laid it on the desk, sat down and grinned as I began to caress the new leather and polished wood. Tears clouded my vision. Here was a gift greater than my benefactor could have imagined. Now, I could walk again without that cursed crutch galling my armpit. I wiped my eyes and held out both hands toward Benton. "God bless you," I said as we hugged each other.

"Okay, John, put on your leg and we'll go for a walk. There's something I want to show you."

We walked a couple of blocks to St. Michael's Church. It is a magnificent structure accented by a towering steeple, which served our enemies in sighting cannons to bombard the city. The edifice escaped except for minimal damage from a shell exploding near the chancel a short time before our surrender.   As a member of the Vestry, Benton possessed a key with which he unlocked the front doors. We walked down the center aisle toward the apse; all the time he commented on how many members sacrificed their lives during the war. We stopped for a moment, placed our hands on The Governor's Pew and said a prayer for General Lee. He occupied it on several occasions when worshiping during the blockade of Charleston. We reached Pendleton's Pew where we knelt, and spent several minutes in quiet meditation.

I concluded my prayer, slipped back onto the bench and waited for Benton to finish. Memories flooded my mind as St. Michael's filled my senses. Subdued blends of green, red, blue and yellow hues from daylight being filtered through stained glass swept the chancel. I sniffed familiar scents emitted only by our beloved house of worship. There were faint aromas of varnished cedar, altar candles, leather-bound prayer books and a mustiness characteristic of old churches. The building seemed to speak to me with faint noises, imagined for the most part. One in particular was Bishop Dossy's voice, rich and full of grace.

My reverie ended when Benton tapped my shoulder. "I promised you something else," he said, handing me an envelope.

"What is this?"

"Open it and see," he said, offering me his pocket knife.

I slit open the envelope and pulled out a ticket for passage to Philadelphia aboard the clipper ship, West Wind, on the fifth of August. I was overwhelmed. I never found it easy to shed tears, having been reared by reserved parents. It wasn't that they didn't have feelings, displaying them was to be avoided. Now, after returning home and experiencing a spiritual and emotional renewal, my shielding armor augmented by war was beginning to fall away. When I failed with another effort to convey heartfelt gratitude, Benton slipped an arm around my shoulder. "It's all right. Tell your Penelope I'm looking forward to meeting her."

"Thanks for being my friend," I said, shaking his outstretched hand. "God bless you."

CHAPTER NINE

Charleston lay behind me — The Battery's scarred remains, St. Michaels Church, my family, Kate and Captain. The West Wind sailed past battle-wasted ruins of forts Sumter and Moultrie, cleared Cumming's Point and headed toward Atlantic's Gulf Stream. A favorable sea and southwesterly winds propelled our square-rigged, three-mast ship at an awesome speed of twelve knots. Captain Wellsley who claimed almost twenty years service as a ship's master was confident we could outrun storm clouds looming over the southeastern horizon.

Following supper, I returned to my cabin, lit a lantern and penned a journal entry for the fifth of August:

> I haven't been aboard a seagoing vessel since finishing my education at Eton College in Berkshire, England. The West Wind is a magnificent British clipper whose voyages include trade routes from Europe to far eastern ports. She travels the world, trading for exotic spices, sugar, tea and coffee, making several crossings to Shanghai, Java, Madras, St.Petersburg, and other European ports. For four years the Yankee blockade kept her from calling on any Southern port until this voyage. Her crew delivered crates of tea and spices — the first Charleston received by any vessel other than a blockade runner since the war began.
>
> If we maintain our present speed, the ship should reach Philadelphia in less than 48 hours. If so, I will arrive at Gettysburg on Monday the seventh.

I opened a porthole to get some fresh air. As I watched white water rolling away from our bow, the ship's bell rang twice. Mariners have a strange method of marking time at sea. Since I didn't possess a timepiece, understanding how they did it was necessary. A bell chart and meal schedule was affixed on the bulkhead above the bunk. It was late evening, so two bells would be seven p.m. I wondered why they didn't ring their bell and call out the real time.

My pondering was interrupted by a bosun's whistle being piped several times. "Deck hands — up and reef topsails," a cockney accented voice called.

A porthole view being so limited prompted going topside to see what was happening. Crewmen were busy collapsing some of the ship's sails. One sailor was manning a windlass nearby — his eyes fixed on a shipmate perched on a yard atop the mizzenmast. I tapped him on the shoulder. "What's happening?"

"We're riggin' for a blow."

"What does that mean?"

He turned his head and gazed at me. I recognized the meaning in his eyes, having experienced it a number of times before going into battle. "Well, mate, we are in for a bit o'weather. Too much canvas can spell disaster in gale force winds."

Gale force winds — a disturbing comment which caused me to scan sky and ocean. Dread squeezed the pit of my belly. Ominous dark clouds and rain squalls obscured the southern horizon. Waves crowned with streaks of white foam surrounded us. Bulging sails and rolling whitecaps spoke of increasing winds, disconcerting signs. "How bad will it get?"

Without taking his eyes off the mizzenmast sailor, he replied, "Any storm in these waters this time of year spells hurricane. A clipper can be dismasted or capsized. You'd best get below and batten down for a wild ride."

He was correct, of course.   Memories of brutal hurricanes that pummeled Charleston and surrounding lowlands before the war were dulled by four years of man-made violence. Those storms were terrifying experiences. Enduring a hurricane at sea was bound to be far worse.

I returned to the cabin, closed and latched the porthole and pondered the sailor's forewarning. We were in for a trying night.   The West Wind might be shipwrecked, casting us into a raging sea with little hope of survival. What agony would one undergo while drowning? Maybe none — or reliving a litany of hellish wartime experiences would escort me past the gates of Saint Peter. I walked with death, a constant companion for four years. Was I spared only to be ushered through his shadow lands into the hereafter?   Was it meant for me to die before seeing Penelope again?   Woeful fantasies grew as I stared at teakwood deck planking.

I paced the deck to ease frustration until increasing angles of pitch and roll forced me to take refuge on my bunk. Disquieting moans emitted by the ship's hull, and screeching sounds from her rigging were foreboding as Wagner's Valkyrie.

If it wasn't for a berth-restraining strap, I would have been evicted from my refuge by the storm. Waves of nausea swathed me in clammy sweat and filled my mouth with salty saliva. Over and over, retching recurred until exhaustion and sleep brought a welcome interlude.

When I awoke, the West Wind was quiet, no pitching and rolling or howling gale, only gentle oscillations characteristic of clipper ships. As I started to get up, the bell rang several times. A cockney voice called, "Eight bells — all's well."

I unlatched, opened and peered through the porthole at a much calmer sea. I guessed it to be past sunup, maybe early morning, so eight bells would signal eight o'clock during a morning watch. Anxious to see how our ship had weathered such a violent storm, I went topside. Only one sail on the foremast remained unfurled, all other sails were furled and secured to their yards. I climbed steps to the poop deck where a sailor was shooting our position with a sextant. "When will we reach Philadelphia?" I asked as he jotted an entry into his navigational logbook.

He looked at me with an incredulous glint in his eyes. "We aren't out of this storm yet, mate."

I gazed upward, saw blue sky, but then noticed we were surrounded by horizon-obliterating rain squalls. The West Wind was in the hurricane's eye — a long time from being out of harm's way. "No — I guess not — any idea where we are?"

"Aye, about one hundred miles east nor'east o'Cape Hatteras, give or take a few nautical miles."

His reply was unsettling for me. "You can't be more precise?"

"That's the best I can do shooting only the sun before noon." He held up his sextant. "These work a lot better when shooting both sun and moon at midday, or stars at night."

"Oh," I said, being ignorant of such matters.

"Aye, mate. There's tea and biscuits in the galley." He then gestured toward approaching squalls. "Better get some afore we're in it again."

* * *

Captain Wellsley and his crew shepherded the West Wind through eight more hours of hellish weather. Raging seas and winds failed to dismast, capsize or sink our sturdy vessel. However, my body and mind were frazzled from being pummeled by a writhing clipper as she struggled to remain upright and afloat.

An interruption to misery came soon after the timekeeper's bell chimed. "Eight bells — all's well."

I opened and peered through the porthole. The sun was shining through a broken overcast above calming seas, certain signs that our ordeal was almost over. "Got t'be four p.m.," I muttered.

A bosun's whistle piped several times. I didn't know what the sequences meant, but thought it might be the first call to supper. We were served only one hot meal after sailing out of Charleston Bay. Biscuits and grog, a mixture of rum and water, were the only fare available during the storm. I did not partake of either. A hazardous trip to the galley, and seasickness prohibited any interest in food or drink. As tumultuous seas and my nausea abated, images and aromas of an awaiting feast filled my senses.

The bosun's whistle piped again. "All hands — up spirits."

Someone rapped on the door. "Mate. Up spirits."

"What's, up spirits?" I called.

"Captain Wellsley ordered two nor-westers for all hands and passengers."

When I unlatched and opened the door, a bearded sailor shoved two mugs into my hands. "Here y'are, mate."

"What is this?"

"Your nor-westers."

"What is a nor-wester?"

He winked and said, "It's supposed t'be 'alf rum and 'alf water."

Before I could reply, he scurried down the passageway, no doubt, heading for his nor-westers. I decided the captain's order was in celebration of our surviving such a horrendous hurricane.

With two potent nor-westers under my vest, I managed to negotiate a trip to the galley where I downed several helpings of salt horse stew. Upon returning to the cabin I fell into the arms of Morpheus and didn't awaken until dawn.

Around noon the West Wind sailed into Delaware Bay. She was under three-quarters spread of canvas, moving along at a brisk speed. Barring any unforeseen problems, we were due to dock at Philadelphia around six p.m. If Penelope received the letter telling her of my Monday the seventh arrival, she would be wondering what had happened. Upon reaching the train station, I'd send her a telegram explaining our delay.

The upriver journey was a pleasant one until reaching Pea Patch Island where smallpox and starvation almost killed me. I wondered if my Gettysburg journal still survived. Was there a marker on the burial site of Private Ian McLean with my name on it? Will his family ever know what happened to him? The time may come when I'll be granted the task.

As that godforsaken island slipped from view, I walked to the ship's bow. Within the hour we would dock near the pier where I boarded The Delaware Queen bound for Fort Delaware Prison. I wondered what had happened to Sergeant O'Hara and Jacob since I escaped from The Old Capital Prison. Then as Philadelphia came into view, anticipation for being reunited with Penelope quickened my spirit. I leaned on the railing and thanked God for His blessed mercy.

* * *

I boarded a train bound for Gettysburg after a restless night endured on a stationhouse bench. Anticipation accentuated every sound emitted by the train as it carried me toward a reunion with Penelope, Todd, and Andrew. A lonesome whistle, ding-donging bell, heavy chuffing wheel cylinders and click-clacking rails reminded me of September in 18 and 63. Then, I listened to similar sounds as our prison train carried me toward a questionable future. They were now conveying me back to Penelope, whose love sustained me throughout my imprisonment, sickness and war.

I gazed through a soot-etched window, counting telegraph poles as miles and time crept past. Our slow progress became maddening. It seemed the locomotive almost attained an acceptable speed when its whistle wailed, bell clanged, and then slowed for another village or city depot. The bell continued to clang and steam hissed while passengers detrained or boarded. Once "All 'board" echoed up and down each station platform, our sound scenario repeated itself. Soon, our conductor, a white headed gentleman, sauntered up the aisle, calling out the next scheduled stop. I hunkered down and sulked.

I was roused when a voice asked, "Excuse me, sir. Is this seat occupied?"

I glanced at my inquirer standing in the aisle. He pointed at a vacant seat next to me. "Do ye mind — if it's unoccupied?"

"I don't mind. It's vacant."

He nodded and started to sit down. His being an amputee with a prosthetic left leg became obvious as he struggled to seat himself.   While he was getting settled, I peered at him. His appearance seemed familiar, wavy red hair, freckled forehead and cheeks, and a well-trimmed auburn beard. "Where are you headed?" I asked.

"Gettysburg — how about you?"

"Gettysburg."

He then stared at me. "Do I know ye? Your voice sounds familiar."

"I think so. Where did you lose your leg?"

"Gettysburg."

I tapped my right thigh. "Mine, also."

Recognition glinted in his eyes as he scanned my face. "You're John Pendleton — the Reb I hoped would get my left shoe?"

"Yes, and you're Timothy O'Brien?"

"It's Tim," he said as we hugged and slapped each other on the back.

The plodding train and frequent stops were no longer of any importance. The next two hours were filled with our reminiscences — also plans for the future.

Tim returned to his home in Lancaster, Pennsylvania, a short time after I was transferred to Fort Delaware Prison. He apprenticed his uncle at the O'Brien Book Bindery, a short distance from Holy Trinity Lutheran Church on Duke Street. He came under the influence of Harvey W. McKnight, a student at Gettysburg Lutheran Seminary, when the company was hired to restore worn reference volumes. McKnight was assigned by Seminary President James A. Brown to assist Tim in selecting books that needed repair. During one of his visits to the seminary library, Harvey and he selected four tomes for rebinding. They were: Books I, II, III, and IV of, *Institutes of the Christian Religion*, by John Calvin, sixteenth century reformist. While reading them, Tim sensed an urging to learn more about the reformation sparked by Luther, Calvin and Wesley. His quest resulted in a personal dedication — become a minister of the gospel.

"Well, Tim, how do you intend to accomplish this?"

"I'm enrolling at the Gettysburg Seminary tomorrow."

"You're going to be a Lutheran pastor?"

"Aye, the Lord willing."

"That is wonderful," I said and fell silent, reluctant to speak of my convictions at the time. A future in Gettysburg was undecided. The main questions involved Andrew's health and other needs, and Penelope. Once again, demons of fear and indecision arose, propelling me into an uneasy mood.

The locomotive's bell clanged and whistle howled as we slowed for our next stop, York, Pennsylvania. Since we would arrive at Gettysburg in about an hour, it was the last opportunity for me to visit a washroom. Some attention to grooming my face and beard might make me appear more presentable. "Excuse me, Tim," I said as the train braked to a stop. "I need to find the station toilet."

"Sure," he said and struggled to stand up in the aisle. "You have only five minutes before the train pulls out."

I nodded and hurried toward the doorway. Once in the washroom, I refreshed myself the best I could. The lavatory mirror's reflection was not reassuring. Two anxious eyes peered at me from pallid and drawn features. There wasn't much I could do to improve appearances. I dabbed some cologne Priscilla gave me on my beard, but the fellow staring back at me from the mirror remained the same. Before returning to the train, I pulled a copy of the telegram, which I sent to Penelope from the Philadelphia station. Its message was succinct: A hurricane has delayed arrival until two-forty five p.m. today. Hope you received my letter posted August first. Love, John.

The whistle howled twice. A voice bellowed, "All 'board." I hurried toward the boarding steps, reaching them just as our train started to move. Tim stood up. I eased past him and sat down. He sniffed a couple of times. "'Tis sweet as a rose you're smellin'."

Having learned a bit of the brogue from Sergeant O'Hara, I decided to respond in like manner. "Aye, a bit of eau de toilette for your beard," I said, handing him the bottle of cologne.

He wagged his head and raised a hand refusing my offer. "On to meeting your true love," he said as the train began to pick up speed.

We settled back in our seats and listened to click-clacking rails. Soon, the conductor would announce our destination: Next stop — Gettysburg.

CHAPTER TEN

I was not prepared for an awakening of emotions lurking within dark recesses of my mind. One of them began to squirm out of its hiding place as our train slowed for Gettysburg Depot. Dismal sadness seemed to fall upon me, a pall suffocating all feelings of joy. The delight of being reunited with Penelope, Andrew and Todd melted like frost on a sunny morning. Instead, a haunting loss of Hank gripped my spirit. Why didn't I return sooner to devote every waking moment in discovering what happened to him? There was no answer, only lingering feelings of guilt for my neglect.

Tim must have sensed my distress. "Why the long face?" he said and flaunted a sly grin. "You're about to meet Penelope again."

His antics jolted me out of distressing doldrums. "Oh, yes, thanks, I was lost in a daydream."

"Aye, war does entitle us to an occasional woe-be-gone."

Our conductor hurried by while calling, "Gettysburg. End o' the line. Gettysburg."

When our train braked to a stop, the passageway filled with excited passengers. Many supported themselves on crutches; others wore arm slings or black eye patches. Injured Yankees, I mused, and wondered whether they would be welcomed by an enthusiastic crowd? The answer came with boisterous cheers as we all stepped onto the station platform. Little did they know I was a Reb, not one of their own.

A travel guide was gathering his clientele of sightseers into a group before touring Gettysburg's Battlefield and Evergreen and National Cemeteries. Penelope, Andrew and Todd were nowhere to be seen. The locomotive bell clanged and steam hissed as we walked toward the depot. Maybe Penelope didn't receive my letter I posted from Charleston. However, she must have gotten the telegram I sent before boarding the train in Philadelphia.

Then, she emerged from the crowd and ran to meet me, her golden tresses bouncing with each step. All of my misgivings evaporated as our arms enfolded each other. "Oh, John," she said. "I've missed you so much."

I have difficulty understanding the contradictory feelings I experienced before and after stepping onto Gettysburg Depot's red-bricked platform. There was an overwhelming sense of joy now lifting my spirit above all emotional scars war inflicted upon me. I held her face between my palms and kissed her. "My dear, sweet Penelope, I love you more than words can express."

She nodded and kissed me. "I love you, too."

I slipped an arm around Tim's shoulder. "Penelope, do you remember the Yank who offered me his shoe?"

"Of course, I do," she said, patting Tim's cheek. "My father says you have applied for admission to the seminary."

"Aye, 'tis true. John, will you be staying in Gettysburg for a while?"

"I hope so," I said and glanced at Penelope. Her smile was all the answer I needed.

"Well, then," Tim said, doffing his hat. "Penelope . . . John, it's goodbye for now. I have an appointment with Doctor Brown at the seminary."

As Tim walked away, Penelope whispered, "He's fortunate to be single. Doctor Brown prefers unmarried applicants."

* * *

A Gettysburg Livery, Ltd carriage being drawn by a team of sleek sorrels pulled up to the station. Its driver appeared to be a Yankee veteran who hadn't replaced his blue kepi and blouse with civilian attire. He tied his reins around the brake lever, tipped his kepi, jumped down and opened the carriage door. "Well, little brother," Andrew said as he stepped from the carriage. "The last time I saw you, there was doubt we'd meet again this side of heaven."

"Andrew," I said, pulling him into a tight embrace. "There was doubt, indeed, but we made it."

"We are both here because of what Todd did for us."

"Yes. Where is Todd?"

"He's waiting at home," Andrew said and embraced Penelope. "We wanted you to meet without any distractions."

The driver fetched my luggage, helped us board the carriage and reined his team toward Todd's home. When we pulled into the driveway, Todd was waiting on the porch.

"Welcome, John," he said, walking down the steps to meet us. "You look a bit thin, but Aunt Gussie will take care of that."

Andrew patted his belly. "That's for certain. She could fatten a shadow."

"Aunt Gussie?"

"She's my housekeeper," Todd said, "and the best cook in Gettysburg."

A rotund, middle-aged appearing woman came through the doorway to meet us. Her corpulent figure was not flattered by a bouncing hoopskirt and white apron. Gray hair swept into a bun atop her head and fluting creases about thin lips reminded me of my grandmother. Before Todd could introduce us, she grasped my hand. "Aunt Gussie Heidelman I am, John Pendleton. Your room all ready I got. A little frail you look, but Aunt Gussie'll plump you up mitt lots of sauerbraten, red cabbage undt strudel."

Her vigorous pumping squeezed most of the blood from my hand. Out of pain more than acknowledgement, I said with a whiff of agony in my voice, "Oh, thank you, Mrs. Heidelman. You're too kind."

"Aunt Gussie you call me, yah?"

"Oh, yes, by all means."

"A good boy you are. Aunt Gussie likes you."

"I like you, too."

"Yah, ist gute," she said, grasped my luggage and disappeared through the doorway.

"Well, John," Todd said, "now you've met the one and only Aunt Gussie."

We sat on the sunroom porch while Aunt Gussie busied herself with household chores. Two years had gone by since Andrew was transferred to Johnson Island Prison. I was impressed with his obvious recovery from a wasting illness brought about by starvation and disease. As I listened to him relate how near death he came, gratitude for Todd's extraordinary efforts to free and heal my brother overwhelmed me.

We were about to walk back into the parlor when Aunt Gussie came bounding through the doorway. She was carrying a large tray stacked with sandwiches and a tureen of borscht. The serving was set before us as she gave out a steady stream of unanswerable conversation. "You eat plenty, John Pendleton. Fat you get not in army. Tell him, Doctor Martin, skinny he is. Aunt Gussie a lot cooks, undt John a lot eats. "

Out the door she swished and I knew for the next thirty days — John, a lot eats.

* * *

Andrew accompanied Penelope home in Todd's buggy while Aunt Gussie led me on a tour of the house, a limestone two-story Dutch Colonial. The parlor was rather long with a stone fireplace at both ends. The study was furnished with leather upholstered chairs and a walnut desk over which hung a portrait of Todd's deceased wife, Kathleen. On the second floor were four bedrooms, each with an alcove and imposing dormer window. It was a spacious and comfortable dwelling built the year of Todd's birth by his father in 18 and 15.

I was soon at home and quite comfortable in a roomy upstairs bedroom. Todd brought me some clothing that belonged to his son, Stephen, who served as a lieutenant in the Yankee army. He was captured during the battle of Second Manassas, and sent to Libby Prison in Richmond where he was killed trying to escape.

I donned Stephen's garments after taking a long, hot sudsy bath with a brisk scrubbing of my back by none other than Aunt Gussie. I was unable to dissuade her from the task. She called through the bathroom door, "Sit in tub, John Pendleton. Aunt Gussie your back to scrub. In I come."

Embarrassment faded as searing pain from her brush spread across my back. Her usual uninterrupted prattle continued: "Dirty, your back is. I find maybe skin sometime. You want more the soap to have, bitte?"

I was grateful beyond expression after she poured the last rinse of cold water over me. Being drained by my reformation, I dressed and crawled upon the bed for a moment of rest. It felt as if I were floating atop a cloud, having forgotten how well a featherbed could feel.

It was late afternoon when I awakened. Todd was talking with someone who had a resonant bass voice. As they continued in conversation, I became curious about the identity of his guest. I arose from bed and stepped through the bedroom doorway onto the stairway landing. Boards creaked with each slow, careful step as I made way toward the staircase railing.

"John, are you up? Come down. Doctor Alonzo Gresham wants to see you."

* * *

I did not meet Penelope's father before I was transferred to Fort Delaware Prison in August of 18 and 63. He provided money and provisions for me soon after my detention; however, the prison riot caused General Schoeph to cancel our first face to face meeting. I often pondered what his reaction would be whenever he became aware of Penelope's and my committed relationship. That happened in Todd's parlor the evening of my arriving in Gettysburg.

"Come and join us," Todd called as I descended the stairway.

They were seated in front of the fireplace. Alonzo Gresham's deep-set eyes were accentuated by bushy black brows. He appeared to be middle aged with silver streaks highlighting his black hair, beard and mustache. An ivory-headed cane lay on the floor beside his bandage-swathed right foot.

"Doctor Gresham," I said, "it's an honor to make your acquaintance, sir."

"I'm delighted to meet you, John." He then slapped his knee. "Please excuse my remaining seated . . . a siege with gout."

"Too much rich food and wine," Todd said, winking at me.

Doctor Gresham wagged a finger. "Not true. Gout is common in my family." He then gestured toward a chair opposite him. "Please, have a seat. I'm anxious to learn more about your family."

Feeling ill at ease I sat down and concentrated on hiding any apprehension. He smiled when I tried to find a quiet place for restless hands. "Thank you, sir."

"Penelope told me about your father's murder. Please accept my condolences. Such violence is unjustified even in times of war."

I thanked him for his concern and began to tell about my growing up on a South Carolina plantation, being educated at Eton College and serving in General Pettigrew's Division. He was attentive and asked many questions regarding plantation life. His mood turned somber when he inquired about our relying on slave labor to produce cotton, rice and indigo. Uneasiness parched my mouth and quickened fidgety hands as I struggled to deal with his questions. I fell silent and prayed Todd would rescue me from Doctor Gresham's taxing interrogation.

Instead, Penelope's father plucked at his beard and said, "The South's position on slavery has been debated by many of its learned men. I find their reasoning flawed to say the least, and unbelievable by most men of conscience. What do you think about owning slaves?"

By the tone of his voice and candor of his question, I knew my answer was of utmost importance. Any hope for a future with Penelope depended on a response he would accept. "Doctor Gresham, I am twenty-one years of age. All but eight of those years were spent on the Cooper River lowlands of South Carolina. Our plantation owned many Negro slaves. We were taught to regard them as part of our family. My father tried to feed, clothe well and provide decent quarters for our field hands and servants. However, many slaves were abused by slaveholders all across the South. Too often they were considered to be no better than domesticated animals without any human rights. That was wrong."

I could tell by his eyes that Doctor Gresham was not pleased with my answer. His reply was slow and deliberate. "You believe owning another human being is acceptable provided they aren't mistreated or abused?"

His question was sobering. My conscience urged me to respond with a resounding denial: No, sir, it is not acceptable. Yet, too many years of moral myopia kept me from such a response. Instead, I replied, "Yes, if all slaves were treated like ours, it would be acceptable."

Doctor Gresham's countenance hardened and sadness filled his eyes. "John, I like you. You're a decent young man, but have an untenable position on slavery."

I could not hide disappointment. He told me in so many words my perception of right and wrong was flawed. "I hope this won't prohibit my continuing to see Penelope."

Doctor Gresham picked up his cane. "That will depend on Penelope. I must be going, Todd . . . John."

* * *

Todd refrained from making any judgmental comments during the ensuing week, for which I was grateful. He must have perceived my dejection and need to ponder the meaning of Doctor Gresham's comments.

I felt duty-bound to visit the place where I was injured. Did all who died or were maimed make those sacrifices in defense of good or evil? Was God on our side, or the Yankee's? I was compelled to seek answers from my brother.

Following a sumptuous supper prepared by Aunt Gussie, Andrew and I met in Todd's study. I did my best to explain Doctor Gresham's and my conversation to him, and then awaited his advice.

"Well, John," he said, "nobody wins a war. One adversary happens to lose more than its opponent. The Yankees didn't win. We ran out of men and resources needed to continue the fight. They didn't. We lost."

"Is there a meaning to that?"

"I don't know. Maybe there's one we refuse to accept."

"Which is?"

"The South will never be the same again — King Cotton — plantation life — slavery — state's rights — all have been nullified, made extinct like dinosaurs."

"Were we right to fight for them?"

"Would you be willing to do it all over again, lose your leg, be imprisoned, humiliated, suffer losses of family and friends?"

"I don't know. Would you?"

"No, little brother, it was a hopeless cause the moment our people fired on Fort Sumter."

We continued with our conversation until time to retire. Andrew's inability to help resolve my dilemma was disappointing. The demons with which I was struggling could only be put to rest by me. Nobody, not even Andrew, Todd, or Doctor Gresham could be my conscience.

* * *

Dejected and frustrated, I climbed the stairway, fell into bed and spent a fitful night filled with nightmares about Hank. The overwhelming theme of each dream was whether he died or suffered disabling injuries fighting for an unworthy cause.

I arose before first light, sat in a chair beside an east-facing window and awaited daybreak. My introspective search continued as predawn purple shadows faded into silhouetted outlines of trees and buildings. From nearby a rooster greeted the coming sunrise with strident cock-a-doodle-doos.

I was swathed in thoughts when a hand touched my shoulder. "John," Todd said, "may I sit with you for a moment?"

"Sure," I said, gesturing toward a chair next to me.

"Thanks. I'm sorry Doctor Gresham was so provocational during your first meeting. I trust you realize he holds no ill feelings toward you."

"I hope he doesn't," I said, but continued to stare through the window, being consumed by a swirling tempest within my mind.

We sat in silence until roused by a neighbor's dog howling its reply to barking in the distance. Night was yielding to morning. A thin layer of clouds glowed as ascending sunrays streaked the sky.

Todd kneaded my tense shoulder muscles and whispered, "Sunup is the most promising time of day. No matter how dark the night, new life begins when morning comes."

The curtains stirred. Early breezes sang muted melodies through the window screen. Subdued sweet aroma of honeysuckle wafted into the room. A new day was being born, but I felt no thrill for its dawning. It seemed to me that the only light which would erase the blackness in my heart was to discover whatever the truth might be. I was desperate for an answer. In anguish, I faced Todd. "Hank and I fought side by side two years for a nation in which we believed. We were committed to give up our lives if necessary. Hank may have done so. Was our cause immoral?"

"If the South had won, would you be asking me that question?"

"Maybe . . . I don't know."

Todd pulled a small leather-bound New Testament from a pocket of his robe and handed it to me. "This may help you discover the answer."

"Where . . . how ...?" I said, realizing it was the one which kept a sliver of shrapnel from killing me.

"Chaplain Janeway left it with me after you were confined in Fort Delaware Prison."

My fingers caressed and then opened the little book. A jagged steel splinter was embedded within the Testament, lodging at the sixth chapter of Luke. These verses seemed to leap from each page as I began to read words spoken by Christ during His sermon on the mount. Was my answer within these pages? I became so caught up in the moment I failed to hear the breakfast bell being rung by Aunt Gussie.

Todd shook my shoulder. "Breakfast time — it's best not to keep Aunt Gussie waiting."

I closed the Testament and shoved it into my pocket. "I know. John, a lot eats."

* * *

With several helpings of Aunt Gussie's griddle cakes, scrambled eggs, and sausages weighing down my belly, I sought definitions of a *Just War* and a *Just Cause* in Todd's library. I was surprised by the number of volumes whose indices listed essays and commentaries on the subject, most of which were written by church scholars. Saint Augustine of Hippo, a staunch man of peace, was the first recorded person to prescribe requirements for a *Just War*. First, the authority to wage war lies with a sovereign entity. Second, a *Just Cause* is required. Third, the belligerents should have a rightful intention.

A Doctor of the Church, Saint Thomas Aquinas, later taught and elaborated on these principles. "The damage inflicted by an aggressor on the nation or community of nations must be lasting, grave, and certain. All other means of putting end to it must have been shown to be impractical or ineffective. There must be serious prospects of success. The use of arms must not produce evils and disorders graver than the evil to be eliminated."

Hugo Grotius, a seventeenth century Dutch secularist, further defined these principles. "The danger faced by the nation is immediate. The force used is necessary to adequately defend the nation's interests. The use of force is proportionate to the threatened danger."

Todd entered the library while I was pouring over these references and writing comments in my journal. "Are you finding any answers?"

"Yes," I said, handing him Hugo Grotius's, *The Law on War and Peace*. "Have you ever read this book?"

He accepted the volume and sat in a chair next to mine. "What have we here?" he said, pulling a pair of reading glasses from his pocket.

"Enlightenment on what constitutes a *Just War*."

"I see . . . yes, I have read some but not all of Grotius' works. So, what do you think about his assertions?"

"They are provocative, worth comparing to our recent struggle."

"I agree. Have you confronted the slavery issue with them?"

"Yes, neither we nor the Yankees went to war because of slavery."

"Not in the beginning, but extremists on both sides used it to promote their causes. It became a burning issue that demanded resolution."

"True, but it wasn't a cause for which we went to war."

"If it had been, would the Confederacy have fought a *Just War*?"

Todd's comment made me question the depth of his meaning. Is slavery a moral practice, one that is proper for slaveholders and slaves alike? Could it be a worthy reason for making war on an adversary who was determined to eliminate the practice? I remained silent while considering these questions. Saint Augustine's second postulate requires a *Just Cause* for which to fight. Since our cause was for the right to secede from a totalitarian republic, the question isn't whether my people fought a *Just War*. It's whether slavery is a humane and proper practice. I was beginning to believe it was not.

CHAPTER ELEVEN

"John . . . stay down . . . you'll get kilt."

Without a doubt, it was Hank's voice. Yet, Andrew and I were alone near where canister killed and maimed many in my division two years earlier. I grasped Andrew's arm. "Did you hear that?"

"Hear what?"

I turned around to face a stone wall where Yankee infantry crouched during our July the third assault. It was only one-hundred yards away, but might as well have been a mile on that hellish battle day two summers before. We were alone except for a touring group well beyond earshot. "A voice calling to me."

"Are you sure? I heard nothin'."

"It was Hank telling me to stay down. I haven't any memory of him saying anything after exploding canister swept our legs from under us . . . until now."

"It could be your imagination. The mind can do strange things."

"No. I heard him. I now remember. He did tell me to stay down or I'd be killed."

Andrew must have thought I was losing my sanity. He patted me on the back and tried to change the subject. "I read in the *Gettysburg Compiler* this morning that a monument honoring your division is being erected."

I was compelled to ignore his comment. For the first time since that fateful day, I was beginning to recall what happened. I gazed across the battlefield toward Little Round Top, the place where Sergeant O'Hara's son was killed. Out of my sorrow for the loss and maiming of friend and foe alike, I began to weep. Pent up anguish and rage erupted from repressed memories into uncontrollable sobbing. I tried to compose myself but was powerless to do so. Dear God, I thought, was all of this carnage necessary? Were all of us victims of past follies? Did slavery do this to us, North and South? Was this blood atonement for our inhumanity? If so, the tap root of our anguish must have been slavery.

My emotional catharsis continued for several minutes, during which Andrew kept saying, "It's all right. Let it out."

The instant it ended, I was free of haunting memories and fears, all of which could not be resolved with never-ending rumination. I was enslaved by these debilitating manifestations until my moment of deliverance. Was it a miracle? I considered it to be so.

"Let's go sit in some shade," Andrew said, pointing at a copse of trees near the stone wall. "We must talk about our plans for the future."

"Sure, I need to explain how things are going at home."

We sat on the wall beneath three trees that survived the battle. "What are you intending to do now?" Andrew said while mopping a kerchief across his forehead.

"What do you mean by, now?"

"Well, little brother, are you going to marry Penelope and settle in Gettysburg or take her back to Charleston?"

"Married?"

"You didn't come up here just to see Todd and me . . . did you?"

"No, I came to see her as well, but getting married at this time isn't the reason."

"I see. You will be returning to Charleston?"

"Maybe," I said and continued to tell him about the circumstances at home. He frowned when I explained the land is all that remains of our plantation. We have no house, barns, sheds, orchard, gardens, fences or livestock, all destroyed by Sherman and his minions. There are no funds with which to rebuild, restock or pay Yankee taxes. Sherman has issued a decree dividing many plantations and farms into forty-acre tracts. Each plot and a mule will then be granted to a former slave. If that happens, the land will cease to be ours. The greatest responsibility for us will be providing for our family. "With all of these uncertainties," I said in conclusion. "How can I consider marriage?"

Andrew stood up, looked down at me and placed both hands on my shoulders as if I were an immature child. "I will take care of everything, little brother. I'll be returning home when Todd says I'm ready."

"I can't let you take on all these problems. I'll go with you."

"No. You need to think about your future . . . which reminds me . . . what are your plans?"

His attitude was assertive and unbending. It seemed as if he were assuming the family's patriarchal role now that our father was deceased. There was but one way for me to escape an in-depth interrogation — tell him about my commitment to ministry.

Andrew's attitude wavered between eyebrow-raising surprise to frowns and skeptical grimaces as I related my story. However, he refrained from interrupting me until I finished, at which time he peered at me in silence for an uncomfortable interlude. "Well?" I said, at last, and waited for his response.

Andrew sat down beside me. "What can I say? You have made a decision to pursue an honorable profession. I agree that taking a wife at this time would be unwise. We have no money. How do you propose paying for several more years of education?"

"I don't know."

"Where . . . which seminary do you plan on attending?"

"I don't know."

"Well, little brother, you have much to resolve. Have you told Penelope?"

"Not yet."

"You'd better right away."

"Yes. Do you think Doctor Gresham will believe me . . . that I now accept it is wrong to own another human being?"

"I don't know, but if that is what you believe, you must try."

* * *

Coming to grips with meeting Doctor Gresham again was not easy. I spent the greater part of the afternoon pacing Todd's parlor, trying to put together my thoughts. I had to get it right. There would not be another opportunity for mending my relationship with Penelope's father. I tried to envision every question with which he might ply my reasoning. He may ask how I managed to change my mind within such a short time span. Or, for a measure of recompense, would we be willing to deed portions of the Pendleton plantation to our displaced servants and field hands — maybe even pay them restitution? These were but two of many questions with which I might be confronted. Could I prepare for every one of them? No. It was time to plead my case.

The walk to Pennsylvania College was pleasant; however, unease over whatever awaited me in Doctor Gresham's parlor was disconcerting. Elm and oak tree canopies shaded streets, brick sidewalks and well groomed yards along the way. Unlike Charleston, few battle scars inflicted during the great conflict remained. The steamy August afternoon brought a sweat to my brow by the time I reached college grounds. As I gazed across campus, its magnificent elms, oaks, and verdant lawns bore no evidence of the fierce conflict fought here only two years before.

A wrought iron bench beneath an oak tree south of the Old Dorm provided me with a welcome respite. My right foot ached in spite of the fact that I no longer had one. Dark storm clouds looming along the northwestern horizon authenticated my absent foot's forecasting prowess.

While resting in the shade, my thoughts returned to July in 18 and 63. I was sitting on this same bench, reading the *Gettysburg Compiler*, when Penelope walked across campus from the college president's house. She was carrying a wicker picnic basket and a pitcher of lemonade. My unarmed guard, a Yankee attendant who was always nearby, met her with a terse challenge. "I'm sorry, ma'am. The prisoner isn't allowed any visitors."

Penelope displayed no signs of being intimidated by his confrontation; instead, she approached and informed him that she was my caretaker. The basket contained a noon meal ordered by my attending surgeon. "Yes, ma'am," he said, stepping back so she could sit beside me. "It's okay since you're tending the prisoner's needs."

"Thank you," she said, sat down and pulled three glasses from her basket. At that moment I realized she was prepared for the task at hand. She filled each glass from her pitcher and offered one to the attendant. "Have some cool lemonade, Private . . ."

"It's Parsons, ma'am, Hiram Parsons."

She nodded and raised the glass toward him. "I'm pleased to meet you, Private Parsons. I'm Penelope, President Gresham's daughter. The day is quite hot."

"Yes, ma'am, it is," he said, accepting the glass.

She retrieved several oatmeal cookies from her basket. "I baked these cookies this morning," she said, offering them to the Yankee.

Private Parsons looked about, no doubt to see whether we were being observed. He took the cookies, slipped them into his pocket and walked away toward the Old

Dorm where he sat on the porch steps and enjoyed Penelope's bribe.

I admired her grit. This was the first time we were allowed any semblance of privacy. The attendant continued to watch us but remained out of earshot on the porch.

Penelope spread linen napkins on our laps. "I hope you like ham sandwiches and deviled eggs," she said, placing them and several cookies on two plates.

I couldn't keep from admiring her beauty — the gentleness of her demeanor — the sweet scent of lilac wafting from her hair. My preoccupation delayed a response, which should have been immediate.

She placed one of the plates on my lap and nudged my conscience. "Well, John Pendleton . . . do you?"

"Oh, yes, I do. Thank you. I haven't enjoyed any food like this for over two years."

All the time while we were ravishing Penelope's picnic, I had to stifle a compelling urge to reach for and hold her hand. My guard seemed to have his gaze fixed on us all the time we were eating. I feared he would report any intimacy between Penelope and me to his superiors. If that should happen, there would be no more picnics.

With the last bite of cookie and sip of lemonade, my caution flew away like dandelion seeds on the wind. When Penelope reached for my empty plate, I grasped and squeezed her hand. "Thank you, so much, for your thoughtfulness."

She smiled, glanced at the guard, leaned over and kissed my cheek. "You're welcome."

Oh, it was a bit of a peck, but ecstasy lifted my spirits into an unknown realm of pure happiness. At that moment, I didn't care what the Yankee might do. But when I glanced at him walking toward us, a bit of trepidation caused me to turn loose of Penelope's hand.

"Thanks, ma'am," he said, handing Penelope his empty glass. "I appreciate the lemonade and cookies."

"There's more," she said, accepting the glass.

"No thanks, ma'am, I got'ta get him back in the ward."

I was roused from reliving the past by a jagged bolt of lightning, rolling thunder and splattering raindrops. I glanced skyward. Dark swirling clouds and lightning flashes were all the warning I needed for seeking shelter. As I stood up to leave, Penelope was running toward me. "John, let's get inside the Old Dorm. There isn't time to reach our cellar."

* * *

We scurried down the hallway toward a ground floor storage closet just as the storm's full furry swept onto campus. There was a crescendo of windowpanes being smashed into glass shards as a barrage of hail stones pummeled the building. Just as I slammed shut the closet door behind us, ferocious winds caused our refuge to shudder, its timbers to creak, crackle and groan. I feared for our lives at that moment. There was little doubt in my mind we were in the midst of a tornado which might bury us under tons of rubble.

Penelope threw her arms around me with such force that we fell against the wall and slid to the floor. There we cowered in each other's embrace and prayed for God's mercy. We were in total darkness, which heightened our fear as the storm's fury roared above us. Its intensity reminded me of the time Hank and I hid under a railroad bridge as an oncoming Yankee troop train sped across its timbered trestle. The sounds were deafening, much like those engulfing us in an Old Dorm broom closet.

With each protest emitted by our sanctuary's superstructure, we tightened our embraces until I was unable to take a deep breath. Neither of us said a word. Being comforted by the warmth of her closeness, an irresistible desire moved me to kiss and tell Penelope how much I loved and cherished her. As our lips met, the sounds of nature's turmoil faded away until they were replaced with blissful isolation.

Passions, consuming and almost irresistible, seemed to quicken every nerve ending in my being. Likewise, Penelope seemed to be yielding to the same emotions. Our ardor was similar to the storm raging across Gettysburg, its intensity mounting until I felt self restraint spinning out of control. To our good fortune, the booming voice of Doctor Gresham seized the moment. "Penelope … John … where are you?"

Penelope pushed me away. "Oh, John … it's Papa," she said with each word spoken somewhere between a whisper and a groan.

Without hesitation, I stood up, opened the door and stepped into the hall. "Here we are, Doctor Gresham."

Penelope's father, standing at the far end of the hallway, raised his cane in a greeting gesture and began to hobble toward me. "Thank God, you're safe."

The hallway was littered with fragments of plastering shaken from ceiling and walls, an alarming indication of how severe the building was pummeled. Fearing the entire structure might collapse, I grasped Penelope by the hand and hurried toward her father. The Old Dorm groaned and emitted several loud popping sounds as if it were about to give way. "We need to get outside — right now," Doctor Gresham called, gesturing for us to hurry.

Penelope and I grabbed her father by his arms and hurried toward the south portico. I was amazed at his agility. He hopped and skipped like a bounding kangaroo, never touching the floor with his afflicted right foot. We reached the iron bench where I rested before the storm just as crashing noises came from inside the Old Dorm. Clouds of dust belched through several broken windows of the stricken edifice — then fell silent as a stalking predator ready to spring upon an unsuspecting prey.

* * *

Damages inflicted on the Old Dorm and several other campus buildings deferred my defining moment with Doctor Gresham until carpenters and masons were hired and repairs underway.

Todd invited Andrew and me to attend St. James Lutheran Church with him on Sunday, the twentieth of August. As we entered the sanctuary, I was surprised at remaining damages incurred during the great battle. Pews were defaced, carpets torn and stained, plastering cracked, and windows broken. Some of the damages were sustained while the church was utilized as a hospital for over a month following Pickett's charge. Only a few repairs, such as new wall frescoing, appeared to be underway, but much was lacking.

Doctor Gresham looked at us and nodded as we sat in a pew across the aisle from him and Penelope who greeted me with a demure smile.

Following scriptural readings by laymen, The Reverend Breidenbaugh stepped behind the pulpit and recited quotes from the Gospels and a prayer. He then waxed eloquent while admonishing the faithful to put *shoulders to the wheel* and restore this house of worship to its prewar grandeur. While the sermon was being delivered, I kept glancing at all of the defacements the church had incurred. It was during this time that I saw an unmistakable blood stain on the carpet. I stared at that crimson spot as the pastor's voice seemed to permeate my entire being. I wondered — could this be Hank's blood? The thought gripped me for a moment, and then I leaned back in the pew, gazed at the altar cross and prayed for total deliverance from my obsession.

Hoping to take my mind off of the stain, I glanced at Penelope. Her golden tresses reflected subtle hues of red, blue and green by morning sunlight diffusing through stained glass. My mind was snared by her beauty. Like a king cobra enraptured by a Hindu flautist, I could only feast upon those scintillating highlights. My hypnotic state ended when Andrew nudged my arm and nodded toward the preacher. "Pay attention, little brother, you might learn something."

His reproach broke the spell, and I was able to concentrate on the good Reverend's homily. Soon, he ended his discourse, blessed the congregation and admonished everyone, "Go in peace and serve the Lord." To which all replied in unison, "Thanks be to God."

"Good morning, Doctor Gresham . . . Penelope," I said, stepping into the aisle.

She nodded and smiled as I reached for her hand. "Good morning, John,"

"Did you enjoy Reverend Breidenbaugh's sermon?" Doctor Gresham said, gripping my arm.

"Yes, very much," I said, choosing not to confess my lack of concentration. "He preaches quite well."

"Penelope . . . Abner," Todd said, "I hope you will join us for Sunday dinner. Aunt Gussie has prepared her and my favorite, sauerbraten and red cabbage."

Doctor Gresham patted his ample girth. "Thank you, that's my favorite, too."

The Reverend Breidenbaugh greeted and shook hands with everyone as we left the church. He was an affable man who seemed to have a genuine interest in each person, inquiring as to their health and needs. He stood upright, was robust, had a trim silver-streaked black mustache and beard, and wore his vestments well.

"Good morning, Pastor," Todd said as they shook hands. "I'd like for you to meet Andrew's brother, John Pendleton."

"Ah, yes," he said, grasping my hand. "So, you're Andrew's brother. He has spoken of and asked prayers for you many times." He then embraced Andrew. "It appears our prayers have been answered."

Andrew nodded. "Without question," he said, leaned closer to the pastor and whispered.

I couldn't hear his comment, but Reverend Breidenbaugh grinned at me. "Ah, John, do come visit me soon. We have much to discuss."

I was taken by surprise and made an awkward attempt to respond. "Oh, ah, yes, uh, thank you, sir."

"Fine, do come by the parsonage anytime. I look forward to visiting with you."

As we left the church, I asked Andrew what he whispered to the preacher. "Oh, little brother," he said, slapping me on the back. "I told him you needed some pastoral guidance."

"Pastoral guidance?" I blurted. "What for?"

"I didn't tell him. He didn't ask."

CHAPTER TWELVE

A coppice of trees near the stone wall where our assault met its downfall on July the third kept beckoning me like Lorelei of the Rhine. For some reason, my thought processes came easier at this spot on Cemetery Ridge where we breached the enemy's line. Since it was the beginning of the end for us, the place would afterward be known as the High Water Mark of the Confederacy. That precise moment came when General Armistead placed his hand on a Yankee cannon, signaling its capture by Confederate forces. He was then mortally wounded by enemy infantrymen and died two days later in a Yankee field hospital. His demise and the death or capture of all the men who penetrated the line with him was a portent of our defeat almost two years later. It was at this hallowed place on Cemetery Ridge that I sought enlightenment, a foreshadowing experience which might reveal an option I ought to take.

I visited this place every morning for several days to ponder my past, present and future. Like the nation for which I served, life as I knew it no longer existed. I was walking into a maze not unlike a London intersection where several roads take their exit. Which road should I choose? Return to Charleston with Andrew? Remain in Gettysburg to be with Penelope? Fulfill my commitment to the ministry? On and on, questions demanded answers but none came. At last, I realized the epiphany being sought — seek guidance from the Reverend Breidenbaugh.

I borrowed Todd's horse and buggy the following morning and drove to Saint James Lutheran's parsonage. "Ah, John," Pastor Breidenbaugh said as he opened the door. "I'm pleased you decided to pay me a visit."

"Thank you, sir," I said and followed him through an atrium into the parlor where he gestured toward an upholstered chair next to a modest rock-faced fireplace.

He sat down in a chair facing me, smiled and glanced at my fidgeting hands. "Andrew says you are considering the ministry."

My response was interrupted as an attractive lady in somber attire befitting a minister's wife entered the parlor. She was carrying a tray laden with a carafe of coffee, some scones, two cups, sugar bowl and a creamer. "Welcome to our home," she said, setting the tray on a serving table next to the pastor's chair.

"Thank you, Elizabeth," Reverend Breidenbaugh said. "This young man is Andrew Pendleton's brother, John."

Without hesitation, I stood up and greeted her with a nod. "Mrs. Breidenbaugh."

Her hazel eyes flashed, reflecting, I thought, a genuine appreciation of my southern greeting. "I am very pleased to make your acquaintance, John." Then she patted her husband on the shoulder. "I'll be in the kitchen, dear, if you need anything."

Before returning to the pastor's question, we spent some time getting acquainted. His genuineness eased my apprehensions and quieted restless hands. Having been informed about my family by Andrew, he expressed condolences for the murder of my father and inquired about Mother, Priscilla and Martin. He expressed pride in his children, a son, Edward, and two daughters, Mary and Annie.

Our conversation was interrupted when their mantel clock's Westminster chimes struck ten times. "Well, John," Pastor said. "I trust you have a deeper purpose in your visit. What can I do for you?"

He listened to me explain my predicament and appeared impressed by the apparition of Bishop Dossy I experienced following my injury during the Petersburg Crater Battle.

"That was a prophetic event," he said. "I can see how it would anoint you with a total commitment to our Lord and his church. It is one you must follow."

"Yes, I'm committed . . . but when . . . how . . . where? I just don't know."

"Well, no man has the answers. If it is the Lord's will for you to become a shepherd of his flock, he will provide the when, where and how. In the meantime, weigh the positive and negative aspects of each problem. The most important one is to determine which seminary offers the best education and preparation for ministry. Have you considered Lutheran Theological Seminary here in Gettysburg?"

"No, sir, I haven't since I am a communicant of Saint Michael's Episcopal Church."

Pastor Breidenbaugh frowned for a moment. He excused himself and left the room. I wondered if my comment was offensive, but he soon returned carrying several books. "Here are some reference volumes I want you to read. I believe you will discover within these pages that our Lutheran theology is quite similar to Episcopalian tenets."

I fell silent while pondering the pastor's claim, which must have been disconcerting for him. How could I, a baptized and confirmed Episcopalian, pursue ministerial training in a Lutheran seminary? The idea was perplexing, and it added another problem for me to consider. The Reverend Breidenbaugh exhibited patience by remaining silent, allowing me to contemplate the meaning of his statement without any interruption. If I were to be considered for admission, would it be necessary for me to become a Lutheran? When I posed this question, he replied, "No, our seminary accepts students of all Christian denominations, such as Methodist, Presbyterian and Episcopalian."

"Thank you, Pastor, for your counsel. You have given me much to think about."

"Study these books, pray for enlightenment and come visit me again, soon."

"Yes, sir, I will. Extend my appreciation to Mrs. Breidenbaugh for the delicious refreshments."

Pastor Breidenbaugh said goodbye as he closed the door behind me. I then walked toward the hitching post toting three large volumes and another weighty problem requiring a solution.

* * *

I spent several days poring over the books Reverend Breidenbaugh loaned me. The most informative was the Christian Book of Concord, a revelation of Martin Luther's protestant reformation movement. When I finished reading the Visitation Articles, I was convinced Episcopalian and Lutheran tenets were almost one and the same. There were differences in systems of governance, but these didn't appear to be of concern for me at the time. The primary question remaining was whether the degree granted from a Lutheran seminary would be acceptable for Episcopalian ordination rites in South Carolina. If not, my remaining in Gettysburg would require conversion to the Lutheran faith — a decision I wasn't ready to make.

I compiled and posted a letter to Benton Dossy asking him to make an inquiry for me with the Rt. Reverend Thomas Davis, Bishop of the South Carolina Diocese.

While walking back to Todd's home from the Post Office, I decided the time was right for me to talk with Penelope's father. He was seated on his porch, reading the *Gettysburg Compiler* as I climbed the front steps. "Good morning, Doctor Gresham."

He pushed aside the newspaper and peered over reading spectacles. "Ah, John — a pleasant surprise," he said and motioned toward a chair next to him. "Come, have a seat."

He tried to calm my unease after I sat down by commenting on the latest news being reported in the newspaper. One disturbing item was concerning a speech delivered by General Howard, President Johnson's recent appointment to head the Freeman's Bureau. The gist of it was for Southern states to adopt a more active role in rehabilitation of former slaves so the need for a Freeman's Bureau would cease.

I pursed my lips and frowned trying to refrain from commenting. I thought but dared not say this was a ridiculous proposition. The war exhausted our treasuries, leaving little for day to day maintenance.

"You don't agree?" Doctor Gresham said, taking notice of my grimaces.

I looked away hoping my eyes would not condemn me. "Where will the money come from?"

Doctor Gresham folded up the newspaper and removed his spectacles. "Exactly," he said, tossing the paper onto the porch. "Howard is simply proclaiming his importance, knowing full well that only the Federal government has the wherewithal for the job."

"Yes, I agree."

"The President is retiring his generals by appointing them to fat places. I suppose it's the right political move, but not one of which I approve."

Noticing Doctor Gresham's foot was no longer swathed in a bandage and hoping to lighten the conversation, I said, "I see your gout has cleared up?"

"Yes, Todd prescribed a round of colchicine pills. I hate to take them, but they work in spite of some distressing side-effects."

I nodded in response to his comment and searched every corner of my brain for a way to bring up the subject of slavery. Doctor Gresham appeared to be aware of my quandary. We sat in silence; it seemed, for an agonizing interval. At last, he gripped my arm. "What's on you mind, John?"

My response erupted as if all thought processes were at a standstill. "I'm not sure I've got one."

"What did you say?"

"I'm sorry, sir, what I meant to say is that I've changed my mind."

"You have? About what?"

"Owning another human being."

"I see and how did you come to that conclusion?"

Now feeling more at ease, I leaned forward in the chair and embarked upon a rather long dissertation on the subject — how I delved into the writings of Hugo Grotius, Saint Augustine of Hippo, Saint Thomas Aquinas and Holy Scriptures. Even though the war was not initiated to resolve the slavery question, President Lincoln made it an issue with his Emancipation Proclamation. As a result, the legal right to own another human ended when Generals Lee and Johnston surrendered their armies. However, the moral issue of slavery required me to search my conscience and the Gospels for an answer. The Golden Rule found in chapter seven; verse twelve of the Gospel of Saint Matthew contains an unqualified admonition. We are to treat everyone like we expect them to treat us. If I am not willing to be the property of another, how can I justify owning any person, no matter their color, race or creed. When finished, I was able to look into his eyes and say, "I am relieved our family no longer owns a single slave."

He grasped my hand. "John . . . you have eased my mind. Being able to consider the validity of your beliefs and discard those that are lacking will serve you well the rest of your life. I'm proud of you."

I expressed heartfelt gratitude for his response, stood up and started to excuse myself when Doctor Gresham raised his hand. "Wait. There is something else we need to discuss."

"Sure," I said and sat back down.

"Pastor Briedenbaugh dropped by yesterday. He said you and he had a long visit regarding your interest in the ministry."

"Yes, sir, we did."

"I trust he was helpful?"

I was reluctant to burden our relationship with all of the questions and decisions with which I was struggling. However, Doctor Gresham's sincerity was compelling. For the ensuing hour I revealed my quandary and he responded by giving me some much needed counsel. Above all, I should follow my conscience relative to seminary attendance, but he assured me Gettysburg's Lutheran Theological Seminary was one of the best in the nation. There were no tuition or library fees. The price of boarding in the seminary building was $3.50 per week, and furnished rooms were provided free of expense. He also assured me that my education acquired at Eaton College qualified me for immediate admission on September the twenty-eighth. We concluded our visit with him admonishing me to give the Lutheran Theological Seminary attentive consideration. If I decided to seek admission, he promised to schedule an appointment for me with Seminary President Doctor James Brown.

"Have you discussed all of this with Penelope?" he asked as I stood up.

"No, sir."

"You should. You'll find her in the Science Building chemistry lab."

* * *

The Science Building was in full view of Doctor Gresham's porch, so I was duty-bound to follow his advice. Disquieting questions as to how Penelope would receive all I was about to reveal filled me with apprehension. I was unprepared for exposing my innermost feelings to her. Unease mounted as I climbed steps to the Science Building. I stopped and glanced back at the president's residence. Doctor Gresham was still sitting on the porch, reading his newspaper. There was no other choice. I reached for the door handle and entered.

Obnoxious odors greeted me as I walked down the hallway toward the chemistry lab. They reminded me of the days spent performing experiments in an Eaton College laboratory. One significant mishap was the time my test-beaker concoction produced stifling fumes of sulfur dioxide which almost asphyxiated me and several fellow students. Chemistry was not my forte.

"Hello, John, come see what I'm doing," Penelope said as I shoved open the lab door.

There was an array of glass flasks, tubing, and a condensation coil interconnected along the full length of a stained work counter. "What is all of this?" I asked, admiring the extensive setup.

"It's an experiment for producing diethyl ether from ethanol and sulfuric acid."

"That sounds dangerous."

"It can be."

"You aren't doing it . . . are you?"

She laughed and shook her head. "No, I'm setting it up for one of Doctor Brighton's graduate students."

"That's a relief. I didn't realize you were interested in chemistry."

She stopped sealing tubing joints and motioned for me to follow her into Doctor Brighton's office. "There's something I want to show you."

From the physics and chemistry student files, she retrieved her folder which listed all of the courses she had completed, which were impressive — general, qualitative, quantitative and organic chemistry. "Are you going to become a chemistry professor?" I asked, scanning the list.

She then pulled a letter from the folder and handed it to me. "No, I plan on attending the Female Medical College of Pennsylvania."

I was stunned. "You are going to study medicine — become a physician?"

"Yes . . . I was planning to tell you, but . . . ."

Contents of the letter, addressed to Felix N. Brighton, Ph.D., could not have been more unsettling for me. As I read the following sentences, all of my expectations for the future wilted like a drought stricken field of Carolina cotton. *We appreciate your letter recommending Miss Penelope Gresham for admission to Female Medical College of Pennsylvania. Our board of trustees has unanimously approved her acceptance into the entering class one year hence on September 28, 1866. With deep appreciation, President Ira L. Milton, M.D.*

Anxiety about revealing my impasse to Penelope underwent a rapid change. In an instant, it was replaced by resentment for her apparent lack of sensitivity. I don't recall whether she kept on speaking. All I could hear were the resounding accusations being voiced within my mind. Then, conscience manifested itself. There was no cause for me to be offended. Tardiness in telling her of my commitment to ministry was of no less an offense. I reached for and pulled her into a tight embrace. "Well," I said, looking into her azure eyes. "I just had a long talk with your father. He said I shouldn't delay any longer in telling you about my commitment to becoming a minister."

She grinned and hugged me tighter. "I've known since three days after you arrived. Andrew told me."

"In confidence?"

"Of course."

"That's a big brother for you."

We walked around campus for several hours discussing plans for the future. Penelope was determined to achieve excellence in medicine. She wanted to receive a Bachelor of Science degree before entering medical college. It was needed since requirements for admission to most medical colleges and subsequent education were undergoing rapid changes. These modifications were the result of inadequate care rendered by too many physicians and surgeons during the war.

Being a female physician was considered to be an unworthy vocation by the general populace. As a result, many medical colleges, proprietary or otherwise, refused to accept women students before the war. But exemplary contributions by women physicians and nurses to the care of sick and injured soldiers were responsible for the dawning of a new era in medicine.

Penelope understood my concerns regarding acceptance of a Lutheran seminary degree by an Episcopalian Diocese. Time was short for me to make a choice. The one year hiatus before Penelope entered medical college became of paramount importance. The only way we could spend it together would be for me to remain in Gettysburg and attend the Lutheran seminary. If Bishop Davis failed to respond within two weeks, I would be forced to make a decision without his blessing.

* * *

When I walked into Todd's study, Andrew appeared to be in deep thought. He glanced at me as I sat down next to the fireplace. "Well, little brother, it took you quite some time to post your letter to Benton."

"I also visited with Doctor Gresham and Penelope."

"Oh, and you're now straight with them?"

"Yes . . . straight."

He leaned back in his chair and handed me a letter. "I've accepted this offer from Transoceanic Cable Company. I think you should know about it."

The letter's content was to the point. *Your application for First Officer of SS New Boston has been approved. She will be docked at Pier 37, New York Harbor on September fourth and will depart on the Sixth to continue laying transatlantic cable. Please report to Captain Roberts no later than twelve noon on September 5, 1865. Welcome aboard, Mister Pendleton. Trenton Meriwether.*

I folded and handed the letter to Andrew. "What about Mother, Priscilla and Martin?"

"It's all right with them. I'll be sending most of my salary to Mother."

At that moment, I struggled to subdue anger toward Andrew for his making such a decision without mentioning it to me. His conduct was a bit cavalier, having passed confidential information to Penelope about my ministry commitment. Did he think his accountability to the family was satisfied by the meager financial support he was pledging to them? Paltry as it might be, I could not match it. The guilt I was experiencing added fuel to my resentment. Who will be taking care of our land? Martin's youth precluded his being able to contribute much. Mother and Priscilla were in no position to manage its maintenance or disposal. We could not expect Benton Dossy to take on such a responsibility. That left me as the only one capable of taking on the task. The more I pondered the situation, the angrier I became. "Well, Andrew," I said, stood up and assumed a defiant stance. "I'll be leaving for Charleston within the week. When are you heading for your new job?"

Andrew stared at me with an incredulous glint in his eyes. "What has gotten into you, little brother?" he said, rising up out of his chair. "What can you do in Charleston? You will only be another burden for Mother. I have commissioned Carrie Dossy's brother, Delbert Hastings, to partition and sell our land. Sherman's ill-advised proposal to divide and delve out our plantation to former slaves was nullified by President Johnson. Sales should go well and will provide for Mother, Priscilla and Martin. Your obligations lie here with Penelope and future seminary studies — either in Gettysburg or elsewhere. Take care of your own needs and leave the rest to me."

Andrew's arrogant remarks intensified my resentment. "Leave the rest to you?" I said, gesturing with a disdainful wave. "You're going to be stretching cable across the Atlantic. How can you manage anything else?"

Andrew plopped down in his chair. "John," he said, which surprised me. It was always, little brother. "Believe me. Everything is arranged. Delbert has dealt in property sales and management for over twenty years. He is trustworthy and capable. Trust me."

I stood there pondering what he said and began to understand how much attention he'd given to the situation. He allowed me to wrestle with my demons and make necessary decisions for the future. "I'm sorry, Andrew, for my inconsiderate remarks. Thanks for all you have and will be doing for the family."

"That's okay, little brother. You are forgiven."

CHAPTER THIRTEEN

Doctor Brown removed his pince-nez spectacles and motioned for me to sit in a ladder-back chair facing his desk. "Welcome to Lutheran Theological Seminary, Mister Pendleton."

I was impressed by the compelling intensity emanating from his eyes. I felt exposed as if he were aware of each character flaw lurking within every niche and cranny of my innermost being. I thanked him for granting me an interview and sat down.

"I trust you are acquainted with our campus?"

"Yes, Timothy O'Brien gave me a tour this morning."

"Ah, yes, he's one of our entering students . . . lost his leg during the battle."

I thumped my prosthesis. "So did I."

"Oh, I'm sorry. You seem to manage it well," he said and handed me a document. "I suggest you study our catalogue and constitution. It should answer any of your questions."

I flipped through several pages without stopping to read anything, a frivolous and nervous action because I knew the answer to my question would not be in it. "My family owned many slaves before the war. Will this influence seminary admission for me?"

Doctor Brown's brow furrowed as he pondered the question. "It might. This seminary was established by Doctor Samuel Schmucker, a staunch abolitionist. Our library was ransacked and many of his writings were destroyed by your people during their occupation of this institution." He then fell quiet for a moment. "If you had won the war, would you still be here?"

"Yes, I would," I said and continued to explain all of the events that changed me from a pampered son of a southern plantation owner to a mature man seasoned by the ravages of war. He was attentive as I explained how a commitment to enter the ministry resulted from an apparitional visit by Bishop Dossy.

Doctor Brown reached across his desk and tapped an innkeeper's bell.

"Yes, President Brown," a grayheaded lady said, opening the door.

"Thank you, Mrs. Keller, please bring me Doctor Gresham's and Reverend Breidenbaugh's letters."

"Yes, sir," she said, closing the door. She soon returned and handed the letters to Doctor Brown.

"I received these yesterday," he said, "both of which informed me of your commitment to become a minister, but were undecided about which seminary to attend — an Episcopalian, or Gettysburg Lutheran. Have you reached a decision?"

"I've written to my bishop. If he gives his blessing, I want to attend this seminary."

He responded by asking about my baptism, confirmation, education at Eaton College, reasons for returning to Gettysburg, and possible marital plans before graduation. I assured him that marriage was not being considered at the present time.

"A wise decision, Mister Pendleton, seminary education is very demanding, which too often causes conflicts between a married student and his spouse."

I sensed the interview was coming to a close when he asked for a clarification of my viewpoint on slavery. He often nodded and voiced agreement as I gave an accounting of how I came to recant previous beliefs on owning another human being. I concluded by saying that I hoped my present stand would be acceptable to him and the seminary's board of directors.

Doctor Brown stood up, walked around his desk, and shook my hand. "I will submit your application to the board as they meet tomorrow morning. They may also wish to interview you before making a definite commitment. When you hear from your bishop, please come to see me."

I felt an unusual sense of elation while walking back to Todd's home. The interview seemed to have gone well, and admission to the seminary appeared almost certain. I could not help but wonder, however, whether Bishop Davis would grant his approval. The thought was disconcerting, one that squelched my enthusiastic mood.

* * *

Spicy kitchen aromas, a combination of apples and cinnamon, greeted me as I climbed steps to the front porch. Aunt Gussie was doing her best to "fatten John up" by preparing and insisting upon my consuming large quantities of her specialties. When I entered Todd's study, a plate of apple strudel topped with a dollop of whipped cream sprinkled with cinnamon awaited me on Todd's desk. "John, a lot eats," she chided, rustling toward me with a carafe of fresh-brewed oolong tea. "There's more on the sideboard."

There was no way for me to refuse even though I was not hungry. The interview went well; however, it squelched a desire for sweets of any sort. "This is more than I can eat."

She shoved the plate into my hand and poured a cup full of steaming tea. "You eat. Skinny you are, but Aunt Gussie fix."

I stared at the plate, trying to muster a desire to consume at least one bite as she pulled up a chair and sat down. "Strudel you don't want? Sick you are?"

"No, Aunt Gussie, I'm not sick."

"Then, John eats."

"Okay, later," I said, setting the plate on the desk.

Aunt Gussie patted my shoulder, leaned toward me and whispered. "Distraught you are. Skinnier you get. Why?"

Her sudden interest in my distress was a surprise. I presumed her curiosity was motivated by my noncompliance with her forced-feeding approach. Instead of replying, I reached for the strudel.

She stayed my hand and pushed aside the plate. "You tell Aunt Gussie — yah."

I complied with her request during the following half hour or so. Without her interrupting for most of the time, I related every question begging to be resolved. When I concluded my story, she handed me the plate of strudel. "John eat unt listen. Penelope need John. John need Penelope. One year you have together. Good seminary here — you enroll — stay here — John, a lot eats. Now, supper I cook."

* * *

On Friday, the fifteenth of September, I found an envelope posted by Bishop Davis that Aunt Gussie placed on my pillow. I sat down in a chair beside the window, tore open the envelope and pulled out the bishop's message. My fingers fumbled with it as I struggled to control my anxiety. I hesitated for a moment, fearing the request was denied, and then gained enough courage to unfold the letter. It was written on official stationery of the Rt. Reverend Thomas Davis, Bishop of the Episcopal Diocese of South Carolina.

> September 1, 1865
> Mr. John Pendleton
> c/o Todd Martin, M.D.
> 210 Carlisle Street
> Gettysburg, Pennsylvania

Dear Mr. Pendleton,

Grace to you, and peace from God our Father and the Lord Jesus Christ.

Your request for approval of ministerial education at the Gettysburg Lutheran Theological Seminary was submitted to me by Mr. Benton Dossy on August 5, 1865.

After prayerful consideration, I have decided to grant my blessing for this undertaking. However, the following stipulations will be required: 1. Documentation of all completed courses of study must be submitted to this office at the conclusion of each semester. 2. At the end of the first year of study, your application must be submitted for approval of the second year. 3. If the second year is approved, a repeat application will be required for the third year of study. 4. Once you are a graduate of the Lutheran Theological Seminary in Gettysburg, Pennsylvania, a final determination regarding Holy Orders will be made.

I have arrived at this determination with the counsel of Mr. Benton Dossy who informed me of the unusual circumstances prompting your application. I trust you will be successful in this worthy pursuit.

In His Service,

Rt. Reverend Thomas Davis, Bishop

The Episcopal Diocese of South Carolina

Never before, nor since that day, have I experienced a comparable portion of joyful release. No longer was I required to vacillate between staying and leaving Gettysburg. I descended the stairway fast as my prosthesis allowed, rushed into the kitchen, embraced, and kissed Aunt Gussie.

"Ach, John Pendleton, vat ist?"

I waved the bishop's letter with a high-spirited flare as though it were a victorious regimental battle flag. "It's here. It's here," I exclaimed, doing my best to dance about on a man-made leg.

"Vat ist here?"

"The bishop's blessing."

"You are blessed?"

"Yes, yes, Aunt Gussie. I most certainly am blessed," I said, handing the letter to her.

She shook her head. "Nein, Aunt Gussie busy. You read."

When I finished reading the letter, she wiped tears from her eyes. "Das ist vonderful. Now, Doctor Brown you tell. Yah?"

"Yes, I will right now," I said, closed the kitchen door behind me and headed for the shed to saddle one of Todd's horses.

* * *

While riding along Chambersburg Pike toward the seminary, my spirit continued to soar as if it were being carried on Icarus's mythical wings into a crisp autumn sky. While basking in the sensation, I recalled how Icarus flew so high the sun melted wax holding his wings together and he plummeted into the sea. It was a fairy-tale, but its example was sobering.

The bishop's letter did not resolve every hindrance facing me. There was the matter of being able to support myself while pursuing seminary studies. Todd assured me

I was welcome to Stephen's room, Aunt Gussies meals and the use of a horse for commuting to the seminary. Could I accept his charity? No! A prideful response? Maybe. If I was going to remain in Gettysburg and pursue an education, paying for it was my responsibility. Would it be possible for me to work and gain a seminary degree? It was a disturbing question. These thoughts brought my high-flying emotions back down to earth by the time I reined up to the seminary's hitching rail.

I reached for and grasped my prosthetic knee, an initial effort necessary for swinging a man-made leg up and over a horse's back. I tugged at the damnable thing several times but nothing happened. The joint remained fixed. There was no way for me to get off, even stand, or climb the entrance steps.

Todd's mare grew more restless with each of my efforts to dislodge a contrary joint. She began to snort and flounce about like an impatient Arabian anticipating the beginning of a race. I had two choices — wait for the inevitable or get off the best I could. The latter appeared to be the best option. While seizing the saddle pummel with both hands, I flung my rebellious limb up over her rump, and yanked my left boot away from the stirrup. The abrupt dismount ended as my body and flailing limbs slammed onto the unyielding driveway. I lay addled in a distorted heap.

I began to chuckle while pondering the irony of dying from falling off a horse two years after experiencing an almost fatal injury just a few hundred yards east of the seminary. Surely God would not be so frivolous and unjust, I thought, trying to regain a bit of composure. "Hey, John, he's brought you through four years of war — hasn't he?" I muttered, struggling to convince myself that my survival was preordained.

The admonition was not convincing. Death and debilitating injuries often occur without any clarification from on high. So, I sat up and pulled up my britches leg to determine the reason for a balky prosthetic knee joint.

The reason was simple and easy to repair. A loose thumbscrew securing the locking latch needed to be tightened. Once the job was accomplished, I got up and dusted myself off. Todd's mare stood next to the hitching rail as if nothing had happened, so I tethered her and entered Schmucker Hall.

I presented my shaken composure before Mrs. Keller, and handed her Bishop Davis's letter. "Would you please give this to Doctor Brown?"

"Yes, of course," she said and nodded toward a Deacon's bench in front of her desk. "Please, have a seat, Mr. Pendleton. Doctor Brown is busy but should be finished soon."

"Thank you, ma'am," I said, sat down and tried to fit into the torturous right-angled oaken bench. Several minutes passed as I squirmed about trying to attain a less painful condition.

Mrs. Keller peered at my fidgeting antics. "They aren't meant to be comfortable, you know."

"I suppose not, ma'am."

"I hate that thing. Your people ruined all of our furniture. It's all they didn't destroy."

Her resentment was unmistakable. If I didn't manage to make amends, the next three years would not be pleasant. I stood, stepped up to her desk and made a slight bow. "If I may, Mrs. Keller, please accept my apology for our barbaric behavior. I am truly sorry for the damages we inflicted upon this institution."

"Please, sit down, Mr. Pendleton. It's not your fault, but you should be ashamed of your people."

"Yes, ma'am, I most certainly am — ashamed," I said, turned around and returned to the Deacon's bench.

She nodded, smiled just a bit, and seemed to ponder my disheveled attire. It was at that moment when I became aware of her absolute candor. "Mr. Pendleton, are you certain you wish to meet with Doctor Brown at this time? Did you realize the seat of your britches is ripped open?"

My face must have conveyed surprise and embarrassment as I twisted about to examine the source of her comment. Sure enough, the seat was torn from waist down to crotch, exposing an ample portion of my unmentionables. "Damn that horse," I blurted, trying to hide the exposé from Mrs. Keller.

"Watch your language. What do you mean by, damn that horse?"

Surprise, concern, relief, and then amusement played across her face as I explained my sudden dismounting accident. "Tisk! Tisk!" she said, "you shouldn't blame the poor horse. The incident resulted from your carelessness."

"Yes, it was my error, not the fault of Todd's mare."

She arose and retrieved a wicker basket from atop a file cabinet. "Lie across my desk and I'll sew up your britches."

Her demeanor reminded me of Sergeant O'Hara, resolute and authoritative. I obeyed and she set about mending my pride and posterior. She was tying a knot when the president's office door swung open. "Well, Mrs. Keller, there seems to be no end to your talents," Doctor Brown said and chuckled apparently at his witty play on words.

Mrs. Keller continued to sew as if there wasn't anything unusual about what she was doing. "Mr. Pendleton just fell off his horse and ripped his britches."

"I hope a tear in your trousers is the only casualty."

"Just my pride, sir."

"Pride does go before a fall," Mrs. Keller said and began to titter as she completed the final stitch. "You can get up now — you're decent."

With restored dignity and Bishop Davis's letter in hand, I followed Doctor Brown into his office to finalize my enrollment.

* * *

The ensuing days following my enrollment were consumed with getting settled in the seminary's dormitory and telling Penelope, Doctor Gresham, Reverend Breidenbaugh and Todd the good news. I was going to remain in Gettysburg as a Lutheran Theological Seminary student. Doctor Brown thought it best for me to live in the seminary's student residence hall instead of commuting from Todd's home. I agreed since there would be no charge for my doing so.

I soon discovered my room mate would be Timothy O'Brien. We were an odd couple whose similarities ended with both of us being amputees who depended on prosthetic limbs. Tim was gregarious while I pursued a more serious demeanor. These traits would prove to be supportive and disruptive regarding our relationship.

When Mrs. Keller learned of my need for part time employment, she suggested I might get a job at Palmer Leiter's harness-horse farm west of town. He often hired seminary students to perform menial tasks, groom blooded harness horses and help with mares during foaling.

As I reined Todd's mare westward along Chambersburg pike toward the Leiter farm, I was reminded of my journey home astride Kate with Captain in the lead. Since I was not returning to South Carolina in the foreseeable future, a longing for my old companions settled upon me like an evening fog over Charleston Bay. An oppressive sense of guilt for having left them behind tweaked my conscience. I would not have survived the war without them. Now, I was setting out upon a new venture that would preclude any reunion with them for several years.   There was no way to have Kate shipped to Gettysburg, but transporting Captain would be possible. Without concern about keeping a dog at the seminary, I vowed to post a letter asking Benton Dossy to build a crate and ship Captain to me. My nostalgia lifted as I reined Todd's mare into the Leiter driveway.

I tethered the mare to Leiter's hitching post and walked toward a white-headed gentleman who was currying a sleek chestnut stud.

"Mister Leiter?"

"Yah, and you?"

"John Pendleton, sir."

"Ah, yah, Mrs. Keller said you would be paying me a visit."

"Yes, that is a fine looking stud."

"Yah, you know horses?"

"Yes, sir, we had many fine horses on our plantation."

He nodded and handed the curry brush to me. "Good, meet Blarney Storm. Show me how you would groom him."

Mister Leiter was proud of being a longtime member of the seminary's board of directors. He was convinced the skills required for taking care of horses were similar to those needed for nurturing a congregation of worshipers, an opinion which he emphasized with considerable vigor. By the time I finished with the curry comb, stiff and soft brushes, and picking each hoof, Palmer Leiter was persuaded of my horse grooming talents. Before we parted, he not only hired me but insisted on my accepting one of his older mares, Della, for commuting from the seminary to his farm.

As I mounted Todd's mare, Mister Leiter handed me Della's halter rope. "She's gentle and easy to handle. I'll look for you Saturday morning for exercising."

"Thank you, sir," I said and reined toward town, embarking upon a new chapter in my life's story.

CHAPTER FOURTEEN

Our entering class of six men, all of whom were veterans of the recent War Between the States, gathered in the assembly room for formal induction Thursday, September the twenty-first. Professor Doctor Krause who was in charge of our matriculation congratulated us for being accepted into the entering class of Lutheran Theological Seminary. After reciting an eloquent prayer dedicating our class to the ministry, he asked each one to introduce himself. I glanced about the room wondering who would break-the-ice. One by one, James Bohler, Henry Crossman, A. J. Johnson and Karl Grobeson stood, recited his name, branch of service, if and where injured and decision to enter the ministry.

I looked at Tim, hoping he would volunteer to be next. He answered by rising from his chair. "Doctor Krause, I'm Tim O'Brien. Only me mother calls me Timothy. I served in Colonel Kelly's Irish Brigade until July the second in 18 and 63. That's the day the Rebs blew off me left leg during the Wheatfield Battle just a ways southeast of here. I promised to dedicate what was left of me to serving the Lord . . . if he spared me from dying there in that bloody field."

Tim sat down and tapped my shoulder. "You're next, Johnny Reb."

Doctor Krause glared at me and then Tim. I didn't know what he might be thinking, but there was no doubt about the intensity emanating from his eyes. He was displeased either with Tim's glib comment or my being an enemy combatant — maybe both. I sensed all eyes were fastened upon me. My South Carolinian accent would reveal I was not one of them. My apprehension didn't make a penny's worth of difference. Doctor Krause frowned, held out his hand, palm up, and nodded. "Yes, Mister Pendleton, please."

I stood up, turned around and searched faces for expressions of enmity. I tried to imagine how each man would feel about a former Reb being one of their classmates. It was a futile exercise. Doctor Krause interrupted my introspection. "Please, we want to hear from you, John."

"Of course . . . my name is John Henry Pendleton. I was born on a plantation in the lowlands between Ashley and Cooper rivers of South Carolina. I served in General Pettigrew's Division during the Battle of Gettysburg. An enemy shell mangled my right leg during Pickett's charge a short distance east of here. Several months afterward a life changing vision caused me to dedicate what was left of me to the ministry of Jesus Christ. Following that dedication and my return to Gettysburg, I experienced a revelation, an epiphany regarding the issue of owning another human being. Thank God my family no longer owns a single slave."

Subdued applause eased my apprehension. "Thanks," I said. "God bless you."

"Welcome, John," Doctor Krause said, stepping toward me.

I was expecting a formal handshake; instead, he embraced me, a gesture seldom practiced by staid gentlemen of northern European extraction. "There is no east, west, north or south in the family of our Lord."

"Thank you, sir."

He stepped back, gripped me by the shoulders and seemed to peer into the depths of my soul. "John . . . Longfellow said it best. *Look not mournfully into the past. It comes not back again. Wisely improve the present. It is thine. Go forth to meet the shadowy future, without fear.* We are blessed by your presence."

* * *

Tim and I became known as the pegleg twins by fellow students. We were assigned to a room at the head of the stairs of Schmucker Hall, better known as the seminary's Old Dorm. The floor planking bore faint stains left from hemorrhaging wounds that refused to be scrubbed away. Their presence was a reminder of the battle during which we lost our legs to a surgeon's saw in another Old Dorm located nearby on the campus of Pennsylvania College.

On the lower level of Schmucker Hall were two lecture rooms, the library, campus steward, and an assembly room where chapel services were conducted. The upper level was dedicated by and large to student housing. Except for supportive courses conducted at Pennsylvania College, all theological classes were held in Schmucker Hall classrooms. On October the second, the first day of classes, we were immersed in subjects with strange sounding names, such as an Introduction to Exegetical Theology. My lack in languages included Hebrew and German, which caused me some reflective pondering. Being somewhat fluent in Greek and Latin, which were two of my courses of study while a student at Eton College, would prove of great advantage as I pursued New Testament studies. Becoming proficient in German was a different matter. When I complained to Professor Krause, he handed me a copy of the Seminary's constitution and asked me to read section five of Article four, which said: *Particular attention shall be paid to the German language, and the course of studies shall be so regulated, that a due portion of them may be pursued in the German language by all the students who wish.* I made the mistake of telling him that I was not one of those, who wish. His response left little doubt where he stood on the matter.

"Mr. Pendleton, this is a Lutheran seminary. Many Lutheran's prefer hearing ritual and sermons in their native tongue, which happens to be German. I suggest you enroll in a German course at Pennsylvania College while there is still time."

I realized compliance was optional, but not to do so could be unwise, even foolhardy. However, the task of becoming fluent in the German language promised to be burdensome. I was Episcopalian. Why should I need to preach the good news in German if I ministered a congregation within any Episcopal Diocese? Was I preparing to serve German speaking Lutherans? It would appear so. It seemed to be an absolute waste of time. I sought counsel and support from Penelope and her father.

"Please come in, John. What's on your mind?" Doctor Gresham said, gesturing toward a leather-upholstered sofa next to the fireplace.

I thanked him and sat down. He remained standing while leaning against the fireplace mantle. I noticed that his right foot was again swathed in bulky bandages. "Another bout with the gout, sir?" I asked.

He grimaced at the question. "Yes, but Todd dropped by with a new supply of colchicine pills this morning. I'll soon have it under control."

"That's good, sir."

"Yes . . . you seem to be troubled."

He had a talent for perceiving my moods. I suppose the expression emitting from my eyes was revealing. "Professor Krause asked me to enroll in a German language course at Pennsylvania College."

He hobbled with assistance of his cane toward a chair facing me. "Asked . . . or insisted?" he said, sat down and laid his cane on the floor.

"Why do I need to read, write and speak German? It's a total waste of time."

His brow furrowed as he contemplated my question while staring at the bookshelf next to the stone-faced fireplace. He finally picked up his cane and pointed at a large leather-bound volume. "Please, fetch me that book."

I retrieved the weighty tome. The gilt title emblazoned on its spine was a bit provocative, being stamped in classic German font. Of course I was unable to translate it. Doctor Gresham took the book, opened its cover and facing page, and began to read the German text. After several lines he paused and asked me to interpret what he had read. "I have no idea," I said, feeling a bit intimidated by his demonstration.

He beckoned me to kneel beside him as he placed his finger on the opening lines. "It says, 'In the beginning, God created the heavens and the earth. The earth was waste and void, darkness covered the abyss.' John, this is a copy of the Bible first printed by Johannes Gutenberg in 14 and 54. It was the first Bible ever printed into book format. This book became the inspiration of men like Martin Luther who fathered the protestant reformation. It was also used to a great degree by English interpreters to compile the King James Version. Preparing yourself for the ministry is a scholarly pursuit. The principal languages of Protestant Christendom are Hebrew, Greek, German and English. You will need a working knowledge of them to interpret and defend Holy Scripture."

"Yes, sir," I said, returning to the sofa. "I doubt there will ever come a time when I will need to preach to a German speaking congregation."

"John, you are a student in a Lutheran seminary. Being proficient in German isn't required but it's highly recommended. Before graduation, you will be encouraged to deliver homilies to local Lutheran congregations . . . some in English . . . some in German."

His admonition weighed me down as if an unwieldy cross had been placed upon my shoulders. My body sank into the sofa while I pondered the severity of his rebuke. A large mantel clock measured the passage of time as I stared at nothing and Doctor Gresham remained silent.

I began to grow uncomfortable with the stillness. I glanced at Doctor Gresham. His eyes were fixed on the Bible lying open on his lap. Not wanting to disturb him, I stood up to leave. Without looking at me, he said, "Penelope has been wondering why you haven't been over for a visit."

His rebuke caused me to sit back down. "I'm sorry . . . getting enrolled and moved into the Old Dorm has been quite consuming."

"I'm sure it has, but take advice from someone older and maybe wiser. Affairs of the heart are fragile. You need to make amends without delay."

"Yes . . . thank you, sir. Where can I find her?"

He pointed his cane toward French doors leading to the patio and garden. "Try the Gazebo. It's her favorite place to read and study."

I expressed my appreciation, left through the garden doorway, and followed a meandering red brick walkway leading to the gazebo amid a golden bed of chrysanthemums. Penelope looked up from the book she was reading. I hesitated for a moment drinking in the view. She was sitting in a lounge chair sheltered beneath an ornate white gazebo. Golden tresses falling in ringlets about her shoulders framed lovely azure blue eyes and angelic features. A pleasant smile and crinkling about her eyes greeted me as I stepped into the gazebo. "Hello, John," she said, closing her book. "I've missed you."

Southern courtesy assumed command of my actions as I lifted her outstretched hand and kissed her fingers.

"My dear Penelope," I said as she giggled. "I fear I have been neglectful and preoccupied. Please forgive me."

"Oh, John, stop your gentlemanly performance. You are forgiven. How do you like being a seminarian?"

I sat down in a wrought iron patio chair and expressed frustrations concerning Professor Krause's request that I become fluent in German. When my lengthy oration ended, she fixed her eyes on me. "Poor, John, learning another language shouldn't be such a bother. You have two years before needing to speak German . . . don't you?"

I pondered the question for a moment. "Yes, I guess that's so, but I won't be required to deliver any sermon's in German."

She shook her head and wagged a finger in my face. "John Pendleton, just what is your problem? Why are you so stubborn?"

Her sudden reproach caused me to search for a response. "Well, I'm not being stubborn," I stammered. "I don't want to waste time in mastering something I will never use after graduation. Is that being stubborn?"

"Why are you so sure? That isn't a reasonable conclusion. You might even decide to become Lutheran . . . then what?"

"Me? Become a Lutheran? Not likely."

She looked away and grimaced. A knot gripped my belly. Penelope, her father, and Todd were all Lutherans. In fact, most churches and the folks living in Gettysburg were Lutheran. *Why am I acting like a thoughtless bore?* "I'm sorry, Penny," I said, trying to sound penitent. "There's nothing wrong with being Lutheran. What you say is true. I'll enroll in a German course today."

"Well, that's the first time you've called me, Penny," she said, jumping up to embrace me. Just as our lips met, she whispered, "I think I like it, Johnnie."

* * *

Tim and I were deficient in the German language, so Professor Krause who also taught German at Pennsylvania College enrolled us in his introductory course. While attending our first class, we got acquainted with a Colored student, Joshua P. Willingham. He appeared to be a studious young man with the physique and bearing of a talented athlete. The musculature of his torso, arms and thighs were indicative of tremendous physical strength. I was more impressed, however, by his intellect.

At first, Joshua and I were hesitant in furthering any social relationships — he being a veteran of the 54th Massachusetts Colored Infantry and I having served in the Army of Northern Virginia. Our reticent attitudes began to thaw during the latter part of the first semester. Test scores for the mid-term examination were posted on a bulletin board outside of Professor Krause's classroom. While Joshua, Tim and I were scanning the list, Tim pointed to T. O'Brien, 90, and then J. Pendleton, 88. "Not bad, fellows," Joshua said, moving between us to find J. Willingham. He chuckled and penciled a circle around his score. "But I beat both of you. Feast your eye's on my 96.

"Yeah, Johnnie Reb, both of us Yankees bested your 88," Tim said, trying to goad me into making an angry response.

I was tempted but thought better of it. Instead, I patted Joshua's shoulder. "Congratulations, that's an outstanding score."

He peered at me and grinned. "Thanks, I appreciate that."

From then on our friendship continued to grow. We often strolled about the college campus after attending Professor Krause's German class. During these walks we talked about our families, wartime experiences, plans for the future — and religion.

Josh was the son of a minister who ran a proprietary school for Negro children in Philadelphia. At the urgings of Frederick Douglass for Negro men to volunteer for service, Josh volunteered when the 54th Massachusetts Colored Infantry was organized at Camp Meigs in March of 18 and 63. I was reminded of Pickett's charge as he described the 54th's attack against Fort Wagner, a Confederate bastion located on Morris Island in Charleston Harbor. Similar to our charge, they suffered a malicious slaughter that killed and maimed half of their regiment, including the loss of his commander, Colonel R. G. Shaw.

It was on Friday, the twenty-second of December, during one of our walks that Josh and I embarked upon a new relationship. He expressed an interest in visiting the Old Dorm room where Tim and I first met following our injuries. As we climbed the stairway to the south portico, memories of the night when litter bearers toted me up those same steps reminded me of the terrible toll the North and South had paid. There were thousands of vacant parlor chairs, shallow graves hiding men where they fell, and broken bodies ravaged by horrendous wounds, disease and starvation — all reminders of our folly.

Once again, a longing for my comrade in arms, Hank Johnson, returned me to those frustrating days following Pickett's charge. My conscience was tweaked by the remembrance. How I longed to see him once again. The emotion of the moment caused me to hesitate as we reached the quarters where I first met Penny and Tim.

Josh seemed to sense my anguish. "We don't have to . . . if it's . . ."

"I don't mind. This place also has some good memories," I said as we stepped into the room. It was furnished with four double-decker bunk beds, a couple of dressers, an armoire and several folding desks similar to the type used by officers in the field.

"Are you sure this is the right room?" Josh said.

"Yes, that's where my cot was located," I said, pointing at the space now occupied by a bunk bed. It was then I noticed JOSHUA P. WILLINGHAM stenciled on a placard attached to the top bunk's railing. I stared at the sign, disbelieving what it meant.

"Yeah, John, this is my room and that's my bunk. Quite a coincidence, huh?"

Tim walked in and slapped me on the back. "Gotcha, didn't we?"

"You knew . . . about this . . . all along?"

A sly grin pulled up the corners of his lips. "Yeah, we decided to surprise you last week when Josh showed me where he stayed."

I was about to get used to Tim's boyish antics by then. "Well, you succeeded. I suppose you told him about the time we met."

"Yep, sure did. Told him about the shoe, but left out the part about Penny."

"You mean, Penelope, Doctor Gresham's daughter?" Josh said, winking at Tim.

Tim plopped into an overstuffed chair and gestured for us to have a seat. "Okay, tell Josh all about Penny . . . don't leave nothin' out."

CHAPTER FIFTEEN

Tree branches scraping to and fro across our window prompted me to get out of bed and do a one-legged hop to see what was going on. I could see by the first light of day that a winter storm was pelting Gettysburg with sleet. Having awakened from a sound sleep, my mind was a bit befuddled. I lit my study lamp and scanned the day's assignments on a wall calendar above the desk. Penciled beneath Saturday, December the sixteenth, was a reminder: Work Day — Leiter Ranch.

I returned to the window to make certain I wasn't dreaming. Wind gusts were buffeting the windowpane with a mix of sleet and rain, much of which was congealing into a frozen montage.

We were in for a disagreeable day, hardly one requiring any of my regular chores to be done at the ranch. The day would be better spent staying home to complete an exegetic evaluation of St. Paul's letter to the Ephesians. In spite of the weather and a need to complete an assigned task, a compelling emotion urged me to fulfill my obligations to Mr. Leiter.

With reluctance I slipped on my prosthesis, dressed and shook Tim's shoulder to awaken him. "Yeah," he said and pulled the covers over his head. "Where're you going?"

"Leiter's farm."

"Oh, don't slam the door."

Tim wasn't in a mood to hear about the weather, so I did as he said.

I headed for Professor Krause's barn to saddle Della. He was gracious in allowing me to quarter her in one of his stalls free of charge; however, I insisted on paying for all of her hay and grain.

As I reined toward the Leiter ranch, a thin coating of ice was already forming on tree branches, fences, and clumps of dormant grass along ditches and fencerows. If icing continued, the road would become too hazardous for steel-shod hooves. I squirmed deeper into my sheepskin parka and pondered the wisdom of venturing forth in such weather. As much as I wanted to turn back, something seemed to be compelling me to continue on toward the ranch.

My mind escaped by pondering other less consuming problems. Combining studies and work hours was a burden. Balancing these obligations was challenging for any first year seminary student. More disquieting thoughts crept out of my subconscious as Della lumbered along Chambersburg Pike. *How can I balance the overwhelming load of assignments with a need for supporting myself? How do I find time to process the mass of information being crammed into my mind? Where does time for Penny and Todd fit into the jumble? How important are excellent grades? Is it worth the extra hours required to obtain them? In the long run, will it merit the effort? I'm hard pressed to settle for anything less.*

Being so involved with ruminations, I was unaware when Della turned off the pike into the driveway. To my good fortune, she knew her way home and didn't need directions from me. When we reached the corral, I noticed a light coming from a barn window. I didn't regard it significant since Mr. Leiter was an early riser and always tended his horses before breakfast.

I tied Della to the hitching rail and climbed over the corral fence. When I slid open the barn door, a light coming from one of the foaling stalls was of concern. "Mister Leiter," I called.

"Yah, is that you, John?"

"Yes, sir."

"Thank God — you're an answer to prayer. It's Goldie. A bit of trouble she's having."

Goldie was one of his prize-winning mares. Her foal's daddy, Thunderbolt, had also won blue ribbons and ample purses during a number of Pennsylvania harness races. "Is it her time?" I said, entering the stall.

"Yah, but too long — no foal — poor dam has run out of steam, I fear."

Goldie was thrashing about while lying on her side. She was in obvious distress. Its probable cause was dystocia, a difficult and often stalled birthing process. My father taught me to anticipate its signs in a mare during labor, because time is of the essence in diagnosing and treating its cause. "Has her water broken?"

"No. We must know why."

"Yes, how can I help?"

"I have ropes, olive oil and soapy water," he said and held up his right hand swathed in a bulky bandage. "I have a deep wound in my palm. You must do it for me?"

I watched and learned from my father but never intervened in a foaling. It was questionable whether I could determine and fix the causes of Goldie's dystocia. My reluctance and apprehension must have been apparent to Mr. Leiter. "Do not worry. I will talk you through it," he said and steadied two lanterns on stools so we would have sufficient lighting.

There was no other choice for me but to do the best I could. I stripped to the waist, scrubbed my arms and hands, and smeared them with olive oil. Mr. Leiter spoke soothing German while patting Goldie as I washed her hindquarters and examined her vulva. There was neither bulging nor the presence of her bag of waters. I glanced at Mr. Leiter. He nodded. I slipped my fingers and hand into the birth canal. There was nothing there. I kept advancing my hand searching for a hoof or nose until reaching a round, quite solid mass. That is when I discovered a rope-like tuft arising from the top of the mass. "A tail?" I muttered, disbelieving what it felt like.

"Did you say tail? It's a rump presentation?"

"Yes, sir. That's what it seems to be."

"We must hurry," he said, making a loop on the end of two smooth cotton ropes. "You must open the membrane and then find and loop a rope around a hind hoof."

I pulled my hand from the birth canal, grasped one rope and advanced it until touching the foal's rump. I found a hoof, tore open the amniotic sac, slipped a loop around the hoof and pulled it into the birth canal. "Got it."

He handed me the second rope. "Now, get the other hoof."

Once I accomplished retrieving the second hoof, we were ready to deliver the reluctant foal. As I began to pull on both ropes, Mr. Leiter repeated over and over, "Careful . . . not to pull too hard."

I tried to obey his admonishments, but the need to deliver the foal soon as possible kept needling me to keep pulling. Goldie's natural instinct took over as a couple of strong contractions, a gush of waters, and one welcome filly was born.

I don't know who was the happiest and most relieved, Mr. Leiter, Goldie or me.   Within a couple of hours, all of the birthing processes were over, and Goldie's filly was enjoying her first meal.

As we started to leave Goldie and her new daughter, Mr. Leiter tapped me on the shoulder. "What do you want to name her?"

"You want me to name your filly?"

"No," he replied. "I want you to name John's filly?"

"You mean . . . ?"

"I feared you wouldn't come — the weather being so bad. I prayed God would intervene. You arrived just in time to save the foal and Goldie as well. The filly belongs to you."

I gazed at the wobbly newborn nuzzling Goldie's udder and grasped a truth demonstrated by the morning's events. *Yes, God is concerned for all of His creatures. Prayers are answered. He used a foaling gone bad, a hazardous winter storm, a husbandman whose wound precluded intervening, and an unskilled seminarian to bring about the fulfillment of His purposes.* "Thank you. Let's name her, Miracle."

Mr. Leiter's eyes lit up as he caressed the newborn filly. "Yah, John, and a miracle she is."

* * *

While basking in the afterglow of participating in a life or death struggle that ended with a miracle, I enmeshed myself in a search for truth. In doing so, I neglected my compelling motive for returning to Gettysburg — to be near Penny.

Mr. Leiter's simple faith in that I was an answer to his prayer caused me to question my own. I never prayed for God to intervene, even during the horrendous battle in which I lost my best friend. To do so should be an obligation of any Christian. On several occasions I heard men who were mortally wounded praying for deliverance, even a drink of water; yet, they received neither request. They were surrounded by soldiers like me who were too consumed to tarry and render aid. Why didn't God use me then to bring about a miracle? Isn't a man of greater value than a horse?

I began to look for the fingerprints of God's hand in everything. In my pursuit I spent more and more time searching for answers. Prescribed courses became burdensome and mundane. There was no joy in parsing Greek, studying church history, liturgics, and systematic divinity. Once certain of my calling to the ministry, I now questioned the authenticity of Bishop Dossy's apparition. I even doubted the reality of being a Christian. Yes, I had been christened as an infant and confirmed at age eleven. I was a faithful communicant until regular attendance was interrupted by the war. I fulfilled all requirements of the church. Yet, I felt something was lacking.

All of these doubts and questions became a driving force propelling me headlong into a quagmire of vacillation. Preoccupation with these demons was turning me into a cold-hearted man who has no love for anything creating happiness. My emotional turmoil began to bring estrangement between Tim and myself. He likened me to Charles Dickens' bah humbugging character, Ebenezer Scrooge, a distasteful characterization I could not abide.

Our relationship continued to deteriorate over most of the school term. I placed all of the blame on what I believed to be Tim's lack of concern for my problems. He was consistent in telling me that I was a bore and wished I would get over whatever was bothering me or move out. Everything came to a head on March 30th, which happened to be Good Friday. I was studying William Wilberforce's writings on Real Christianity when Tim returned after turning in a Greek assignment to Professor Krause. Without speaking, he sat at his desk, picked up a couple of pencils and began to rap the desktop as if it were a snare drum. This seemed to be his favorite way to release frustrations. I'd learned to ignore the racket and let him get it out of his system. However, this time the intensity began to be quite disturbing, so much so that I closed my book and stared at him. "I can't study with that racket going on."

"Sorry," he said, but kept the rat-a-tat-tat going.

"Do you mind?"

He tossed the pencils on his desk and turned to face me. "John, I've got something to tell you."

"Oh, what is it?"

"You've changed a lot the past several months. You spend all your spare time with your nose in a book, researching in the library, or working for Mr. Leiter."

I sensed by the tone of his voice there was a deeper problem than my study and work habits. "That bothers you?"

"Yeah, not only me, but . . ."

I waited a moment for him to finish the sentence, but he just looked at me and wagged his head.

"But, who else?"

"Penny."

I couldn't believe what I was hearing. I tried but was unable to mask the disdain in my voice. "How would you know?"

I listened while Tim confessed he had been visiting Penny after classes and on Saturdays for the past two months. I doubted his assertion that he was trying to calm her concerns for my negligence. His visits became a daily occurrence — even attending church together on Sundays. Why would he do this all the while claiming to be interceding for me?

As he continued to speak, I fantasized Penny repeating Pricilla Mullin's reply to John Alden in Longfellow's poem, *The Courtship of Miles Standish*, "Why don't you speak for yourself . . . Tim?"

On and on those words kept repeating themselves. Tim was a close friend, but so was Miles Standish's friend, John Alden. My anger and resentment toward Tim mounted until I could contain my ire no longer. "A fine fellow you are," I yelled, slamming Wilberforce's book on the desk. "You were just taking advantage of our friendship to court Penny behind my back. Don't sit there claiming to intercede for me."

"I'm sorry, John," Tim said, standing up to face me. "It began as an innocent effort to help you."

I stood up and wagged my head in disgust. "One visit with her would be an act of a friend. Instead, you kept going back."

"You're right," he said, holding out his hand. "I was wrong to keep visiting her, but . . ."

I stared at Tim's hand as he thrust it toward me. I began to realize much of the fault lay with me. I was allowing emotions to consume my mind and spirit. I recalled his urging me from time to time to get out of my bad mood and spend some time with Penny. I didn't have any reason to question the truthfulness of his confession. She was a delight, a girl with whom any fellow could fall in love. I'm certain that is what happened with him. My anger melted as I gripped his hand.

* * *

I stood on Doctor Gresham's porch with hat in hand. Disquieting emotions caused me to hesitate, to question whether the damage from my negligence was repairable. In a moment of uncertainty, I glanced at Della standing at the hitching rail and was tempted to make a speedy retreat. The moment was similar to the day Hank and I fell into formation for our assault on the Yankee's line along Cemetery Ridge. Apprehension squeezed my chest until breathing required a concentrated effort. I pondered the hour, which was close to midmorning, a time when Penny and her father might not be at home. The thought quieted my uneasiness enough for me to reach for the door knocker. I prayed there would be no response as I rapped several times.

I waited for what seemed a proper time before donning my hat and hurrying down the steps. Just as I was untying Della's reins, the front door opened and Doctor Gresham hobbled onto the porch. "Sorry I took so long to answer," he said, gesturing at his bandaged left foot. "The cursed gout has returned."

I retied the reins and climbed porch steps to plead my case. "I'm sorry to bother you, Doctor Gresham."

"No bother," he said, pointing his cane at a portico glider. "Let's sit here. It's a pleasant spring day."

We sat down almost in unison, Doctor Gresham struggling with his swathed foot and I with my prosthesis. I glanced about trying to collect my senses before speaking. Penny's father said nothing until he must have thought I was rendered speechless. "Well, John, we've missed seeing you."

"Yes, sir," I stammered, trying to gather my wits. "Is Penny . . . Penelope home?"

"No, she left for Philadelphia a week ago."

"Oh . . . I didn't know."

"No, I suppose not."

I wanted to ask how she got to the depot since Doctor Gresham had been incapacitated by his infirmity, but I already knew the answer. My good friend, Tim, stepped in for me—again. "Sorry," was all I could utter.

"She hoped you would come by before she left."

"Sorry."

While I was wrestling with embarrassment and Doctor Gresham's terse attitude, Todd reined his buggy up to the hitching rail. "Hello, Alonzo, he called. "I've brought you some more colchicines pills."

"Ah, thank you," Doctor Gresham said. "Look who's here."

"Yes," Todd said, climbing the steps. "How are you, John?"

I stood up to shake his outstretched hand. "Getting by."

Todd's arrival was a blessing. The tense atmosphere surrounding Penny's father and me melted away as Todd pulled up a porch chair. "Alonzo, I see you've been enjoying your sherry and port."

Alonzo frowned at the inference. "Now, Todd, gout runs in my family."

"I know, and so does the love of fermented grapes. You keep this up and you'll develop a bladder stone before you're fifty."

"Both my father and grandfather had gout. Neither developed a stone."

"That won't stop you from getting one. Cut down on the wine and rich foods."

"All right, I'll do my best."

Todd glanced at me and pinched my bearded cheek. "Well, John, you've lost weight. You could do with a better diet."

Doctor Gresham slapped my shoulder and chuckled. "He just needs some of Aunt Gussies victuals."

Todd leaned back in his chair, grew somber and looked me up and down as if he were considering the purchase of a horse. "You seem weary, John. How are you doing at the seminary?"

I felt resentment for his asking. Things were not going well because of reasons I was not prepared to discuss with him, Doctor Gresham or anyone else. My best friend betrayed me. I was feeling guilty for neglecting Penny, Todd, and even Aunt Gussie. I was too embarrassed to ask her father how long Penny would be away, an answer I should have heard from her. How was I going to respond to Todd's question? My reticence must have caused discomfort as I pondered all of the woes haunting me.

Todd finally broke the silence. "John, I've been concerned about you for several months. Mister Leiter tells me that you are an excellent hand, but you've grown distant. Mrs. Keller says you aren't cordial and seem preoccupied. Even Aunt Gussie is disappointed by your long absences. Now, Alonzo and I are here to help, but you've got to take us into your confidence."

His reproof stung like a switch striking bare skin. I needed help, but pride was clouding my ability to accept it. I recalled Mrs. Keller's words as she repaired my torn britches, *pride does go before a fall.* Putting aside my inhibitions, I explained the list of problems consuming me. They responded by laying out what I should consider doing about them. I was to seek counsel from Reverend Breidenbaugh and try to make amends with Penny. Todd also urged me to consider moving from Schmucker Hall back to Stephen's room where he and Aunt Gussie could lend family support.

I thanked them for their concern and advice. "You're welcome," Todd said, pulling an envelope from his pocket. "I have something else for you."

"What is it?"

A letter from Kathleen's brother, Shawn O'Hara."

I stared at Todd in disbelief. "Sergeant O'Hara?"

"Yes, go ahead . . . read it."

A cornucopia of mixed emotions stoked and restrained my fumbling fingers each time I tried to unfold the letter. "What does he say?"

Todd explained that the Library of Congress employed Sergeant O'Hara following the war to assist in listing of all prisoners held in U. S. Army prisons during the war. Being concerned with my distress, Todd asked him to search for every Henry and/or Hank Johnson. Shawn wasn't successful in his search until the past week when he came across a list of wounded Confederates captured north of the Potomac River during General Lee's retreat. It was a rear guard action in which General Pettigrew was mortally wounded and many of his division captured. "Now, read what Shawn has to tell you."

The letter was addressed to Dr. Todd Martin and John Pendleton. *Dear Todd and John, I have some news of which I leave to your considerations as to whether it be good or bad. I recently came across a prisoner of war listing submitted by General Kilpatrick to the War Department on August 1, 1863. The listing included 276 Confederate infantrymen of Pettigrew's Division captured July 14th. One of the prisoners in the wounded column was an H. Johnson, Private. I have no follow-up information at this time, but will let you know soon as I have any additional data. Your Obedient Servant, Shawn O'Hara.*

"This is good news," Doctor Gresham said, patting my shoulder.

"I hope so."

"Yes, now, you need to know that Penelope will arrive tomorrow on the three o'clock train."

"I'll be there."

CHAPTER SIXTEEN

Tossing pride aside, I set about doing whatever was required to atone for my sins of neglect and jealousy. Todd loaned me the use of his sleek new Physician's Phaeton carriage to meet Penny at the depot. Della was stepping out like a proud harness racer, no doubt because she was drawing the fanciest carriage in Gettysburg. I was late and prayed the train from Philadelphia would also be overdue.

The town hall clock chimed three times as I tied Della to a hitching post and headed for the ticket office. I tapped the agent's bell to get his attention. "Pardon me, sir," I called to a white-headed gentleman wearing a banker's visor who was scribbling on a pad. He continued to write until the clattering telegraph receiver fell silent. He tossed his pencil aside, peered at me and asked whether I needed a ticket. Several blasts of a locomotive's whistle in the distance answered my intended inquiry. "No, sir," I replied and hurried out to the station platform.

A crowd of greeters gathered as the locomotive's whistle, clanging bell and chuffing wheels signaled the train's arrival. While searching the faces of passengers in each of the windows as the train slowed, dread began to swirl from the depths of my mind like eddies in a spring-fed pool. Would Penny be relieved to see me? How was I going to explain my lapses? Would she be receptive to my pleas?

All fear left me as I caught sight of Penny's blue eyes looking at me from behind a coach window pane. As the train slowed to a stop, I stepped closer to get a clearer view. She was smiling — a sure sign she was happy to see me. Excitement urged me closer until I could place my palm on the sooty window. She kissed her fingers and tapped where my palm was striving to make contact through a few millimeters of glass. I called an enthusiastic greeting "Welcome home, sweetheart. I love you."

Her voice was muffled, but her lips shaped each word. "I love you, too."

In my excitement, I rushed toward the coach doorway only to be met by a surly conductor. "Step aside," he said, dropping a footstool beneath the stairwell. "Make way for passengers."

It was a chore to obey his churlish command, but I held fast to my place at the front of the waiting crowd. One by one, arriving travelers pushed me aside, but I was determined to hold my ground. There seemed to be an endless stream of strangers stepping from the stairwell, gentlemen waving at greeters and ladies being assisted by a now pleasant conductor. Then, my vigil was rewarded by the sight of Penny stepping down from the stairs. The conductor was still clutching her arm as I reached for Penny's hand. "Patience," he said, feigning an introduction of sorts. "Here's your young lady."

She stepped into my embrace as I pulled her away from the brash conductor.

"Am I really your young lady?"

"The one and only."

"I prayed you would meet me."

"I believe in prayer, but it wasn't needed."

She hugged me tighter. "I knew you would be here."

We walked hand in hand to the baggage car, picked up her valise and headed for Todd's carriage. I pretended not to see Tim as we walked past a group of greeters near the depot waiting room. Penny glanced at him but said nothing. *He doesn't give up easily*, I thought and felt a twinge of jealousy trying to squirm from its hiding place.

"Where did you get such a fancy carriage?" Penny said as we reached the hitching post.

I opened the door and gestured for her to step up into its leather upholstered interior. "I borrowed it from Todd. It's his new Phaeton."

I could tell she was impressed by the opulence of it as she caressed the patent leather dashboard. "My, my, this is really nice."

"Nothing too good for my lady," I said and kissed her.

She smiled and her azure eyes glistened. "Oh, can we go for a ride; it's such a nice day?"

I assured her that we could and reined Della north on Carlisle Street. The day was warm and sunny, perfect for driving into the surrounding countryside. Penny tucked her hand around my elbow and slid closer to me. My apology promised to come easier as we settled into a pleasant jaunt toward the edge of town. Della kept up a quick pace as I reined her down the Harrisburg Road toward the Adams County Almshouse. After passing by Barlow's Knoll and crossing Rock Creek Bridge, Della quickened her tempo. A pleasant breeze swept through both open side windows, stirring Penny's golden tresses from beneath her green bonnet held fast by a silk scarf tied under her chin. *How blue her eyes are,*" I mused. Her beauty captivated me so much that my glances toward her became obvious.

"You need to keep your eyes on the road," she said, patting my arm.

"Sweetheart, you are the prettiest girl in Gettysburg . . . Pennsylvania . . . the whole world. I can't keep from looking at you."

"My, my, you do turn a girl's head with such flattery."

"Not flattery. It's the truth."

She cuddled closer and kissed my cheek. "You're sweet."

The time seemed proper for an apology. I wanted her to know how sorry I was for my negligence and would never let it happen again.   I pulled back on the reins.

"Whoa, Della." The carriage stopped in the middle of the road. I turned to face Penny and doffed my hat. "There is something I want to say, so please hear me out. I am very sorry for having neglected our relationship the past several months. I have allowed problems, scholastic and personal, to dominate my every waking moment."

"Please, Johnnie," she said, gripping my hand. "An apology isn't needed. I know how distressed you have been. Tim told me all about it."

Her mentioning Tim and his unsolicited intervention caused me to stop and ponder his claim to having my interests at heart all the time he was seeing Penny. Maybe in the beginning, but I still was unable to fully accept his claim. However, it seemed that she believed Tim's intercession was out of friendship for her and me. Since she felt that way, I needed to accept Tim's assertion. "But, I do need to apologize to you, Tim, Todd and Aunt Gussie, because I have allowed problems to push away those whom I love. Will you forgive me?"

"You are forgiven. Now, I have something to tell you."

The thrill of her forgiveness was fleeting, being replaced with dread for whatever followed. "Not anything bad . . . I hope?"

"I went to Philadelphia to enroll at the Women's Medical College. I will be moving in August just before the fall session starts."

My mood changed from being overjoyed to wretchedness. I felt as though my hopes for the future were being torn up and cast aside. I'm certain my disappointment was not hidden, but after a moment of reflection, I put my arms around her and drew her closer. "I'm happy for you. Medicine has been your dream and now it will be coming about."

"I hoped you would understand. This doesn't change our relationship . . . does it?"

I assured her that it wouldn't, but there was doubt and disappointment in my heart. I reined Della about and headed back to town, wondering all the while just how strong our love would be in sustaining us during the coming months — and years.

* * *

A thunder storm came the night after my meeting Penny at the depot. The next morning, it was still raining. I, for some peculiar reason, felt tranquil as rain pitter-patted against the roof. I was compelled to remain in bed, listening to the clatter of rain overhead. It was during such times I have always been able to reason and put aside trivial thoughts. *There'll be few and far between visits with Penny if I stay in Gettysburg. Tim's interest in Penny won't cease, but her assurances were convincing. I can't afford to transfer to a seminary in Philadelphia . . . and Bishop Davis would have to approve. I'd better stay in Gettysburg for my second year. I'll accept Todd's invitation to move into Stephen's room after the winter session ends in June. I'll tell Tim — maybe he'll move with me. I hope so.*

As I pondered these things, I was reminded of Todd and Doctor Gresham's recommendation for me to seek counsel from Pastor Breidenbaugh. There were personal questions needing resolution before another year of seminary training. *It's a good day to go see him.*

I got out of bed, dressed and headed for Professor Krause's shed to saddle Della. The rain ceased as I reined her down Chambersburg Pike. By the time I arrived at St. James's parsonage, the overcast sky was breaking up allowing the sun to shine through.

I climbed porch steps and rapped the door knocker several times. When no one responded, I walked around the house to look for Pastor Breidenbaugh. His favorite hobby was caring for rose beds alongside and in the backyard of the parsonage. The bushes were putting on new growth, having been awakened by recent spring showers and warmer days. As expected, I found him pulling up noxious weeds from around his adored rose bushes. "Good morning, Pastor," I said, opening the backyard gate.

"Ah, yes, John. It is a good morning. How are you?"

"That's why I'm here."

"Oh, how may I help?"

"Do you have time to talk?"

"Of course, let's go sit in the gazebo."

The gazebo was a pleasant shelter surrounded by rose beds. While walking along the pathway, Pastor pointed out a number of varieties he and previous pastors had developed. Soon, pink, red and yellow hued blossoms would invite bees and humming birds to savor their nectar.

As we sat in white wicker rockers, he smiled and tossed his weathered straw hat onto the floor. "I've missed seeing you in church. Have you been ill?"

"Yes and no. My health is fine, but other matters have been besetting."

"I'm sorry. Feel free to tell me about them."

"Thanks, Pastor," I said and began to tell him about the distresses with which I was struggling. He listened without commenting as I related how I came to question my being a true believer and whether I should continue to be a seminary student. When I finished, he remained silent and seemed to be in deep thought. I became more uncomfortable as he began to rock back and forth. Finally, he reached over and grasped my hand. "John," he said, looking into my eyes. "If you believe in and have accepted God's gift of his only son, Jesus, you are an heir to eternal life. It's just that simple. Your parents dedicated you to that truth through your baptism. You accepted that commitment at the time of your confirmation. We all who call ourselves Christians are born into God's kingdom as babes in the faith. Like our human bodies needing to grow and mature, our spiritual beings grow through nurturing of the Holy Spirit, the Holy Scriptures and Christ's Holy Church. God requires us to search our hearts every day for His enlightenment. I'll not quote scripture and verse verifying this. You are a student of the bible and know the references to which I am alluding. Jesus himself proclaimed He was the Light of the world. In order for us to walk in the Light, Christ must have freedom in every niche and cranny of our hearts and minds. Too often, we commit a crippling error by keeping Him in an isolated room separated from everyday dwelling places of our minds and hearts. When we perceive a need, we go to His room and seek counsel. We thank Him for His help and shut the door as we leave. The solution is to remove that door and invite Him to always walk and talk with us without any restricting locks and doors. Then we can bask in His Light that enlightens. I believe if you do this, your demons will vanish."

I thanked him for wise counsel and promised to follow his suggestion. Then Pastor Breidenbaugh stood up, placed hands upon my head and said a short prayer asking for a renewed anointing of the Holy Spirit. He beseeched God's Grace for me in all of my days to come. Before he finished his prayer, the load of my crippling burdens lifted and was replaced with peace and assurance of my calling to the ministry. Yes, I was a servant of our Lord — no question about it.

* * *

From that day on I tried to fulfill my promises to Penny, Tim, Todd, Aunt Gussie and Pastor Breidenbaugh. Tim and I moved into Stephen's room. He accepted my apology, but also promised not to interfere in Penny's and my relationship again. To be honest, I doubted whether he could abide by his promise if he felt the need was present. However, I was happy he and I would remain close friends.

I also dedicated myself to never give up in determining Hank's fate. As the winter session at the seminary ended, I committed myself to do some research into the data Todd had received concerning a H. Johnson being captured in southern Maryland.

Part of my rehabilitation involved the fulfillment of a commitment to my trusty wartime companion, Captain. I sent a letter earlier to Martin asking him to ship Captain to me whenever he could. That had been several months ago, so I was unprepared for his arrival.

* * *

I was reining Della down the driveway on my way to the Leiter ranch when a freight wagon from the railroad station pulled into the drive. "Got a crate for you," the driver called. I didn't have to guess what was in the crate. Captain detected my scent and began to raise a ruckus. He was frantic as I helped the driver lower the crate to the ground.

"Hey, old friend, how are you doing? I'm sure glad to see you again."

The driver pulled a hammer from the wagon toolbox and handed it to me. The crate was no match for my frenzied effort to remove the lid. After several wood splintering whacks, I was able to pry up the lid. Captain completed its removal with a lunge that propelled him up and out of the crate. My beard became wet from sweeping licks of his flapping tongue as he kept leaping up on me. I managed to subdue his enthusiasm with a tight embrace, but as my grasp loosened, he jumped away and began a ritual of racing about the yard to show this was his new territory.

Aunt Gussie hustled through the front door onto the porch. "Vat ist, John Pendleton?" she bellowed.

"My dog, Captain, just arrived. You remember me telling you about him?"

"Yah, Aunt Gussie remembers. A miracle dog he was. Velcome, Captain miracle dog," she called, raising her hands toward Captain as he raced by the porch another time on his way around the house. She followed her welcome to Captain by bellowing at me. "Herr Leiter's now you go. Snell, quick, late you are, John Pendleton."

I stepped in Della's stirrup and called to Captain. "Come along. Let's go."

Aunt Gussie waved as Della trotted toward Chambersburg Pike. Her departing words rang up and down the street as Captain raced by Della to take up his customary lead point. "Not the late for supper, you be, John Pendleton."

* * *

Mrs. Keller mailed the grades I received for my courses, including German, to Bishop Davis on the ninth of July. She included a letter from Doctor Brown, requesting approval for my second year. I was confident of a favorable response since my grades were better than most of the other students.

Tim and I were awakened early the next morning by Aunt Gussie's clanging bell and bellowing voice. "Outen zie bed for the breakfast. Snell . . . snell."

Tim was still unaccustomed to Aunt Gussie's call to breakfast. He sat up on the bedside, rubbed sleep from his eyes and scowled at me. "That woman is a witch from hell."

"Maybe, but she cooks like an angel."

While strapping on his prosthesis, he continued to grumble inaudible protests. I did the same without any grumbling, got up and donned my robe. "Better not be late," I said, heading for the stairway. "Aunt Gussie abhors tardiness."

"I abhor clanging bells and loud voices while I'm sleeping."

"No matter. You want breakfast, snell . . . snell."

"Yeah, yeah, I know what snell means."

"See'ya downstairs."

Tim managed to sit at the table before Aunt Gussie was about to remove his plate and flatware. "Late you are, Timothy O'Brien," she said, filling his cup with coffee.

"Ich bin reue, Tante Gussie," he said, sounding apologetic. "Erfordert es ein langfristiges, dieses prothetische Bein anzubringen."

She stared at him while clucking her tongue. "Speaking the German you are dumkopf. Speak the language I understand."

"I'm sorry, Aunt Gussie, I was trying to tell you it takes time to put on my peg leg."

"Yah, what you meant I know. Much time to put on leg, John Pendleton too. But on time he is."

Tim grimaced at her rebuke and set about smearing butter and gooseberry jam on his potato cakes. I gloated a bit at his comeuppance. "Next time," I muttered, "ask her how to say something in German instead of showing off your ignorance."

"I wasn't trying to be smart."

"Well, you failed on that score, my friend."

"Okay, I'll turn on me Irish wit and charm the old biddy."

"Try that and you'll be eating table scraps with Captain on the back porch."

"Yah, mein herr. Ich bin ein dumkopf."

"You've got that right," I said and then called to Aunt Gussie, "Is Todd up, yet?"

"Nein . . . Gone all night. Herr Gresham sick."

"What's wrong with Herr Gresham?" Tim called, reaching for another helping of potato cakes.

"Ask I did not. He not say."

I was certain Doctor Gresham's recurring gout wouldn't require Todd's attendance all night. Some cholchicine pills and rest were all the treatment he'd required before. When I visited Penny's father recently, I heard Todd warn him about developing a stone if he didn't quit the wine and rich foods.

While mulling over Todd's overnight call, I heard his carriage coming up the driveway. "I'll go help Todd unhitch and park," I said as Tim was reaching for another bratwurst.

Todd appeared a bit disheveled and weary as he stepped out of his carriage. "It's been a long night. I could use some coffee and a hot bath."

"Aunt Gussie has breakfast on the table. I'll unhitch and park the carriage."

"Thanks, John," he said, pulling his medical bag from under the carriage seat. When you're finished, come on in the house. I have something to show you."

All while I was tending to Todd's mare and carriage, I pondered what he was going to show me. Would it be something good — or bad? When finished with the chores, I walked to the back porch where Captain greeted me with frisky tail wagging and a whine. "Good morning, old friend," I said, giving him a vigorous patting about the head and neck. As we finished our good morning ritual, Captain returned to his bowl of table scraps and I to the dinning table where Todd was sipping coffee and talking with Tim.

"How is Doctor Gresham?" I said, pouring myself another cup of coffee.

"He's comfortable now, but spent a miserable night passing a kidney stone."

"Has he sworn off the wine?"

Todd wagged his head and sipped more coffee. "Oh, yes, he did, but that vow will be forgotten soon as he's up and about."

"He does like his grape," Tim said, shoving back his plate. "Penelope is about the only one who can get him to swear off."

Todd frowned and peered at Tim. "Oh, no, she's tried harder than I have. It's up to Alonzo. Tim, if you don't mind, I need to visit with John . . . in private."

"Sure," Tim said, pulled out his watch and flipped open its cover. "I do need to be getting over to the library. Meetin' Josh Willingham at eight."

As Tim disappeared up the stairway, Todd pulled an envelope from his pocket and handed it to me. "This arrived yesterday."

"Who's it from?" I said, noting the return address was only a Washington postal box.

"Shawn O'Hara."

"Is it about Hank?"

"Maybe. It concerns H. Johnson, the prisoner named in General Kilpatrick's report."

I pulled the letter and three other documents from the envelope.

Dear Todd and John,

I am enclosing copies of documents discovered while I was researching General Kilpatrick's prisoner report to the War Department. As you can see, the first page is a hospital record which lists prisoners who were cared for by the Third Cavalry Division Field Hospital on July 14, 1863. Midway down the column of names is, H. Johnson, Private. The second page is a roster for Confederate prisoners that were incarcerated at Point Lookout Prison. It is dated, July 23, 1863. H. Johnson, Private, is listed as number 143. The third page is another prisoner of war roster, which lists Confederate prisoners who were scheduled for exchange on August 15, 1863 for Federal prisoners. As you know, the prisoner exchanges were abandoned close to that date; consequently, it probably never came about.

I have not been able to find any other documents containing H. Johnson at this time; however, I shall keep looking. I hope this finds both of you well.

Your Obedient Servant,
Shawn O'Hara.

With this assurance in mind, I decided it was time for me to help determine whether Hank could be the H. Johnson listed in these papers. "I must go to Washington City. I can't wait any longer to find out if Hank is alive. I owe that to him . . . and myself."

CHAPTER SEVENTEEN

I squeezed Penny tighter and tighter. Her tears spilled down my cheek. A wellspring of self-belittling thoughts tweaked my conscience. How can I leave Gettysburg at this time on a mission holding little chance for success? I might as well be embarking on a safari into the jungles of Africa. Only a few days have passed since I promised never to neglect our relationship again. Yet, when I explained the compelling need to search for Hank, she gave her blessings for my journey. I can't help but wonder whether she will change her mind if I persist in searching for Hank's survival or demise. What if the hunt becomes a maze of blind alleys that lead to nowhere? Will I be able to set aside the quest, or might I be compelled to keep charging windmills like Don Quixote?

My interlude of hesitation ceased as the conductor slid a stool beneath the train's coach steps. "All 'board for York, Philadelphia and Washington City."

"I love you," Penny said as I loosened my embrace.

"And I love you . . . forgive me."

"Don't worry."

"I do worry. I don't want to go, but must."

"I know. Let me hear how you are."

I picked up my valise. "I'll write."

She began to cry. "Come back . . . soon as you can."

I hugged her again. "Please don't cry."

"Give me your ticket," the conductor said, tugging my sleeve.

I boarded the train, found a seat, stowed my valise and searched for Penny through the window. She was lost within the crowd of well wishers who were waving and shouting goodbyes. Just as the locomotive's whistle blew and the coach jerked into motion, I spied her. She was waving a white handkerchief. Her lips shaped unmistakable words, "Goodbye. I love you."

* * *

At six o'clock that evening, the thirty first of July, my taxi driver reined his carriage up to Willard Hotel's Pennsylvania Avenue entrance. As I stepped to the pavement, I gazed upward at the multistoried structure and tried to recall how it looked the last time I saw it. More than two years had gone by since Todd and I departed the hotel on my journey to freedom. Everything appeared the same, except there were no uniformed Yankees milling about. For that, I was grateful.

I signed the hotel register and the clerk handed me a key to room 210. When I unlocked the door I realized it was the room where Todd readied me for my trek homeward. What a difference a few years can bring about. No longer was I a prison escapee who could be arrested, charged as a spy and shot. Instead, I was a seminary student embarking on a discovery quest for the closest friend with whom I endured the ravages of war. Anyone who has suffered such can understand the bond which compelled me to undertake my mission. I was prepared to experience any heartache or cost to complete the task, but prayed it would not alienate those I loved.

I unbuckled my valise and pulled out a copy of the telegram Shawn sent in reply to my inquiry.

> TO: JOHN PENDLETON
>
> FROM: SHAWN O'HARA
>
> I WILL HELP ALL I CAN TO DISCOVER THE FATE OF HANK JOHNSON (STOP) A ROOM IS RESERVED FOR YOU AT THE WILLARD FOR JULY THE THIRTY

FIRST (STOP) I WILL MEET YOU IN THE LOBBY AT SEVEN PM (STOP)

As directed by his message I was sitting in the lobby as the hotel's clock chimed seven. I looked around, but Shawn was nowhere to be seen. I picked up a copy of the New York Times lying in a chair next to me. I began to read a front page article about President Jefferson Davis being placed in irons by command of Secretary of War Stanton. I became very upset that our former Confederate President was being humiliated by such behavior.

I failed to see Shawn until he tapped me on the shoulder. "Hello, Laddie, it's been a while."

I stood up fast as my prosthesis allowed and grasped his outstretched hand. "Aye, Sergeant O'Hara, it's been too long."

"No, Laddie, I'm no more a sergeant . . . just your friend, Shawn."

I gripped his hand tighter. "And, my friend, I'm thanking you for all you've done and are doing for me."

"You're welcome, Laddie. Now, let's have supper. I've reserved a table in the dining room."

As I followed Shawn to our table, I thought how rare such a relationship could be between a prior warden and one of his former prisoners. It all began as we stood face to face on the snow-covered quadrangle of Fort Delaware prison. My expressed sorrow for the loss of his son and promise to pray for him forged a bond between us. How fortunate I am to have such a friend — one who risked his life in helping me escape from a squalid prison, even death. Now, he is helping me discover whatever became of Hank.

I was scanning the menu when Shawn whispered, "The roast leg of lamb is excellent. They serve it with the most delicious currant jelly."

"That sounds good to me."

"Aye, I'll order for you."

The waiter, a dapper fellow sporting a waxed handle-bar mustache, leaned over Shawn's shoulder. "Mister O'Hara, may I suggest an excellent Claret aperitif?"

"Aye, please do."

"The Bordeaux 1861 is our best."

"Aye, please serve it."

"Yes, sir, and might I suggest the roast red head duck entrée?"

"No, thank you," Shawn replied, "we want the roast leg of lamb with current jelly."

"An excellent choice," the waiter replied. "Vegetables?"

Shawn glanced at me. "Laddie?"

"I'll take whatever you have."

He nodded and ordered mashed baked potatoes, squash, and orange angel food tortes for dessert. Wine with supper was P. Rogers' Ohio Still Catawba, vintage 1862 and Old Otard Brandy afterward. I never anticipated such an elegant fare for the evening.

While enjoying our supper, we discussed the purpose of my visit to Washington City. Shawn thought our best option would be to visit Point Lookout Prison, especially its cemetery, and Hammond Hospital which cared for many incarcerated prisoners. The prison was closed down in June of 18 and 65, so locating records on the premises might not be possible. However, he thought it was our best option at the time.

After we finished eating, the waiter cleared our table and served us each a dram of brandy. Shawn seemed lost in thought as he sipped from his snifter. At last, he roused. "Would ye be carin' for a smoke?"

"That would be nice."

"Good," he said, sliding back his chair. "The tobacconist has the finest Havana cheroots."

The waiter hurried to our table with his receipt book. I pulled out my wallet, but Shawn wagged his head. "No, Laddie. Tiz my treat."

The men's lounge was mahogany paneled and furnished with comfortable leather-covered chairs and sofas. Framed paintings and lithographs along with shelves of books lined the walls. While Shawn visited the tobacco shop, I strolled around the lounge looking at pictures. I noticed a unique lithograph hanging above the fireplace. Point Lookout, MD — A View of Hammond Hospital and U. S. Depot for Prisoners of War was printed along the bottom margin. All of the structures and other locations were numbered with references as to their usage. I was quite engrossed with examining the lithograph when Shawn tugged my sleeve. "Aye, that's the prison where H. Johnson was incarcerated."

"It appears to be larger then Fort Delaware Prison."

"Aye, Laddie, there were upwards of twenty thousand prisoners held there until the war ended."

"I wonder if Hank was one of them."

"Wonder indeed is all we can do for now. Only time and luck of the Blarney Stone will give the answer."

We sat in chairs facing the fireplace, and enjoyed our cigars while spending the better part of an hour discussing much of what happened to both of us since my escape. Shawn became the assistant provost at the prison until after the hanging of Major Wirtz on the tenth of November in 18 and 65. He requested and was granted a discharge at that time. He expressed great regret for participating in the execution, knowing how terrible the Yankees treated prisoners of war.

When our smokes grew cold and conversation waned we decided to call it a day. Shawn promised to secure a team and carriage so we could leave on the sixty-mile trip to Point Lookout the next morning.

Upon entering my room, I took pen in hand:
My Beloved Penny,

I arrived Washington City without incident this evening and experienced a most delightful supper and visit with Shawn O'Hara. We will be traveling to Point Lookout, Maryland in the morning. I pray we will be able to discover whether Hank actually was the H. Johnson whose records Shawn has discovered.

I detest visiting any place of incarceration, Yankee or Rebel, but am compelled to do whatever is required.

I love you more than life itself and pray the moment of our being together again will come very soon.
Yours,
Johnnie

* * *

Shawn reined our carriage into Maryland's Point Lookout Prison complex Thursday afternoon, the second of August. It was situated on a narrow peninsula between the Potomac River and Chesapeake Bay. Whoever selected the prison's location could not have found a more secure setting. It was placed on a tapered strip of ground about one quarter of a mile wide at the mouth of the Potomac River. The shorelines were populated by sooty terns and smoky-winged white gulls. Intermingled tern *wacky-wack* and gull *key-rack* screeches competed with rhythmic sounds of waves surging along the beaches. The air was intense, laden with a dank stench common to swampy environs during dog days of summer.

I shielded my eyes from the sun and gazed across the river, but could only make out a slim landfall along the distant horizon. "That would be about a ten mile swim,"

Shawn said, gesturing toward the formidable stretch of water. He then pointed eastward at the Chesapeake Bay. "And it's thirty miles to land in that direction."

"That would be suicide."

"Aye, Laddie, if you look about two hundred yards off shore, you'll make out the dead line." On both sides of the peninsula, a row of timber pilings projected above the surface like vigilant pickets. "Anybody swimming past those posts would have been shot."

Only buttresses remained where demolished structures once were utilized by the Yankees to incarcerate my fellow countrymen. My heart sank as we approached Hammond Hospital, a quite large building whose design was that of a tropical facility. Only three of its original sixteen two-storied wings remained intact. They projected from a central hub like spokes of a broken wheel. Nothing was left of the other wings except rotting poles upon which they had been supported two or three feet above sandy soil. This was a certain indication the area was water-logged much of the time — a miserable environment during freezing winter and scorching summer months alike.

With our team tethered to a hitching post, we walked along a pathway leading to the main hospital entrance. The afternoon was quite hot and humid — a reminder of what the prisoners must have experienced in July and August. A corpulent, solemn-faced guard was posted at the entrance. He wasn't wearing a uniform or outward identification, but a holstered revolver hanging from his ample girth was a clear sign of authority. He raised his hand, challenging us as we climbed steps to the front portico. "Only authorized persons are allowed," he growled, appearing to be aggravated by our presence.

Shawn stopped short of stepping onto the porch, pulled a document from his pocket and handed it to the guard. "I'm Shawn O'Hara. You'll see my authorization is signed by Colonel Meeker to review all Point Lookout Prison records."

The guard looked over the document and handed it back to Shawn. His demeanor turned pleasant as he smiled and opened the door. "You won't find much, Mister O'Hara. A lot of the files were hauled away last week. But you'll find what's left in several boxes at the end of the hallway."

I experienced strange sensations creeping up and down my back as we walked down the dingy corridor. The building was empty but I felt as if unseen eyes were fixed upon us — eyes of those who resented our being there. For a moment, I had an urge to turn about and leave; however, the quest to discover Hank's fate quickened my pace toward what remained of Hammond Hospital's records.

Within a few minutes we were probing through boxes of musty, mildew splotched documents whose script was faded and difficult to read. The horrific environment was taking its toll, which would soon render most of them useless. Since many prisoners were illiterate, clerks often spelled a name according to its phonetic sounds. With this in mind, we gathered every entry that could be a variant of Johnson into a stack for assessing at a later time.

We were delving through the last box of records when the guard sauntered down the corridor toward us. "It's five o'clock, Mister O'Hara, gotta lock up for the night."

Shawn did not look up. "We'll finish in another ten or fifteen minutes."

"I have to lock the door now. You can come back tomorrow."

"What time in the morning?"

"Eight o'clock."

Shawn gathered up the records we set aside. "All right, I'll return these in the morning at eight."

The guard's eyes grew somber as he wagged his head. "Can't let you take 'em out of the hospital."

"I have Colonel Meeker's authorization to review any and all of these records, sir," Shawn said, handing the guard his permit."

Our reluctant inquisitor looked over the document again and returned it to Shawn. "Well, I suppose you can — but have 'em back at eight sharp."

"Any suggestions where we can spend the night?"

"You might try the lighthouse on the point south of the hospital."

We thanked him for his assistance, returned to our carriage and headed for the lighthouse. It was a white framed single-storied building with a red shingle roof. A conical tower in which the keeper maintained a signal light projected above the rooftop. Like other structures on the peninsula, it was supported about two feet above ground on timber pylons. As we climbed steps to the porch, someone pulled aside the curtain in a window to the left of the door for a second and then turned it loose. Shawn rapped on the door and waited. There was no response. He rapped again, louder this time. Still, no one responded. "Strange," Shawn said, "lighthouses are always attended."

"Yes," I said, pointing at the window. "Somebody pulled aside the curtain when we started up the steps."

"Well, Laddie, we'll roust 'em out," he said, and then bellowed, "Ahoy, the lighthouse keeper."

The door eased open. A young man, appearing to be in his late teens, peered at us. The expression of his features seemed strange — a distant stare — present in body but absent in mind. "Evenin'," Shawn said. "Are you the keeper?"

The young fellow nodded, hesitated and then shook his head. "No, Miss Olga's the keep . . . I help."

"Might we be speaking with her?"

"Wait," he said, closing the door.

Shawn tapped his forehead. "He seems a bit daft."

We didn't have to tarry long before the door opened and a pleasant middle aged lady greeted us. "Hello, I'm Olga Roland, what can I do for you?"

We introduced ourselves, and Shawn explained our mission and need for a night's lodging. "Of course, you're welcome to spend the night," she said and gestured for us to enter.

After entering the living quarters, Olga introduced us to her nephew, Alphonse, the strange fellow who first answered the door. He followed as she gave us a tour of the lighthouse, but said nothing until we were seated at the kitchen table. "Ashley Cooper Lowlands," he said, pointing at me.

Olga seemed to ignore his outburst. "I've prepared a pot of Irish stew for supper. Would you like some?"

"Aye, dear lady," Shawn said. "A bit o' Ireland would be to me likin'."

"Thank you, ma'am," I said. "It would be to my likin', too."

"Mister O'Hara speaks with a brogue but you don't, Mister Pendleton." she said, stirring the contents of a large stewpot atop the kitchen stove.

I glanced at Alphonse, wondering how he came up with Ashley Cooper Lowlands. "No, ma'am, my family emigrated from England."

Alphonse's eyes squinted as he glanced at me, but he didn't speak. Olga poured stew into a large tureen and set it on the table. Its spicy aroma wafting through the room tweaked my appetite and filled my mouth with anticipation.

"Please, set the table, Alphie," she said, placed a ladle beside the tureen and sat down.

Alphonse set a large bowl and a soupspoon on the table in front of me, pulled a napkin from his pocket and tucked it under my chin. He performed the same ritual for Shawn, Olga, and then himself.

Olga nodded at Alphonse and waited for him to say grace. He folded his hands and spoke in a monotone while gazing at his bowl. "Bless us, oh Lord, for these gifts which we are about to receive from Thy bounty. Help us to be mindful of all our blessings, and the needs of those who have less. Amen."

While enjoying supper our conversation turned to the environs of Point Lookout Prison. Olga hesitated for a moment when I asked if she ever met any of the prisoners. Her reply was unexpected. "Where did you lose your leg?"

"Gettysburg," I said, not wanting to question her evasive response. "I was captured and sent to Fort Delaware prison."

Her features softened as she dawdled with her spoon. "Were you exchanged?"

"No, ma'am, I managed to escape."

"With help?"

I felt a brisk nudge of Shawn's boot against my ankle. "Yes, ma'am," I said, "but I'm not at liberty to say who it was."

Her gaze penetrated into the depth of my soul. "Neither am I able to say whether I knew any of the prisoners here on this godforsaken sandbar."

Shawn slid back his chair and patted my shoulder. "Laddie is only interested in finding the fate of his best friend who may have been captured during the Rebel retreat from Gettysburg."

She nodded at Shawn. "His name?"

"Johnson . . . Henry . . . he probably went by Hank."

Olga glanced at Alphonse and shook her head. "No . . . I don't recall any prisoner with that name."

"Any Johnsons?"

"No, none."

Either Shawn's interrogation or Olga's responses caused Alphonse to become agitated. He toyed with his napkin, leaned forward in his chair and began to utter unintelligible sounds. At first I thought he was choking, but Olga expressed no concern.

"You are excused, Alphie," she said, stood up and began to clear the table. As Alphonse left the room, we thanked Olga for sharing their supper with us.

"You are quite welcome," she said and headed for the stairway. "I have to tend the lamp . . . make yourselves at home."

CHAPTER EIGHTEEN

Shawn and I were poring over prison records when there came a rapping on our bedroom door. With raised brows, Shawn glanced at me. "Aye, who is it?"

The door opened. Alphonse's familiar features peered at us. The light from our lamp accentuated his misshapen face. At that moment I judged him to be an imbecile — his expression vacant — apathetic.

I jumped up and hurried toward him intent upon excusing his intrusion and then to shut the door. "I'm sorry, Alphonse . . . we're busy."

"No. No," Shawn called. "It's all right . . . come in, Alphonse."

He walked past me, waited beside the table where we were perusing documents, and spoke in monotone. "Five Johnson prisoners were from South Carolina — A. H., Wendell, H. C., H. L. and Sam."

I was too stunned to comment, but Shawn motioned toward a chair. "We appreciate your help. Please, sit down."

Alphonse obeyed and sorted through the stack of papers. He laid aside and pointed at four pages. "Those are buried out there," he said, gesturing toward an eastward-facing window.

"Pull up a chair, Laddie," Shawn said, handing two pages to me.

I hesitated, dreading what I might discover, and then A. H. Johnson's listing leapt from the first page. I tried to remember whether Hank ever told me his full name. Henry and Hank were the only ones I could recall. I turned to the next page and found Sam Johnson. Just as I laid it aside,

Shawn shoved a page toward me. "There's H. C. Johnson," he said, tapping the penned entry.

Fear squeezed my insides as I pondered the initials. We weren't discovering anything other than that these men were buried in the prison cemetery. A. H. or H. C. might be Hank, but the record listed only their initials. The remaining records did not record H. L. Johnson, the only other prisoner who might prove to be Hank.

Shawn glanced at Alphonse. "Did you know any of these prisoners?"

Alphonse stared at the doorway leading to the keeper's quarters. "Some," he whispered. "But Aunt Olga says we can't tell anyone."

I began to question my perception of Alphonse's mental capacities. "Is that because she helped some of them?"

He nodded but said nothing.

"Provided them with food and drink?

Again, he nodded.

"How about escaping this godforsaken place?"

Alphonse looked away and nodded.

"How many prisoners did you and your Aunt Olga help escape?"

He glanced at the door, and said nothing, but replied by holding up a total of twenty two fingers.

"What about H. L. Johnson?"

"Escaped."

"When?"

"July fourth . . . sixty four."

"How?"

"I helped him strap on floats."

"He tried to swim across the Potomac?"

"Yes . . . after dark."

"That would be a ten-mile swim," Shawn added, "a long distance at night even with floats."

"What did the H. L. stand for?" I asked.

"Henry Lewis."

"You knew him?"

"Yes."

Such rational responses belied his nitwitted appearance. If for any reason I could not view Alphonse's distorted features, there would be no question about my speaking with a normal person.   My prejudgments started to evaporate like dew on a summer morning.   "Can you describe Henry L. Johnson?"

"He was grizzle-headed, tall and skinny, and spoke like a Carolinian." Alphonse then patted his right eye.   "He wore a leather patch."

So, Henry Lewis Johnson's right eye was blind. Hank could have suffered such an injury during our charge. He might also be grizzled, having started to turn gray during our last year in the field. He could be Hank — if so — he might have survived a ten-mile swim from Point Lookout to Virginia.   I seized upon the possibility and didn't want to pursue the likelihood of Hank being A. H. or H. C. who were buried in the prison cemetery.

"Did you know any of the prisoners buried out there?" Shawn asked, interrupting my preoccupation.

Olga swung open the door. "Why aren't you in bed?" she yelled, wagging her finger at Alphonse.

Shawn stood up to intervene.   "Please, dear lady, Alphonse has helped us narrow our search down to three prisoners, one of which can very well be Hank Johnson."

Ire flashed in her eyes as she stepped toward Alphonse. "I told you we didn't know any prisoner by the name of Johnson." She grasped Alphonse's ear and lifted him up from his chair. "Now get to your room."

Alphonse grimaced as he grasped Olga's wrist. "Y-e-e-ow. I'm going."

"See that you do, and stay there," She said, shoving him toward the door. She then spun about to confront Shawn. "You're no longer welcome . . . both of you . . . get out."

Shawn started to gather up the prison records. "Dear lady, I think you don't understand your nephew's affliction. He's not what he appears to be."

"What do you mean? Alphonse is a nitwit. You can't believe anything he says. He lies just to get attention."

"Maybe, but he has an exceptional capability, one that persons who are mentally crippled sometimes possess."

"Oh, and what would that be? Most of the time he's dumb as a goose."

"How many prisoners have you helped escape from Point Lookout?"

Olga, gulped and glared at Shawn — then me. "None. Who are you . . . Pinkerton agents?"

"No. Does twenty-two sound right?"

Color drained from her features as Olga slid onto a chair. "You can't believe Alphonse."

"I think we can. Now, we are willing to forget what we learn here tonight provided you tell us everything you know about Henry Lewis, H. C. and A. H. Johnson."

Olga's shoulders slumped as she gazed at the bedroom floor.

"Alphonse said he strapped floats on Henry L. Johnson when he began his swim across the Potomac after dark on July the fourth, 18 and 64."

"He makes up stories all the time. You can't believe him."

"Do you know H. C. Johnson's full name?"

"No."

"Alphonse is good with names isn't he?"

"No. He can't even tie his shoes."

"Dear lady, my younger brother was mentally crippled like Alphonse. In every way he was slow except with numbers, dates, names and events. He possessed extraordinary abilities in such areas, but was unable to learn simple tasks. I'm certain Alphonse has information about A. H., H. C. and Henry Lewis Johnson that we need. We'd be beholden for another chat with him."

Olga's fingers toyed with her apron as she pondered Shawn's request. The fear of revealing her and Alphonse's treasonous activities to strangers must have been intense. Mary Surratt, one of the convicted conspirators in President Lincoln's assassination, was hanged only a year before. Her demise must have been a reminder that a woman was not immune to capital punishment when convicted of subversion.

Olga's cheeks grew more pallid and jaw muscles clinched as she wrestled with how to respond. I glanced at Shawn, hoping he wouldn't press the matter any further.

"Dear lady," Shawn said, pulled up a chair and sat down to face Olga. "I know what you are dealing with . . . for you see . . . I planned and carried out the escape of a Reb prisoner from Fort Delaware and Old Capital prisons. If I were found out, even to this day, the punishment would be severe." He then pointed at me. "That escaped prisoner stands there before you. His name is John Pendleton. Now, his purpose is to find what happened to his closest friend who fought beside him at Gettysburg. His friend is Hank Johnson . . . who may well have been captured and imprisoned in Point Lookout Prison. There is no bond any stronger between men than the one experienced by soldiers who fight side by side. As I promised earlier, your secret is secure if you tell us whether Hank Johnson was here . . . buried in the prison cemetery or escaped."

Olga smoothed the wrinkles from her apron. "Alphonse knows whether any of the prisoners named Johnson went by Hank. I don't recall any prisoner named A. H. Johnson. H. C. was shot and killed by a guard when he swam past the dead line. Alphonse begged him not to try an escape before dark . . . but he wouldn't listen."

The bedroom door creaked as it eased open. Alphonse's face peered at us from the darkened doorway.

Olga stood up and wagged her finger at him. "Have you been eavesdropping on us?"

"Yes, Aunt Olga. The only one who went by Hank was Henry Lewis Johnson."

* * *

After returning to Washington City the next morning, Shawn accompanied me to the B&O station where I boarded the train for my return trip to Gettysburg. He promised to continue searching for any records that might cast light upon whether Henry Lewis Johnson had succeeded or failed in his escape. The odds against finding any were significant, but I was confident he would be true to his promise.

The entire return trip was overshadowed by continuing frustrations about our failing to discover whether Henry Lewis survived swimming across the Potomac – if so, was he the soldier with whom I served?

The locomotive's whistle moaned, steel wheels clacked, and the coach swayed as I pondered my unfulfilled quest. The countryside sliding past the window seemed bleak and colorless. Being lost in my thoughts, I paid little attention to the panorama unfolding before me. I was vaguely aware of Amish barns, farm dwellings, and dairy cattle grazing verdant meadows. I wasn't a stranger to disappointment, but to have gotten so near without getting the answer for which I sought was more than depressing. Hank probably escaped Point Lookout Prison — but did he survive?

I continued to be immersed in disquieting thoughts until the locomotive's clanking bell signaled another stop. I roused and leaned closer to the window as the conductor called, "Gettysburg. End o' the line."

While the train slowed, I scanned the waiting greeters' faces for Penny's effervescent smile. "Where is she?" I muttered, trying to locate her in the crowd. Brakes squealed and the coach jolted as the train stopped. I grabbed my valise and stepped into the isle that was by then becoming clogged with passengers. When I reached the station platform, I walked toward the depot entrance. Since I'd sent Penny a telegram from Washington City informing her of my arrival time, her absence was disturbing.

"Welcome back, John," Josh Willingham said as he hurried toward me. "Sorry I'm late. Penny asked me to meet you."

"What's happened?" Is she all right?"

"She's fine," he said, reaching for my valise. "She's in Philadelphia."

"Why? Her classes won't begin for a couple of weeks?"

"Dad's only tutor came down with consumption, requiring her to enter an upstate New York sanitarium. He asked Penny to tutor his students in exchange for room and board while she's attending medical school.

* * *

The following morning I boarded the eight o'clock train bound for Philadelphia. I arrived at the Willingham Boarding School shortly before noon. A tall mulatto lady greeted me at the front door. "I'm Mrs. Willingham. May I help you?"

I introduced myself and inquired about visiting with Penelope. "Yes, yes, Mister Pendleton, do come in," she said, gesturing for me to follow her. While we walked down a long corridor, she gave me a continuous description of the school's facilities and how her husband's father established and operated the only boarding school for Colored children in Philadelphia. We ascended a stairway to the second floor, and then walked down another hallway until reaching a door with Jeremiah Willingham, Headmaster etched in its glass pane. Opening the door, she motioned toward a chair beside a large oak desk. "Please be seated, Mister Pendleton. I'll tell Mister Willingham you wish to see Miss Gresham."

While waiting I decided to look over several framed documents and pictures hanging on the wall. At the center of the display was a Writ of Release from Illegal Bondage certificate. Beneath a British Union Jack embossed at the top was penned the following:

Writ of Release from Illegal Bondage

> *Let it be known by all men that Hezekiah Willingham, a freeman of color and citizen of His Majesty's Colony of Jamaica, who was abducted, incarcerated and illegally sold into slavery, has prayed to His Majesty's servant, Sir Thomas Coltrane, for relief from unlawfully imposed servitude. By the authority vested in me as the commanding officer of His Royal Majesty's Frigate Surprise, I grant and bequeath the relief for which Mister Willingham pleads. From this day forward, said Hezekiah Willingham is forever declared a freeman of color. Attest: Sir Thomas Coltrane, Capt. HMS Surprise. Dated on September 4, 1812 and the 52nd year of the reign of His Majesty George III, King of Great Briton and Ireland.* Beside his signature was a hot wax seal of the crest of Sir Coltrane's signet ring.

My rapt interest in the distinctive document was interrupted by a melodious tenor voice. "Ah, Mister Pendleton, welcome to our school."

I turned to face a tall, colored gentleman as he came through the doorway. "Thank you, sir. I was quite taken by this certificate," I said, gesturing toward the writ.

"Yes . . . it is unique . . . a treasure of which I am most proud. You see, it is an irreplaceable piece of paper that freed my father from bondage. I must tell you about it sometime, but now I understand you wish to visit with Miss Gresham?"

I couldn't free my mind of the ordeal Hezekiah had endured. I was compelled to hear more about how he was enslaved, and established this boarding school after securing his freedom. "Yes, sir, that is why I'm here . . . but first . . . ."

"There is something else?"

"If you agree?"

"Of course . . . what is it?"

"Was your father born a slave?"

"No, he was a freeman before being captured by pirates in Jamaica and sold into slavery at Charleston, South Carolina."

"I was born and reared on a plantation in the lowlands of South Carolina. My father owned many slaves. Could your father have been one of them?"

He pursed his lips and frowned. "No. He was owned less than a year by a Charleston merchant before obtaining his freedom."

I was relieved by his answer, but something deep within caused me to pursue how his father was able to found a boarding school that prospered for many years. "What happened after he was freed?"

Jeremiah nodded, pulled a book from his desk drawer and handed it to me. "Please take and read my father's accounting of his life's journey. Then we will talk."

"May I take it with me?"

"Of course . . . just return it on your next visit. There will be another visit?"

Although he did not reveal any confidences, I was certain he knew much about me through conversations with Josh. Otherwise, he wouldn't be willing for me to take the journal back to Gettysburg. "Oh, yes, there will be many more."

Jeremiah grinned and slapped my shoulder. "Good . . . now . . . didn't you come here to see Miss Gresham?"

CHAPTER NINETEEN

The moment Penny opened her door, all apprehension faded. "Hello, Johnnie," she said, stepping into my arms.

"Hi, Penny, I've a lot to tell you."

"What about Hank?" she asked, squeezing me tighter.

I explained how he tried to escape Point Lookout Prison by swimming ten miles across the Potomac to Virginia.

"Nobody could do that."

"Frantic men try desperate things."

"Let's go to the kitchen — I'll brew some tea while you tell me all about it."

By the end of our second cup of oolong, my story concluded with Josh greeting me at Gettysburg depot.

"I'm sorry," Penelope said, squeezing my hand. "I had to be here yesterday, so I asked Josh to meet you."

I opened Hezekiah Willingham's accounting. "You're forgiven."

"What is this?" Penelope said, sliding her chair closer.

"Hezekiah Willingham's memoir."

"Hezekiah?"

I pointed at the introduction and picture of Hezekiah. "He's Jeremiah's father . . . and Josh's grandfather."

Time seemed to stand still from the moment we began reading his cogent handwritten entries. The story began with his growing to manhood on a sugarcane plantation in Jamaica. His father, a freeman of color and the plantation overseer, sent Hezekiah on an errand across the Blue Mountains to Spanish Town in 18 and 11. He was captured, gagged, bound, and cast among other prisoners into the hold of a renegade pirate ship. During the ship's voyage to Charleston Harbor, he became ill with a raging fever. It was during an episode of delirium and utter exhaustion that he prayed for God's intervention.   His screams and raucous pleadings aroused fellow prisoners to the point of violence.   They beat him with such hostility that he was rendered unconscious.

During this incident he experienced a profound vision. The remainder of his story is in his own words, copied from his accounting.

> *My prayer for God to intervene was answered. Out of blackness came a bright light, so brilliant I had to shield my eyes. From the overpowering radiance emerged a man whose raiment was whiter than beaches of Montego Bay, and trimmed with bands of purple. I was awestruck by his passionate eyes and the compassion emanating from them. I liken it to a lighthouse beacon beckoning storm tossed seafarers toward a safe haven. "Is that you, Lord?" I called, standing up to greet him.*
>
> *"Yes, it is I, the risen one."*
>
> *I fell prostrate before him and grasped the hem of his garment. "Have mercy on me."*
>
> *He knelt and placed his hand on my head. "Arise, Hezekiah, I have a mission for you."*
>
> *He arose as I stood up to face him. "What will you have me do, oh Lord?"*
>
> *"Care for my little ones."*
>
> *I peered past him. There were no children. "Where?"*
>
> *"The place you are going. There you will be my messenger to the little ones in*

bondage. Teach them and I will abide with you . . . always."

"Yes, Lord," I said as he turned and walked back through the brilliant portal from which he appeared.

When I awakened, my fever was gone and new strength surged through me.

After the pirate ship docked in Charleston Harbor, all prisoners were led in chains onto the pier. Most were freemen of color before being captured — now we were about to be auctioned to the highest bidder.

Twenty six, all young men, were herded into wagons and transported to the Exchange Building where a crowd was gathering. The auction master ordered me to strip off my shirt so the crowd could ogle my physical attributes. I was ordered to step up on the auction block and turn around to face the bidders. Strange hands squeezed the muscles of my legs and arms, a usual practice in determining a slave's worth. I was ordered by the trader to open my mouth so one buyer could settle on whether I had a full set of teeth. I glanced skyward pleading for divine intervention, but nothing happened to interrupt the trader's exhortations directed toward obtaining a higher price.

Penelope's features grimaced as if in pain. "That's humiliating. Have you ever been to a slave auction?"

"Once, when my father bought Lizzie."

"Lizzie?"

"Mother needed a mammy for Pricilla . . . my sister."

"How old were you?"
"About ten."
"Did it bother you?"
"No, Mother needed a mammy."
Penelope shook her head, but said nothing.

Hezekiah continued to describe how each slave was subjected to the same humiliating evaluation.

> *We were then lined up according to height, the tallest on the left with the shortest on the right. I was first since I was the tallest nearing six feet four inches; or, as the trader bellowed, "Nineteen hands in height of sinew and muscle. What am I bid for this fine specimen?"*
>
> *When the bidding was concluded, I was sold to Benjamin W. Harris, a wealthy Charleston merchant, for sixteen hundred and fifty dollars — a rather high price to pay for a coachman.*
>
> *B. W. Harris was a shrewd merchant who always looked to turning a profit. Owning a slave for him was no different from buying and selling a bale of cotton. If offered a higher price than what he paid for an item, or slave, the sale was quick in coming. This bit of his character was bound to cost him dearly. It happened during the war with Britton in 18 and 12, less than a year following his purchase of me, when a British frigate, HMS Surprise, sailed into Charleston Harbor. Her captain, Sir Thomas Coltrane, needed supplies, so he sent his first mate and a squad of sailors ashore to find a warehouse where his needs*

could be obtained. B. W. Harris, Ltd., being located on the wharf, was an obvious choice for the acquisitions.

The British contingent selected a substantial inventory of supplies, and promised to pay Harris in British pound sterling for their purchase if delivered without delay. Eager to turn a sizeable gain, Harris agreed and ordered me to drive the loaded wagon to the pier where the supplies would be stowed on the ship. He directed me to board the ship, and collect twelve hundred and fifty pounds before allowing the goods to be transferred.

Benjamin Harris was brilliant, but lacked moral integrity and knowledge of British law. Otherwise, he would have never allowed such an arrangement to take place. The British had no intention of honoring a purchase from a citizen of a belligerent nation with whom they were at war. Once the goods were on the pier, they would have no compunction in seizing it as spoils and sail away laughing at the stupid Yankee. Neither was Harris aware that Briton outlawed slave trading on the twenty fifth of March in 18 and 07. Any freeman of color who had been illegally enslaved since that date could be declared a free man simply by stepping foot aboard a British man-of-war.

When I asked permission to board, the first mate agreed and escorted me to the captain's quarters. When I entered, I stated my purposes, which were to collect for my master's goods and to request a writ of release from illegal bondage. As expected, the captain denied my request for payment, declaring all property to be spoils of war seized by His Majesty's Frigate Surprise. The second request was readily granted as he penned the writ, signed and certified it with his seal. I had gone aboard a slave and returned to the pier a freeman of color.

With the writ in my pocket, I returned the empty wagon to its owner who erupted into a fit of rage when informed of the captain's actions. He threatened to charge me with theft of his goods. But when I stated his agreeing to sell goods to a British captain was tantamount to treason, he accepted my terms. I was henceforth a freeman of color who could pursue whatever course in life I wished.

Penelope started to giggle. I stopped reading Both of us were soon consumed with laughter.   She finally caught her breath. "Oh, that is hilarious."

"Yes, a well deserved comeuppance for Harris."

I was no longer a chattel of B. W. Harris. However, as a free man I was without shelter or sustenance. Also, I was prey to any slave trader who might have me overpowered, shackled and sold into slavery again. The writ issued under British law could be challenged in a federal or state court. I was free for the moment, but there were no guarantees of it lasting another day, hour or minute.

In my quest for shelter I rapped on St. Michael's rectory door.   The vicar, sympathetic to my situation, invited me to stay the night. The following morning, the vicar accompanied me to the home of Jethro Niles. He was a freeman of color, a member of the Methodist Episcopal Church, who owned and operated a successful freighting business.   He also helped start the Minor Society in Charleston that established and operated several schools for Negro orphans. Mister Niles employed me to drive one of his freight wagons and provided living quarters in his warehouse on East Bay.   This arrangement assured my remaining a free man without being harassed by B. W. Harris.

When Niles asked whether I would be willing to help with the Orphan School at the Methodist Episcopal Church, I knew this was why the Lord brought me to Charleston. During the ensuing ten years the school grew from a mere six students to over one hundred and fifty.   I advanced my own education by serving an apprenticeship under the Reverend Nathan Weir, Bishop of South Carolina. It was during this time that I dedicated the rest of my life to educating orphaned and needy children of color. Multiple blessings came my way until a fateful day in 18 and 34 when the South Carolina legislature passed an act to amend the law relating to slaves and free persons of color. From the effective date on April 1st in 18 and 35 no slave or free persons of color *could be taught how to read or write by white persons, slaves, or free persons of color. It was a devastating law that forced me to close my school and move to Philadelphia. There I established the Willingham School at the corner of Arch and North Second streets.*

I stared at Hezekiah's fluid cursive script but was unable to read any further. His haunting message refused to go away.

"What's the matter?" Penelope said as I closed the journal.

"Nothing," I lied, not wanting to voice the turmoil boiling up in my insides.

"When does your train leave?"

I glanced at a kitchen clock setting atop the pie safe. "Five thirty," I said, noting it was now a quarter 'til three.

"We have time for me to show you the Women's Medical College. It's close by."

"Okay. Then I'll need to catch a trolley to the depot."

* * *

My entire second year at the seminary was overshadowed by uncertainties. Penelope was becoming more involved with her medical career and less interested in our relationship. Subsequent visits to see her diminished because she was spending most weekends at the Women and Children's Hospital. My interests were in flux, vacillating between academics and an ethical awakening. Was I pursuing the true meaning of Bishop Dossy's apparition? Hezekiah's experiences caused me to dwell more and more on this question. I was having difficulty in balancing obligations to the Leiter stables with seminary and family responsibilities. Shawn, being unable to find any more records, wasn't able to determine whether Hank survived the Potomac swim. By the final day of the winter term, I was overwhelmed by my battle between will and will not. I found succinct down to earth advice from none other than Aunt Gussie.

* * *

I was reading Hezekiah's accounting while spending time with Captain on the sun porch when Aunt Gussie came bustling from the kitchen. She set a platter of scones and a carafe of tea on the table. "Plenty there is for you and Captain dog. The scones he likes, yah."

"Thanks, er ah danke schon, Aunt Gussie."

"Bitte sehrl. You are reading what?"

I held it up for her to see the title. "This is Hezekiah Willingham's memoir. He's Josh's grandfather."

"Oh, yah, Josh tells me about his family. A good boy he is."

"His grandfather was a very special man. Would you like to read his accounting?"

She wagged her head and sat down in a chair facing me. "Nein, but for you to read it to me I will like."

"Sure," I said and began to read from the beginning. By the time all of the scones had been eaten and the carafe emptied, the memoir reading was completed. I shut the book and laid it on the table.

Aunt Gussie remained silent as her chair rocked back and forth. She often rocked whenever undecided about which dishes she needed to prepare. She stopped rocking, leaned forward and wagged her finger at me. "Aunt Gussie thinks John Pendleton is wandering, nein, that not the word — gone astray in his head. You are walking in forest, trees too tall, trees too thick so you don't know where to go."

I was stunned by her rebuke. How did she arrive at such from my reading Hezekiah's experiences to her? "I don't understand."

"Nein, but your face I watch while you read."

"My face revealed something?"

"Yah! You want to do, but how you not know. In your voice and in eyes, you want to do, but a decision cannot make."

"Aunt Gussie, you've lost me. What decision?"

"You remember Aesop's fables, yah?"

"Yes, which one?"

"The donkey unt haystacks."

"I don't recall."

"Between two haystacks a hungry donkey ist standing. He will starve if unable to decide which stack ist the better to eat. Or he will founder and die if both stacks he decides to eat."

"I see . . . but what two stacks am I between?"

"Bishop Dossy unt Hezekiah."

I was beginning to understand Aunt Gussie's analogy. *Bishop Dossy said my ministry is to be among the lost and afflicted. That was, and remains, the ministry Hezekiah established — schooling and nurturing orphaned children of color to accept and follow the teachings of Jesus Christ. Who could be more afflicted than these children?* "Thank you, danke schon, Aunt Gussie. I don't have to choose one over the other. Their missions are the same. Bishop Dossy was pointing me toward serving among the lost and afflicted . . . same as Hezekiah."

"Bitte sehrl, John Pendleton. Here to help Aunt Gussie is," she said, picking up the empty tray and carafe. "The supper I have to cook, yah?"

Even though there were other questions to consider and decisions to make, I felt as if a great burden had been lifted from me. "C'mon, Captain," I said, heading for the door, "let's take a walk over to visit Penny's father."

* * *

We found Doctor Gresham dozing in the gazebo with his muslin-swathed right foot elevated atop a wrought-iron garden stool. It seemed that he would never accept Todd's advice — give up wine and rich foods. I hesitated in disturbing his snooze, but Captain was not so inclined. He nudged his cold muzzle against Doctor Gresham's hand.

"Stop that," Doctor Gresham grumbled, pushing Captain away.

Captain responded with a conciliatory whine. "Oh, sorry old friend," Doctor Gresham said, patting Captain's shoulder. "Hello, John, pull up a chair."

With the usual pleasantries out of the way, I inquired whether Penelope would be coming home any time soon.

"No, John, she's apprenticing between terms. You haven't heard from her?"

"She hasn't answered my last two letters."

"She's busy with college and tutoring."

Too busy to write? I thought. "I asked for a good weekend to visit."

"She'd be glad to see you any time."

"Uninvited?"

Frowning, he peered at me. "Of course. Is there something you need to tell me?"

"No, sir . . . well . . . maybe."

He kept staring at me as I pondered how to say what I was feeling. "Well?" he said and waited for my response.

"I'm wondering . . . "

"Yes?"

"Does Penelope think our careers are incompatible?"

Doctor Gresham looked away as if avoiding my reading the answer in his eyes. "I don't know, John. You need to ask her."

CHAPTER TWENTY

On the thirteenth of July in 18 and 68 I climbed the steps to Schmucker Hall for a meeting with President Brown to determine whether I would be granted a degree. The other members of my class received their diplomas during our graduation ceremonies, but mine was being delayed until the faculty could review the defense of my thesis. Two professors were antagonistic to a fault during my presentation. They seemed to be at odds with scriptural references and even the title, *Racial Prejudice, the taproot of slavery, which remains unresolved by war, a proclamation, and a constitutional amendment.*

As I entered President Brown's office, Mrs. Keller peered at me over a copy of *The Gettysburg Compiler.* "Well, John, have you heard the news?"

"No . . . what news?"

She handed the paper to me. A large headline in bold print proclaimed: **South Carolina Ratifies 14th Amendment.** "You have time to read it. Doctor Brown's in a board meeting."

I picked out the only comfortable chair and began to read how South Carolina's deciding vote completed the constitutional requirement for ratification. The author was quick to point out the irony of my native state being the first to adopt articles of secession in 18 and 60 — and then on July 9th, 18 and 68, cast the final affirmative vote needed to ratify equal rights for persons of color. While reading his comments I recalled how the country had changed; especially, the adjustments in my life during the previous year.

Josh Willingham enrolled as a seminary student and assumed my responsibilities at Leiter stables, which included the training of my filly, Miracle. Mister Leiter provided Josh quarters and I gave him Della so he could commute to classes. He and Captain became very close, so I agreed for Captain to live at the farm where he would have the freedom to roam about, chase critters and do whatever pleased him.

I accepted Doctor Gresham's suggestion — ask Penelope whether she felt our career choices were in conflict. The opportunity to do so happened on Christmas Eve as she arrived to spend the holidays with family and friends.

Todd loaned the use of his carriage for me to meet her at the railroad station. I tethered his mare to the hitching rail and walked along the station platform toward greeters waiting for the three o'clock from Philadelphia. My apprehensions diminished as I gazed at festive greenery and listened to carolers singing, *Joy to the World.* However, I remained uncertain about revealing my concerns to Penelope. As the approaching locomotive's bell clanged and steam spewed from wheel cylinders, I searched for her in each passing coach window.

When Penelope stepped down from the coach, I tried to speak but words would not come. It was dreamlike, weird, and distorted. The experience was maddening, yet, emphatic in its effect. As she walked into my arms, the soft warmth of her body against mine was intoxicating and overwhelming like a hypnotic drug. She was all I could think about. I dared not, could not separate those feelings from reality. I came to the depot intent upon clearing the air, but left with my arm about the waist of the only person who mattered.

"Doctor Brown will see you now," Mrs. Keller said, rousing me from my reflections.

I entered his office with hat in hand, ill at ease and wondering what he was about to tell me. Were my thesis and its defense refused? If so, what recourse will I have?

"Hello, John, please have a seat?" he said, opening a file folder. "I trust you are well."

"Yes, sir."

He pulled a sheet from the file, studied it for a moment and handed it to me. "As you can see, this letter is from the Reverend Breidenbaugh. Go ahead and read it."

> July 8, 1868
> The Rev. Dr. James A. Brown, President
> The Lutheran Theological Seminary
> Gettysburg, Pennsylvania.
>
> Dear President Brown,
>
> I am flattered that you prized my opinions enough to ask me to peruse and comment on John Pendleton's master thesis. Without the benefit of hearing John's defense, I must rely upon the substance and proofs he has included in the body of this work. My conclusions also are tempered by my knowing and counseling him for the past three years.
>
> First: I find the title of his thesis to be challenging, a reminder of the writings of William Wilberforce who championed the abolition of slavery in Briton.
>
> Second: His scriptural references are apropos and germane to the subject. There are others he could have used, but were not necessary.
>
> Third: I believe he presented the underlying causes for slavery, especially in

the United States. Each enslaved person, man or woman, has always been considered inferior or less than human by his or her slave master.   The prevalent prejudice is racial, mostly against the Negro race in this nation, north and south.   If you are of a colored race, you should be subservient to your superiors, namely whites of European extraction.

John has undergone a significant process wherein he honestly addresses the subject in his thesis. I recommend its acceptance by the seminary.

Your Obedient Servant,
The Rev. Breidenbaugh, Pastor
St. James Lutheran Church.

I handed the letter back to Doctor Brown. "Thank you for allowing me to read Reverend Breidenbaugh's letter."

"Yes, a master's thesis deserves unbiased and substantive reviews by those responsible for considering its merit." He then replaced the letter, closed the file and handed me my diploma. "Congratulations, John. Will you be returning to Charleston?"

"Yes . . . next week."

"I trust Miss Gresham will be going with you?"

"I hope so."

"I'll have Mrs. Keller send your transcript to Bishop Davis."

"Thank you, sir."

"Via con dios, John Pendleton."

I grasped his outstretched hand and wrung it with more vigor than I should have. "Thank you, President Brown."

* * *

With many farewells said I sat beside a window in the room Tim and I shared for two years. I gazed at the seminary's familiar outline along the western horizon, trying to recall how it had influenced my life since I first sighted it over five years before. The halls and rooms served my people as a refuge during three horrible days in July of 18 and 63. And, it nurtured and allowed me to find meaning in my life since returning to Gettysburg. Leaving Todd, Tim, Doctor Gresham, Aunt Gussie, Josh and Captain behind was heartrending. I was so deep in thought that footsteps on the stairs were barely noticed.

Todd entered carrying a tray of sandwiches and hot tea. "Well, John, Aunt Gussie says you refused to come down for lunch."

"I'm not hungry."

He set the tray and carafe on the table beside my chair. "You'd better eat or Aunt Gussie will be spoon feeding you."

"Yes . . . I remember . . . John a lot eats?"

"Why are you so melancholy?"

"Oh, leaving is not easy."

"No . . . what about Penelope?" he said, filling two cups with tea.

"I had a long talk with her and Doctor Gresham last evening."

"Will she be going with you to Charleston?"

"She's thinking about it. Her classes begin in six weeks."

"I see. Are you going to stay in Charleston?"

His question reverberated inside my head. *I've been trying to determine the answer for the past year. Before I can make a decision, Bishop Davis needs to be consulted. He approved my preparation for ministry and accepted the degree granted to me by the Lutheran Seminary. I'm certain he will insist upon me being ordained and added to the diocesan roster of ministers. That was my goal until I became acquainted with the works of Hezekiah Willingham. I then began to search my soul for God's inspiration. My heart continues to undergo a spiritual transformation. Before returning to Gettysburg, I was a prejudiced son of a slave master. Today, I am laden with guilt for my people and myself.*

"John," Todd said, handing me a cup of tea. "You seem distraught. What can I do to help?"

"I'm in a sticky situation."

"How so?"

"I received this from Jeremiah Willingham," I said, handing Todd a letter in which Jeremiah described how impressed he was with my master's thesis. He went on to say that he took the liberty of sharing it with General Samuel C. Armstrong who was establishing a new normal school for Negroes in Virginia. After studying my thesis, he asked Jeremiah to convey his interest in my considering a position on his faculty at Hampton Normal and Agricultural Institute.

Todd removed his reading spectacles and peered at me. "Just who is this General Armstrong?"

"President Brown says General Armstrong and Doctor Schmucker are close friends, both having been active in the abolitionist movement."

"Come with me. There us something I wish to show you," Todd said, hurrying toward the stairway.

When we reached his library, Todd pulled a leather-bound directory from a bookshelf. We sat at his desk and began to scan the index. "Here it is," he said, pointing at *The Freedmen's Bureau* listing. "I remembered reading about a Samuel C. Armstrong being appointed to the bureau by President Johnson."

We turned to General Armstrong's entry and discovered President Johnson had indeed appointed him to the bureau. But of greater interest was that he and I shared similar experiences. He served in the Second Corp defending Cemetery Ridge during our assault on July the third. Following the battle for Gettysburg, he commanded the Eighth U. S. Colored Troops, which later participated in Grant's siege of our lines at Petersburg. I wondered what kind of man this former commander of colored troops would be. He may not be interested in me after discovering my role during the war.

Todd closed the directory. "What now, John? Are you going to be a preacher or a teacher?"

* * *

On Monday, the tenth of August, Penny and I arrived in Charleston. It had been three years since I sailed on the clipper ship, West Wind, bound for Philadelphia. The return journey required frequent transfers between trains, ferries and stages. Only short stretches of rail service existed in most of the Carolinas and Virginia.

As our rail coach rolled past once burned out buildings, I pondered on my meeting with Bishop Davis. How would he respond to my interest in becoming a professor at a school dedicated to training Negro teachers? Our people had sacrificed lives, treasury and blood defending our homes and way of life. There was very little doubt in my mind concerning their attitudes toward persons of color, all of whom were now free and considered equal. My insides churned at the thought of asking the bishop for permission to become a professor at Hampton Normal and Agricultural Institute.

Penny tugged my sleeve. "A Yankee dime for your thoughts."

"Oh, I'm just a bit apprehensive about tomorrow."

"Your meeting with the bishop?"

"Yes . . . I wish he were Bishop Dossy instead of Bishop Davis?"

The train's abrupt braking signaled our arrival at the depot. I spied Mother and Martin waiting on the station platform as our coach came to a stop. "There they are," I said, grasping Penny's arm.

As we stepped from the coach, Mother reached for Penny's hand. "This is your Penelope? What a pretty young lady."

"Yes, Mother, this is Penny, or, ah, I mean, Penelope."

"Welcome to Charleston, my dear," Mother said, embracing her. "I feel as if I already know you. John has written so much about you in his letters. Thank you for carin' for him when he was so injured."

"You're welcome, Mrs. Pendleton. We cared for all of them, Southern as well as Northern."

Mother nodded. "Yes, my dear, but your carin' for John was special."

"Yes, ma'am, he is to me, also."

I glanced at Martin. He was smitten by Penny's beauty and charm — no doubt about it. "Come, Martin . . . little brother," I said, emulating how Andrew always addressed me. "Meet the lady of my dreams, Miss Penny Gresham."

I thought Martin's response was a bit exaggerated as he lifted her fingers to his lips. "I'm most pleased to meet you, Miss Penny. Welcome to Charleston."

"Thank you, Martin, for your hospitality. John tells me you are studying medicine."

"Yes, ma'am, at the Medical College of South Carolina."

"I'm starting my final year at Pennsylvania Women's Medical College."

Martin lifted his brows and stammered, "Oh . . . ah . . . you're goin' to be a doctor?"

Penelope grinned and patted his hand, much the way a mother corrects a wayward child. "Is that surprising?"

"Well, yes, ma'am, we don't have women students or . . . doctors."

Mother glanced at me. The expression in her eyes was unmistakable. *Change the conversation.* I obeyed. "Well, Mother, where's Benton?"

"Bishop Davis assigned him to St. Thaddeus in Aiken following his ordination at St. Michael's last month."

"And, Priscilla?"

"Prissy's abed with a female agony," Martin interjected before Mother could respond.

Penelope grimaced, appearing to be disquieted by Martin's crudeness. "Don't you mean dysmenorrhea?"

"Well, yes, I didn't think any of you knew what the word meant."

"Martin!" Mother scolded. "Penelope is almost a doctor."

Martin scraped the toe of his boot against the red brick platform. "Sorry, Miss Penny," he said, trying to sound repentant. "I'm not used to any woman even wanting to be a doctor."

I had heard enough of Martin's prejudice. "Why is that, little brother? You seem to have forgotten women proved themselves during the war."

Mother gripped and shook his shoulder "This is no way to welcome John and Penelope. Apologize this minute."

"Yes, ma'am, I'm sorry, Miss Penny, for my ignorance." He held out his hand and stepped closer to her. "Am I forgiven?"

With Penny's forgiveness granted, Martin and I picked up our luggage and we all climbed into Mother's carriage. As we traveled along live oak-canopied Church Street, my ears shut out grinding steel rimmed wheels and clopping hooves as I pondered my meeting on the morrow with Bishop Davis.

* * *

Dark semicircles beneath Thomas F. Davis's eyes, drawn features and sallow complexion bespoke a state of infirmity. However, his sharp intellect soon became evident as I met with him in the parlor of his home. With the usual pleasantries out of the way, he opened a file folder and studied its contents. Several minutes passed while he perused it and I entertained myself by studying several portraits lining the walls. At last he closed and laid the file aside. "Well, John, your professors seem to value your intellect quite highly. I presume you are ready for ordination?"

"Yes, sir."

"And, for assignment?"

"I'm not certain."

His quick response seemed to ignore my equivocation. "We have an opportunity for you at St. Bartholomew. Rev. Stone was forced to retire . . . consumption . . . a dastardly affliction."

"I'm sorry to hear that, sir . . . the consumption."

"Yes, we lose too many good clergy from this scourge. You are well, aren't you?"

"Yes, quite so, sir."

"Excellent! Now, shall we plan for your ordination?" He picked up a desk calendar and studied it. "Say . . . on the twenty second?"

I sensed the situation was spiraling out of control. "If I'm ordained, do I have another option besides a pastoral appointment?"

He peered at me with intensity. "Option? To what do you refer, John Pendleton?"

My hasty question had brought about an abrupt response. "Maybe . . . a professorship . . . at Hampton Normal . . . sir."

He glared at me, at first, and then his gaze softened. "Professorship? Hampton? Where's that?"

"Virginia, sir. Hampton, Virginia."

"I'm unaware of this institution. Tell me about it."

I spent several minutes in describing the new school for former slaves; its purpose being the education of Negro teachers and craftsmen. He appeared to be impressed. "That is all well and good, John, but we are in the business of being 'the Church', nothing more and nothing less. You have spent much time and effort in preparing to be a cleric. Why being a professor?"

"We, the Confederacy, embraced slavery as a legitimate rationale for sustaining our way of life. It was not only in error, but immorally perceived."

"Quite so, John. William Wilberforce's perseverance certainly prevailed. Too bad, we were unable to follow his lead . . . without bloodshed."

"That is why I must become a professor at Hampton, sir."

His gaze underwent a transition from skeptical to acceptance. At last, he said, "A noble pursuit, John. Permission is not only granted, but receives the blessing of this office."

* * *

Penny found favor with the family by successfully treating Pricilla's disabling dysmenorrhea with doses of amyl nitrite and elixir of belladonna. By the end of our two-week visit, she had convinced Martin of a simple truth: women physicians were not inferior to men because of gender.

No lesser task was for me to persuade Mother, Martin and Pricilla I made an appropriate decision to seek professorship in a Negro school instead of accepting a clerical appointment. Our luggage was packed and ready to load for our trip to the railroad depot when Mother asked me to meet with everyone in the parlor. Her comment was, "Before you and your Penelope leave, the family needs to hear why you refused a clerical appointment by Bishop Davis?"

While everyone gathered in the parlor, I became quite apprehensive as to how they were going to react. Mother had lost Father and her home to Sherman's minions. Andrew would continue his maritime profession. At the time he was somewhere in the Atlantic, laying a transoceanic cable. I'd been away throughout the war, and for another three years at Gettysburg Lutheran Seminary. Now I was opting for a future that would separate us for an unknown period of time. I was quite aware she wanted me to accept a clerical appointment in or near Charleston. How was I going to convince her that my accepting a teaching position at a school dedicated to educating emancipated Negroes was the proper thing for me to do?

"Well, big brother," Martin said as I walked into the parlor where everyone was seated and awaiting what I had to say. "Please enlighten us."

"May I, little brother?" I said, gesturing toward a chair next to the fireplace.

""Please do," he said.

I sat down and collected my thoughts. "I am aware of your questions regarding my decision not to accept a clerical appointment. I understand why each of you has an issue concerning my reason for making such a decision. The answer is not simple. Neither is it easy for me to formulate. I suppose the clearest response is that I am following my conscience. There is a need for all of us who are of a Christian persuasion to reach out to the oppressed. The Negro, above all others, has been the most oppressed of any who have lived in this nation we call the United States. We Southerners who have been the most oppressive are responsible for the rehabilitation of those whom we oppressed. I am deeply aware of that responsibility. I fought to keep our previous way of life — a plantation maintained through slave labor. I since have come to regret my participation in the recent war. Now, I've an opportunity to condone for all of my guilt. Teaching former slaves to survive and prosper in our land is of the utmost priority. That is why I am dedicating myself to being a teacher instead of a preacher."

While subdued applause led by Mother brought her truth-seeking gathering to an end, I thanked them for their support. In departing I felt an overwhelming sense of sadness as I embraced each one. While holding Mother tightly, I pondered whether it would be the last time I would be with her. Her features portrayed a striking portrait of a woman who had experienced overwhelming tragedies. "Goodbye, John," she whispered, "don't worry about Martin, Pricilla and me. We will be just fine. You must follow the path that our Lord has laid out for you."

* * *

Like our journey to Charleston, the return trip was exhausting. Southern railroads were in a shambles with only a few cities and towns connected by them. As a result we spent many hours aboard railroad or stage coaches before arriving in Richmond, Virginia.

Our moment of separation became imminent as the rail coach rolled past partially reconstructed outskirts of the former Confederate capital. Penelope was going on to Philadelphia, but I would board a stage bound for Hampton, Virginia. I had mixed emotions regarding a meeting with General Armstrong, President of Hampton Institute. If he asked me to accept a professorship, a lot of time and miles would separate Penny and me. If he decided a former Rebel was not suitable for his school, what options did I have?

Penny grasped my hand as we peered through the coach window at what once was a beautiful and thriving city. Much desolation remained. Unsupported sooty brick walls of many fire-gutted buildings stood like inanimate watchmen amid mounds of blackened rubble. Three long years following General Lee's surrender had failed to remove the ravages of a futile war. I could not help but wonder whether Richmond would ever experience a rebirth. Little had been accomplished by the nation's reconstruction.

Penny squeezed my hand. "I'm going to miss you — so very much, my darling Johnnie. You will write — often?"

"Of course," I said, pulling her into a tight embrace. As our lips met, my mind melted together the present with all of the past days since I first met Penny in the Old Dorm. Her love had sustained me through many hours of imprisonment and war — and nurtured me during my years spent in seminary. Going on without her seemed unimaginable. The locomotive's clanging bell roused and reminded me that the time of our parting was near. I loosened my embrace and peered into her bonny blue eyes. "I will love and cherish you forever," I said, holding her face between my hands. "I pray God keeps us near even though we are far apart."

CHAPTER TWENTY ONE

While I was walking along a cobblestone walkway, leading to the front porch of General Samuel C. Armstrong's residence, a sense of apprehension slowed my pace. Awkwardness about meeting a former Yankee general refused to go away. I wondered what his response would be when I confessed to being one of Pickett's soldiers.

The day was hot and humid with a weighty, musty aroma, which reminded me of an August afternoon in the lowlands of South Carolina. Feeling the need for a time to collect my senses, I spied a white, wrought-iron garden bench beneath a live oak beside the walkway. I sat down, loosened my collar and mopped sweat from my brow. Out of a need to review the reason for my visit, I unfolded and revisited the general's letter I received before Penny and I left for Charleston.

> July 2, 1868
> Mr. John Pendleton,
> Lutheran Theological Seminary,
> Gettysburg, Pennsylvania
>
> My Dear Mr. Pendleton,
>
> Mr. Jeremiah Willingham, a Negro educator with whom I have consulted regarding the establishment of a normal school for freed slaves, favored me with a copy of your master's thesis. I was impressed by your in-depth coverage of the problems our nation experienced relative to

slavery. I am in complete agreement with every aspect of your learned work.

I have taken the liberty of sending an inquiry to Dr. Brown, President of Gettysburg Seminary, concerning your education and qualifications. My purpose stemmed from the need for establishing a quality faculty at Hampton Normal and Agricultural Institute. After receiving President Brown's reply, I have determined you would be an excellent member of our faculty.

I would appreciate your prayerful consideration of my invitation to visit me here in Hampton, Virginia at your earliest convenience.

Your Obedient Servant,
Samuel C. Armstrong

I stuffed the letter back into my pocket and climbed several steps to the general's porch. I tapped his brass doorknocker and waited. There was no response. I tapped the knocker again, a bit louder this time. After I took several deep breaths, the door opened.

Except for sideburns, a clean-shaven gentleman, whose erect posture disclosed a military bearing, extended his hand as he stepped onto the porch. "I'm Samuel Armstrong, and you are …?"

"John Pendleton, sir," I said, gripping his hand.

"Welcome, Mister Pendleton. I've been looking forward to your visit."

His pleasantness was calming, for which I was grateful. "Thank you, sir."

The intenseness of his eyes grew as he examined me more closely. "Yes . . . you are quite welcome, Mr. Pendleton. May I call you John?"

"Yes, sir."

"I'm Samuel. Close friends call me Sam."

Calling a former general by his abbreviated Christian name seemed somewhat insolent; however, I intended to comply since it was his request. "Thank you, Sam."

My hesitancy must have amused him. A grin lifted his cheeks and crinkled the corners of his eyes. "Well, John, let's sit here on the porch," he said, gesturing toward a ladder-back swing.

I nodded, sat down and released the flex lock on the knee of my prosthesis. Sam frowned as he sat beside me. "Battle injury?"

"Yes, sir."

"Where?"

"Gettysburg. July the third."

"Pickett's charge?"

"Pettigrew's Division."

He grimaced, appearing to question how to respond. "My division, the 125th New York, helped repulse your charge. How were you wounded?"

"Canister."

"Canister is barbaric, but so is war, I suppose. It's too bad so many of your men suffered and died defending slavery."

"Agreed. That's the reason I'm here. I'm bound to honor the premise of my thesis by helping overcome prejudice, the taproot of slavery."

"A noble commitment," he mumbled, "but . . . this is a school to educate freed slaves. They may find it difficult to accept a former Rebel. Your accent would be a reminder of their being owned and exploited by your people."

I understood his reluctance. Could I defeat reverse prejudice, the attitude I was committed to overcome? It would be daunting, but possible. "May I make a suggestion?"

"Please do."

"I could meet with your students, read my thesis to them, and explain my repentance for the past."

His brows arched upward as he pondered my suggestion. "Possibly . . . no harm in trying," he muttered, nodding acceptance.

* * *

Standing in front of more than twenty former slaves whose black faces reflected skepticism and repressed anger was a daunting task. General Armstrong placed his hand upon my shoulder. "Please welcome, Mr. John Pendleton. He has agreed to join the faculty of Hampton Institute provided you deem him worthy of the task. Please listen to what he has to say."

I felt sweat trickling down my back similar to the morning Hank and I lined up for our charge toward General Armstrong's 125th New Yorkers. "Thank you, General Armstrong," I said, trying to hide my Carolina accent.

I unfolded a copy of my thesis, spread it atop the lectern and paused while trying to look into the eyes of each student. Streaming thoughts surged through my mind, some of which were questions concerning just why any of them would accept what I was about to say. Others involved how I would be able to convey the spirit of my thesis — regrets for the past — remorse for the sins of my people — a dedication to correcting the wrongs inflicted upon them, their families, and their race. Those tumbling trepidations stilled my tongue until a young fellow in the front row whispered loud enough for me to hear his acidic comment. "Don't wanna listen to no white slaver."

His comment cut through me swift as a scythe reaping indigo. The comment, and some more severe, undoubtedly were harbored within the minds of my audience. Realizing the immensity of the task before me, I spoke to the young man. "Yes, my family enslaved some of your people. I took up arms in defense of that practice. I lost a leg trying to defend my people at Gettysburg. After being captured, I experienced mercy and healing by my adversaries. Incarceration on Pea Patch Island awakened my appreciation of and a desire for freedom. Escape became possible through the aid and comfort of family, friends, and even former enemies. At the war's end I returned to the town where I discovered love and compassion. There I found God's response to questions roiling within my spirit. Would you like to hear them?"

Silence, overwhelming and deafening greeted my question. Finally, the young man who questioned my presence, said, "You got somethin' t'say, say it."

"Thank you," I said, looking into his eyes. "What is your name . . . sir?"

His brows rose, expressing surprise. "Thomas. Don't have no other name."

"I'm pleased to make your acquaintance, Thomas."

"What you gotta say t'us?"

"I wish I could erase the past, but that is impossible. I lost my father, home, closest friend, and right leg, but you and your people lost much more. I cannot replace your or my losses. I can only express my remorse for them and dedicate myself to a future of freedom without prejudice for you and your people."

"Hum, you talk good. Maybe you be a liar . . . like all slavers."

"I have been many things in my life, but never a liar. I was required to research and write a proposal in order to graduate from a seminary. I entitled it, *Racial Prejudice, the taproot of slavery, which remains unresolved by war, a proclamation, and a constitutional amendment.* I would appreciate your allowing me to read it to you."

Silence again settled over our gathering. I waited, determined to remain mute until permission to proceed was granted. There ensued scattered sounds of unease — several "hums" and "ohs" and at last one student said, "Well, go'head."

"Thank you. How about you, Thomas? May I proceed?"

His gaze was defiant until nodding a silent approval.

I began to read, mindful that these students who lacked formal education would probably become bored and cease to listen. About half way through the document, I stopped and glanced at upturned black faces who seemed overwhelmed. I pondered the wisdom of proceeding. How was I going to prop up my case, and convince them of my premise? With this determination, I flipped to the last page and read my concluding statement. "President Lincoln's emancipation proclamation, General Lee's surrender at Appomattox and the thirteenth amendment to the constitution have brought an end to slavery in the United States of America. However, racial prejudice, the taproot of slavery remains, waiting to sprout anew and spread its poison throughout our nation. Consequently, we are a divided people, whose divine destiny cannot endure. Unless we uproot and destroy racial prejudice from the very subsoil of our country's soul, freedom for every person regardless of color or station will cease to exist. We stand at the gate of decision. As for me, I will spend the remainder of my life doing whatever the Almighty commands until the stain of slavery and prejudice is removed from our beloved land. So help me, God."

I folded the thesis, slipped it into my pocket and waited for a response. Their only reactions were downcast expressions and utter silence. Like a sail collapsing from a sudden calm, my spirits sagged. Embarrassed by their overwhelming rejection, I left the meeting hall and headed down a cobblestone walkway toward the ocean. I had no idea where it would lead me. There was simply an irresistible need to separate myself from an offensive situation.

I followed the pathway until reaching a wooded park where I found a stone bench close to the waterfront. The seclusion was what I needed to ponder the intensity of my disappointment. A kaleidoscope of emotions tumbled out of the depths of my being. Sorrow, anger, embarrassment, and resentment swept over and plunged me with the force of an ebb tide into a dark void of despair. I had been so certain that the students would recognize and accept what I felt in my soul. It seemed impossible that they would not understand and believe the basis of my confessions.

I sat there for some time bathing myself with self pity. Swarms of gull-billed terns emitting their "kay-wek" calls and pulsating waves splashing along the waterfront were hypnotic. Why hadn't I accepted Bishop Davis's appointment to St. Bartholomew? How could I have imagined that former slaves would believe any conclusions brought about by three years of soul searching and research by the son of a slave owner? It was impossible for them to understand my journey, and I was beginning to realize I could not comprehend theirs. It was pure folly on my part.

My trip into remorse was interrupted with a searing comment spoken by a familiar voice. "Why does you want t'teach colored folk?"

I stood up to face my accuser. "Thomas?"

"Yes, suh, I be Thomas. You be a Rebel, a slaver, what you doin' here?"

"Didn't I make that clear to you?"

"You said a lotta big words . . . words we don't know. Can't you say it plain out?"

"I thought I did. I spent a lot of time crafting a thesis, so it would be completely understood."

"What's a thesis?"

His riveting question caused me to pause, to fathom his meaning. "You don't understand what a thesis is?"

"No, and a lot other words you used."

So . . . my premise hadn't been rejected. They had no idea what I said or meant. I felt a great burden being lifted. "Come, Thomas, sit down and let's talk."

"Awright," he said and we sat down together.

"Well, Thomas, how can I say what I need to?"

"Just leave off the fancy words . . . you had slaves . . . right? Talk to me like you did to them."

My years at Eton College and Gettysburg Seminary had conditioned me to communicate with others who were equally educated. This fact sank in as I tried to relay what my thesis said in simple words — a daunting challenge. "Well, Thomas, let me say it this way. We white folk enslaved colored folk to do our work without us paying them any wages. We prospered off of their sweat and years. In doing this we had to convince ourselves that only colored folk deserved to be enslaved, because they were an inferior class of folk. They were so simple that we were favoring them with our being their masters. Otherwise, we could not have accepted the practice if we were enslaving white folk. So, prejudice against colored folk became a normal attitude for white folk. Owning another human being fouled the master's character. Obedience became his demand, so he punished his slaves if they disobeyed or rebelled. Consequently, the slave masters justified their actions and slaves seethed with rebellion and vengeance. My family owned many colored men and women. I grew up believing I was better than any colored person. When the war of rebellion came, I fought to keep things the same. I and my family paid a great price during and following the war. But our defeat brought about the freeing of every folk who had endured being a slave. After the war, through much study and soul searching I came to a conclusion that slavery and prejudice were wrong. My decision was made out of the need to say to you and your people, I'm sorry, Thomas. I can't change the past, but together we can change the future. May I be your equal, your teacher and friend?"

Thomas peered at me with a steely gaze. It was intense as a soldier who was intent upon piercing his enemy with an eighteen inch long bayonet. "Is you a liar?"

"No, Thomas, I am not a liar."

"You wanna be my friend?"

"Yes, I do."

"You ain't better'n me no more?"

"Not for a long time."

He held out his hand. "Then we's friends?"

I gripped his hand between both of mine to convey my sincerity. "We are friends. May I be your mentor, your teacher?"

"Yes, Marse Pendleton."

"No more Marse. Call me Professor John."

I sat down on that stone bench in utter defeat and arose from it beside a friend with whom I could build the future. We talked together on our way back to the meeting hall as if we had been lifelong friends. Thomas had asked all of the other students to wait while he went to question me about what I told them. Once in the hall, I repeated the meaning of my thesis in simple words and sentences. When I was finished, General Armstrong stepped before the students. "If you want Mister Pendleton to be one of your teachers, say, yes. If not, say, no."

The students stood up, voiced approval and applauded — but all clapping ended when a solitary voice cried, "I votes, NO! Go home slaver."

* * *

Within the week I was scheduled to begin my teaching assignments at Hampton Institute. However, my first priority was to secure room and board close to the campus. General Armstrong suggested that I might find pleasant accommodations in the home of Mrs. Mary Arthurs. She lived alone in a two-story stone cottage close to the campus and waterfront. Her husband who was killed during the battle at Cold Harbor in June of 18 and 64 had provided a modest trust for her, but she needed a supplemental income.

I wondered whether she might be related to Sarah Arthurs, the lady who helped me during my escape from Old Capital Prison. This idea was foremost on my mind as I headed down a winding pathway toward the waterfront and an appointment with Mary Arthurs. Sam described her as a petite lady in her mid twenties who met Herbert Arthurs when he was a cadet at Virginia Military Institute. They married soon after he graduated and was commissioned in the U. S. Army. When shots were fired at Fort Sumter, he resigned his commission and volunteered to serve the Confederacy. Within three years he had ascended to the rank of Colonel and was assigned command of a brigade in the First Corps. His death at Cold Harbor ended their marriage that had spanned less than seven years.

As I neared the Arthurs' cottage, clanking navigational buoys in the bay fractured the still morning air. The lonesome chimes reminded me of the waterfront along the Battery in Charleston — home and family. The remembrance awakened a feeling of regret for having disappointed Mother by my decision to teach former slaves instead of accepting a clerical appointment at St. Bartholomew.

I made a halting climb up more than a few porch steps — a task made more difficult by a perverse prosthetic leg. Mrs. Arthurs must have observed my difficulty, because the door flew open and she hurried toward me. Her hazel eyes crinkled as brilliant white teeth peeked between smiling lips that silently bespoke a friendly greeting. "I apologize for my steep porch steps," she said, starting to reach for my arm.

"No need, ma'am," I said and slapped my right thigh. "It's this balky excuse for a real leg, not the stairs."

She clasped her hands together and nodded. "Oh, I'm so sorry."

After apologizing for my intrusion, I handed her an introductory note from Sam Armstrong. "General Armstrong sends his greetings."

"Thank you, Mister . . . ?"

"I'm sorry; it's Pendleton . . . John Pendleton."

She swept black tresses away from her face, which was pristine as a cameo carved in ivory, and studied the note. "Sam says you are seeking room and board."

"Yes, ma'am, I have accepted a professorship at the Institute, so a long term arrangement is needed."

With the reason for my visit stated, Mrs. Arthurs invited me into her parlor. "Do you have references?" she asked as we sat in large leather chairs facing each other in front of an ornate marble fireplace.

"I don't understand."

"Character recommendations by reliable people."

"Will the General's comments suffice?"

She frowned and peered at the note. "Yes, I suppose so."

Above the fireplace was a portrait of a balding gentlemen attired in a Confederate uniform. "Colonel Arthurs?" I asked, nodding at the painting."

"Yes, did you know my husband?"

"No ma'am, I served in General Pettigrew's division."

"You would have loved Herbert. His men adored him."

"We thought highly of all our commanders," I said, feeling somewhat guilty for gilding the truth. "I'm sure your husband was held in high esteem."

"He most certainly was. Is your General Pettigrew well?"

"He was killed during my division's retreat from Gettysburg."

"Oh, I'm so sorry," she said, wringing her hands, and then fell silent while staring at her husband's portrait. "So many . . . such a tragedy . . . ."

"Yes, ma'am, do you have children?"

Her features became somber as the Sphinx of Giza as she looked at me with intent hazel eyes. "No. Herbert and I were not blessed with children, but we adored our nephew . . . a fine young man . . . we lost him in sixty-three."

"Was he killed in battle?"

"No . . . he was captured and died a prisoner. So, sad."

"Do you know where he was captured?"

"Gettysburg."

The coincidences were overwhelming. Could her nephew be my bunkmate in Delaware Prison? It was like a déjà vu experience, otherworldly, an impossible recurrence. With reluctance, I asked, "Was he a cavalryman?"

"Yes . . . why do you ask?"

"I was wounded and captured at Gettysburg, and sent to Delaware Prison on Pea Patch Island. Was your nephew incarcerated there?"

"Yes," she muttered, frowning. "My aunt said it was a terrible place."

"Yes, ma'am, it was as close to Hell as any place on earth."

As tears welled up in her eyes, she fingered the hem of her apron. "Did you happen to know my nephew, Cade Arthurs?"

Her question confirmed my suspicions. "Yes, ma'am, we were in the same barrack. He came down with smallpox and they carried him away to the hospital. That was the last time I saw him."

"You must be the young soldier that spent a week with my aunt, Sarah Arthurs?"

"Yes, ma'am, I met her during my escape from prison," I said and continued to tell Mary about meeting Cade, his death, my escapes from Delaware and Old Capital prisons, and how Sarah gave me shelter, her mare, Kate, and Cade's beloved dog, Captain. At the end of my story, Mary held my hand and wept. "Thank you," she said, gripping it as if letting go would doom her to oblivion. "You will be pleased to know that Aunt Sarah is coming Christmas to visit me. She will be so happy to see you again."

CHAPTER TWENTY TWO

If I were Robinson Crusoe trying to survive on a remote, cannibal infested island, Thomas would have become my man, Friday. My future at Hampton Institute became uncertain when overcoming the students' deep seated ill will began to falter. A turning point came on the morning I decided to take Thomas into confidence and seek his advice.

Dawn was breaking with an array of clanking buoys, surging surf, chattering terns, and crimson streaked clouds hovering over the eastern horizon. I found him sitting alone on a bench near the waterfront. He appeared to be in deep thought as I sat down beside him. "Good morning, Thomas."

"Mornin', Prof John," he said, gazing toward the bay.

"This is peaceful place."

"It's good for thinkin'."

"You sound troubled."

His eyes, piercing and questioning, gazed at me. "Can't read much . . . don't write. A letter came yesterday . . . gotta be bad news."

"Let me read it for you."

Thomas nodded, pulled an envelope from his pocket and handed it to me. The letter within was from Benjamin R. Cathy, Esq., Attorney at Law, 214 6th Street, Tuscaloosa, Alabama. To the best of my recollection, it read as follows: Dear Mister Thomas, I represent the administrator of the Cornelius Waite estate. Mister Waite died March 6, 1868 after making his last will and testament. The directives of said Cornelius Waite bequeathed certain real and personal properties to you, which the Tuscaloosa County Probate Court has considered and granted without contest. From his estate you are the recipient of forty acres of land, two mules, one plow, one cultivator, one boar and two sows. I have prepared the proper deed and papers for you. When you forward certified legal tender in the amount of $15.75, I will complete the transfer of these properties to you. Your Obedient Servant, Benjamin R. Cathy.

Returning the letter to Thomas, I wondered why he'd become the recipient of an estate in Alabama. "Who was Cornelius Waite?"

Thomas stared at his hands clinched together with such force the knuckles were almost white. "I was one o' his field hands . . . and . . . mamma say he were my daddy."

What a travesty. Cornelius Waite was unwilling to acknowledge him as his son, but sought amends with forty acres of land, two mules, some machinery and three hogs. Could any words console the troubled man sitting beside me?

"Now, my friend, at last you have a legitimate name . . . Thomas Waite."

"Don't want that name. He weren't a daddy to me."

"It's a name."

"Thomas be my name. Don't need another."

"Are you going to claim your inheritance?"

"Don't know 'bout that, Prof John. I ain't got fifteen dollars and seventy five cents, and no way to manage two mules, three hogs and forty acres down in 'bama. Jus' don't know."

My problems waned considering how Thomas's life was being changed. He was a former slave without any known family. His white father denied him, and he didn't have any support other than being a Hampton Institute student. His inheritance in Alabama might be more of a burden than a windfall, but it could be a new beginning for him. "Well, now, we can resolve that question. I'll write a letter for you to make an arrangement with lawyer Cathy. If he agrees to sell your inheritance, I'll pay the fees for you."

Thomas made an emphatic gesture with his hands. "The letter be okay, but money's my job."

"It would be a loan, not a gift. You can repay me when lawyer Cathy sells your property." Thomas frowned, slowly wagged his head, but then agreed after further persuasion.

Mentoring Thomas was fulfilling for me, but my need to obtain his advice remained — how could I become an adviser to the other students? Would he feel recompense was my motive if I brought it up? The quandary settled upon me like a fog rolling across the bay. Thomas appeared to sense my dilemma. "You looks puzzled."

"I suppose," I said, stood up and walked toward the pier where several boats were moored.

While staring at the bay, I felt Thomas's hand squeeze my shoulder, "You helped me, Prof John . . . maybe I can help."

I turned about to face him. His eyes never wavered from my gaze. "Yes, you can," I said and explained my need for a closer relationship with all of my students, especially, the former slave who had admonished me to go home.

His response was unexpected, but the one I needed to hear. "Be yo'self, Prof John. My mamma say the golden rule be true. You 'member that and you gets your answer."

* * *

I finished reading, *A Christmas Carol*, by Charles Dickens before retiring for the night. I laid the book on the bedside table, blew out the reading lamp and crawled between the sheets. I pulled the comforter up to my chin and gazed into the darkness, unable to shake Dickens's depictions from my mind. While vivid characters who were explicitly described by him paraded in my mind's eye, the ghost of Christmas Past tarried at the foot of my bed. Pondering his airy specter, my mind returned to festive childhood days. We spent many joyous hours exchanging gifts and experiencing tantalizing aromas emitting from goodies being prepared by Mother. This memory gave way to Christmases spent in the field during the war. There was nothing pleasant about them. Hank and I considered ourselves fortunate if we had a hot meal, canvas over our heads and a warm fire. How I missed him and wondered where he might be. The bleak memory faded as festive days spent in Todd's home at Christmastime unfolded before me. Aunt Gussie's strudel and gingerbread cakes were special, and sitting beside the fireplace while holding hands with Penny and listening to Doctor Gresham reading from the second chapter of Luke warmed my spirit. While dwelling on these recollections, sleep soon closed my eyes.

Tantalizing aromas of biscuits baking in the oven, a pot of hot spiced apple cider atop the stove, and smoked Virginia ham frying in a skillet ascended the stairway to my room. They reminded me of past Christmases spent with Todd, Aunt Gussie, Penny and Tim. While I lay half asleep expecting to hear the Lutheran Seminary's carillon playing, Oh Come All Ye Faithful, Mary Arthurs called, "Christmas gift, John Pendleton . . . breakfast's waiting."

I slid from a warm and tranquil bed, strapped on my prosthetic leg, dressed and started down the stairway. When I reached the bottom step, a melodic duet singing, Joy to the World, came from the kitchen. As I began to sing with them, Mary and a white-headed lady stepped from the kitchen into the hallway. It had been four years since Mary's aunt sent me homeward astride Kate with Captain leading the way. I suppose my surprise was etched into my face as Mary cried, "Surprise, look who arrived last night."

Sarah's captivating smile filled me with a blessing from the past. "Miz Sarah . . . ma'am," I said, reaching for her embrace.

A mischievous glint filled her eyes. "Forget the ma'am, John Pendleton. It's Sarah."

I glanced over her shoulder at Mary Arthurs. "Why didn't you tell me Sarah was coming?" I said, sounding more chastising than intended, and then continued in a more mollifying manner, "I would have met her at the station."

Mary wagged a reproving finger at me. "Aunt Sarah wanted to surprise you . . . and Thomas volunteered to fetch her from the station with General Armstrong's carriage."

"Ham, biscuits and redeye gravy's awaitin'," Sarah said, slapping my back. "Let's talk while we're eatin',"

As we sat around the kitchen table, Sarah reached for Mary's and my hands. "Since you're a bona fide preacher, John . . . would you say grace?"

Nodding, I prayed a common blessing. "Bless us, O Lord, and these your gifts, which we are about to receive from your limitless bounty . . . through Christ our Lord . . . Amen."

Sarah squeezed my hand and said, "Lord, thank you for answering my prayers for John to live through the war, and bringin' us together again."

Aromas wafting from platters of ham and redeye gravy tweaked my appetite, so much that I nodded with each offering Sarah ladled onto my plate. Once no more food could be stacked in front of me, I held up my hand. "That's plenty, thank you, Miz Sarah."

As she filled her plate, I noticed how much Sarah had aged. Her hair was white as autumn frost blanketing her bluegrass meadow. Deep furrows between her brows bespoke burdens experienced since we said farewell the morning Kate carried me homeward. My telling her about her grandson's imprisonment and death surely added depth to her burdens. Despite the joy of seeing her again, a melancholy mood settled upon me. This dear lady had played a major part in my surviving the war. A somber frame of mind stayed my hand as I stared at the bounty of food before me.

"Better eat – starin' at your plate won't put any get-up on your ribs," Sarah said, patting my hand.

I nodded and pierced a chunk of ham with my fork, but a sudden coughing paroxysm overwhelmed me. While trying to stifle the fit with my hand, Sarah kept slapping me across the back. "Spit it out. Get rid of it."

Her admonition, of course, wasn't the solution. I'd experienced similar episodes during the previous month, but passed them off as being due to a simple case of catarrh. Once the attack resolved, I pulled my hand away. Sarah stared at me as she dabbed her napkin across my lips. "How long you been coughin' up blood?" she said, wadding up her napkin.

"Blood?"

"Blood," she said, unfolding the evidence.

I starred at telltale stains, trying to collect my senses. A flood of emotions stilled my tongue as dread for what the irrefutable facts meant. Consumption, the illness that squelches hopes, futures and lives came crashing through my mind like a swirling dervish. Sarah and Mary seemed to be experiencing the same emotions. Mary kept saying, "I'm so sorry."

Sarah grasped my hand. "Now, now, Mary. Blood don't always mean somethin' bad. John, you need to see a doctor. Do that afore you think the worst."

"Thanks, Miz Sarah, I'll do that tomorrow. Now, let's enjoy this wonderful Christmas breakfast."

"No, John," Mary said. "Please go see Doctor Bigelow right after breakfast . . . not tomorrow."

* * *

Doctor Bigelow kept grunting, "hum . . . hum," as he thumped, and then listened to my chest with his cold, steel stethoscope. Occasionally, he would glance at me and ask questions. Several of which were, "Have you been having night sweats? Lost weight? Had any chills? Fever?"

I honestly replied, "No, sir," to each of his questions. The examination and questioning ended when he pulled a large book from a shelf above his desk. While he was studying, I dressed and waited. He finally closed the book, leaned back in his chair and peered at me, seeming to be pondering the situation. I became quite uncomfortable with his demeanor, and began to fear the worst. I assumed he was trying to break bad news gently. At last, he gestured to a chair beside his desk. "I apologize, John, please sit down. I'm unable to arrive at a diagnosis at this time. My examination fails to reveal any definitive findings that would confirm tubercular phthisis; however, it remains a strong possibility."

"What else could it be?"

"Well, since you've only had one episode of hemoptysis . . . coughing up bloody sputum, the possibilities run from a simple vessel rupture because of extreme retching to vessel erosion within a tuberculous cavity."

"I've assumed my coughing was due to a simple case of catarrh."

"Well, John, that may be. I'm going to prescribe some medicine for you to take. If your cough fails to clear up, bloody sputum returns, or you experience chills, fever or night sweats, I want Doctor Herman Michaels to examine you."

"Doctor Michaels?

"He practices in Richmond and is experienced in the diagnosis and treatment of Tuberculosis."

With a bottle of Doctor Bigelow's medicine in hand, I returned home, hoping there would be no need for a visit to Doctor Michaels in Richmond.

* * *

I prayed for Doctor Bigelow's foul-tasting medicine to contain a supernatural force capable of performing miracles. That came into question as I hurried toward St. John's on Sunday morning, February 2nd. Anxious to be on time for the Feast celebrating Christ's Presentation in the Temple, I rushed along the paving toward America's oldest surviving church. A sudden and overwhelming coughing paroxysm ended my efforts to reach services on time. I leaned against the sturdy trunk of a live oak while trying to rid the offending demon from my lungs. With each coughing spasm, bloody sputum soiled my kerchief. The attack finally ended, leaving me shaken and depleted.

I spent several hours walking along the shore while struggling with reality. My illness was no longer a mystery. The symptoms and signs seemed without question to be indicative of consumption. If so, how long would it take to destroy my lungs and bring about my death — a question I could not answer?

Once again, Sarah Arthur's became my sustaining angel. Thank God, she decided to stay until springtime before returning home. I knew deep within my soul that she lingered because of her concern for my health. That dread caused her to come looking for me after I failed to return for dinner. I was sitting on a park bench near the shore, pondering the disquieting options I was facing when Sarah's voice roused me from my dark thoughts. "What's wrong, John?" she asked, sitting down beside me.

"Doctor Bigelow's concoction isn't working."

She grasped and squeezed my hand. "I'm so sorry . . . another attack?"

"Much worse, and . . . there's more blood."

"Tomorrow, you must go to Richmond and see Doctor Michaels."

"I can't, Sarah. I have classes in the morning."

"Oh, tut — tut, John Pendleton, you must go tomorrow. General Armstrong can teach your students."

Several more minutes passed as we argued about whether an immediate journey to Richmond was necessary. Sarah's wisdom finally prevailed and I agreed to tell Sam Armstrong about my illness, and the need to consult Doctor Michaels.

* * *

The greatest hurdle of my lifetime loomed before me, stark, foreboding and intimidating. The overwhelming emotions wrought by battles and imprisonment did not compare to the devastating hopelessness I was experiencing. Again and again, I muttered, "Why, me . . . why, me?" as I climbed a creaking stairway to Doctor Michael's office.

A frumpish, middle-aged woman greeted me as I closed the office door behind me. "Good morning, sir. Is the doctor expecting you?"

"Yes, ma'am, I'm John Pendleton."

She ran a finger down a ledger listing until reaching the intended entry. "Yes, Doctor will see you now. Come with me."

She escorted me down a dark hallway whose walls were decorated with portraits of austere appearing gentlemen. I paused to study an especially interesting man who was apparently pondering a patient lying beneath a white sheet. "That's Doctor René Laennec," she said, opening a door bearing a Herman Michaels, M.D. inscription on a brass nameplate. "He was Doctor Michaels' mentor." Her claim meant nothing to me. My only concerns were the demons within my lungs and how to rid myself of them.

Doctor Michaels, a white-headed man who appeared to be nearing seventy years of age, hobbled into the room with the aid of an ornately carved walking stick. His reticent countenance conveyed nothing but gloom. I suppose his experiences with patients who were suffering from debilitating afflictions had shaped his demeanor. "Well, now, Mister Pendleton, what brings you to Richmond . . . and my services?"

"Did you receive a letter about my illness from Doctor Bigelow?"

"Yes. He wasn't able to make a definitive diagnosis. Tell me about your illness."

I explained how my coughing paroxysms with bloody sputum developed during the past several weeks. He inquired about night sweats, fever, and loss of weight. My denial to these questions caused his brow to furrow as he thumped my chest, and then searched for mysterious noises with the cold steel bell of his stethoscope.

At last, he pulled his stethoscope from his ears, told me to redress, and left the room. Several minutes passed before he returned. "Now, John," he said, patting my shoulder. "I must tell you that you have consumptive lung disease; however, it is in an early stage."

"You are certain?"

"Yes."

"Can it be cured?"

"Only arrested . . . a high and dry climate is your only hope."

His succinct response caused me to pause, to ponder my future, and consider the man who was predicting my future. "Just who is Doctor René Laennec?"

"I spent a year studying diseases of the lungs with him. He invented the first stethoscope and taught me all of the diagnostic signs of Tuberculosis."

"Very impressive," I said, standing up to leave.

He stood up and grasped my hand, but hesitated. "I'm sorry, John," he then said, unable to look at me. "There is no question. You have consumptive lung disease. Go, west . . . without delay. Good bye and God go with you."

* * *

I experienced crushing sadness during my return trip to Hampton. Sarah was waiting for me as I struggled up the stairway to Mary Arthur's porch. "You look tired, John. Let's sit in the swing and talk."

"Thanks, Sarah, for being here. It's been difficult."

"You want to tell me about it?" she said, massaging my back like Mother used to do when I was sick or suffering difficult times.

"I suppose so, but there's not much to tell."

"What was your impression of Doctor Michaels?"

"He's a bit old and crotchety, but seemed to be expert in lung diseases."

"Did he diagnose your illness?"

"Early stage tuberculosis. No cure, but advised going west to high and arid country."

"You must let your Penelope know right away."

Sarah's counsel hit me cold as a wintry wind. I sat dumbfounded, unable to speak while pondering the dread of telling Penny. What could I say — I have an incurable illness — got to go to the mountains, but even that won't assure any benefit? At last, with emotions under control, I said, "Yes, I must tell Penny. I don't know how, but I have to do it."

"Go to her, right away, John. She will want to be with you when you give her the news."

I embraced Sarah and wept. She whispered consoling words while patting my back. I composed myself enough after several minutes to speak, "I will go see General Armstrong in the morning . . . and, I must tell Thomas . . . I owe that to him . . . then I'll leave for Philadelphia."

CHAPTER TWENTY THREE

I arrived at Woman's Hospital of Philadelphia at 9 a.m. where a medical student escorted me to a conference room. "Miss Gresham will be with you soon," she said and closed the door behind me. I sat down, pondering just what I was going to say whenever Penny came through the doorway. Minutes crept by slow as a meandering terrapin while I stared at restless fingers. Self-pity consumed my thoughts until her voice awakened me. "Johnnie! What brings you to Philadelphia?"

I stood up fast as a wooden leg allowed and welcomed her into a warm embrace. "You look tired," she said, caressing my bearded cheek. "Is anything wrong?"

"There is something."

"Are you ill?"

"Do you know of Doctor Michaels in Richmond?"

"Yes, he specializes in pulmonary diseases . . . mainly tuberculosis. You've been examined by him?"

"Yes . . . last week."

"Why?"

"Coughing up blood tinged sputum."

Tears welled in her eyes and trickled down her cheeks. My heart ached as she pressed her forehead against my chest and sobbed. "I'm so sorry, Penny," I said, over and over, wishing I could comfort her in a better way.

The experience depleted both of us. We sat together holding hands and waiting for something to pull us from a chasm of despair into which we had fallen. A moment of relief came as Penny squeezed my hand. "It's going to be all right, Johnnie. We'll overcome this."

I nodded and winked at her. "Of course . . . Doctor Michaels said it can be arrested by a high, arid climate."

"Where will you go?"

"I hope to start a school in Nevada for miner's children. General Armstrong has a close friend, Mr. George Stone, in Virginia City. He is writing a letter of introduction for me."

"Oh, dear," Penny said, frowning. "Nevada is a long way from here. I need to go with you . . . but."

"You must finish your training . . . then I'll send for you."

"I need to go with you, now."

I gripped both of her hands. "You must complete your studies."

Silence engulfed us again as we searched for a solution. I desired Penelope's presence more than anything, but she had worked too long to give up a career in medicine. Somehow, I needed to convince her of that fact. I didn't know what she was thinking, but I had to dissuade her of making a rash decision.

Penny dabbed her eyes and smiled at me. "You can't go to Nevada alone. You just can't."

"I won't be alone. Thomas, one of my students, insists upon going with me. He's a fine young man and will be of great help starting a school. Now, see, I'll be in good hands."

Penny's gloom changed to joy. "Oh, Johnnie, that is wonderful. Tell Thomas I will forever be grateful. No, I'll tell him myself when I come to Nevada."

* * *

Thomas and I were rump-sprung, frazzled and in need of a hot bath by the time we reached Virginia City, Nevada. Our westward trek was coming to an end, but had I made the right decision? Could I overcome the malady consuming my lungs and also build a school in this place? The answers were in the hands of the Almighty.

The journey had taken its toll on my general health. We were jarred and pummeled as the stagecoach's steel-rimmed wheels dropped into potholes and bounced across rock-strewn washes populating western stage roads. For more grueling hours than I wish to recall, we traveled across sage-covered high plains traversed by windswept mesas inhabited with scrub junipers that were bent and distorted by prevailing winds. Stifling acrid dust churned by hooves and wheels rolled into the coach. It permeated our clothing, and scorched my lungs which sent me into miserable coughing fits. The only things making the journey worthwhile were panoramic vistas of snowcapped mountains, bounding herds of deer, antelope, and bald eagles circling high above the arid terrain.

Virginia City was a surprise. As our stage approached the station, we were greeted by clanking piano keys, boisterous laughter and profane expletives emanating from saloons spanning both sides of the street. The main street was barely wide enough for our three-teamed stage to pass through unobstructed. Obnoxious odors from roadside garbage barrels mingling with palatable kitchen aromas wafting from neighborhood eateries were an unappetizing combination.

Thomas gripped my arm as he pointed toward a buxom individual attired in a fringed leather jacket cinched at the waist by a cartridge belt and holstered revolver. A weathered cavalryman's hat, and striped britches tucked inside high mule-eared boots barely disguised her perceptible feminine physique. "Prof John, I know that woman."

"Are you sure that's a woman? Looks like a man."

"She's sure enough a woman," he said and then called, "Hey, Big Belle, It's me, Thomas."

"Well, I'll be damned," she cried, waving a red bandanna. "Is that you, young Thomas?"

"Yes'm, this be me," he yelled, jumped from the coach and hurried to greet Big Belle.

When the stage stopped in front of the International Hotel, I was greeted by a swarthy gentlemen attired in a black frock coat. He tipped his narrow-brimmed Stetson and handed me a *Territorial Enterprise* newspaper. "Welcome to the best hotel west of St. Louis," he said, smiling like a Yankee carpetbagger. "I trust you need help with your luggage?"

I assured him I did since we packed all of our belongings in two passenger trunks. He pointed at a grubby fellow loitering on a bench in front of the hotel. "Herby'll take care of your trunks, sir."

While Herby was loading the trunks onto a dolly, Thomas and his full-bosomed friend walked into the hotel lobby. She was handsome in spite of her contrived masculine appearance. I was reminded of a woman serving in Pettigrew's Brigade who passed herself off as a man in order to be with her husband. After he was killed at Chancellorsville, she deserted since the reason for her masquerade had ended. *Why, otherwise, would any woman want to hide her true identity by dressing like a man?*

"Prof John," Thomas said as we met. "This be my friend, Big Belle."

Ashes fell from a cigar jutting from the corner of Big Belle's mouth as she spoke. "I'm Annabelle," she said, gripping my hand. "Most folks call me Big Belle." I glanced at Thomas as she tweaked his cheek. "Now, Thomas and I go way back." Without hesitating, she continued, "He says you're goin' t'start a boardin' school for miners' kids."

"Yes, ma'am, ah, " I stammered, "that is our intention."

"You're wastin' your time, John. Ain't many kids in Virginia City. We got drunks, miners and whores, but only a smidgen of wives. That's why there ain't many kids."

I was taken aback by her crude remarks, but soon recovered enough to ask, "Is there someplace we can have a cup of coffee and get better acquainted?"

She nodded and gestured toward a building across the street. "The Delta Saloon's a good place to sit and palaver. Don't know about coffee, but they have good booze . . . can't say that for most o' the saloons in Virginia City."

My education into how the world turns in a western boomtown began when we reached the Delta Saloon doorway. I asked Big Belle to explain why the entry doors were hinged so they opened in both directions. She replied, "Folks going in are in a hurry and them that's leavin' ain't sober enough to manage a doorknob." She further explained the practicality of having the swinging doors only shoulder high — it kept folks from slamming the door into those who might be coming as well as drunks who were leaving. She continued to enlighten me about the workings of a western saloon as we walked among faro, poker, craps tables and roulette wheels toward a barroom table. As I slid back a chair and waited for Big Belle to sit in it, she peered at me as if I were in need of further education. "I can handle a chair without any help," she said and gestured for me to use it instead. She pulled up another chair and sat down while continuing to enlighten me. "Married and single ladies don't frequent saloons . . . just whores, barmaids and a female stage driver like me. You'll soon learn you're in a different place out here where most folks live by their own law backed up with guns and knives. I can count every legitimate lady and gentleman in Virginia City on one hand. You left civilization when you crossed the Mississippi. That's why folks out here wear a Colt." She then patted her gun. "There ain't much government. Churches are far between and mostly used for buryin'."

A barmaid, whose bodice exposed ample skin, sauntered up to our table and tapped me on the arm. "Well, now, handsome stranger," she breathily uttered like a Charleston prostitute. "What are you folks goin'ta have?"

Before I could answer, Big Belle proclaimed, "Gertie, bring a jug of my whiskey and three glasses."

"Make it just two," I said, holding up two fingers. "I'll have a cup of coffee."

Gertie frowned, nodded and set her wiles upon poor Thomas. "Hey, handsome, you appear t'be new in this armpit of the west?"

"Watch it, Gertie," Big Belle scolded. "You're speakin' to my good friend."

"Well, pardon me," Gertie quipped. "Does your friend drink whiskey . . . or would he rather have a sarsaparilla?"

Big Belle responded by standing up to face Gertie. "The order was for whiskey and three . . . er, ah two glasses and a cup o' coffee. Any questions?"

At first, Thomas appeared too shocked to respond, but soon gathered himself. He stood up and offered Gertie his hand. "I'm pleased to make your acquaintance, Gertie. You can call me Thomas."

"Sure, Thomas," she said, winked and slapped his palm. "I'll bring your order right away."

Thomas plopped down in his chair, appearing to be overwhelmed by his encounter with Gertie. "Don't pay any attention to her," Big Belle said, leaning back in her chair. "She's a two-bit whore . . . keep your coins in your pocket."

Gertie slid a cup of coffee, two glasses and a jug of Jack Daniels onto the table. She squeezed Thomas's shoulder, tipped his cap aside and began to muss his hair. "Anything else, Thomas, just whistle."

Big Belle laughed while filling two glasses with booze. "May we always sleep 'neath a rain-tight roof, and eat high on the hog ev'ry day o' the year," she said, lifting her glass.

As my cup and two glasses clinked together, I pondered the event prompting my decision to come west for a cure. The day Doctor Michaels placed his stethoscope against my chest, the expression on his face was unmistakable. Tuberculosis had achieved a serious foothold within me. His advice was succinct and unequivocal. Seek a high, arid climate or you won't live another year.

My quest for healing brought me to a boomtown, which now seemed to be the most unlikely place on earth for pursuing my commitment. *Why here ?* I thought, sipping coffee from my cup.

Confusion and perhaps a bit of regret shut my ears to what was going on around me. Big Belle continued to utter a steady stream of advice to Thomas while he remained quiet. My thoughts were centered on where Thomas and I might find reasonable lodging. My coughing episodes were too disquieting for us to occupy a single room — and I needed open windows with plenty of ventilation. "Do you know where Thomas and I can get room and board," I said to Big Belle, interrupting her discourse of advice.

"Sure, I get room and board at Ma Ingram's. It's clean and she's the best cook in Virginia City."

"Where is her place?"

"Next door to the *Territorial Enterprise* . . . well, I gotta go," she said, slapped me on the shoulder and slid back her chair. "I'm drivin the 2:15 to Carson City."

I marveled at the aura surrounding Big Belle as she headed toward the swinging front doors. Every man stepped aside as she walked through the crowd of miners who were busy plying their luck at various games of chance. "That's my friend," Thomas said, pouring more of Big Belle's whiskey into his empty glass.

As I peered at Thomas, his face exuded an expression of pride. Excessive curiosity prompted me to seek an answer to his relationship with Big Belle. "Just who is Big Belle?"

"Oh, Prof John, Big Belle is Mars Waite's daughter."

"His daughter?"

"That right."

"Then, you're her brother?"

Thomas pondered his glass as I gazed at him. "I don't know," he said, "but she is the best friend I ever had. And, don't you worry, Prof John. Big Belle'll help us start our school."

* * *

The first thing I did after obtaining lodging for Thomas and myself at Ma Ingram's boarding house was to visit George Stone, President of Virginia City Bank. If I was going to have any chance for starting a school, I needed a letter of credit. Sam Armstrong assured me that Stone could provide whatever was needed, but I wasn't prepared for my first meeting with him. As he peered through reading spectacles at Armstrong's letter, I sensed a baleful aura emanating from him. Ordinarily, I paid little attention to such feelings, but this spirit seemed most provocative. All I had to my credit was a letter from a former Yankee general who was vouching for my character. Would that be enough to persuade a hardnosed banker to grant me a blank check to finance a school? Big Belle claimed there were not enough children in Virginia City to warrant such an adventure. Would George Stone agree?

"Well, Mister Pendleton, it's been a spell since I last heard from General Armstrong," Stone said, laying aside my letter. "How is Sam?"

"Quite well, sir."

"I guess you know that we served together during the war? How about you?"

"No, he never mentioned that, sir. I was in General Pettigrew's Division."

Steely blue eyes peered at me. "You were a Reb?"

"Yes, sir."

"At Gettysburg?"

"Yes, sir . . . that's where I lost my right leg . . . and my best friend."

Stone nodded, removed his spectacles, and retrieved a bottle of whiskey from his desk drawer. "That was a bad day for us all," he said, pulling the cork. "Shall we toast the end of that battle?"

I sensed a new spirit emanating from him as our glasses clanked together. "Here's to all who fought, sacrificed and died during that terrible fight."

"Hear. Hear," I agreed, hoping our encounter at Gettysburg had become a catalyst for building a new friendship—and funding the school.

My hope was dashed after Stone sat down, replaced his spectacles, and studied Sam Armstrong's letter again. He finally laid it aside and toyed with his graying beard. "If you can get the Virginia City miners' union to vouch for your proposal, I will consider granting assistance . . . but they will have to come up with some guarantees."

"Who should I contact?"

"Harry DeQueen, Gold Hill union's chairman, and Dub Blakemore. He's president of the Virginia City union, but he also deals poker at the Boston Saloon."

"Would that be a good place to catch him?"

"Do you play poker?"

"Not much . . . some . . . during the war."

Stone counted out ten double-eagles from a drawer. "Meet me at the Boston Saloon around eight this evening," he said, handing them to me. "I'll be sitting at Dub's table. The rest is up to you."

"What if I lose your stake," I said, slipping the coins into my pocket.

"I get half of your winnings. You lose . . . you owe me. Be there at eight."

* * *

The Boston Saloon's reputation of being an establishment devoted to lust and avarice became obvious as I walked through its darkened doorway. A buxom barmaid greeted me with a sensual smile. "Hi, I'm Lola. What's your name, handsome?"

"John," I stammered, a bit embarrassed by her greeting.

"Welcome, John, to the best saloon in Virginia City," she said, slipping her hand around the crook of my elbow. She then escorted me into a beehive of activity — clanking glasses, clattering roulette wheels and squealing barmaids. A small alcove at the end of the gambling section was being used as a stage. Meagerly clad women flaunted bare flesh while tunes were fingered by a gaunt fellow on a black and gold upright piano. I stopped and stood awestruck by this literal den of iniquity. Lola squeezed my arm and breathily asked, "What'll it be, Johnnie, poker booze, me or all three?"

"I'm meeting Mister Stone."

"That'll be Dub's table," Lola said, ushering me toward a dimly lit alcove.

Pungent cigar smoke billowed from the shadows as George Stone intoned, "Pull up a chair, John. Meet dealer Dub Blakemore and my friend, Harry DeQueen."

A chorus of "Howdy, John," greeted me as I sat down and shook hands all around. Dub Blakemore flashed a toothy grin while peeling the wrapper from a new deck of cards. "Welcome, John, my game is fair and the rules are simple. All bets are hard currency . . . no paper. All antes are on the table before I deal. Y'got any questions?"

"No, sir."

"You playin' gold, silver or both?"

"Gold," I said, stacking my cache of double-eagles on the table.

He began shuffling cards. "Okay, the game's five-card stud with a two dollar ante, and Lola'll bring change when y'need it."

I haven't seen, before or since anyone shuffle a deck of cards with more speed and dexterity than Dub Blakemore. While Dubs hands were moving quicker than it was possible to follow, he spoke between drags on his cigar. "George tells me you're planning on startin' a school here for miners' kids?"

"Yes, sir, that is my intention."

"Y'spoke to anyone besides George."

"No, I just arrived two days ago."

"John came by the bank this morning," George said, pulling two cigars from his vest pocket and handed them to Harry and me. "I told him he needed to talk to you and Harry about his plans."

"I don't talk business durin' a game," Harry said, striking a match. "Any objections, Dub . . . George . . . John?"

We all voiced agreement as Harry lit his, and then my cigar.

I pondered my situation as each card slid in front of me. It didn't look good. Asking for support following a poker game when the majority will probably be losers held little promise.

During the ensuing hands, wagers, raises, calls and folds, my mind was occupied with how to open a conversation regarding my quest for funds. The result was a persistent pattern—loss after loss, and increasing apprehension.

Between asking Lola to bring more change and watching my cache dwindle away, I displayed absolute ignorance of how to win at poker. I habitually called when I should have folded. It only took a couple of hours to almost exhaust my stake. I was all but broke, and had a two-hundred dollar gambling debt.

At last, Harry DeQueen unknowingly came to my aid. "Y'aren't goin' into the mines with that wooden leg are y'John," he said, chewing on his smoldering stogie.

"No, I'm a schoolmaster and my only interest is to build a school."

"Well, I hope you are better at that than y'are at poker."

I chuckled. "So, do I, Harry."

Out of any more double-eagles, I folded on the last raise by George. "That's it," I said and slid back my chair.

"Not quite," Dub said as George raked in the pot. "You need to convince Harry or me about our needing a school. Virginia City, Gold Hill, and Silver City are booming. We got churches. But don't see a need for a school anytime soon. What do you say, Harry?"

Harry's brow furrowed as he chewed his cigar. "Well, I reckon what you say is a fact. If we did, where would we build it?"

Dub's deep-set eyes peered at me. "What's your plan, John?"

I handed copies of my plan to each one. "It needs to be a boarding school, and I believe Virginia City is the place to build it . . . but the unions must agree to support the school before we can proceed."

"Okay," Dub said. "We'll consider your plan."

"Until you hear from us, stay away from poker," Harry chided, "It ain't your game."

CHAPTER TWENTY FOUR

I awaited word from Dub and Harry for over three weeks. Each passing day without any response seemed to be a harbinger of their rejection. I was becoming annoyed with George Stone who kept admonishing me to remain patient. The few dollars I'd earned at Hampton were being depleted with no prospect of any future income. Thomas insisted on going to work as a guard for the Comstock Mining Company, which would barely provide enough to pay Ma Ingram for our room and board. Big Belle's attempts to sway Dub and Harry fell on fallow ground. Nothing was going well.

Before departing Philadelphia I promised Penelope to abide by Dr. Michael's advice — get plenty of high country fresh air. To my good fortune, Ma Ingram rented me her airy screened-in sunroom, fulfilling my need for a healing environment. Also, her front porch provided an open-air place for me to spend reading and getting acquainted with passersby. Because of my healing endeavors, I was getting better in body and spirit as each week passed. Unlike severe ravages of smallpox, a much slower recovery was being taken by my affliction. I was experiencing fewer coughing attacks and a progressive gain of weight. However, like my venture at Dub's poker table, starting a school wasn't paying off.

The fear of failure haunted me. Time seemed to be running out like remaining sands in an hourglass. Once again, a desire to find Hank Johnson resumed. I became preoccupied with discovering his fate; consequently, I sent a telegram to Todd asking him how I might contact Shawn O'Hara.

Todd's reply was prompt. Shawn was still in Washington, D.C., working for the War Department. I straight away sent a wire asking whether he had any up to date information regarding Hank. His reply soon came. He hadn't been able to determine Hank's success or failure in swimming from Lookout Point Prison across the Potomac River to the Virginia shore.

I was contemplating Shawn's telegram when Big Belle tapped me on the shoulder. "Bad news?"

"Just disappointing," I said, stuffing the telegram into my pocket.

"Well, what I got to tell ya ain't going to help."

Since Thomas told me Big Belle was going to the union meeting the previous evening, I feared her news would be bad. "They turned down the school?"

"No, Harry wanted to postpone it . . . he didn't believe they could back up the building costs."

Out of frustration I slammed the chair arm with my fist. "Why can't they see it's needed?"

My tirade was interrupted as Dub reined his horse up to Ma Ingram's hitching rail. Stepping down from his stirrup, he called, "Howdy, John . . . Big Belle. We need to palaver."

As Dub sauntered along the pathway, I whispered to Big Belle, "He's probably going to deal me another losing hand."

Big Belle champed her cigar and rolled her eyes. "Yeah, it may be time to fold 'em. He'll connive ya, if y'let him."

"Big Belle," Dub said, climbing the porch steps. "Did y'tell John 'bout the meetin'?"

"Yeah, I did."

"John, have y'thought about opening the school in a church?"

"A church? No, can't say I have."

"It could be a startup. Once going, we would fair better in getting financing."

Big Belle let out a guffaw, spat and wiped tobacco stained spittle from her chin. "How are you goin' t'get them Presbyterians t'attend school in a Catholic or Episcopal church . . . nor the other way 'round neither? Ain't likely t'happen."

"Aw, Big Belle," Dub scolded, "We don't know that for a fact."

Big Belle rolled her eyes again. "If you believe that, your shadow ain't ever darkened the door of a church house," she said, sitting down on the porch railing.

"Well, what do you think, John?" Dub said.

"The problems between Protestants and Catholics are considerable, but it might work if their clergymen agreed to support the school."

"Well, Guys," Big Belle, said and spat. "I hate t'rain on your parade, but that'll be like gettin' them t'back a school upstairs over the Bloody Bucket Saloon."

"Ha, yeah, they could use the Madam's parlor during the day and she could show off her soiled doves at night," Dub said, gloating over his supposed cleverness.

"Tain't funny," Big Belle chided. "What do y'plan on doin', John?"

The prospects for getting a school started seemed to be dissolving like foam on warm beer. However, I was determined to try one more time. There were only three churches in Virginia City — St. Mary's Catholic, St. Mark's Episcopal, and First Presbyterian. "I'll talk to the rector of St. Mark's?"

"That would be Reverend Locke," Dub said. "You'll find him at the rectory."

* * *

I rapped several times on the front door of St. Mark's rectory the day after Big Belle, Dub and I met.   As the door eased open a short, silver haired lady greeted me. "Good afternoon, sir. May I be of assistance?"

"Is the Reverend Locke at home?"

"Yes, he is," she said, stepping aside while gesturing toward an overstuffed chair facing a rock-faced fireplace. "Please be seated while I summon Reverend Locke."

I settled myself into the leather-bound chair and waited. The silence was punctuated by a slow-ticking grandfather clock standing next to the fireplace. Its subdued rhythmic cadence calmed the uneasiness of my visit. While waiting I pondered whether to reveal I was a seminary graduate. If so, would it help my cause? My pondering was interrupted by a resonating bass voice, "Good morning, I'm Charles Locke."

"I'm John Pendleton," I said, starting to stand.

"Please . . . don't get up," he said, eying my prosthetic leg.

He possessed a restless nature which was shown all during our meeting. Between his trips to stoke or add more wood to the fireplace, I managed to reveal the reason for my visit. He listened without commenting most of the time, except interspersing at odd times with, "I see," and, "interesting." When beginning to explain our need to use St. Mark's for classes, the grandfather clock began its chiming ritual. Several clanging notes ascended and descended the scale before pealing the arrival of four o'clock. "Ah," he intoned, "it's tea time. I trust you take milk and sugar with your tea?"

"Just a dash of each," I said, reluctantly accepting the unwelcome intermission.

"Wonderful, I'll have my housekeeper fetch it for us," he said and left the room.

I sat ill at ease staring at that damnable clock while waiting for Reverend Locke and his housekeeper to serve four o'clock tea and crumpets. It was a custom for which I never cared or observed — except at Eton College and in Mother's parlor before the war.

I was so disgruntled by my loathing for four o'clock tea, a chiming clock and an edgy clergyman that abandoning my mission became an attractive alternative. However, by the time tea was served I was able to continue with my plea. The calming influences of sweet tea worked wonders with Charles Locke. He became tranquil and inquired about my school building plans. At last, feeling the time to be right, I made my request. "Would you consider my holding classes in St. Mark's until we can obtain a permanent building?"

He set his cup on the tray, glanced away, and then at me. "Only the bishop can make that decision."

"Will you ask him?"

"We don't have a bishop. He was transferred to Indiana."

"No bishop? Who's in charge?"

"California's Bishop Kip is provisional."

Renewed frustration seized me. "Well," I blurted. "Will you ask him?"

"I'm sorry. I can't until the Nevada Conference appoints our new bishop."

"When will they meet?"

"In six months."

* * *

Three weeks later I was scanning a copy of the *Territorial Enterprise* when a lone rider tied his horse to Ma Ingram's hitching rail. He was an imposing hulk of a man attired all in black — black felt hat, leather vest, pants and boots. The rowels on his spurs jingled with each determined step as he strode along the pathway. His demeanor was worrisome, foreboding. "Howdy, I'm Sheriff Hodge," he said, pulling aside his vest exposing a bright silver star. "I'm looking for John Pendleton?"

I laid the newspaper down and stood up to greet him. "That would be me."

"Do y'know a negro man who goes by Thomas . . . no last name?"

"Yes, sir, he's my assistant. Why do you ask?"

"We've got him in the Carson City lockup. It seems he decided to take up another trade."

"Doing what?"

"Thievery."

"Thievery?" I said, sitting down. "I can't believe that, Sheriff Hodge."

"I reckon it's so. We caught him and Big Belle stashing Comstock's gold and silver in an abandoned shack between Silver City and Carson City."

"Red Handed?"

"In the act. They weren't aware of me and my deputy following out of sight behind the stage."

"You don't think I had anything to do with such a scheme . . . do you?"

"Well, did you?"

"No, sir, I'm unaware of any plan to steal gold."

"Well, I'll be checking out what you're sayin'. Big Belle spilled the whole story. She claims she talked Thomas into helping her deliver gold and silver ingots to the new mint in Carson City. She got the stage company to assign him as her guard. Her plan was to hide all of the ingots in an abandoned mine shack. Upon their arrival at the mint, she would claim the stage was attacked and robbed by a half-dozen masked bandits. Thomas's role was to verify the incident and claim he was unable to resist, being overpowered and outgunned."

"When can I see Thomas and Big Belle?"

Sheriff Hodge's eyes grew somber. "I reckon tomorrow, but be certain that following a short trial everybody involved will be swinging pickaxes in the prison quarry."

As Sheriff Hodge mounted and reined away from the hitching rail, I cringed at the thought of Thomas and Big Belle resorting to thievery — probably believing it was for my benefit. Hodge's visit wasn't made simply to tell me they had been caught trying to steal a gold shipment. There was little doubt that he thought I was a partner in their conspiracy. Many folks, including Reverend Locke, Dub, Harry and George Stone were aware of Big Belle's and Thomas's commitments to raise financing for the school. If Hodge hadn't queried them already, he soon would.

My musings ended as Ma Ingram called, "Supper time. Come and get it."

* * *

After a sleepless night I climbed aboard the stage bound for Carson City at eight o'clock the next morning. An hour later the stage pulled up in front of the Great Basin Hotel on the corner of Carson and Musser streets. It had recently been purchased from Abram Curry by Ormsby County to house the courthouse and jail. As I climbed steps to the front porch, Sheriff Hodge greeted me. "Good morning, Mister Pendleton, I've been expecting you."

"I've come to see Big Belle and Thomas."

"Sure," he said, gesturing for me to enter. "First, I'd like to visit with you in my office."

There was no other alternative. Hodge was in charge. I followed him down a hallway toward his office where he offered me a chair in front of his cluttered oak desk. "What can I do for you?" I asked.

"Just need to clear up some things."

"Such as?"

"For one thing, how are Big Belle and Thomas connected."

"I believe they are siblings?'

He sneered at my response, tossed his hat onto a hat tree and sat down behind his desk. "She's white . . . he's black. How do y'account for that?"

After explaining the background for my opinion, I said, "It really doesn't matter. They are very close."

He nodded without saying anything for several minutes, and then glared at me. "Where were you night before last?"

His abrupt inquiry caused me to hesitate before answering, "Ma Ingram's."

"I've learned you've been trying to get money from the unions . . . and the bank. Is that right?"

"Financial backing," I replied. "I'm trying to start a school for miners' children."

"Yeah, that's what I've been told. Y'ain't succeeded have ya?"

"Why don't you come to the point by asking whether I am a conspirator with Big Belle and Thomas?'

"Well . . . are you?"

"It's still, no, Sheriff Hodge."

"Well, Mister Pendleton, you seem like an honest man. For now, I'm prepared to accept your denial. Y'aren't armed are ya?"

"No, I don't own any guns or knives."

"My deputy'll take you to see Big Belle and Thomas after he verifies you're unarmed."

Thomas and Big Belle were caged in separate but adjoining cells. Hodge's deputy rapped on the bars of Thomas's cell door and gestured for me to wait. "Hey, Darky . . . y'got a visitor."

"Who is it?"

"Prof John," I said.

"Hold up there," the deputy said, pulling me aside. "Before I unlock the door, y'got t'give me any weapons y'are carryin'."

I pulled off my jacket and handed it to him. "You can see I'm unarmed."

He nodded, unlocked the cell and gestured for me to enter. "Yell when you're ready t'leave," he said, locking the door behind me.

The cell was saturated with despair and gloom, being dimly lit with scant sunlight entering through a single window secured by heavy wrought iron bars. Since Sheriff Hodge showed up on Ma Ingram's porch, I had wrestled with this moment. How was I going to intervene in what appeared to be a hopeless situation?

"Hey, Big Belle, told ya Prof John'd come," Thomas said, grasping my hand. "Ain't got any chairs but we can sit on my bunk and talk."

Pictures of my Fort Delaware Prison's louse infested blanket flooded my mind. "Are there any vermin hiding in your bedding?"

Big Belle poked her face between the cell bars. "Better not sit 'cause this jail is crawlin' with all sorts o'bugs."

Determined to stay vermin free, I opted to remain standing. "Okay, let's talk. First, both of you need a lawyer. Second, I'd like to know why you stole Comstock's gold and silver shipment."

"Don't blame Thomas. It was my idea. You weren't goin' t'get any backing from the unions, the bank, or anywhere else. It's that simple."

"You thought I'd accept stolen money?"

"No, I inherited some money from Daddy's estate; however, we needed a lot more. The opportunity came along. I convinced Thomas to go along as my guard. That's all he's guilty of."

"And if successful you would claim it all was your inheritance?"

"Yes."

Raw and overwhelming anger surged through me. "Why, Thomas," I said, punching a finger against his chest. "I can't believe you agreed to such a stupid scheme? Why didn't you realize that I would also be accused if you were apprehended?"

"I'm sorry, Prof John."

Out of frustration, I slammed my fist against the cell bars. "Sorry! Sorry doesn't help one iota."

"Don't blame Thomas," Big Belle said. "I had no idea the sheriff would be trailing us. I hadn't said anything about stealin' the gold to anyone. I ain't that stupid."

"It weren't me," Thomas said, wringing his hands.

Big Belle's eyes bore into mine. "I'm thinkin' we've been set up. I bet the sheriff figured he would get a reward or somethin' for claiming he caught us stealin' the gold. "

"You may be right, but you played right into his game when you stopped at the abandoned shack."

"Humph," Big Belle said, turned away and lay down on her bunk. "We ain't got a chance against him."

Thomas grasped my hand and shook it while starring at the floor. "I be real sorry, Prof John. I did wrong."

"There's no need to apologize for a crime you didn't commit. All three of us need a lawyer," I said, and then yelled, "Okay, Deputy, I'm ready to leave."

CHAPTER TWENTY FIVE

Phineas J. Benjamin, Attorney at Law, listened as I explained my need for legal counsel. His physique reminded me of a bloated bullfrog, one like those inhabiting marshland along the Ashley and Cooper rivers in South Carolina. His ruddy features and baggy, bloodshot eyes scrutinized me like a mule trader considering a long eared purchase. While listening to my story he pulled an ornate snuff box from his vest pocket, flipped it open, placed a pinch atop his wrist and sniffed it, first into one nostril, and then the other. "Well, Mister Pendleton," he said, his voice low and rasping. "In my opinion you are not in jeopardy. However, I have no doubt about your friends being charged. Under the circumstances, a plea bargain would be the best course of action. If you so desire, I'll talk to the county attorney."

"Don't you want to talk to Thomas and Big Belle before meeting with the county attorney?"

Benjamin appeared puzzled by my question. His swivel chair squeaked as he leaned back and pulled a pouch of chewing tobacco from his pocket. After stuffing a sizable wad into his mouth, he offered a helping of it to me.

"No thanks, I don't use it."

"Too bad," he said, jamming it back into his pocket. "I find it calms the nerves and helps me think. Now, to answer your question, I will certainly visit with your friends before agreeing to any compromises, but this case doesn't appear to be winnable. They were apprehended in the act of stashing Comstock gold and silver ingots in a vacant shack by Sheriff Hodge and his deputy. I can't imagine any circumstances that could bring about a successful defense. Even though the shipment was recovered, Comstock will want to drive home a conviction so as to discourage any more robbery attempts."

I didn't want to believe Benjamin was right. A logical defense appeared unlikely at best. Why did Big Belle decide to commit robbery? She may have wanted to help Thomas by securing money for me. But, why would she take such a risk? Even if they hadn't been caught, a stage robbery involving such a large amount of gold and silver would be tirelessly investigated by Comstock officials. I believed Thomas's involvement resulted from his loyalty to Big Belle. I'm sure he knew she is his sister, and he would be easily swayed by her. The situation appeared bleak, but Thomas, a freed slave, deserved more than a plea bargain. "Mister Benjamin, I grew up on a slave owner plantation, and spent four years fighting to preserve slavery. I was convicted of the evilness of slavery, and dedicated myself to educating former slaves, but consumption altered my commitment. Now, I am faced with rescuing a former slave, a true friend and companion from being cast into prison. I owe him more than a reduced prison sentence."

Benjamin snorted like a wary bull. "That may be the most you can do for him."

"I can't settle for that. We have to find an effective defense."

"When you come up with one, let me know," Benjamin said, standing up to shake my hand. "In the meantime, there will be a hearing before Judge Simmons. We need to be prepared for a pleading by your friends. And also there's the question of bail."

"Bail? I hadn't thought of that."

"Well, if bail isn't set and met, they'll sit in the pokey until trial. You need to get on this right away, if not sooner."

* * *

"You've gotten yourself into a pretty pickle," George Stone said, reading lawyer Benjamin's case evaluation. "He recommends plea bargaining for both defendants."

"Thomas deserves better."

"Why? He's guilty as sin. You have to know that."

"Big Belle pressured him into helping her."

"Maybe so, but he did agree to participate in the theft. You had better thank your maker you weren't charged as a conspirator."

"Sheriff Hodge has no evidence, because there isn't any of my being involved. What is most important remains the culpability of, Thomas, a recently freed Negro slave. Thomas grew up living his entire life in servile obedience. The only laws he knew were those made and enforced by his master. Everything he had was owned by the person to whom he was enslaved. He does not understand what theft involves. He must not endure more enslavement for participating in what he considers a favor for his sister."

"A question the prosecutor will ask him and Big Belle is whether the gold and silver was being stolen to benefit you."

"That could be their defense," I said, grasping for a faint glimmer of hope. "They weren't stealing to gain themselves. Their motive was pure . . . the establishment of a school for miner's children."

"Stealing from Comstock to help the needy is still against the law."

"Well, you are right, but Thomas deserves leniency."

"It will be up to Judge Simmons. He has a lot of latitude in how this will turn out."

"I hope he's wise as Solomon. Right now, I need to arrange for bail. The hearing is at ten o'clock in the morning."

George picked up a quill, dipped the nib into an inkwell and penned his signature on a bail bond. "The court clerk can enter whatever Judge Simmons decides," he said, handing the document to me.

"I don't know how to thank you. Thomas and I will be eternally indebted to your kind generosity."

"It's the least I can do. Sam Armstrong would have me shot if I didn't help."

I stuffed the bail bond into my pocket and stood up to leave. "What about Big Belle? Thomas will not leave her locked up in the Ormsby County jail."

"You can include her on the bail bond, too. If she skips leaving me holding the bag, you're in deep trouble."

* * *

Phineas J. Benjamin possessed a conniving, determined and creative mind. Six weeks after Thomas and Big Belle walked out of the Ormsby County jail, they and I were sitting in Benjamin's office. Trial was scheduled to begin at 9:00 a.m. the next day. Benjamin was now preparing for the reading of charges, jury selection, and his opening statement. His determination to bargain for lesser charges in exchange for shortened sentences remained on his mind. "It's . . . not too late . . . for bargaining . . . with the prosecution," he said, between puffs on a pungent Havana stogie.

Big Belle patted Thomas on the shoulder and mussed his hair. "Thomas ain't guilty of nothing. I stole the ingots, well, I was going to before Hodge caught me. You can bargain all you want as long as you get my brother out of this mess."

Thomas, Benjamin and I gaped at Big Belle. Her confession was an absolute surprise, but it confirmed her being Thomas's sister. Thomas bowed his head, buried his face into the palms of his hands and began to weep. Big Belle and I knelt beside his chair and tried to comfort him. "I've known you were my brother for a long time," Big

Belle said, massaging his back. "I think you've known it, too."

"Yes, since we was kids, but Massa Waite would've sold me if it got said. Sure didn't want that."

"Nor I," Big Belle said as she wiped tears from her cheeks.

Benjamin slammed his fist on the desk. "Why didn't you tell me this before now? Big Belle, you said you were trying to steal the ingots when Hodge caught you. Under the law, trying is attempting, not committing. Attempted robbery is a whole different charge for me to defend. Dammit, tell me exactly what happened . . . I want the whole story . . . don't leave out anything."

Big Belle sat back in her chair and slid it closer to Thomas. "Y'got another one of them stogies? I could use a smoke right now."

Benjamin pushed a humidor across the desk and flipped open the lid. "Sure, help yourself," he said, tossing her a box of matches.

As smoke rolled out of her nostrils, Big Belle began her story: "Well, there weren't anything turning out about getting any backing for the school. I felt I had to help my brother. He also was like a brother to John, so it came down to being a family thing. I inherited some from my daddy's estate, but not near enough to start a school. If we didn't get some money, all would be lost. Then the stage master asked me whether I would be willing to drive the gold and silver to the new mint in Carson City. I was scared to take that on without some protection. There had been several stage robberies in the past along the road to Carson City. I told the stage master that I'd do it only if a guard rode with me. He agreed and asked if I knew anyone who would be willing to take the risk. Sure do, I told him. Thomas agreed to ride with me. I hadn't decided on stealin' nothing when we left Virginia City. Then when we were passing the old Holder mine shack, the impulse hit me. I stopped the stage and told Thomas what I was going to do. He started to climb down from the stage when I told him to stay there. I didn't need any help. That's when Hodge rode up with his deputy. What y'up to, he yelled, stepping down from his stirrup. Before I could answer, he pulled out his Colt and yelled at Thomas to throw down his shotgun. That's it. You know the rest, I reckon."

"Well, I'll be damned," Benjamin said, clapping his hands. "Why, didn't you tell me this six weeks ago. We wouldn't be sittin' here right now if you had."

"I didn't think it mattered. I figured whatever Sheriff Hodge claimed, that was it. That's the way it was in Alabama before the war."

"Well, not here. That's why we have a court of law so you can be defended from false charges. Leave the rest to me. We'll have to be in court Monday morning, but I guarantee it's going be a lot better than it could have been."

* * *

"Hear, Ye, Hear, Ye," the bailiff called. "The Superior Court of Ormsby County, State of Nevada is now in session. "Draw near all ye who seek justice in this honorable court."

Then as the judge, robed in black, entered, the bailiff called again, "All rise, Judge Herman Simmons presiding." After the judge sat down behind the tall oaken bench, the bailiff said, "Please be seated."

That was the beginning of Monday, October 24th in 18 and 70, a day I shall never forget. I looked around the courtroom. It was quite small, having recently been constructed by remodeling the original dinning room of Abram Curry's house. Benjamin, Big Belle, Thomas and I crowded around a table on the left side of the courtroom. The prosecutor, Attorney Omar White, a skinny, sallow complexioned fellow appearing to be around thirty years of age was seated alone at a small table to our right.

When the judge called for the clerk to read the charges, Benjamin stood up. "Your honor, I, Phineas J. Benjamin, defense attorney of record, request that counsel be permitted to approach the bench."

Judge Simmons appeared quite irritated by Benjamin's request, but nodded and said, "Mister Benjamin and Mister White, you may approach the bench."

Judge Simmons and White were distraught by whatever Benjamin said to them. Their conference went on for quite a few minutes before the judge rapped his gavel. "This court is in recess until ten o'clock. Counsel for the state and defense will meet with me in my chambers."

Thomas, Big Belle and I left the court house and sat on a wrought-iron bench in the yard. We busied our conversation with various topics, mostly about the mysterious aura of court procedures, judges, lawyers and such. I glanced at my watch as Benjamin walked toward us. It was ten minutes until court would reconvene and come to order. Benjamin was jovial and grinning as he sat down. "The charges have been changed. Big Belle will be charged with attempted robbery, and Thomas's charge will be accessory to robbery. Then he slapped my knee and gazed at me. "Now don't get upset, John, but I had to agree to your being charged also as an accessory. Otherwise, White wouldn't go along with reducing the charges against Big Belle and Thomas. Don't worry one iota, because I can successfully defend these charges, and I'm confident all of you will be acquitted."

True to his word, Benjamin performed like he promised. He and White agreed to changing from a trial by jury to a judicial proceeding with Judge Simmons hearing the evidence and rendering his verdicts. The actual procedures required less than a day. White called Sheriff

Hodge and his deputy, Jim Colbert, as witnesses for the prosecution. Benjamin destroyed their claim that Thomas and Big Belle were caught stealing the ingots with brilliant cross examination. Hodge had to confess that no gold or silver ingots were removed from the stage before he made the arrests and took them into custody.

Benjamin didn't call any witnesses and concluded with: "Your honor, theft did not happen since my clients never even moved the shipment from the stage. Wanting to steal something is not a crime. Coveting the gold and silver is all of which Big Belle can be guilty. Thomas performed his duty well as a guard protecting the shipment from theft until ordered to surrender his weapon by Sheriff Hodge. Cross examination of prosecution witnesses has proven he had no prior knowledge of Big Belle's intentions. John Pendleton wasn't involved in any way, and the prosecution hasn't presented any evidence that even remotely suggests otherwise. I, therefore, move for dismissal of all charges against my clients."

"It is so ordered," Judge Simmons said, banging his gavel.

Omar White looked careworn and defeated as he closed his valise and stood up to congratulate Benjamin. "Brilliant cross, Phineas."

"Yes, it was. Next time, do you homework."

"Humph," White said, heading for the door.

* * *

Being strapped for money, paying Benjamin two-hundred dollars for his services was impossible. I wired Todd Martin, hoping he would come to my aid. I had no one else I could turn to for help. I received a letter from him containing a bank draft for three-hundred dollars.

> Dear John,
>
> I am pleased you asked me for help in this time of dire need. I am enclosing a draft

to help with your present expenses. Penelope came home yesterday from Philadelphia. Her studies have concluded and she now is free to join you in Nevada. She and I are very concerned about your health. She plans to leave within the week. In fact, by the time you receive this letter, she will be on her way.

We also have a surprise and some exciting news of which you will be most happy to hear. But, Penelope wants to give it to you when she arrives. In the meantime, may the Lord bless and keep you.

Your cousin,
Todd.

"What a difference the truth can make," I said to Benjamin as I handed him two-hundred dollars. "You saved Thomas, Big Belle and me from a great injustice. For that I am most grateful."

His swivel chair gave a familiar squeak as he leaned back, pulled two cigars from his humidor and handed one to me. "It was fun, time to celebrate."

"Yes, time to celebrate," I said as he lit our cigars.

"There is a possibility we could go after Hodges. I discovered yesterday that he asked Comstock for a reward if we lost our case. He's crooked as a desert rattler."

"He probably is, but he'll get his comeuppance without any help from me. Let him hang himself."

"I agree. Now what do you plan to do?"

"The lady I hope to wed is coming to Virginia City right away."

"Oh, that will be wonderful, but what about Thomas?"

"He has a good job with Comstock. I want him to forget about my plans and concentrate on his future."

"He's a fine young man. He'll do well."

"Yes, he will. He and Big Belle have each other now."

Benjamin stood up and offered me his hand. "Stay out of trouble, my friend, but if you ever need a lawyer again, call on me."

CHAPTER TWENTY SIX

When I awoke the following morning, I sat on the bedside and pondered what all had transpired since Thomas and I arrived in Virginia City. It was that moment when I realized my coughing spells had ceased. I looked into the mirror above my washstand. The fellow looking back at me didn't look like a poor soul dying from consumption. I raised my hands, jubilant for what appeared to be signs of my affliction being arrested. "Hallelujah," I yelled.

"John!" Ma Ingram shouted in return. "Are you all right?"

"No, I'm better than all right."

"That's good. Breakfast's ready."

Like Aunt Gussie, when she said a meal was ready, I needed to get to the table pronto. So, I strapped on my prosthesis, dressed, washed my face and headed for the kitchen.

Ma Ingram piled my plate with golden pancakes, sizzling fried ham and buttery scrambled eggs. "What's all the shoutin' about?" she said, pouring coffee into my cup.

"I'm not coughing anymore, and I'm getting stronger . . . no more night sweats."

She poured herself a cup of coffee, sat down and watched as I devoured her repast. She reminded me of Sarah Arthurs. Like her, Ma Ingram was silver haired, compassionate, ready to listen and give advice. "Yes, you haven't been hawking the past couple of months . . . I've noticed that . . . and you've been cleanin' up you plate. Fact is, you're plumpin' out some."

"It must be your cooking and the high, dry air of Nevada."

"May be, but I expect the Lord's got more to do with it."

I laid my fork down and patted her hand. "You're right. After what has been happening, I should be knocking on the grim reaper's door."

"You should, but the Lord does intervene. You just gotta ask. I've been doin' a lot of askin' and so has my pastor, Reverend Locke."

"God bless you, and Reverend Locke, too."

"The Lord does, every day," she said, picking up my empty plate. "What are you going to do, now?"

"I'm undecided. Thomas and Big Belle have their lives to live without dealing with my problems. My intended, Penelope Gresham, will be arriving any day now. Then we will make that decision."

"No more school?"

"No, it wasn't meant to be."

"Well, John, remember what I said . . . y'gotta ask."

"I will," I said, leaving for the stage station. "Maybe there will be a telegram from Penny waiting for me."

The rising sun, a crisp autumn breeze, and anticipation for Penny's arrival lifted my spirit as I walked along C Street. What could I do now that there was no longer a valid reason for me to remain in Virginia City? Professor Krause's admonition the day I became a student at the seminary came to mind: *Look not mournfully into the past. It comes not back again. Wisely improve the present. It is thine. Go forth to meet the shadowy future, without fear.* Somehow, I reminded myself, God always provides. He is the captain of my soul.

My life had taken many turns over a short span of time. My destiny underwent multiple changes — beginning with the secession of South Carolina, meeting Hank the day he and I joined the army, our enduring over two years of battles, losing my right leg and the uncertainty of Hank's fate at Gettysburg, falling in love with Penny, escaping from prison and enduring the final months of the war, a life altering vision of Bishop Treetor Dossy, returning to Gettysburg and three years at the seminary, a new commitment to educating freed slaves, being smitten with tuberculosis, and suffering failure trying to establish a school.

I hardly noticed a six-horse drawn stage approaching from the south, because I was so preoccupied with my musings. It wasn't until I reached the International Hotel that I became fully aware of the stage as its driver, Big Belle, yelled, "Whoa, you knot heads. Hey, pilgrims, welcome to Virginia City." I cringed recalling how close she came to spending a lot of years in prison.

The doorman rushed from the hotel carrying a wooden step and plopped it below the stagecoach door. Big Belle pulled several carpet bags and valises from the luggage rack, tossed them to the doorman, and jumped to the ground. "Okay, pilgrims watch yer step," she said, yanking open the door.

An unfamiliar hunch caused me to tarry. My attention was riveted on the passengers as they stepped down from the stagecoach. The doorman welcomed each one with his usual spiel. "Welcome to the best hotel west of St. Louis," he said, handing them a copy of the *Territorial Enterprise*.

As the next passenger appeared in the doorway, I muttered, "Shawn O'Hara? What's he doing in Virginia City?"

Just as I moved nearer to get a better view, a toothy grin lifted his auburn mustache. "Hello, Laddie," he called. "I've got something to tell you . . . first, though, welcome your bonny lass."

He moved aside. Penny, radiant and smiling, appeared in the doorway. I shoved the doorman aside as I rushed to meet her. "Dear Penny, please be careful," I said, reaching for her hand. "Oh, I've missed you so much."

"I've missed you, too, John Pendleton," she said as I pulled her into my arms. "How have you been feeling?"

"Praise the Lord, the coughing and night sweats have gone away."

"Yes, indeed, praise the Lord," she whispered, squeezing me tighter."

My reverie was interrupted by Shawn's hand gripping my shoulder. "Let's go some place where we can visit. I've got something to tell you, Laddie."

With her bonny blue eyes gleaming, Penny squeezed my hand. "So do I."

I glanced at Big Belle who was helping the doorman with luggage. She had played a significant role in my efforts to start a school. She and Thomas deserved to be included in whatever plans I would make for the future. "Do you recall my telling you about Thomas, one of my students at Hampton, who came with me to Virginia City?" I asked Penelope.

"Of course I do."

"I'd like for him and his sister to meet you and Shawn."

"I would love to meet them, too," Penny said.

"So would I, Laddie," Shawn said, nodding toward the hotel entrance. "The restaurant should be private enough."

Big Belle welcomed my request, promising she and Thomas would join us after she parked the stagecoach at the stage station.

* * *

I peered at Penny, wondering how she would react when Big Belle and Thomas arrived. Being certain Big Belle's crudeness would be shocking, I decided to tell Penny and Shawn everything occurring after Thomas and I arrived in Virginia City. As my story ended, Big Belle and Thomas entered the dinning room.

I should not have been concerned about the encounter. Following usual pleasantries, it was evident Penny and Shawn were comfortable, even pleased to becoming acquainted with Big Belle and Thomas.

Penny opened her purse, pulled out an envelope and handed it to me. "This letter came to Todd two weeks ago."

I slipped the letter from the envelope. It was written on the Bishop of South Carolina's stationary. Its message was succinct.

October 5, 1870
Rev. John Pendleton,
c/o Dr. Todd Martin,
210 Carlisle Street
Gettysburg, Pennsylvania

Dear Rev. Pendleton,
Grace to you, and peace from God our Father and the Lord Jesus Christ.

The Reverend Trent Clegg, Rector of St. Michael's Church, suffered a fatal accident on October 1st. Consequently, the Diocese is in need of a replacement. I found your résumé in Bishop Davis's files while searching for a qualified minister. Since you are a son of Henry Pendleton, was christened by Bishop Dossy and granted ordination during Bishop Davis's tenure, I prayerfully ask you to consider filling our need at St. Michael's. I would appreciate your acceptance.

In His Service,
Rt. Reverend C. O. Forsythe, Bishop
Episcopal Diocese of South Carolina

I pondered the letter longer than I should have. I was certain my body was overcoming the consumptive disease in my lungs, but it would require a physician's verification. Penny patted my hand, a comforting gesture. "Are you worried about your illness?" she asked.

"Yes, I must know whether it is arrested?"

"I can determine that for you. How do you feel about the bishop's invitation?"

"It was an honor for him to ask me to accept the appointment."

"Yes, but is it something you wish to do?"

Big Belle must have been stressed by my deliberation. "Y'ain't got any future here. Anything would trump this. I'd say jump on it. How 'bout you, little brother?"

Thomas glanced at Big Belle, and then me. "Prof John, you're a good teacher, but I believe this is what the Lord wants you to do. Remember when you told me about your vision of Bishop Dossy? He anointed and dedicated you to be the Lord's messenger."

Big Belle grimaced. "I wouldn't know, but you ain't good at what you've been up to here."

"Well, Laddie, you may find it easier to make a decision after I tell you the reason I accompanied Penelope across the United States to see you. I have located Hank Johnson."

"You have? Where is he?"

"He made it across the Potomac and managed to get back to Charleston. He lost his right eye at Gettysburg, but otherwise was uninjured. At present, he works on the docks and is the custodian for St. Michael's. I spoke to him a week before leaving for Nevada. When I told him you survived the war and was in Nevada, he slapped his knee and shouted, 'Whoopie. Tell that whipper snapper, John, to come and see me.' I might add that Hank was really excited when I told him about your surviving prison and the war. Whatever you decide, go see him."

"Thank you, Shawn O'Hara for finding Hank. I'm going to accept the appointment if Penny verifies my consumption is arrested."

"I will be going with you," Penny whispered, slipping her hand into mine.

To: Historical Archives of South Carolina,
        Charleston, South Carolina..
From: Henry Lewis Johnson, III, Ph. D.

Former Bishop John Pendleton's prisoner of war journal arrived at the history department of the University of South Carolina on September 1, 1929. It was discovered among the meager belongings of a deceased elderly Negro, Jacob Pendleton, who resided in Washington, D.C. I am convinced after reading the journal that he was the runaway Pendleton slave who befriended John Pendleton while serving as a Yankee guard at Fort Delaware and Old Capital prisons.

I have a special interest in this discovery since I am a professor of history at the University of South Carolina, and am the grandson of Henry "Hank" Lewis Johnson. He and John Pendleton served together in the Army of Northern Virginia for two years. Both were severely wounded during Pickett's charge on July 3, 1863. My grandfather told me how they were wounded, captured, and incarcerated in different prisons. However, I was unaware of their full story until reading Reverend Pendleton's journals and biographical manuscript following my interview with him.

I was able to interview Bishop Pendleton at his residence in Charleston two days prior to his death. The following notations were recorded by me during that interview on September 3, 1929. The Reverend fell silent as he searched his shirt pocket for a match to relight his pipe. I retrieved his old journal, now musty and stained, whose entries on yellowing pages were dim and difficult to read. As he lit his pipe, I opened the journal and read aloud an inscription on its opening page, "Private John Henry Pendleton, Heth's Division, Pettigrew's Brigade, Army of Northern Virginia."

I handed the journal to him. "Reverend, is this the diary you left behind when you escaped from Old Capital Prison during the War Between the States?"

He stared at it for a moment, and then reached for the journal. He tried to open it with halting fingers, but their stiffness brought about only a faltering effort. "Young Henry, I need your assistance."

I read some of the entries to him. He listened, puffed on his pipe and said nothing until I finished reading an underlined entry, "Andrew has been sent to another prison. His gaunt frame haunts me day and night. He is dying, I fear. God, help him."

Reverend Pendleton nodded. "And God did."

I closed the journal and toyed with my pen for a moment. One question persisted in my mind. "How did my grandfather escape from the field of battle that Friday afternoon so long ago?"

"Well, young Henry," he said with his voice rasping and strident. "He told me that two of our people managed to pull him out of the tangled mass of our dead and dying men. I suppose they thought I'd suffered mortal wounds since I was unconscious and lying in a pool of more blood than a body should contain. It was a natural mistake."

"What would you like for me to do with your journal?"

"What do you suggest?"

"The university museum would be an excellent choice."

"Why not," he said and gestured toward one of the bookshelves lining the walls of his study. "You are welcome to my other journals, also."

We spent several hours together while reading and discussing entries in all of his journals. The clarity of his records was most impressive. In spite of advanced age, his recollections about each notation painted a vivid picture, one that could have happened only yesterday. His spiritual journey, which traversed a lifetime, had its profound onset when Bishop Dossy appeared to him as an apparition following John's grievous head injury suffered at Petersburg. When I asked him who influenced him most during his life, he did not hesitate to respond. "Oh, there are many," he replied. "Martin Luther, St. Francis of Assisi and Penelope, my dear departed wife come to mind. Luther admonished every seeker to learn to know the crucified and risen Christ. Learn to sing to him and say, Lord Jesus, you are my righteousness, I am your sin. You have taken upon yourself what is mine and given me what is yours. You have become what you were not so that I might become what I was not."

"And St. Francis of Assisi?"

"His prayer became my prayer. Each morning, when I awake, I say his prayer before I open God's word. The greatest reward we mortals can enjoy this side of being with the Lord Jesus is to experience the privilege of being an instrument of His peace. To counter hatred with love — pardon each injury — replace discord with union, doubt with faith, error with truth, despair with hope, sadness with joy, light for darkness — to console, understand and love. In giving, we receive, and in pardoning we are pardoned. In dying we are born to eternal life. In following these admonitions, I have discovered where my Lord resides. For many years, I had a room deep within my soul where I kept Him. When a need arose, I knew where He would be. I soon discovered the error in living such a way. You see, I was insisting upon being in charge. And then one day during my seminary studies, I discovered a simple truth. Jesus admonishes every one of us in his word to open the doorway to our soul so he can enter and abide within. We must not keep the Lord in a convenient place, a little room accessed only when we feel the need. Since then He has been my soul's companion."

"And your wife, Penelope?"

"Penny was my constant companion for fifty eight years. She was like Ruth who swore a vow of total commitment to Naomi: Do not press me to leave you or to turn back from following you! Where you go, I will go; where you lodge, I will lodge; your people shall be my people and your God my God. Where you die, I will die, and there will I be buried. May the Lord do thus and so to me, and more as well, if even death parts me from you. I lost her a little over a year ago. I thank the Lord every day for the years we had together. She was my counselor, confidant and ever-present helpmate. Praise the Lord, we shall meet again when I lay down this mortality."

"You have expressed great wisdom, Reverend Pendleton. You should write an accounting of your life's journey?"

He pointed toward a thick sheaf of papers on his desk. "I already have. It's written down in that manuscript. I've entitled it, *No Lesser Measure*. Those of us who yielded our blood and lives for a nation in which we believed sacrificed in no lesser measure from our brothers who fought for the other side. Would you like to read it?"

"Yes, sir, I most certainly would."

"Very good, as long as it stays with my journals, the university may keep it."

I assured him of the university's gratitude while placing note pads, his journals and manuscript into my valise. He nodded and tapped ashes from his pipe into a tarnished brass ashtray. In parting, I wanted him to know how moved I was by my visit with him. "Reverend Pendleton, your story has stirred my heart. Thank you, sir."

He remained silent while filling his pipe and again searched for a match. After finding one in his shirt pocket, he slipped the pipe into his mouth and struck the match across an edge of an ash try. His tremulous fingers lifted the match above his pipe. With each draw of air he sucked through the stem, the flame bent itself into the tobacco. Billowing smoke began to waft its way upward until the burning match consumed itself close to his fingers. He dropped it into the ash tray and sat holding his smoldering pipe. I picked up my valise and turned to walk through the doorway. I was compelled to pause for a moment when he called to me, "God bless you, young Henry."

His admonition spoke well of the depth of his spirit. There was no sadness at all in his voice. Indeed, his tone was joyful and I knew he really meant it.

"And you too, sir."

His reply came as I closed the door behind me. "He does every day."

Respectfully Submitted,
Henry Lewis Johnson, III, Ph. D.
Grandson of Henry "Hank" Lewis Johnson.